SOMETHING
Wilder

ALSO BY CHRISTINA LAUREN

Dating You / Hating You
Roomies
Love and Other Words
Josh and Hazel's Guide to Not Dating
My Favorite Half-Night Stand
The Unhoneymooners
Twice in a Blue Moon
The Honey-Don't List
In a Holidaze
The Soulmate Equation

THE BEAUTIFUL SERIES

Beautiful Bastard
Beautiful Stranger
Beautiful Bitch
Beautiful Bombshell
Beautiful Player
Beautiful Beginning
Beautiful Beloved
Beautiful Secret
Beautiful Boss
Beautiful

THE WILD SEASONS SERIES

Sweet Filthy Boy
Dirty Rowdy Thing
Dark Wild Night
Wicked Sexy Liar

YOUNG ADULT

The House
Sublime
Autoboyography

CHRISTINA LAUREN

SOMETHING

Wilder

GALLERY BOOKS

New York   London   Toronto   Sydney   New Delhi

G

Gallery Books
An Imprint of Simon & Schuster, Inc.
1230 Avenue of the Americas
New York, NY 10020

First Gallery Books hardcover edition May 2022

GALLERY BOOKS and colophon are registered trademarks of Simon & Schuster, Inc.

For information about special discounts for bulk purchases,
please contact Simon & Schuster Special Sales at 1-866-506-1949
or business@simonandschuster.com.

The Simon & Schuster Speakers Bureau can bring authors to your live event.
For more information or to book an event, contact the Simon & Schuster Speakers Bureau at 1-866-248-3049 or visit our website at www.simonspeakers.com.

Interior design by Davina Mock-Maniscalco

Manufactured in the United States of America

10 9 8 7 6 5 4 3 2 1

Library of Congress Cataloging-in-Publication Data

Names: Lauren, Christina, author.
Title: Something wilder / Christina Lauren.
Description: New York : Gallery Books, 2022.
Identifiers: LCCN 2021048419 (print) | LCCN 2021048420 (ebook) |
  ISBN 9781982173401 (hardcover) | ISBN 9781982173425 (ebook)
Subjects: LCGFT: Novels.
Classification: LCC PS3612.A9442273 S66 2022 (print) | LCC PS3612.A9442273
  (ebook) | DDC 813/.6—dc23/eng/20211018
LC record available at https://lccn.loc.gov/2021048419
LC ebook record available at https://lccn.loc.gov/2021048420

ISBN 978-1-9821-7340-1
ISBN 978-1-9821-7342-5 (ebook)

For Violet:
You asked for a book with horses.
We also included a woman who is brave and smart
and industrious, a lot like someone else we know.
We love you very much.

Author's Note

JUST BEYOND MOAB, Utah, Canyonlands National Park is one of the most spectacular places in the continental United States, with high desert vistas spliced by the Colorado River, Green River, and endless serpentine tributaries. Lucky visitors get an eyeful of wide blue sky and the spectacular view of red rock stretching for miles and miles. There are areas within the park that are remote and nearly impassable, and there are other areas that are hikeable, drivable, and wildly enjoyable for tourists.

After months of research and visits, we both became intimately familiar with this landscape and terrain. We even hired an expert expedition guide to draw us maps of a possible treasure hunt. But, dear reader, sometimes story must come before accuracy, and so—despite all that we've learned about the geography of this area . . . we made up a lot of stuff anyway. In some places, we have condensed distances; in others we've created settings and structures where none exist.

All this to say: we wrote this book to be a fun, swoon-filled escape from the real world, not to serve as a guide to your own adventure. (If you follow our route, you will die, lol.) Of course, we'd love to think Leo and Lily's love story will inspire you to get out in the wild and blaze new trails, but even if you're happier staying curled up in your reading nook, we hope we've given you one hell of a good time.

With love,
Lauren & Christina

SOMETHING
Wilder

Prologue

Laramie, Wyoming
October, Ten Years Ago

LILY WILDER'S BOOTS crunched through smooth gravel as she made her way from the barn to the lodge, surveying her favorite place on earth. Behind her, horses stepped up to slurp from the water tank, thirsty after a long night out in the pasture. Smoke drifted from the chimney of the big house and into the clear gray sky. The dawn was cool, the sun just breaking over the mountains.

She'd already been up for hours.

On the porch, a long shadow waited for her, holding two mugs. Her heart gave a heavy, infatuated jab at the sight of Leo—sleep-rumpled and grinning, bundled up in sweats and a fleece. Without question, this was how she wanted to start every morning; she still couldn't believe that from today on, she would. Lily jogged up the three rickety steps, stretching to fit her smile against his, feeling like it had been days, not hours, since she'd last touched him. His lips were warm, soft against her wind-chilled ones. The heat of his fingers on her hip ignited bottle rockets inside her chest.

"Where is he?" Lily asked, wondering if her father had left the ranch without saying goodbye. It wouldn't be the first time, but it would be the first time she didn't care.

Leo pressed a warm mug into her hand and nodded to the caretaker's cabin across the river. "He walked over the bridge to Erwin's," he said. "Saying goodbye."

Was it odd that she had no idea where her father was headed or how long he'd be gone? If it was, Lily didn't let the thought penetrate very deeply; more demanding was the way her pulse banged out a celebratory blast of a song: her life was finally starting, and somehow, this summer, while she'd learned how to manage nearly every aspect of the ranch, she'd also fallen in love. It was a love that surprised her—anchored and assured, clothes-shredding and fevered. She'd spent the first nineteen years of her life being tolerated and planned around, but here, with Leo, she was finally the center of someone's world. She'd never smiled so much, laughed so freely, or dared to want so ferociously. The closest she'd felt before was saddling her horse and racing across her family's land. Those moments were fleeting, though; Leo had promised he was here to stay.

She tilted her chin to gaze up into his face. He'd inherited his Irish father's build and his Japanese American mother's features, but the soul inside was all his own. Lily'd never known anyone as quietly, firmly grounded as Leo Grady. She still couldn't believe this steadfast man was willing to uproot everything for *her*.

She'd asked him "Are you sure?" a hundred times. Wilder Ranch was her dream; she knew better than to expect running a guest ranch year-round to be anyone else's. It certainly hadn't been her father's, though at least he'd put in the bare minimum to keep it solvent. For Lily's mother, the ranch was just another thing she gladly left behind. Sometimes Lily felt like she'd spent every day of her life waiting for the moment when she could make this ranch her forever. And now it was here, with Leo to boot.

"I'm sure, Lil." Leo's free arm came around her shoulder, guiding her right up into his side, where he tucked her close and bent to kiss her temple. "You sure you want a rookie like me here, though?"

"Hell yes." The words were loud in the quiet morning. In the distance, her new foal whinnied back. Leo looked at her with adoring eyes. He was new to ranching, true, but he was also a natural with the horses, capable in a million tiny ways, and a convenient top-hook-in-the-tack-room kind of tall. But none of that was why she wanted him there. She wanted him there because Leo Grady was undeniably hers, the first *hers* she'd ever had.

He smelled clean from the shower, and she curled in, pressing her face into his neck, searching for some hint of his sweat, the intensely masculine scent she'd felt gliding over her skin late last night.

"I made you breakfast," he murmured into her hair.

She leaned back, smiling hopefully up at him. "Your mom's scones?"

This made him laugh. "You act like she invented them." He bent, covering her mouth with his, and spoke around the kiss. "She usually makes us rice and fish. Pretty sure these are Rachael Ray's scones."

Duke Wilder strode across the frosty grass and onto the porch, a small twitch of his bushy salt-and-pepper mustache the only indication he'd seen how pressed together they'd been.

But then the moment passed, and his eyes brightened. Duke was always happiest when he was on the cusp of leaving. When Lily was little, his work took him as far as Greenland, but his radius of adventure had shrunk dramatically when her mother left them seven years ago and Duke became anchored down by a daughter and—in the summers, at least—the guest ranch in Laramie. Now she was grown, and he was finally free to enjoy being a niche celebrity who was deeply fixated on his childhood dream of finding the piles of money some outlaws hid in the desert more than a hundred years ago.

Lily wasn't the only one who was glad she was finally old enough to take on the burden of his family's land.

He shifted his gaze over her shoulder, and Lily watched Duke's face as he carried on some silent exchange with Leo. Sometimes Lily thought she barely knew her father; other times she could read him like a book. Duke had no love for Wilder Ranch, but right then Lily could hear his thoughts as if he'd spoken them aloud: *That kid doesn't look like a cowboy.*

Because Leo wasn't a cowboy. He was a college student, a math whiz, a New York City boy who had come to the ranch for a summer job, fallen in love, and upended his life to stay on with her in the off-season. Shy and quiet and thoughtful, he was everything Duke Wilder wasn't. Only twenty-two, staring at a fifty-year-old man with the local reputation of Indiana Jones and the confidence of Captain Jack Sparrow, Leo Grady didn't shrink or shift at her side.

"We'll be fine, Duke," she said, snapping the moment shut.

"You'll look after her until I'm back," Duke commanded,

eyes still fixed on Leo, so he missed his daughter's exasperated grimace.

"I will," Leo assured him.

"I don't need looking after," Lily reminded them both.

Duke reached forward, mussing her dark hair. "Sure you don't, kid. I left y'a note in the dining hall."

"Great." A riddle. A puzzle. Some cipher for her to decode. Her father had raised her on the games he loved, always poking at her like a kid prods a beetle, unable to understand how she ended up so different from him. A wrestling match between resentment and curiosity would ensue until necessity would beat them both, and she'd finally sit down to solve whatever puzzle he'd left for her. It was entirely possible that the note would translate into something asinine like *See you later* or *Don't eat all the oatmeal cookie dough*, but it was just as likely that he'd left some critical piece of information just out of her reach that Lily would require in order to run this place. Everything Lily had ever wanted or needed had always been hidden somewhere complicated, sometimes miles from home, and if she didn't have the motivation to look, Duke had figured she hadn't needed it after all.

Maybe today she wouldn't bother. Maybe she and Duke would finally agree that they didn't have to love the same things—they didn't even have to love each other—to coexist. For the first time, that sat fine with her. Maybe Duke would go back to his world, where he hunted artifacts and dug up lost treasure, and Lily would stay at the ranch with her horses and her land and her love and ignore the note on the table forever.

The tension stretched and then snapped when Duke took one last sweeping glance at the lodge, the barn, the rolling hills beyond. His parents had bought this land and raised two boys here—Duke and his brother, Daniel. Daniel had turned it into the Wilder Ranch, living here year-round and welcoming guests each summer until he died two years ago. Lily and Duke kept the business limping along, but it was never his priority and always her dream to be here full-time, to take it over, to bring it back to what it had been in the golden summers of her childhood. Seventy-eight horses and two hundred acres of glimmering Wyoming beauty were her idea of perfection, but Duke resented every single fence on the property like he was a cat in a cage.

Her larger-than-life father fit his cowboy hat on his head and nodded to the two of them. "Well. I'm off."

There weren't hugs. Leo and Lily didn't even step down from the wide porch. They silently watched the long, strong shape of Duke Wilder stride over to his old hulking truck and climb in.

Lily turned to Leo, bouncing on the balls of her feet, joy bubbling up inside her with a force that might shoot her off into the gray-blue sky.

"You ready for this, boss?" he asked.

Lily answered Leo with a kiss she hoped told him the things she sometimes still struggled to say.

She let it all sink in. Right now, everything was exactly right. No one and nothing rushed her past this single, perfect moment. With the dust of Duke's truck still swirling in his wake, all that mattered was the love at her side and the bejeweled galaxy of land around her. Her galaxy. She took a breath to speak but was caught in a double take at the tender expression on Leo's face as he looked down at her. "Lovesick

City Boy," all the cowboys had called him from that very first day he met her, five months ago.

Laughing—*blissful*—Lily cupped his cheek and stretched to kiss him again. "Promise me we'll be happy here forever."

He nodded and brought his forehead down to rest against hers. "I promise."

Chapter One

"IN HINDSIGHT," LILY said, wincing, "I know better than to ignore a bar fight going on behind me."

Archie extended a meaty hand, passing her a dripping cloth full of ice. "I'm more concerned you took an elbow to the back of the head and barely flinched."

"Is that a joke about me being hardheaded?" She sucked in a breath at the shock of ice against the nape of her neck.

Archie leaned over the bar. "I'm saying you're a tough little cowgirl, Lily Wilder."

Lily shoved him away with a laugh. "Kiss my ass, Arch."

"Any time you want, Lil."

With an elbow resting on the scuffed wood, she held the ice in place and watched condensation track in slow, fat streams down her pint glass. But as soon as she dragged a finger through it, the glass got muddy. All day long, wind worked the red desert dust into the creases of her clothing, into her hair. Hands, arms, face. Thank God for showers and sunscreen. With the kind of crowd one found at Archie's, though, it was never worth showering before coming in— whether Lily was sitting at the bar with a beer or working behind it in the off-season. The errant elbow to the back of her head was proof enough.

The door opened, briefly blasting the dim room with light, and Nicole arrived in a flash of messy blond hair and checked red-and-blue flannel. Sliding onto the stool beside Lily's, Nicole lifted her chin to Archie in both silent greeting and beverage order. He pulled a lager into a questionably clean glass and slid an even more questionably clean bowl of peanuts toward the women. More starving than fastidious, Lily dug in.

Nicole gestured to the ice pack. "What the hell?"

"Petey and Lou were at it. I was collateral damage."

"Need me to kick their asses?" She moved to stand, but Lily stopped her with a hand on the arm.

Nicole was taller and stronger than Lily, and her loyalty made her nearly feral when provoked. Lily wagered that Petey and Lou would have a pretty fair fight on their hands. If Lily gestured for Nic to go at it, she'd die trying. But Nic was all she had, so Lily tipped her head instead toward the small stack of papers on the bar near her friend's arm. "Is that the new group?"

Nicole nodded. "Arriving tomorrow."

"Dudes?" Lily asked. Their clients were almost always men coming out to hunt treasure and play at being outlaws. A group of women felt like a breath of fresh air. Those trips were quieter, more easygoing. They almost made the job worth it. Almost.

"Yeah. Four of them."

"Bachelor party? Birthday?"

Nic shook her head. "Looks like it's a group of friends just taking a trip together."

At this, Lily groaned. At least bachelor parties were on some kind of mission, usually to sneak booze and have a week of debauchery they'd talk about for years to come. But the groups that came to Lily's tourist expedition company, Wilder Adventures, just to "get away" always needed more babysitting, more structure. Sometimes that was fine—helping people enjoy a vacation on horseback had been Lily's joy growing up and was to this day—but right now she was running on fumes.

"All of them signed the waiver?" Lily asked.

Nic scratched her cheek, hesitating. "Yeah."

Pointing, Lily asked, "What's that mean?"

"Well," Nicole said, "it kind of looks like they were all signed by the same person."

Lifting her beer to her lips, Lily muttered a quiet "Shit."

"Dub, it's a formality."

"Unless it isn't," she said. "I can't afford a lawsuit."

"Girl, you can barely afford this beer." When she ducked to catch Lily's gaze, Nic's wild hair fell over half her face, leaving one glimmering blue eye free to study her best friend. "How are you thinking this will be our last trip out?"

Lily squinted down at the whorls in the scuffed wood bar. Truthfully, she had been hoping more than anything that this would be the last hurrah for Wilder Adventures. She *wanted* this to be the last time she took city slickers out into the desert to team-build and "rough it" and hunt for fake treasure. She wanted to put her dad's journal away and never have to look at it again. She wanted to live where no one asked her about Duke Wilder's maps or his stories and she could forget all about Butch Cassidy. Lily wanted to never again see a man wear polished dress shoes while riding a horse or hear another woman wearing a Prada "western" shirt complain how sore her ass was after a half hour in a saddle. She wanted to be running a ranch, to tack up Bonnie at sunrise and wrangle her own horses across sagebrush and frost-tipped grass that glimmered like diamonds and crunched beneath hooves. She wanted enough money to move out of her dad's old run-down cabin and leave this dusty shit town. She wanted this to be her last trip out more than anything.

But wanting didn't get her anywhere. She'd learned that lesson a long time ago.

Still, quitting this gig consumed Lily's every waking thought; seven years into this business and she felt trapped. She scraped by leading tourists around the desert, but horses were expensive, and Lily needed horses to lead tourists around the desert in order to scrape by. Chicken, meet egg.

"How did things go at the bank?" Nic asked, coming at it from a different angle.

Lily shook her head.

"Again?"

"Who's going to give someone like me a loan? What's my income going to be if I stop leading treasure hunts?"

Nicole leaned in again. "Did you *tell* them that was your plan? What do they even know?"

Lily looked over at her. "I didn't, Nic, but they're not dumb. The guy said, 'So if you buy some land and start up a new outfit, how are you going to make money until it's solvent?' And I told him that it would take a couple years but that I knew the area, knew the business, and knew what people wanted in a Wild West vacation, but it didn't matter. It doesn't matter what I say; I'm not a good investment."

Nicole blew out a breath and stared down at her hands. It was then that Lily noticed an envelope with her name poking out of the stack of mail and liability waivers. She'd recognize the return address anywhere. It used to be hers.

Immediately, she was buried under a deluge of memories—the astringent, crisp punch of sagebrush; herding horses as the sun tipped its hat over the top of the mountains; fat, warm butter biscuits in the mornings; the precise moment she'd laid eyes on *him*, and, weeks later, the heat and fever of his body—

Rubbing the ache beneath her breastbone, Lily cut those thoughts off at the pass, pointing at the envelope. "What's that?"

Nic tucked the envelope away again. "Nothing."

"It's from Wilder Ranch. And it's got my name on it." She reached for it. "Give it."

But Nicole slapped her away. "You don't want it right now, Dub, trust me."

Right now?

"Is it about the ranch?"

"Let it go, Lil."

A rare fire ignited in Lily's veins. "Did you open it? I swear to God, Nic, you are the nosiest little—" She went for it again, but Nicole dodged to the side, evading.

"I said *no*."

Lily's blood turned to steam at the implication that she couldn't handle whatever was in there. Nic was the hothead; Lily was the measured one. But suddenly, she'd never wanted anything more than she wanted to see the contents of the nondescript white envelope.

Lily shoved Nic's arm, but Nic knew it was coming and leaned in, caging around the papers, unmoving. Diving for her midsection, Lily knocked Nic off the stool and tackled her onto the floor. Suddenly paling in importance, the liability waivers rained around them, landing among the discarded peanut shells in the layer of sticky beer on the floor. Behind the wrestling women, men hooted and clapped, cheering them on. Normally Lily would get up and take this argument elsewhere, but she had a singular focus, and it was to dig that envelope out from under where Nicole had rolled onto her stomach, covering it with her body.

"No fucking way," Nic yelled into the floor, even as Lily smacked uselessly at her shoulders, tickled her ribs, and then began to punch her ass.

"It has *my* name on it, you dick."

"You don't want it!"

"You're committing a felony!" Lily glanced over her shoulder. "Petey! You're a cop."

"Off duty," he answered, laughing into his beer. "Punch her in the ass again."

"I'm gonna punch you in the dick next if you don't help me."

"Honey, you're welcome to hit on any part of me."

With a savage growl, she dug with all her strength under her friend's body, reaching blindly for the envelope. She got her fingers around it, tearing off a corner as she yanked it free. Lily scrambled up and away, hiding behind Big Eddie near the dartboard in case Nicole decided to come for her.

"I'm telling you," Nic warned, "you don't want it." Defeated, she stood, swiping bar floor grime from her cheek with the back of her hand. She returned to her stool, and her beer, and the bowl of nuts. "Just don't come pouting to me when you see what it is."

Back in the corner, Lily pulled the letter free. A bar full of eyes lingered on her as she read it, at first uncomprehending— the words swam in swirls of black and white—and remained glued to her face as she returned to the beginning to start again. Sentences took shape, meaning coalesced, and all of the ache and loss and empty blackness she'd packed into a solid brick in her chest broke free, becoming a swarm of horseflies.

The letter was from the man who now owned her family's land. A man she'd met only once, barely a week after that other, brutal heartbreak. As much as Lily hated Jonathan Cross, she'd wanted to read these words every day for ten years.

. . . retiring . . . ranch up for sale . . . like to give you the first opportunity . . .

It didn't matter how good a deal he was offering her. There wasn't a single thing she could do to get her family's ranch back.

Once something was gone, it was gone. Lily thought she'd dealt with her sorrow, her longing for that place, but she felt bruised all over again.

It took every ounce of physical strength she had to maintain her composure. She tacked her lower lip to her teeth, nailed her jaw shut. She forced her shoulders steady, working to keep them from rising up around her neck, to keep her back from curling. No one alive—at least, no one in this room— had ever seen her break. Finally, when everyone had lost interest or turned away out of respect, she made her way back to the bar.

Nicole had already ordered her friend a fresh beer and pushed it over as Lily settled onto the stool beside her.

"Told you," Nic said.

"You did."

"What're you going to do about it?" she asked.

"I'm going to do a whole lot of nothing," Lily said, and brought the glass to her lips.

Chapter Two

New York City
May, Present Day

THE DOWNSIDE TO leaving for JFK at 8:15 a.m.: in the past twenty minutes, the tangle of morning rush-hour traffic had not once moved faster than ten miles an hour. Potential upside: Leo was free to answer the litany of questions his boss could ask literally anyone else still at the office . . . but wouldn't.

When his phone chimed with the tenth text in five minutes, Leo closed his eyes, groaning.

"Just put it on silent," Bradley said, rolling the cab window down as far as it would go, then quickly rolling it back up against the plume of truck exhaust that barreled inside.

Leo typed out a quick reply. "It's fine."

The phone immediately chimed again.

"Leo, this happens every year."

Typing, Leo said, "It's just how Alton gets when I'm going to be out of the office."

"Exactly my point. He acts like there's no one else in the tristate area who can use a calculator."

This time, the phone rang in Leo's hand.

Bradley gave him a warning look. "Leave it."

Shrugging helplessly, Leo gestured to Alton's name on the screen. "They're making decisions about the VP role next week and I'm on vacation. I can't not answer."

"Leave it."

Leo brought the phone to his ear. "Hello?"

Bradley groaned and leaned forward to tell the cabdriver—who absolutely did not care—"He never lets his boss go to voicemail."

"I do," Leo whisper-hissed before returning to Alton on the other end of the call and telling him, "The code for the Daxton-Amazon algorithm is in the C drive under the folder named 'Daxton-Amazon.'"

Bradley turned and gaped at him, but Leo waved this off, continuing the call. "That's right. You can forward it directly to Alyssa or save it to the cloud—"

Bradley yanked the phone from Leo's hand and bent, pressing his mouth close and faking static. "Can't"—*crackle*—"hear"—*crackle*—"tunnel"—*crackle*. He hit End and slid the phone into his own coat pocket with a smirk.

Leo stared blankly at him. "Dude, seriously?"

"My year, my trip, my rules. Rule number one: no phones."

Leo reached for it anyway, explaining, "He was calling to find out where the—"

Bradley slapped his hand away. "If your boss can't find an algorithm named Daxton-Amazon in a folder also named *Daxton-Amazon*, I really have no idea how he ended up in a corner office."

Leo turned to stare out the window, unable to argue. It was time to stop worrying about work anyway, and start wondering where Bradley was taking them. This annual trip with his two best friends from college was his only time away, and as their lives had gotten busier, the status quo had transitioned from *It's my year to do the planning* to *Absolutely no details will be shared until we arrive at our destination.* Knowing they were flying into Salt Lake City told Leo nothing, and whenever it was Bradley's turn, the other two men were justifiably wary. Bradley prioritized telling a good story down the road over personal comfort and common sense every time.

His phone rang again, and Bradley pulled it out, grinning when he saw who was calling. "It's your other boss." He turned the screen around, showing Leo.

Cora.

Bradley swiped to answer. "Leo's phone, Uncle Bradley speaking."

Leaning in again, Leo tried to take it from him.

But Bradley put his entire hand on Leo's face and pushed him away. "How are you, darlin'?"

Leo could hear nothing but the tinny hint of his sister's voice through the line. Resigned, he deflated into the seat. Cora adored Bradley. Even if Leo managed to grab the phone, she'd just tell him to hand it back again.

"Congratulations on graduating, Cor. That's incredible." Bradley nodded, smiling at whatever she'd said. "Is that right?" He turned and looked at Leo. "And Paris tomorrow? No, your brother absolutely did not tell me that he was sending you and a friend to *Paris* for your graduation gift."

Shit. Bradley would be relentless about this.

"I bet," Bradley said, eyes widening as he stared at Leo in mock alarm. "That does sound like a special night." He paused, listening. "I will definitely pass that along. You have an amazing trip. Love you too, kiddo." He ended the call and, with a derisive grin, finally handed Leo his phone. "That was enlightening."

Dropping it into his backpack, Leo leaned his head against the headrest. "Let it go."

"Cora wanted me to let you know that she stopped by your place and got the cash you left for her." Bradley paused, stroking his five-o'clock shadow. "I must say I'm disappointed you didn't invite me to her graduation dinner last night," he drawled. "Certainly one more person wouldn't have broken the bank if you'd already invited twelve people and are flying her to Paris tomorrow."

The cab pulled up in front of the terminal at JFK, and they climbed out, retrieving their bags from the trunk. "Cost wasn't what kept me from inviting you," Leo explained as they made their way into the terminal. "Your habit of hitting on my little sister's friends was."

"They're legal," Bradley reasoned.

Bradley was his oldest friend, the one who'd picked Leo up when his world fell apart a decade ago and stood by him while he found his footing again. He was the teasing stand-in uncle and the joking, lighthearted counterbalance to Leo's over-protective and overcompensating tendencies. He was also a shameless player.

"But still ten years younger than you," Leo reminded him.

"Ten years means less when you're older."

"It still means a fair bit, Bradley."

He smirked at Leo. "You're changing the subject. You spoil her."

"A man wearing a Rolex and a Prada crossbody should be the last person giving me a lecture on spoiling someone. It's not like you need a free meal, either."

"No, but I'd *like* one."

Leo laughed at Bradley's winning grin. "Cora's moving to Boston. You know it was my job to get her through school." Get her through school, yes, but also be her brother, father, mother, and benefactor, and make up for every tiny bit of adoration that had been robbed from his baby sister ten years ago.

"And you did that. Along with a weekly allowance, no student loans, and an apartment four blocks from the Columbia campus."

"Which she shares with three other people," Leo reminded him. "She's not rolling around in a penthouse."

Bradley waved this off. "Where we're going, she won't be able to call you. Will she be able to function without Big Brother?"

Leo was already sick of this conversation. "She'll be fine." At least, he hoped she would. "She'll be too busy enjoying Paris to worry about checking in anyway."

"But how will *you* be?" Bradley pressed.

"What do you mean?"

"Leo, this is the first trip we've ever taken where we can't check work email or take calls."

Dodging around a family repacking a suitcase at check-in, he cut a glance at Bradley. "Don't worry about me. I've been mentally preparing for isolation based on your horrible packing list."

"Horrible?" Bradley repeated, feigning offense.

They stepped up together to the ticketing counter, handing over their IDs.

"I don't own cargo pants," Leo told him. "And 'heeled boots'? Are we talking *Purple Rain* or construction worker?"

"You know the rules. Don't question, just pack."

"I do know the rules," Leo said, "but when I saw 'hat with stampede string,' I didn't even know what that meant."

In fact, Leo knew exactly what it meant, but the thought of *why* he might need a heeled boot and a hat with a stampede string made his stomach turn. Which was why he'd put off packing until this morning, when he finally—frantically—shoved everything into his duffel bag. Each of the three friends had a set of rules for these trips, spoken and unspoken. For example, Bradley refused to travel to Key West because the family of a woman he'd drunk-proposed to in 2012 owned nearly a quarter of the restaurants in town. Walter refused to visit any state with a real possibility of tornados. Leo's unspoken rule had always been *No horses.* Bradley knew better than anyone *why.*

So even if this vacation didn't take them to Wyoming, being near horses would undoubtedly take Leo back to a mental place he had—according to several ex-girlfriends—not emotionally unpacked.

The annual vacation tradition had begun the spring after he'd returned from Laramie, hollow and heartbroken. Bradley, acting on an equal number of good and bad intentions, had planned a guys' trip hiking upstate while Cora was at YMCA camp in Vermont. On that trip, Leo had laughed out loud for the first time in seven months.

The following year, the three of them went away again, on

a road trip to Maine that Walter planned. After that, as their incomes improved, so did the trips. There had been wine tasting in Oregon and cheese making in France. They'd swum with dolphins in Ensenada and kayaked through glaciers in Alaska.

Given that Bradley's last getaway, three years ago, was a week in Ibiza, when Bradley had put "bail money" on the packing list—and good thing Leo and Walter had taken him seriously—they'd been mildly trepidatious about this year's plan.

Leo was pulled from contemplating this any further when a voice from behind them boomed, "*What's happening, pussies?*" They were surrounded by at least a hundred other travelers, and there was no reason to assume these words were directed at them, but Leo didn't have to look to know that they were. While every traveler in the vicinity turned to see who had just shouted the word *pussies* in the middle of a goddamn airport, Leo turned to gape accusingly at Bradley.

"Seriously?" he hissed. "You invited him?"

Bradley immediately shrank back.

A reluctant glance over his shoulder revealed exactly what Leo expected: Terrence "Terry" Trottel—a man who had never served in the military yet was decked out in full camo gear and carrying a military-grade pack slung over his shoulder— sauntering straight toward them. Tall, thin, impulsively tattooed, and ineptly bearded, Terry was the kind of book that could be accurately judged by its cover.

Bradley winced. "He asked me outright. I couldn't say no."

"You could, though. It's easy: 'No, Terrence. You're not a part of this tradition.'"

Terry—Bradley's roommate from freshman year—remained

only tenuously connected to the group, given that he was absolutely the friend one had to apologize for, no matter the situation. Here was a man who once showed up uninvited for beers wearing a shirt that had a picture of a woman with a piece of tape over her mouth and the words *Enjoy the silence*.

But although Bradley might give Leo shit about Cora and his job and his nonexistent love life, he didn't do actual conflict; he was everyone's friend. Leo was the calm center of the group so Bradley could trash-talk in safety. In contrast, Terry was a hothead, finding insult whether or not one was intended. And here they were, about to be trapped with him somewhere clearly remote enough to require the ability to live without cell service.

Awesome.

They pretended not to see Terry wave before he stepped up to the check-in counter a few yards down. While the agent tagged their minimal luggage, Leo glared at Bradley.

"He didn't use to be this bad," Bradley argued under his breath.

In college, Terry's version of weird had manifested as a penchant for collecting bottle caps and not washing his lucky shirt. Present-day Terry collected vintage ammunition and considered *feminist* and *terrorist* to be roughly synonymous. Bradley wasn't wrong that Terry hadn't always been this bad, but it was moot, because Terry was definitely terrible now. Leo had already been semi-dreading this trip, and now he was convinced it would be interminable.

"Walt sent me screencaps of some scary shit that Terry's posted online," he told Bradley. "Terry spends all day in some pretty dark corners of the internet."

"I know. But when it's all of us, he tones it down."

Leo let out a one-syllable laugh. "Does he?"

Their agent handed over the tickets, and the two men stepped away from the counter.

Bradley glanced to the side. "I think he'll be pretty chill."

"Because that's Terry?" Leo asked, pointing to where Terry appeared to be "educating" the airline agent on the correct way to tag his luggage. "Pretty chill?"

"Are *you* going to tell him no?"

"Bradley, he's checking in for the flight. Of course I'm not telling him no now."

Under his breath, Bradley mumbled, "I don't know why you're judging me. You won't even tell Cora no."

"I heard that."

"That's why I said it out loud."

They turned to make their way to the security screening, but when Bradley lingered to wait for Terry, Leo kept moving, making it through in only a few minutes. In the end, he was glad he went ahead, too, because Walt was already at the gate and would need to be prepared for the Terry news. Specifically, if the stress of Terry joining the trip was too great, Walter would want time to hit the restroom before they had to board.

Walter sat with his backpack in his lap, headphones in, bopping happily to music. A gentle soul who rarely prioritized things like haircuts or replacing holey T-shirts, he was always the first to call to check in on a friend having a hard time. Put simply, he was the anti-Terry.

Leo hovered at the periphery, hating that he was about to ruin Walt's good mood. But when Walt looked up and over Leo's shoulder, his expression crashing, Leo realized he was too late.

Walter tugged out an earbud, staring wide-eyed at Terry's approach. "Wait, why's Terry here?"

Leo supposed there was one reason to be grateful for Bradley's nonconfrontational nature: with Terry along for the ride, at least there was something Leo was less excited about than riding a horse for the first time in a decade.

Chapter Three

JOLTED ABRUPTLY AWAKE, Leo angled forward in the unforgiving bus seat, reaching back to cup his neck.

"What happened?" Bradley asked, slowly straightening from his slumber across the aisle.

"We stopped."

Bradley groaned. "Where?"

"No idea." All Leo knew was that the bus, which reeked of soil and ethanol, had just come to a hard, abrupt stop seemingly in the middle of nowhere.

"What the hell, dude?" Bradley called to the bus driver, crossing his arms over the seat in front of him. "How about a little warning the next time?"

The driver's raspy response barely reached them: "This is as far as I take you. Climb on out."

Focusing his gaze through the window, Leo could distinguish nothing but vague shapes in the blue-black darkness. He would have sworn the sun was up only a few minutes ago, but

he'd drifted off somewhere outside of Green River, Utah—
worn thin from an unending travel day, including three hours
delayed on the JFK tarmac, a bumpy and crowded flight, and
this bus ride to who knew where.

Leo felt like he'd slept crammed in a box, but despite the
interminable travel for whatever Wild West adventures might
lie ahead, Bradley looked entirely untouched. For a man wearing leather driving shoes and a cashmere sweater, he was surprisingly game for the great outdoors. Beside Bradley, leaning
awkwardly against the window and wearing an ancient green
T-shirt that read MIDDLE EARTH'S ANNUAL MORDOR FUN RUN,
Walt remained blissfully comatose, snoring softly.

Behind them, Terry's perpetually flushed face split into an
unsettling grin before he reached forward and sharply slapped
Walter on the back of the head, jolting him awake.

"Come on, man," Leo said. When Leo first met Terry, he
thought he was perpetually sunburned, then Leo wondered
whether he drank too much. Now, of course, Leo knew Terry
was just chronically pissed off. Worked up all the time, angry
at women, socialists, his mom.

Leo shifted and threw Walt a commiserating *Wow, do I hate
Terry* look before turning his attention down to his phone,
mumbling, "One bar already? Did we drive to 1992?"

"Should've brought a satellite phone," Terry said, stretching in the aisle. "Cell service is gonna be sketchy at best."

"Come now, gentlemen." Bradley stood, too, pounding
his chest. His thick blond hair fell away from his forehead in
easy, travel-immune waves. "Where we're going, we won't
need phones."

Bradley led the group off the bus to collect their various

bags. About twenty feet from where they stood, Leo could make out a small, rickety wind shelter cupped around a handful of weathered wooden benches. A tumbleweed somersaulted by on the dry cement, a small cyclone of dust following in its wake. As Leo's eyes adjusted, the sky slowly turned purple; the ground was swallowed up by shadows that seemed to stretch uninterrupted for miles.

The bus rumbled to life again, and the group of men watched it trail away, the taillights fading into darkness.

Walter's brows furrowed in worry. "Does he know we're— I wonder if he—" He looked over to Leo, stating the obvious: "We're not on the bus with him."

"Maybe now is when you tell us what we're in for, Bradley," Leo said.

"All you need to know is we're in for *adventure*. Don't worry, guys, we're not going to be out here alone for long."

As soon as he finished the sentence, a coyote howled and its pack followed with eerie, rallying yipping.

Leo stretched and his back cracking sounded like a stack of dominoes falling. "I fell asleep but am willing to bet we haven't passed anything for hours. Can you at least tell us where we are?"

Terry freed a GPS unit from one of several cargo pockets. "We're at thirty-eight degrees north and—"

"Thank you," Leo said dryly.

"God, fine, nobody enjoys mystery, I see." Bradley pulled out his phone, and the screen illuminated his frown, making his pampered skin look oddly lined and spooky. "We should be just outside of Hanksville, Utah, but I'll read you the brochure information if I can pull it up." He turned the screen to face them, pointing to the way his mail icon spun uselessly. "It's an adventure guide company," he explained defensively. "We'll be riding horses and camping and hunting for *treasure*. Tell me that doesn't sound like a fucking blast."

A vague memory clouded Leo's thoughts, and his stomach tilted queasily.

In the distance, a pair of yellowed headlights sliced through the dark.

"See?" Bradley said, vindicated. "There's our ride now."

They watched in anticipatory silence as a Bronco that was more rust than metal barreled down the pocked two-lane road. It showed no signs of slowing as it approached.

Apprehension made Leo's voice louder than normal: "They're coming pretty fast . . ."

Alarm swelled in his chest as the driver jerked onto the shoulder, bumping over gravel and careening directly toward them. The men pressed back against the benches, letting out a chorus of *Are we about to die?* exclamations before the vehicle came to a dusty, screeching halt only inches from Walter's feet.

"I have never been that close to pissing myself," he whispered.

As they all took a few careful steps away from the Bronco's grille, Bradley happily waved to the outline of the driver. "Told you someone would be here soon."

The engine cut off abruptly and the lingering notes of Dolly Parton's "Jolene" echoed in the answering silence.

Leo squinted as the driver slowly climbed out and rounded the front of the vehicle, their footsteps crunching through the gravelly dirt. The driver was still backlit by the headlights, but Leo could make out long legs as the figure leaned back against the hood.

Their face was hidden by a dusty cowboy hat, but when they tipped their head up, Leo was surprised to see a woman—midtwenties and pretty—almost six feet tall and wearing a smile that suggested she'd be up for a party or a bar fight, no big difference to her. She was in boots and jeans, and her chin-length blond hair curled over the collar of her worn button-down shirt. "I'm Nicole. You must be the suits I get to whip into shape this week."

At Leo's side, Bradley reached out, clutching the collar of Leo's shirt in a fist and releasing a happy moan. Leo shoved him away.

Everyone else remained noticeably silent, so he stepped forward and offered a hand. "I'm Leo."

"You the one who signed your friends up for this?" she asked in a flattened twang, taking his hand in her strong grip.

"No, that'd be Bradley." When she released it, Leo put the hand on Bradley's shoulder before pointing around the group. "And this is Walter." He hesitated before gesturing to Terry, who remained a step outside their small circle. "Terry's over there."

Walt offered a small wave. "Miss . . . um, is it 'miss'? 'Mrs.'? Or would 'ma'am' be better?"

"It's Nicole, but 'miss' would be a lovely change of pace. 'Miss Nicole' has a particularly nice ring to it."

"Okay, Miss Nicole?" he said then, looking around the growing blackness. "Where are we, exactly?"

"Bus depot." She circled them, inspecting. "Bus doesn't go all the way to camp, so I'm here to get you." She let out an abrupt, unimpressed grunt. "You wore loafers to the desert?"

"They're driving shoes and they're orthopedic," Bradley explained. "Recommended by my podiatrist."

"A butt doctor?"

A laugh tore from Leo before he could hold it in.

Bradley paused. "Never mind."

Walter's bag sat on the nearest bench, and Nicole did a double take at something visible through the open flap, reaching in and pulling out a bright blue plastic gadget with a nozzle on one end and an accordion-shaped bottle on the other. "The hell is this?"

"It's a Tushy," Walter explained, reaching for it and shoving it back inside. "A portable bidet."

"A bidet?" In the glare of the headlights, Nicole's eyes were bright with amusement. She tipped her hat back, and Leo felt the rustle of awareness pass around the group: she was even prettier with her whole face visible. "I've seen folks bring some crazy shit out here," she said, "but that's a new one. Had one guy think he could wear nipple clamps the whole ride. A bachelorette party brought at least a dozen vibrators. I promise neither of those things pairs well with a week on a horse." She leaned forward, lifting a booted foot to rest on a wooden plank. "Besides, honey, I can just toss you in the river if you like your bottom scrubbed, and that don't take up space in your backpack."

Bradley preened. "I told you this trip was going to be awesome."

"I'm sorry," Walter cut in, holding up a shaking hand, "but it sounds like you just said something about a week on a horse."

"That's why you're here, precious. To be cowboys. We take you to the Outlaw Trail on horseback. You leave all your smartphones and loafers and smart toilets behind. There'll be

open sky and meals by the campfire. Games and puzzles and—
if you're lucky—real-life hidden treasure."

"Games?" Terry asked gruffly. "Puzzles? What the fuck
kind of operation is this?"

Unruffled, Nicole gave him a good once-over and then
winked. "The kind that's gonna keep you alive out here."

A long day of travel rendered Leo too tired and cranky to make
small talk, but as Terry droned on in the back seat about topographical maps, the formation of slot canyons, and God knew
what else, Bradley eagerly peppered Nicole with questions.

"Where are we going?"

"To camp."

"Who else will be there?"

"The boss is getting the horses situated."

"You're not the boss?"

"I am when Dub's not around."

"Are there cabins?"

"Tents."

"Are you single?"

Ignoring this, Nicole slowly pulled a knife still wrapped in
its leather sheath from her side and set it on her thigh.

Walt leaned in. "Just to clarify, will there be flushing toilets
out on the trail?"

At this, Nicole laughed for a long time, but the answer was
unfortunately no.

Unfazed, Bradley leaned back in his seat, face turned up to
the wind. "Smell that air, ye lads. No pollution, no exhaust.
This is the life of the adventurer, the life of the man out on the

frontier." He lifted his shirt, slapping his ribs. "My chest hair is growing. I can feel my fangs coming in."

Walter stuck his head out the window and unleashed a trembly roar before ducking back in, coughing. "I inhaled a bug."

"Some big ones out here," Nicole confirmed.

"I'm telling you," Bradley said, ignoring this and turning around in the front seat to face his friends, "this is going to be fucking awesome. A week with no responsibilities. I may never leave. Plus"—he motioned to himself—"you've got a real-life Howard Carter on your team."

At Nicole's questioning glance, Leo clarified, "The guy who found King Tut. Bradley's a professor of archaeology."

Terry scoffed and the wind whipped his wispy beard. "Yeah, but he doesn't go out into the field. I'm the only one here who's ever spent actual time in a slot canyon."

"What's a slot canyon again?" Walter asked.

Terry leaned back, happy to spout off to a captive audience. "They're long, narrow gorges and channels caused by thousands of years of water penetrating cracks in soft sandstone."

Bradley looked from Terry to Walter. "Did anyone else think that entire sentence was unnecessarily suggestive?"

Nicole met Walter's eyes in the mirror and clarified, "Like a really long, skinny hallway carved into the rock."

"Oh!" Walter said, satisfied. "That could be cool."

Terry cleared his throat. "Anyway. Stick with me. I know what I'm doing."

"I'll stick with the guides," Leo replied with quiet calm.

Nicole winked at him over her shoulder. "Smart man."

Leo knew that even if Bradley had chosen a trip decidedly

outside of Terry's interests—treasure, canyoneering, and red-neck Bear Grylls–style roughing it—Terry would still act like the resident expert. In the end, was it better or worse to hear him go on and on about something he knew a lot about or something he didn't? Leo steadied his own anxiety and irritation with a deep breath.

And there was nothing else to do, anyway, but try to turn his horseback-related dread into the sweet anticipation of a week away from the office; they couldn't see much as they raced through the dark. Leo thought he spotted a pair of glowing eyes in the brush as the headlights bounced and dipped, cutting a path of light through the empty road ahead. At a particularly high spot, his stomach soared and then dropped as the tires left the ground, connecting again with a bone-jarring clank that sprayed soil and gravel into the stillness behind them.

When the Bronco finally came to a clattering stop, the men climbed out with varying degrees of enthusiasm. Leo's first step was a dizzy, dusty one; a cloud of dirt kicked up as his shoe met the ground. The breeze was cool and almost uncomfortably dry, the air heavy with the smells of sagebrush and woodsmoke, of earth cooling in the blissful absence of the sun.

Beside him, Walter dropped his bag at his feet and squinted into the distance, fists planted on his hips as he surveyed the landscape. It wasn't likely he could make out much—the sky was more black than purple now, a backlit bruise with only a hint of the mountains beyond—but he slowly took it all in. A row of lanterns lit the path to where a small camp had been set up about forty yards away.

Nicole had already told them they'd be camping, but even the roughest of their previous excursions had included, at the very least, running water. As they followed her, a hushed awareness set in: this was *rustic*. Six glowing tents circled a crackling campfire; the soft whinny of horses carried through the darkness. It was beautiful. The closer they got to the fire, the better Leo was able to make out an iron corral with a corrugated metal overhang, a small building, and what looked like an outhouse nearby.

A large stake had been pounded into the ground near the fire, and Nicole reached for a clipboard hanging from a bent nail. "This is base camp, so there are more amenities here than we'll have the rest of the trip." She swatted at a mosquito and then pointed to the semicircle of tents. "Soak up the luxury, kids. Inside your tent you'll find a pack with some food and water to get you through the night. Might even be a few cold ones in there, but that depends on how generous the boss was feeling. As a rule, there's no drinking unless we're back at camp for the evening, and only what we provide. Can't have any messy cowboys."

Her gaze landed meaningfully on Bradley, who jerked upright at attention. Beside him, Walt jumped at something rustling in the dry grass nearby, clutching for Leo. On instinct, everyone but Leo and Nicole took a step back.

"What the fuck was that?" Bradley whispered.

"Just a kit fox or jackrabbit," Nicole said without taking her eyes off the clipboard. "It's not gonna hurt you."

Walt didn't seem reassured. Even Leo had to admit it was hard not to feel exposed when surrounded by nothing but black sky and unending stars. The closest he'd ever been to this degree of isolation was his summer at Wilder Ranch, and at least that property had electricity and toilets. Here they were out in the middle of nowhere with just the moon and the stars and a few torches to light their way. Leo assumed it was safe at camp, but so far there'd been no sign of Nicole's boss, and he wouldn't exactly say Nicole seemed overly concerned about their well-being.

"I will ask you not to wander around, though. It's flat here, but it won't be for long. We don't want anyone tumbling over a cliff because they got disoriented taking a leak in the dark." She pointed to a small cluster of buildings. "For tonight, the tack shed and outhouse are that way, but stay inside the boundary of the lanterns. If you can't see the ground, we can't see you."

Terry stood with his arms crossed over his chest. "What's the mountain lion situation 'round here? I've read they hunt in this area. I assume you have some kind of perimeter fence set up."

Nicole bit back an amused smile. "Fence wouldn't keep 'em out if they really wanted in."

"A gun would," Terry countered.

"I got no problem turning a rooster into a hen with one shot," she said, "though it's my experience that guns usually cause more problems than they solve. But if you're worried, just know mountain lions don't have much use for us and are usually following the mule deer this time of year, anyway. Just do what we ask, and we'll keep you safe."

" 'We' being just you and your girlboss?" he asked, and the rest of them took a step away, distancing themselves from Terry's mouth. Apparently he hadn't seen Nicole's knife.

"Why do you assume my boss is a girl?" Nicole asked, arching a brow at him.

When Terry inhaled to answer, Bradley quickly cut in. "I'm sure he just meant, like, we don't imagine a man would just leave you out here alone with a bunch of guys."

Nicole laughed at this. "I can handle myself just fine."

Leo had no doubt this was true.

But Terry couldn't help himself: "Can you?"

Nicole took a step forward, eye to eye now and staring him down. "We've been capably taking care of tourists for nearly a decade. There are a few cowboys who use this camp when they need to, and we have a guy who jumps ahead to leave supplies along the trail, but you won't see them and you won't need them." She paused, gazing evenly at him. "That going to be a problem? I can call someone to come pick you up before we head out tomorrow."

Terry laughed but took a small step back. "Nah. That's all right."

"Good." She held his gaze for a beat longer. "You'll meet Dub in the morning." Nicole smirked. "I invite you to run these questions past her as well."

She gave each of them a set of handouts, and in the flickering light Leo could just make out what he assumed was a list of rules stapled to a brief trip itinerary. All for him to look over tomorrow. For now, at the top of the first page and circled in red was his tent number. Nicole told them to turn in for the night and that breakfast would be served at seven o'clock sharp. "Get some sleep," she said with a wink. "You'll need it."

Leo moved to follow the scattering group when a figure just out of the firelight caught his eye, a mirage at the edge of the moonlight, stepping out of the small horse pen. Stick-straight hair sparked the memory of fall leaves and naked skin on the bank of the river. It was a hazy memory, or maybe he was already half out of it, already dreaming. Shaking his head, Leo climbed into his tent and tumbled onto the sleeping bag there. He didn't even kick his shoes off. The sense of déjà vu was gone before he could get a solid hold on it, and within minutes, he was asleep.

Chapter Four

TO LILY, THERE was no such thing as sleeping in. There were no holidays, only the special workdays with clean jeans—not dirty ones—at the dinner table. Even as a little girl she was up with the sun. In the summer, feed needed to be put out and troughs filled, meals prepped, and guests tended to. In the winter, the work changed, but no matter what, the horses came first, the humans came second, and self-care specifically fell somewhere much further down the line.

With the rest of the camp still asleep, Lily stepped out of her tent in time to catch the first spark of light in the sky. She loved the location of the tour's base camp. At the edge of Horseshoe Canyon, it was remote enough to feel like wilderness but still close enough to town in case a guest sensed the true isolation they'd be facing and got cold feet. Not to mention, it was beautiful. City folks seemed to always expect the desert to be burnt and barren, but here it was as alive as any garden. There were pictographs on rock walls and clusters of cottonwoods that grew with their feet in the fitful stream in the sandy canyon bottom. Lichens clung to sandstone in clumps of bright red and orange, yellow and green. Cacti clawed their way through crusty soil; wildflowers erupted, and grasses swallowed trails, reclaiming. The sharp brine of juniper filled the air.

The morning was cool and damp from a rare streak of spring rain during the night. It was a welcome break from the heat of the last few days, but rain could be worrisome out here. High-walled canyons sent water rushing off and down, so it wasn't the storm above that was necessarily dangerous, it was the rain miles away falling on higher ground. Lily taught people to listen for the obvious signs of floods, and to watch for the smaller ones, too: currents suddenly full of sticks and twigs, previously crystal-clear rivers turning muddy. Last night's rain didn't amount to much, but any rainfall meant mud and a doused fire. No fires meant no food, and any guide would agree that guests would write off a sore ass and a stiff bed, but they wouldn't overlook an empty belly. At the dude ranch, Lily's dad used to say, "You gotta keep 'em tired and full." It had been true there and was even truer out here.

She stoked the fire back to life, watching the coals flicker and glow before finally catching. When the smoke spiraled overhead, Lily set the water to boil and got the coffee ready to brew.

The horses were fed and inspected, their hooves cleaned. Lily owned eight in all, each with their own quirks and temperament—which made it easy to assign them to riders of any skill level—and each one far more pampered than Lily herself.

Bonnie, her ten-year-old bay mare, was in a feisty mood,

tolerating the comb through her tail but pawing the ground impatiently, ready to get started. It was rough country, but these horses were conditioned to riding it, preferring the slower pace and varied terrain—and extra treats—that came with a day on the trail over a quiet day in pasture back at Lily's cabin. Some outfits used four-wheel-drives and ATVs to travel the Outlaw Trail where it was passable, but most of the maps Duke Wilder drew could be followed only on foot or on horseback. "If it was good enough for the outlaws," he used to say, "it's good enough for me."

Lily's father had been obsessed with these canyons and spent years chasing the same myths and legends she now exploited to take groups on guided tours and fake treasure hunts. Unlike Duke, however, the wannabe weekend warriors who hired Lily went home at the end of the ride, back to jobs and family and reality. Duke might have physically walked through the door at the end of a dig, but he was never really with his family, always dreaming about finding long-buried treasures while the rest of his life—his wife, his health, and his family's ranch—eventually fell away.

Footsteps crunched through the brush, and Bonnie whinnied softly at Nicole's approach. "Is Bossy Bonnie ready to go?" she cooed, stroking the mare's soft nose.

"Someone knows she gets a peppermint at the end of the day."

Nicole had come to Utah from Montana, in search of a job and a life away from a mean family and a meaner boyfriend. Lily met her while bartending at Archie's; Nicole was hired into the tiny kitchen to clean dishes and prep greasy bar food. She'd been sleeping in her truck at the time, and Lily dragged her home, gave her a place to stay. They were both broke and totally alone, and they quickly bonded in a way only two women can when they've had enough of their lives being turned upside down by the impulses and bad decisions of men.

When Archie suggested Lily as a guide for a crew scouting film sites in Moab, there was no one else she trusted to come along but Nicole. That first trip led to another, and when someone asked about the history and myths around the area, about Butch Cassidy and his gang using these trails to run from the law and hide their loot, and whether it might still be out there, it was like Duke's ghost coming back to haunt her. Lily had immediately thought of his goddamn tally journal— filled with random notes and riddles and stories and maps. It was one of the few things of his with any value whatsoever, and she decided, hell, *something* good should come of growing up in the shadow of *the* Duke Wilder. Who knew so many people wanted to play cowboy?

But now she'd been at it for seven years, which was a long time to be at something she'd started out of necessity and barely liked to begin with. The money was enough to quit bartending from May to September, buy back some of the horses she'd had to sell, *and* pay Nicole, but she was still just treading water. Lily's truck and horse trailer were ancient, and Bonnie wasn't getting any younger. Frankly, neither was Lily. She loved this wild country, but she wanted a real house with kids and land for horses to run. She wanted to put down roots, but growing roots wasn't easy in the desert.

"How's the new group?" Lily asked.

Nicole picked up a bucket and filled it with weed-free pellets. At the sound, hooves pounded through the dirt as a black-and-white paint trotted happily toward them, head thrown back as he shook his mane. It would be cliché to say horses were like their owners, but look at either Snoopy or Nicole the wrong way and they would knock you on your ass with a convenient tree branch and not think twice about it.

"Nothing we haven't seen before." Nicole ignored Snoopy nibbling on her shirt before he ducked his head to help himself to the bucket. "There's a loud one, a sweet potato, a creep, and a—"

Lily stopped, comb in hand. "Creep?" She and Nicole could handle themselves, but once they got out on the trail, they would be well and truly alone. "He wasn't a problem, was he?"

"Nah." Nic pulled out a handful of barley and offered it to Bonnie. "Just annoying. There's also a quiet one, and he's real cute."

Lily lifted a brow, making Nicole bark out a laugh. "I like the occasional quiet one," she said, "but he looked a little too tame for me. Spent most of the ride here gazing at the sky out the window."

Before she could stop it, a memory filled Lily's head: of a sweet, sweaty, lovesick city boy moving with purpose above her, a blanket-covered pile of hay beneath her back, the stars visible through a crack in the old barn roof. Leo whispered for her to be quiet, but he didn't stop. If anything, he went harder, swallowing her sounds and biting back his own. "Quiet doesn't necessarily mean tame."

It was Nicole's turn to look scandalized. "Story time? I haven't heard this one before."

"Yes, you have," Lily said, and tossed Bonnie's comb into her tack box.

"Which of them was quiet and not tame?" Nic tapped her lips with a finger, her hands already covered in dirt.

"None you're thinking about."

"The accountant from Quebec?" She held up a hand. "Wait. That architect from Oregon."

Lily shook her head, shoving the images away. "Sun's coming up, and we've got breakfast to make."

Nicole paused as awareness landed. "Oh, you mean him."

"Yeah."

With conversation temporarily stalled, they both word-lessly moved to the cooking fire. The birds were still mostly silent, more cold than hungry in the breaking dawn, but the song of a canyon wren filled the air.

They poured themselves some coffee, got cleaned up again, and started on breakfast prep, knowing the smell of bacon would be enough to rouse the sleepy campers from their tents even if it wasn't quite enough to lure the sun over the mountaintops.

"So, what's the plan if we stop doing this?" Nicole asked, redirecting—but not necessarily in a direction Lily preferred. She knew money and the prospect of a future without any weighed heavily on Nicole's mind; frankly, it was all Lily could think about, too.

"Don't know yet. We can always work at Archie's until we figure it out."

A pat of butter hissed as it hit the hot griddle.

"What about the rodeo?" Nicole asked. "For the ranch. I used to make more barrel racing than a week working at Archie's. I could enter, just to try?"

"I don't know if Snoopy has it in him anymore," Lily told her with a wince. "But I love you for thinking of it."

Nicole growled, taking her frustrations out on the potatoes in front of her. "This is why people in movies do stupid shit for money. Maybe Cassidy had it right, and we should just rob a bank."

"Didn't work out so well for him," Lily reminded her.

"Because he wasn't a woman. Men are idiots."

Lily laughed, dropping a handful of chopped onions into the hot cast-iron skillet. "Even if we have to pour beers and swindle every wannabe cowboy who walks in the place, we'll figure it out. It's you and me, remember?" Nicole nodded. "Let's just get through this week and we'll go from there."

The rustle of canvas tent flaps cut through the sound of Nicole humming over the camp stove. When Lily glanced up, her gaze snagged on the shape of a man stepping through time.

The breath was knocked clear out of her.

Lily knew all about mirages in the desert, when light bent and refracted and moved through warmer air, causing the eye to see something that wasn't there. She'd seen this particular mirage before, so it took her a moment to get her bearings and realize that this time was different. This time, it wasn't a trick of the light or the air, or even wishful thinking.

This time, Lovesick City Boy was walking right toward her.

Chapter Five

SO, SHE BOLTED.

Without a word of explanation, Lily threw the wooden spoon onto the table and sprinted back over to where Bonnie lazily grazed. Ducking behind the horse, Lily hid from view, resting her forearm on her mare's soft flank and working to get her pulse under control.

What in the hell?

Leo Grady was here.

Leo—the man who'd made her believe in happily ever after and then vanished without a word—was *here*?

Needing confirmation, she peeked over Bonnie's back, and her heart vaulted into her windpipe. It was him, without a doubt.

Tall, lean, smooth honeyed neck visible above the collar of his North Face fleece. She'd know that neck anywhere; she'd recognize that posture and that long stride from half a mile away. The rest of him autofilled in her memory, and Lily squeezed her eyes closed, pushing away another deluge of images. It had taken her years to shove them out and here they were, roaring back like a flash flood, uninvited.

She would pray to a god if she believed in one. She'd take off in her truck if she didn't mind leaving Nicole on her own. A glance down at her jeans revealed how worn and dusty they were; her shirt was faded blue chambray, with a big bleach stain on one sleeve. Immediately, Lily felt shabby. Her hair was braided for practicality, not style, and she was wearing more sunblock than makeup. She looked young for her age, but not really in the way most people meant when they said that. If her quick glimpse told her anything, it was that Leo had grown into a full-on *man*. Meanwhile, here she was, looking poor and unpolished and exactly like the girl he'd left behind all those years ago.

That is, if he even remembered her. Five months together had been wiped out in a single morning. One minute he was over her, cocooned in a blanket next to the river—eyes locked on her mouth, his bottom lip trapped tightly between his teeth—and the next they were inside, staring down at the ranch's old answering machine with a red *29* flashing in insistent, mechanical panic.

The rest of that day unfurled in a blur: His mother had been in an accident. She would be fine, the messages said, but was in the hospital, and Leo needed to come home. Leo'd bolted to the bedroom, throwing things in a suitcase. He only managed to pack half of his things before it was time to go, before he sealed his mouth tightly to hers, promising he'd come back.

His last words to her that morning had been "I'll call you when I land."

He hadn't.

With his mom in the hospital, things had undoubtedly been busy, she'd assumed. His sister, Cora—ten years his junior—had been only twelve; his mother had an important career and many responsibilities to juggle. But when Lily called Leo three days later, there was no trace of the soft-spoken, adoring man she'd come to know. Instead, he'd been abrupt with her for the very first time. "I can't do this right now, Lily. I'll call you in a few days."

That had been the last time she'd heard his voice.

A pathetic late-night Google search a few years back told her Leo Grady had graduated from NYU a year later. That he'd been quickly hired at a small tech company in Queens, then at a bigger firm in Manhattan. He didn't have Facebook. Didn't have Instagram. Didn't even have a head shot in his company profile. She didn't know if he'd married or had kids. Lily both loved and hated how impossible Leo had been to stalk online.

Now, when the ghost from her past disappeared inside the small wooden outhouse, she jogged back over to where Nicole was tending the sizzling pan of potatoes.

"What was that about?" Nic asked. "You get bit?"

"Yeah. Big . . . bitey thing," Lily answered vaguely. "Hey, do you want to do orientation this morning?"

Wearing a bewildered frown, Nicole looked at Lily from under the brim of her hat. Nic always did pickup. Lily always did orientation. Not once had they ever traded these roles.

Nicole scooped a big pile of crisp potatoes and onions into an aluminum tray, saying, "Dub, you know the only thing I'd like less than doing orientation is putting my face directly onto this hot pan."

With a sigh, Lily reached for the clipboard. One of Nicole's other responsibilities was to pair guests with horses based on the information they provided about height, weight, and riding experience. Unfortunately, the two of them had been doing this so long that Lily rarely looked at the guests' names and assignments until she was gathering them around the breakfast table to begin orientation. Now she glanced down at the assignment sheet.

Rider: Bradley Daniels	**Horse:** Bullwinkle
Rider: Walter Gibb	**Horse:** Dynamite
Rider: Leo Grady	**Horse:** Ace
Rider: Terrence Trottel	**Horse:** Calypso

Lily let out a quiet "Well, shit."

Maybe it's a different neck, a different set of squared shoulders, a different Leo Grady. Frantically, she flipped through the folder of guest forms. On only the second page her hand froze in midair; the stapled-together photo and form for a man named Bradley fluttered to the ground as Lily stared down at the face of the man she used to know.

She closed her eyes to absorb the final blow. A deep-rooted self-preservation instinct made her scratch around to find a legitimate way out of this. Could they cancel this excursion, cite an incoming storm? Could they claim one of the horses was lame? Could she fake illness?

They could . . . but long ago Lily had learned it was a waste of everyone's time to fake anything.

Staring down at the photo, Lily wondered what he was like now. And she wondered why he was here. Her company was called Wilder Adventures, for Christ's sake. Lily wasn't exactly hiding.

"Do you remember what you said earlier?" she asked, looking up at Nic. "About the guests? You said there was a loud one, a sweet potato, a creep, and . . . ?"

Nicole gazed to the side, thinking. "A quiet one?"

The quiet one—and what else had Nicole said? That he was cute? Lily looked down at his photo again. Twenty-two-year-old Leo had been cute. He'd been shy and sweet and perpetually lost in thought, but this Leo—he must be thirty-two years old now—was devastating. In the photo, he appeared to be standing on a balcony somewhere, holding a beer and laughing at the photographer. His hair was still the soft, dark mess she remembered, always sticking up in the morning, falling forward on its own. Glimmering dark eyes. His face had lost the softness of youth and sharpened in the years they'd been apart, at once more delicate and more masculine. His cheekbones were sharper, his jaw more angular, his neck still as long as a summer day, his lips just as full as she remembered.

Shiiiiit.

Nicole leaned in, peeking over Lily's shoulder at what had her so transfixed, and Lily slapped the folder shut, tossing it on the table. Aggressively, she picked up a slab of bacon and started hacking it into thick slices. Each one dropped into the hot cast-iron skillet with a satisfying sizzle.

"You okay there, Dub?"

Not even a little bit. "Yeah, I'm good."

The group began filtering out one by one, stretching as they stepped out of their tents and pausing to take in the view they hadn't been able to see when they'd arrived.

"Oh, man, it's gorgeous here."

From over near the campfire, Leo's voice filtered to Lily, and goose bumps broke out along every inch of her body.

He would see her. He would see her, and she would have to react, and Lily Wilder was a woman who worked her hardest at everything, including remaining at least an arm's length from any emotional entanglement. Leo would be in her space for the next week, and she had no idea how to handle any of it.

So, she kept her head down, hiding beneath the brim of her cowboy hat as she carried steaming trays of potatoes, eggs, and bacon to the wooden picnic table in the center of camp. Nicole rang the dinner bell and footsteps scratched sleepily through dry dirt. When a husky laugh echoed behind her, Lily's stomach absolutely fell to her feet. She knew how a rattlesnake sounded in the brittlebush on the ranch and the raspy croak of a passing raven. She knew the trickling of water in a spring and the impatient huff of Bonnie when she was done for the day. And Lily knew—even after all this time—the deep, vibrating sound of Leo Grady's voice in the morning, the way it warmed up slowly, from rocks to gravel to a smooth, polished stone.

Taking a deep breath, she pulled herself together before she turned to face the men lined up for breakfast. "Morning, everyone."

Lily didn't have to be looking straight at him to feel Leo's wide gaze swing her way.

He sucked in a breath, eyes stunned, and it took every bit of her practiced indifference to appear oblivious. "Go ahead and fill up your plates. Once you're settled, I'll go over the game plan." She smiled as naturally as she could manage, adjusting the skillet and straightening a stack of forks. "We've got a big few days ahead of us, and there's more than enough food for everyone."

Three men crowded around the table, exclaiming about the food and the view. Everyone but Leo. Lily wasn't even sure he'd moved yet. After several seconds, he jerked to life, finding a spot at the far end of the picnic table and slowly lowering himself onto the bench. He didn't bother to take food; he just sat there, pulling a baseball cap on and using it to shield his eyes as he stared down at the wood.

God, it was unbearable. Lily's heartbeat was a jackhammer on concrete.

"You all met Nicole last night," she said, slowly finding her footing in the words she'd said at least a hundred times before. Nic waved from where she was pouring herself a cup of coffee, and Lily was pleased to see everyone's posture straighten in response.

"I'm Lily Wilder, 'Dub' to Nicole. Welcome to Wilder Adventures. I hope you're all ready for some good food, great horses, one-of-a-kind adventure, and some of the most beautiful country you've ever seen."

The guest Lily assumed Nicole had labeled "the loud one"—a fit, tanned white guy with prep-school hair and perfect teeth—slammed a hand on the table, cutlery clattering. "Bring it on!"

"You're here for a guided tour of some of the most remote and beautiful canyon lands on earth. In the late 1800s, outlaws like Butch Cassidy famously used a long trail that stretched across the West to evade the law. On that trail were Hole-in-the-Wall, Brown's Park, and Robbers Roost. You'll be riding some of it just like they did," she said. "Along the way we'll have some fun games, some home-cooked meals, a little history and geography, and at the end you'll get to use your newfound skills with the terrain to find hidden treasure."

A tall, tattooed man let out a derisive laugh, and Lily glanced over at him as he passed a hand across a thin mustache and wispy beard. Must be the creep.

Ignoring him, she continued. "I've been in and out of these mountains all my life. I know every trail, every landmark and plant out here. As long as you do what we say, I promise you'll be safe and have the best trip of your life. That said, I'm in charge on the trail, and when I'm not around, Nicole is. You may have noticed that we are women. If you have any problems following a woman's lead, taking instructions from us, being respectful, or keeping your hands to yourself, you should say something now while we can still call someone to come get you."

Nicole placed her comically large knife on the table and smiled at each of them far too long to appear completely sane. "Anyone got a problem with that?"

All but one of them shook their heads, muttering politely. The one Lily could only assume was the "sweet potato"—soft dark curls, enormous green eyes, and full, ruddy cheeks—swallowed audibly, whispering, "No, ma'ams."

The lone holdout crossed his arms over his chest, leaned back, and let out a single dry laugh.

"Question?" Lily asked him. He was relatively fit, early thirties, wearing an expression of unmasked disdain. They almost always had at least one of these: men who came out here thinking they knew everything, that she and Nic were just two cutie-pies playing at being tough.

They got over these misconceptions by the end of the trip.

"I'm good." He sucked on his teeth and gave her a brief once-over. "Just sitting here being respectful, sweetheart."

"Glad to hear it." Lily clapped her hands, wishing they could skip this next part. On instinct she looked to Leo, startled to find his dark, direct gaze pinning her. Eye contact was a streak of fire shimmering through her from head to toe. She felt her neck heat.

Damn it.

Blinking away, she looked to the sweet potato, who was wearing a bright orange shirt with bold green letters spelling HOWDY!

"Why don't we go around, and you can tell me your names," Lily said, "a little about your riding experience, and what you hope to get out of this trip, so we can make sure it happens. Walter?" She looked around at each of them. "Why don't you start?"

"That's me," Sweet Potato said, raising a hand and then dabbing at his mouth with the corner of a paper napkin. "Walter Gibb. A little experience riding when I was a kid but haven't been on a horse for a long time." He cleared his throat. "I'm a Gemini and single, and I work as a pet health and wellness facilitator—"

"He manages a Petco," the Beard cut in with a sneer.

"Is your name Walter?" Lily asked.

He looked up at her, annoyed but confused. "No? I'm Terry."

"Then I suggest you stop interrupting and wait until the name Terry is called. Sound good?" He gave Lily a gruff look but, unfazed, she turned back to Walter. "Go ahead. Tell us a little about your hobbies."

"I have a small plot in a community garden," he said, shrugging. "Mostly lettuces and flowers. Tomatoes." He looked skyward, thinking. "I have brunch with Leo and his sister, Cora, on Sundays, but otherwise I don't have a ton of regular activities."

Lily's heart pinched painfully at this mention of Leo's life back in New York, but she pushed past it. "And what are you hoping to get out of this trip?"

"Hmm. Well, when I was a kid, I used to go to sleepaway camp every summer and hated it. I'd spend more time dreading the day my parents would drop me off than I physically spent at the camp. I was an anxious child, so I never canoed or did the obstacle course . . . or anything but ceramics and campfire songs, really. Last night, I really didn't want to be here. But after sleeping on it, I'm thinking of this as a camp do-over." He glanced at the others before doing a little bow in his seat. "Thank you."

Nicole snorted. She had a weakness for the soft, earnest ones. He'd already won her over.

"Terry?" Lily said. "Now it's your turn."

He took his time setting down his fork, folding his napkin, holding court. "I've been out here a number of times," he said, reaching up the sleeve of his camo T-shirt to scratch his shoulder and expose his relatively unimpressive biceps. "Depending on where we're headed, I might have some suggestions on more efficient routes. In my day-to-day life I run the Cabela's in Newark."

"He works in the stockroom," the loud one interjected.

"—with a flourishing side business of my own."

The loud one again: "He sells hacked iPhones."

Lily was tempted to remind everyone that they'd get a

turn and to stop cutting in, but Terry was already on her shit list; she just let them roll with it.

For his part, Terry easily ignored the interruptions, leaning back as though holding their rapt attention. "I consider myself an adventurer overall. A hunter. I like getting outside, shedding the bullshit of society. Lately it's too much homo everything and gender-neutral whatnot. Jesus Christ. Outside, at least I can embrace what it means to be a man."

Lily felt her fists instinctively curl with anger.

"So far I'll admit he's my least favorite," Nicole said, voicing Lily's thoughts, without any attempt to lower her voice. Leo choked on a bite of bacon.

Lily gave her a warning glance, and Terry continued. "I attended the fourteen-day Ultimate Man primitive living course in Boulder, paddled a couple hundred miles up the Colorado River, and did a bungee jump off the Bloukrans Bridge in South Africa."

"You all did these together?" Lily asked incredulously.

The loud one pulled back in alarm. "Are you kidding me? Hell no."

"*No*," Terry clarified. "These pussies wouldn't have made it out of the parking lot. These were trips I organized with the Cabela's boys."

"Terry doesn't usually come on these trips," Walter murmured.

Ignoring him, Terry glanced at Lily. "Sorry, am I allowed to say 'pussies,' boss?"

"What do you think?" she volleyed back.

Lily didn't miss the way the other three guys seemed to want to vanish into the ether.

"How would I know what a chick likes?" he said, laughing cockily.

The loud one barked out a laugh. Lily gaped at Terry, wondering if the world had ever witnessed a self-own that slapped that hard. He hadn't seemed to hear it, but out of the corner of her eye, she could see Leo bring his hands up to his face. She watched Terry pensively. "Are you going to be a problem?"

He smirked at her. "Wasn't planning on it."

"Glad we agree on that." And Lily was officially ready to move on. "Blondie?" she said, turning to the loud one. "You're up."

The same age as the others and good-looking, with wavy blond hair and blue eyes, he stood, smiling a dramatically sexy smile. He knew it, too. In another world and on the right night down at Archie's, Lily could imagine herself going home with him, primarily because she usually chose the terrible hot ones.

"I'm Bradley. I don't answer to 'Brad.' I'm a professor of archaeology at Rutgers." A professor of archaeology. Interesting. Lily had met her fair share of them through Duke's work back in the day, and Bradley did not fit the type. Rather than wearing head-to-toe weathered North Face or Patagonia gear, Bradley was in a button-down western-themed shirt with the word BURBERRY emblazoned across the chest and boots that were made of soft black leather with polished hooks and eyelets. What a knob. Those boots would be so covered in God-knew-what by the end of the week that they'd no doubt be left behind.

"I've been on a horse once or twice," he continued, "but

not for years, and even then, I'm sure I was pretty terrible at it. I play softball on the weekends, am the greatest uncle in the world to Miss Cora, and run once in a while with that loser down there." He pointed to Leo. "Basically, I'm here because I just want to be a goddamn cowboy for a week. Do I pass the test?" He dug his hands into the pockets of his very blue, very new jeans.

"Works for me," she said with an easy shrug, and Walter gave him a sweet *yay* as Bradley took his seat.

The enormity of the situation really hit her when she glanced down at the clipboard and registered that there was only one name left. Lily took a slow inhale, steadying herself. "I guess that leaves . . . Leo," she said as steadily as her throbbing pulse would allow.

With a resigned nod, he stood, and Lily mentally pleaded with her heart to stop its renewed, frantic pounding.

He cleared his throat, and she hoped he wouldn't let on that they knew each other. She wasn't proud of what his leaving had done to her. She didn't need that ugly scar put on display today.

"My name is Leo. I'm thirty-two." He paused, avoiding her gaze. "I have experience with horses." Silence seemed to swallow the air around them for a few moments before he continued. "I live in Manhattan and I work in IT."

After a beat where they were all clearly waiting for more, Bradley burst out laughing. "Riveting, dude. Don't be shy."

While the IT job didn't surprise her, this manifestation of it did. This version of Leo seemed more remote and detached than sweetly shy. The Leo she knew had been a numbers geek but gently reverent about them the way a painter is about art.

He'd tried his hardest to make her fall in love with math. He had a favorite *equation*, for Christ's sake—something about cutting up the surface of a sphere that Lily was sure she still wouldn't understand even if he'd spent the last decade explaining it.

She searched for the tiny clues that he was real, that he was the same man she'd known in that other life—a former lover with skin and bone and muscle right in front of her. When he reached to adjust his hat, Lily could see calluses across the insides of his palms. Not the roughened skin of someone who worked with his hands for a living, but the kind one got from hours at a gym or the occasional home remodeling project. The ruddy color in his cheeks meant he didn't spend all day in an office; he probably took a bike out every weekend or ran in the park. His watch was bulky and expensive, telling him not just the time but date, direction, altitude. Lily wondered how often he really needed to know any of that in his day-to-day life. He wasn't wearing a ring, and the fact that she noticed this—as well as the rush of relief it brought—made her want to break something.

Leo paused, like he was deciding how honest to be. The old version of him had been an open book, at least with her. She had no idea what this one was thinking. "Hobbies . . . I read a lot. I like biking, running—"

"Working," Bradley cut in with a sharp laugh.

"Right." Leo nodded with a wince. "As for what I hope to get from this . . ."

When he trailed off, she focused on the abused wood of the table. It had been worn smooth over the years, scored and burned in some places and buckling from the weight of time in others. Lily could relate.

"I guess I'm looking for adventure. My day-to-day life is pretty routine." He turned his baseball cap over in his hands and seemed to note that the mood had grown solemn. "But maybe let's set the low bar of just not dying," he added, and his lips curved into a small grin when the others laughed at this. Even this tiny glimpse of his crinkly-eyed smile made Lily's heart fall like a weight into her stomach.

Walter clapped again, louder this time.

"Okay, well." Lily floundered a little and motioned for Nicole to come forward with a small metal box. "I need your phones." If they'd read the orientation material ahead of time, they'd all know this was coming. But Lily found that it didn't matter how much they warned guests; a collective wave of griping and moans would always ripple through the group. Nicole walked along the table, thanking each man as he reluctantly set his device inside the box.

"You can keep whatever medicine you have, of course," she continued. "And if there's anything else you need—within reason—just let us know. We're supposed to be roughing it; the point is for it to be hard."

Terry let out a crude snicker. This one was going to be a handful.

She nodded toward where she spotted a small GPS unit sticking out of a pocket in his complicated vest. "You might want to lock that up in the tack shed. It won't do you any good."

Terry closed his eyes, sighing. "It's a global positioning system, honey. Working in the middle of nowhere is literally its job."

"Well, whoever sold it to you didn't ask where you'd be using it."

He ran a hand down his beard. "Do you understand how GPS works?"

Lily pointed to where spires of red rock could be seen in the distance. "We'll be going there. Batteries run out, cell phone coverage is nonexistent, canyon walls block satellites, and out there under the sun? Those tiny digital displays are almost impossible to see. You have a paper map in your backpack. You'll need to pay attention to it and to me. Not a GPS. Is that clear?"

"She's scary, but I kind of dig it," Walter stage-whispered to Leo, who, she noted, managed to hide any reaction at all to this.

Picking up a backpack identical to the ones she'd left in each of their tents last night, Lily began to unload it. "You've each been given a pack filled with things you'll need. You can use the one provided or your own, but if you use yours, make sure to move every single thing over, including the sleeping bag on your cot. You'll need it all. Anything you want to leave behind will be locked up securely in the tack shed."

She smoothed a map flat on the table's surface. A glance around reassured her that she had everyone's attention, including Leo's. It was an enlarged printout of one of the dozens of maps Duke had drawn in his lifetime. Her father knew the American Southwest better than almost anyone, and his expertise had been wildly in demand. Too bad it had rarely been lucrative. At least, not for him. Museums benefited, native lands were returned their artifacts, but Duke was never in it for the money. He might have received a small finder's fee to help pay the bills, but it was the thrill of the chase that excited him, untangling clues and slowly unearthing history. It was the hunt.

Lily tapped the printout near the ridge where Duke had once carefully written the word *Horseshoe*. "This is where we are now." She slid her finger down along the trail, pointing out some of the stops. "Tonight, we'll camp at the edge of the spur in Robbers Roost, then on to French Spring below Hans Flat.

"Now, this part is important." She pulled out another map of the area with elevation lines; there were a *lot* of them. "Stay away from the edge of any canyon. I guarantee it's not as solid as it looks, and you're not as athletic and steady on your feet as you think. Don't learn the hard way."

Eyes wide with mild terror, Walter nodded earnestly.

"Throughout the trip, you'll get to solve some clues and use your maps to find the path and eventually find the treasure." She straightened. "We'll talk more about the rest as we go, but first things first, we're getting you acquainted with your horses. I want everyone to roll up their tents and pack while we clean up breakfast, and then meet us at the corral. Does anyone need a good pair of boots?"

The men shook their heads, murmuring quiet *no*s. Only one person remained noticeably silent.

Leo ran uneasy hands over the thighs of his jeans, finally admitting, "I do."

The last thing Lily wanted right off the bat was a reason to talk to him alone. "Right." Her voice was sharp; Leo knew how important good boots were out here. "Get your stuff packed and meet me in the tack shed near the horses."

He blinked at her, no doubt hearing the razor in her tone. "Okay."

Lily began stuffing everything back into the pack and noticed that everyone was chitchatting, lingering over their cold coffee. "What are y'all waiting for? You need me to carry you?"

They scattered, but Nicole stood there, quietly studying her. "You wanna tell me what's going on?"

Lily glanced at her and then away. " 'Going on'?"

Nic's blue eyes went wide, and she pushed her hair off her forehead. "Oh, we're playing the bullshit game?"

It wasn't worth trying to keep this from her. "I know him."

"The quiet one." It wasn't even a question.

"Yeah. Leo." She looked down at her boots and dragged a line in the dirt.

Surprised, Nic straightened and looked back over her shoulder. "Holy shit. That's him? It's that Leo? From the ranch?"

"Yeah."

"Did he track you down?"

Lily was already shaking her head. "I'd bet Bonnie that he had no idea I'd be here."

Nic sized her up quietly. "Should I worry?"

"What? No, I'm fine," Lily assured her. "It was forever ago. It's fine. I'm really fine."

"Sounds like it's fine," she said dryly.

They both knew it was a lie, but Nic didn't bother to ask again.

Chapter Six

LEO WALKED TO his tent in a daze, heart racing and palms clammy. With every step, his feet landed unsteadily on the ground—he felt like he'd walked onto a moving platform or into a wormhole. Seeing Lily wasn't unlike being transported back to that first day at the Wilder Ranch, when she'd emerged from the barn and his world had instantly tipped upside down.

Except this time there was no anticipation, no immediate head rush of a dream that this woman could someday want him—only the stark recollection that he'd had the perfect love once and had pushed her away.

He was supposed to be packing, but instead he sat heavily down inside his tent, shell-shocked. Leo hadn't heard her voice since the morning she'd called him, checking in when he'd failed to. He hated how brusque and sharp he'd been—he'd tried to reach her later, tried to fix it, but by then it was too late.

Now she was *here* and his blood felt electric for the first time in a decade, his head awash with anticipation and guilt . . . and something else. Hurt. Belated confusion. Why hadn't she ever called him back?

After years of actively working to not obsess about where she was and what she was doing—envious of some imaginary man who got to love her and live the life he wanted—here he was, face-to-face with his first love, in the middle-of-nowhere desert. Leo had no idea how to proceed like everything was fine.

Minutes later, when the ringing in his ears eased and he trusted his legs not to buckle, Leo shoved his things into the roomy expedition pack Wilder Adventures provided and exited his tent. The remnants of breakfast had been cleared away, and Bradley was trying to figure out how to pack his tent into a bag the size of a coat pocket. Almost everyone wore jeans and long-sleeved shirts, but when Terry emerged from his tent, he'd changed into yet another set of camo military-style pants—the front pockets bulging with who knew what—and a vest with Velcro and straps and, somehow, even more pockets.

"You ready to do this thing?" Bradley asked Leo, who looked over at the shed, feeling deeply unprepared for the next ten minutes of his life.

"I have to grab boots."

"If you'd paid attention to the packing list," Terry said, "you wouldn't be on your way to see teacher right now."

Bradley smacked him in the stomach. "Have you seen teacher? She can bend me over her knee in the barn anytime she wants."

Just then, Nicole passed by, eyes narrowed, and Bradley straightened immediately, muttering, "My bad." Walter, who had just emerged from the outhouse, didn't seem to know what to do with his arms and settled on some kind of salute.

"Knock it off," Leo muttered to Bradley before setting his pack aside with the others and making his way to the opposite end of camp.

The tack shed was a twenty-by-twenty wood building next to a corral filled with a handful of excited horses who clearly knew it was almost time to go. Leo reached out, petting a soft nose as he passed, and stopped at the door. The shed leaned mildly in the shade of a spindly Russian olive tree, a wash stall with an ancient truck and trailer parked just behind. The door was wide enough to accommodate saddles or fifty-pound bags of feed and fitted with what looked like a sturdy lock for when they'd be out on the trail. It was meticulous inside, and he was hit with a bittersweet nostalgia at the heady scent of alfalfa and leather.

Lily was toward the back, working on something next to a big hook heavy with nylon halters, and Leo cleared his throat, wondering if he imagined the way she stiffened. He wished he could access the right words, the right way to open the most impossible of conversations, but his brain was a tangle. Why was she out here? Why was Lily Wilder, of all people, leading fake treasure hunts when she'd resented Duke's relationship with real ones more than anything?

"You need anything other than boots?" She didn't turn around, instead reaching for a lighter to melt the end of a piece of nylon rope.

Leo stared at her back, taking her in. Her braided hair was longer than when he'd known her, just past her shoulders. Her sleeves were rolled up, exposing the same toned arms, those perfect, calloused hands. Lily had beautiful hands; long fingers—almost delicate. But capable and strong. He remembered how gentle they were when she stroked the head of her favorite gelding, how steady when handling a spooked horse. Her habit of tapping her fingers restlessly when she was lost in thought.

He remembered the way it felt when those fingers danced across his bare skin.

Wave after wave of realization left Leo wondering if he would ever get over the fact that it was Lily. Right there. Lily Wilder was just *right there*.

But, he noticed, she seemed to have no reaction to him whatsoever.

"I realize this might be a weird thing to ask," he hedged, "but do you remember me?"

"Of course I remember you, Lovesick City Boy." She turned, and the flatness in her hazel eyes read *short on time and patience*. It was an expression Leo had seen dozens of times . . . just never directed at him. With him she'd been standoffish at first, pushing him away, almost—he'd realized in hindsight—to test the strength of his attraction. But once she'd given in, she'd been as vulnerable and wide open as the sky outside. She'd given him everything without hesitation: her body, her innocence, her trust.

"So?" she prompted, impatient. "Do you need anything besides boots?"

He had to swallow before he could answer evenly. "No."

Lily tossed the rope down and walked to a cabinet, opening it to reveal a tidy collection of boots in various states of wear and tear. She hadn't asked him what size he needed, but Leo figured he'd take whatever he got. Lily stretched for a pair on the top shelf, then walked over to dump them at his feet. A small cloud of dust kicked up around him.

"Those should work." She'd already returned to what she was doing.

He bent to pick them up and froze halfway. Holy shit. "You kept these?"

"Waste not, want not."

She was as difficult to crack as the Riemann hypothesis.

Straightening, he moved to sit on a dusty trunk and slipped off his sneakers. After a few moments of tense silence, he risked it. "I didn't know this was your business." Leo paused, trying again. "I mean, I didn't even know where we were headed until we got to the airport. We never—"

"Trust me, Leo," she interrupted quietly, "I believe you had no intention of ever running into me again."

"That's not . . ." He closed his mouth, not trusting what might come out. What was happening here? He'd always known she'd be hurt that he hadn't returned, but what had she expected him to do?

With words failing him, he picked up the first boot, staring down at it. The brown leather was smooth in his hand, the heel scuffed but still solid. Years ago—maybe a month before he'd laid eyes on Lily—when Duke told him over the phone that he'd want to get a pair of riding boots, Leo hadn't had the faintest idea what differentiated a riding boot from a hiking boot. In town, Duke took one look at Leo's Timberlands and sent him into Martindale's, where the woman said a good pair of boots could last ten years if he took care of them.

As Leo slipped his foot into one now, he could see she was

right. They'd obviously been worn, but when he stood, the instep gripped like it should, and the heel was snug enough not to slip. "Still fit perfectly."

She hummed in the corner: acknowledgment, not interest.

The familiar, stubborn set of Lily's shoulders creaked open a time capsule buried beneath Leo's ribs, sending a stabbing ache through him. He reached up, rubbing the spot just beside his breastbone. He'd loved Lily so deeply that it changed his biology. Standing here now, it seemed his love for her hadn't gone away, it had just been vacuum-sealed and stored. Back in her presence, the physical memory of his infatuation was released in a deluge, gasping to life, and adrenaline flooded his bloodstream.

He knew he'd been excused, but his feet wouldn't move. A heavy, knowing silence stretched between them. "How have you been?" he finally said.

"We're not doing that, Leo," she said, not bothering to turn around. "We're not long-lost friends. I am the guide, and you are the guest. We're only talking right now because you're paying me."

Well, then. He bit back a reply, knowing it wouldn't be helpful; there was a canyon of hurt between them on both sides, and five minutes in a toolshed wasn't going to bridge it.

Besides, they were standing in a room full of sharp ranching implements. The Lily he remembered knew how to use every one of them—there was a pitchfork right next to her, for God's sake.

And yet he had so many questions. Lily had always hated these stories, this trail, hated the word *treasure*. Duke might've been a wanderer, but the Lily he'd known would've had to be buried in the barn at Wilder Ranch before she'd let someone else run things. She'd never willingly leave.

"I just wondered what you were doing here," he managed, finally. Something ugly settled in his gut. "Why are you out here instead of getting the ranch ready for the season?"

Lily turned on him and instinct propelled him back a step.

"It's not my ranch anymore." She lifted her chin. "Now get your boots on and head out. We're done in here."

Chapter Seven

AFTER A BRIEF orientation to the gear they'd be using, Lily led the group over to meet the horses. Dynamite was patient enough to keep steady as Walter worked up the nerve to step into the saddle. Bullwinkle—as big a jokester as his rider—had Bradley on his ass twice before they'd even left the corral. In a stroke of irony, Terry was matched with Calypso—a grouchy, bitey mare—and after only a moment of hesitation, Leo managed to swiftly mount Lily's most sensitive horse, a beautiful black gelding named Ace.

Lily held back a flash of irritation. She would have liked to have seen him fall on his ass, too.

They worked on steering, halting, and dismounting. Once they were all comfortable enough for a walk, they tried a trot. Leo and Bradley even attempted a lope, all in the safety of the small fenced arena.

But once the guides and guests were out on the trail, the landscape swallowed up the camp behind them, and the guys seemed to realize that every step took them farther and farther from the safety of their everyday lives. No phones, no computers, nobody else to depend on but Lily and Nicole.

Lily had the sense that it was going to be a very long week.

Because no matter what she did—no matter how hard she blinked, or how savagely she pinched her own thigh or stared at the sun to burn something else into her vision—she couldn't seem to shake herself out of the stunning reality that Leo Grady had popped back into her life.

A couple of hours into the ride, she could take him in without her stomach clenching. He was still lean, but subtly bulkier in the way swimmers are—broad-backed, long-limbed, toned. Looking at him now, she could see nothing of the colt still growing into his frame. This Leo was a man who moved with ease in his body. His riding posture was as instinctively solid as it had ever been: hips forward, back straight but relaxed, heels down in the stirrups, with one hand resting on his thigh, the other loosely holding the reins.

Eager, hyperattentive, twenty-two-year-old Leo faded into a childish fever dream, paling in comparison to this man.

That summer, it had taken her forever to realize that the way he chased her wasn't standard for him. For weeks she'd assumed he was a player, a flirt pretending to be shy. No one who looked like that and came after a girl with such bare intentions could possibly be as sincere as he seemed.

But he was. And the more she'd gotten to know him, the more she'd realized that he was usually reserved to the point of stoic silence. That Leo trusted only the people closest to him with the quiet, raspy flow of his thoughts. And right now, being reminded of how carefully controlled he was—how that same control meant that he would spend hours figuring out her body in ways she hadn't even understood yet, how that control meant that when he'd decided to stay at the ranch with her she knew he'd thought about it from every angle, but how that control also must have been what allowed him to disappear entirely, like a ghost into fog—made Lily want to knock him off Ace and onto his ass.

"It's fitting I'm riding an Arabian," Terry said out of nowhere, dragging two fingers over his dusty mustache. He kept moving his horse to the front of the group, and Lily kept telling him to fall back in line.

"Calypso is an American quarter horse," Nicole cut in breezily.

"Given that in ancient times," Terry continued, ignoring her, "Arabians were reserved only for men to ride."

"Do you just make bullshit up all day long?" Nic asked. Clearly she had already entered the Tired of a Guest's Garbage phase. It had barely been twelve hours; a new record.

"It's not bullshit." Terry took a long pause to clear his throat and launched a thick ball of phlegm to the side. "The Arabian bloodline is the only pure bloodline left in existence."

"That's—*no*." It was the first thing Leo had said in hours. "There are lots of other pure-blood breeds, Terry."

"He's right," Nicole said, impressed.

Walter angled himself in the saddle to glance back at him. "Did you learn that when you worked on the ranch, Leo?"

Leo's eyes briefly flickered to Lily, then away. "I—well—"

"Ease up on Calypso's reins, Terry," she interrupted, saving them both. But she was relieved to discover that Leo hadn't tipped his friends off to what had gone down between them years ago. She suspected it was just a matter of time before the other three figured it out, but the longer she had without them gossiping about her, looking at her differently, the better.

Terry huffed out an annoyed breath. "Calypso is a mare who needs a strong hand."

"She's my horse," Lily reminded him, "and you'll ease up or you'll walk the rest of the way on your own feet."

"Today is our shortest day on horseback," Nic said, glancing nervously between Lily and Leo before turning her attention to the rest of the group. "In part because you'll be sore. We'll reach tonight's camp in about a mile or so."

"Another *mile*?" Bradley whimpered and tried to find a comfortable position in the saddle. "I already can't feel my balls."

Just as he said it, they came around a bend and the second night's camp came into breathtaking view in the distance: a dramatic outcropping of wavy brilliant-red rock hugging a small open pasture of russet earth and clumps of spiky green sagebrush. Lily squinted to see the four hay bales with fresh targets for the archery competition and four others with iron bullhorns protruding for the lassoing. In a locked chest nearby, there'd be four sets of locks to pick, four books with code to solve, and four slide puzzles.

Usually, this was Lily's favorite day of the trip. It was the first full day out in the crisp air and unreal landscape. Everyone was excited to be riding but happy to get off the horse after only a couple of hours. Guests were getting used to the idea that they'd done this for fun, gamely ready for adventure until the end. Tonight's dinner, chili and cornbread, was Lily's specialty. She loved the games, loved watching the guests with their newfound confidence, loved the usually friendly competition. But this time, she was filled with vague dread because whatever Terry thought was going to happen when the games came out, he was mistaken. He'd probably never seen Leo in this element.

They reached camp in a lazy, dragging single-file line, the horses faking being tired so they could get their treats, the men genuinely sore and overheated. All except Leo, whose posture remained straight and balanced atop Ace. Damn if he didn't look like he was made to ride that horse.

While Lily dismounted and headed to retrieve lunch items from the cooler dropped ahead for them, Nicole guided them over to the short fence where the horses would be tied for the night and have easy access to shade and grass and water. The men climbed down with varying degrees of grace; Leo slid easily from Ace and tied him loosely to the post. Lily ripped her eyes away just in time to catch Terry falling in a tumble and landing on his ass with a satisfyingly rough impact. He pretended to have done it intentionally as he plucked out a long piece of grass and stuck it between his teeth.

"The horses pee over there," Lily told him. "Just so you know."

Terry dropped the grass.

Her attention was drawn like a magnet to the left, to where Leo stretched out sore muscles and his shirt rode up. She wanted to look away, she really tried to, but it was like that small, exposed swath of honeyed skin had her eyes under some Vulcan death grip. When he turned to begin taking the saddle off Ace, the fabric of his shirt stretched taut across his back muscles.

That body used to belong to me, Lily marveled. *That man was mine.*

"Okay!" she shouted, oddly loud. Everyone startled, turning to look over their shoulders at her. With a flapping hand, she pointed to the sandwich spread she had begun unloading, the lunch they needed to devour before the games could begin. "Eat."

Ignoring her abrupt tone, they descended on the table like they hadn't seen food in a week. She absolutely did not stare at Leo's forearms as he reached for a piece of lettuce to drop on his sandwich, or at the tight clench of his jaw as he took a huge, ravenous bite.

"Who can tell me about Butch Cassidy?" she asked, redirecting her brain away from sexy things and toward work, and professionalism, and the fact that *Leo had abandoned her*, for crying out loud. Lily held up a preemptive hand. "Someone other than Terry."

He laughed at this, grabbing a pile of ham by the fistful. "Why? You afraid I might know more than you?"

Lily blinked, biting back a sharp reply.

"He was a bank robber," Walter called, clearly the peacemaker. "He also robbed trains. And he had a gang. The Wild Bunch."

"He did," Lily said, folding a couple of pieces of sliced turkey on her bread.

Bradley wiped at his mouth with a paper napkin. "So, if this is the actual trail, were they using it to run from the law? Right here?"

"That's right," Lily said. "And we're headed to one of the places Cassidy supposedly hid money to come back to later. A lot of people say it's still out here."

"That's because it is, sweetie."

"Thank you for proving my point, Terry," she said evenly.

"Walter, do you remember what I said about the Outlaw Trail?"

"That it stretched across the West. Hole-in-the-Wall, Brown's Park, and Robbers Roost?"

"Exactly." Lily nodded. "That's where we are, near Robbers Roost. A spot used by many bandits to lay low between heists or hole up during winter. The goal for this trip is to have a good time with each other, to enjoy one of the most beautiful spots in this country, and to follow clues to find the hidden treasure at the end." She cringed inwardly, hating how cheesy and manufactured this all sounded. It hadn't ever sounded that way to her before, but *before* there was no Leo, who knew better than anyone how Lily thought Butch Cassidy's still-hidden money was one of the stupidest legends to live out here. Walter raised his hand.

"Yes, Walter?"

"If a lot of bandits knew to come here, how did nobody else ever find this place?"

"The Outlaw Code," she told him.

Bradley spoke around a bite of sandwich. "Honor among thieves."

Lily nodded. "If word got out, it'd be ruined for everyone."

"I guess that makes sense," Walter said. "Hey, if we find treasure, do we split it?"

"Nope, anything you find is yours to keep," Lily said.

He frowned. "I say we split it. That seems more in keeping with the code."

"I like that," Bradley said.

"Great. But in order to do that," she continued, "you'll need to solve codes and puzzles, pick some locks, and maybe even see if you can hit a few bull's-eyes. We're going to practice all of that today."

"Archery?" Terry's chest puffed. "I once took down a ten-point buck with a single arrow."

Ignoring this, Walter shot a hand into the air again. "She said puzzles. I call Leo."

Bradley leaned forward, nearly launching the crust of his sandwich at Nicole in his rush to battle this out. "Fuck you. I call Leo."

"You're all working solo," Lily cut in, raising her voice over their bickering. "It's a friendly contest. No teams."

Amid their overlapping protests—*But I've never shot a bow and arrow— Everyone knows Leo is the code master— Don't be so sure, Walt— Puzzles like on* Survivor, *you mean?*—Lily stood and cleared out the lunch spread, avoiding the way her ancient lizard brain wanted to remind them all that no matter who called dibs today, Leo had been hers first.

Chapter Eight

"THERE ARE FIVE stations," Lily told them as they stood in front of the field full of games. "The slide puzzle, code deciphering, lassoing, archery, and lock picking."

"What about fire building?" Terry asked. "You're telling me that isn't important out here?"

She slowly turned her eyes to him. "You want four amateurs to set fires in the desert, Terry?"

He shifted on his feet, falling silent, and she continued. "There's a tool kit at every station." She walked them through the basics, knowing archery would need to be a little more hands-on. With a tilt of her chin, Lily beckoned them over to the archery setup and showed each of them how to hold the bow, how to nock the arrow, how to aim and release. Only Terry and Leo seemed to have any experience with it; as long as Walter and Bradley didn't shoot the arrow directly overhead or at each other, they'd be okay.

"What do we get if we win?" Terry asked.

Nicole grinned around a toothpick. "A chance to die like a man."

"An extra clue," Lily corrected. "And an extra beer tonight."

That got their attention. Gathering them at the start of the course, Lily blew her whistle and the men jumped into action toward the slide puzzles. All but Leo. He carefully approached his puzzle, observing, but didn't touch it. While the other three frantically shifted pieces, turning the board to various angles, Leo stood, staring.

"What's he doing?" Nicole stage-whispered out of the side of her mouth.

"Solving it."

As expected, Leo stepped forward, leaning down, and after ten decisive moves, stepped back.

"Check."

Lily walked over; the image of the red rock landscape had been assembled perfectly. Of course. She gave a stiff nod. "Go on."

With a little smirk, he was at the code. Leo leaned in, pen in hand, surveying again. This time, he tried a few things out, but Lily witnessed the moment it clicked.

"Oh, he got it," Nicole said.

They watched him write the answer and then flip his paper over so Bradley, who had just finished the puzzle, couldn't see.

"Wanna check?" he asked, looking up at her with amusement in his eyes.

Lily set her jaw, shifting her attention to the side as she tamped down the unsettling combination of irritation and attraction. "Just go on."

He struggled a bit with the lock picking but still made it out before Bradley solved the code. Terry made it through the code quickly, but there was no hope for anyone else. Lily didn't think anyone in the history of Wilder Adventures had finished the sequence of challenges faster than Leo. He had a lasso made and wrapped around his hay-bale steer's horns in under a minute, and surprised even Lily when he hit his third bull's-eye in archery and then slowly turned, lowering the bow in his arm as he looked over at her.

"Is that everything?" he asked.

"You showing off?" she replied.

He reached up, scratching his eyebrow and squinting at her, backlit by the sun. "Maybe a little." His gaze burned briefly, only a flicker of heat, but she caught it. "Had to remind myself that once upon a time I was good at something other than sitting at a desk."

The unexpected vulnerability in his tone hit her like a punch to the stomach. "And? Are you satisfied?"

"Satisfied?" Finally, a real smile. "Not yet."

Her breath froze in her chest. Lily had been all wrong; she'd been worried that the pieces of Leo that differentiated him from every other man were gone, muted somehow in the intervening years. But present-day Leo wasn't cold, he'd just been stunned into silence at their unexpected reunion. That shock was ebbing. She could see with her own two eyes that he was still the paradoxical brew of hot-blooded and restrained she'd fallen for years before.

And heaven help her. It was warm out and he was all male physicality and testosterone. Leo had changed into a black T-shirt and the sleeves hugged his broad shoulders. His jeans hung low on his hips, well-worn and soft. The size thirteen boots Lily had tossed at him only this morning were dusty, soft brown leather.

Lily couldn't help the laugh that came out of her like a celebration. She *wanted* to hate him. She *wanted* to resent this man forever. But how could she? Whether he was aware of it or not, he was looking at her like she was the prize at the end.

She blew the whistle again, and all around her, activity stopped. "Gentlemen, we have a winner."

Walter let out a delighted laugh. But Terry narrowed his eyes, throwing down his rope. "You didn't check his code."

"Didn't need to," Lily said, and turned her eyes to Leo. "What's the answer?"

He lifted one side of his mouth into a smile. " 'Whatever Lily Wilder says, we do.' It's a ROT cipher."

"Goddammit," Bradley said. "How'd you know all that?"

"Eagle Scout," he said, still looking right at Lily.

They were staring at each other. It was probably too long. Then it was definitely too long, but something happened in the depths of it. A tether, connecting them across time.

"Hello?" Walter said quietly, waving a confused hand in the air.

When they failed to look away, a murmur of awareness passed around the group.

"Wait," she heard Walter whisper. "Bradley, her name is *Lily Wilder*. Wasn't that—?"

"Oh shit," Bradley whispered. "You're right. She owned the ranch he worked at, didn't she?"

"She sure did," Lily said. Anger, attraction, and confusion created friction in her bloodstream. The cat was out of the bag, and it was her fault. She knew it. But what could she do?

She'd been completely unraveled watching Leo in his element like this. "Leo and I go way back, don't we?"

Leo nodded slowly, exhaling. "We do."

And even with their past out there for everyone to see, the heated moment didn't immediately break off. Unfortunately, for her own sanity, she needed it to.

"All right, then," she said, wrenching her gaze away. "Y'all read the code. Gossip time is over, and Lily Wilder wants you to get cleaned up and set up your tents."

Chapter Nine

AFTER DINNER—TOO much chili, too much cornbread, an extra beer for Leo, and Lily's wickedly delicious spicy hot chocolate for everyone else—the group of guests slowly stood, creaking, groaning. In the firelight and stooped over from saddle soreness, they all looked ten years older.

Walt walked to where Lily and Nicole were going over notes for tomorrow's route.

"I wanted to tell you good night and see if there's anything I can help with before bed." His eyes scanned the area, pausing on the old leather notebook—Duke's journal—on the table. "Cool," he said, reaching down and fingering the faded yellow leather strap used to hold it all together. "That looks vintage."

"Neither cool nor vintage, I promise," she told him with a laugh. "Just old."

Terry dropped his mug in the washbasin and nodded toward the book. "Can't find 'em like that anymore."

"Sure can't," Lily said, closing the journal and slipping it into her bag. She had no deep love for the words and drawings that lined the pages but felt protective of the journal anyway. "And thanks for the offer, Walt, but there's nothing else to do. You guys should get to bed."

Walter mumbled a grateful "Good night," and headed off in an exhausted shuffle. Bradley and Terry looked ready for a few more beers, but they eyed Lily, and then Leo sitting alone at the firepit, and seemed to silently agree to file away.

Only Nic lingered. When she caught Lily's attention, she tossed an eyebrow skyward and cocked her head, wordlessly asking if Lily wanted her to stay or go.

Tilting her chin toward the tents, Lily said a quiet "Night, Nic."

Lily supposed it was time to do this.

Once Nic left, she took a seat next to the fire, unsure where to start. She'd initiated this conversation in her head so many times, but it was never satisfying. Her imagination never got it right. The balance of understanding and hurt, of consolation and castigation.

Thankfully, he didn't make her. "We don't have to talk about it, you know."

Lily released a husky, wry laugh. "I don't see how there's any way around it. We're going to be up in each other's business for the next week. Let's just get it over with."

She'd been terrible at having emotional conversations before him. But to be fair, Lily'd been the only daughter of a man with the emotional depth of a teaspoon and a woman who couldn't take the isolation of living in the middle of nowhere with a husband who was never present, even when he was. Her uncle Dan taught Lily everything she knew about horses and ranching, but his sensitivity bucket was only slightly deeper than Duke's had been. Feelings were never a priority.

Lily knew she'd grown up hard, but Leo had made her soft. Over the five months they'd spent wrapped up in each other, Leo had broken her down one day at a time until she would tell him practically anything. It had taken some prodding, but with him Lily would open her mouth and everything would come tumbling out.

Truthfully, she hadn't done that in a long time.

"Okay." Leo let a thoughtful handful of seconds pass and then pulled out a proverbial two-by-four and took a swing. "So, what happened? After I left, I mean."

She glanced into her tin mug before taking a sip of the hot chocolate that had long since gone cold. "Starting small, I see."

"I didn't think you wanted to do the long-lost-friends thing," he said, looking over at her. "But maybe it'd be better if I started with 'How are you?'"

Lily kept her attention fixed on the fire, but the press of his gaze was unnerving. She turned and met his eyes. Dark and searching. So familiar it hurt. "Actually, yeah. Maybe that's easier."

"Okay, Lily," he said, and his playful smile tapped against a tiny, vulnerable well of feelings inside her. "How are you?"

"I've been better." Lily laughed thickly, pushing back the heavy swell of anger and sadness that rose in her throat. "I guess I was wrong. 'How are you' isn't an easier place to start."

His gaze swept over her face, from her hairline down to her mouth, pausing there. That vulnerable well began to upend, spilling dangerously, and Lily turned away.

When he spoke again, Leo's voice was so strained it came out as a whisper. "Then maybe I'll just start where I really want to: What happened to the ranch?"

She settled her gaze on his when she answered, wanting to see how it would land. "Duke sold it right after you left."

Leo went still. "What? Why?"

"About a week after, in fact, he handed over the keys." Lily turned her attention down to her hands, where her fingers were knotted together. "I'm not sure if you remember, that last morning, Duke was heading out of town."

"I remember," Leo said. "For a dig."

"Turns out he wasn't going on a dig," she told him. "I can't tell you how many times I tried to remember if he told me that, or if I just assumed. He was going to sign papers at a title company. He sold the ranch to a local guy named Jonathan Cross."

"I don't—" Leo cut away, understandably confused. "He'd already planned this when he left that morning? It felt like he was leaving everything in your hands."

"I know," Lily said, remembering how naive she'd been. How excited she'd been to see him go. "I thought so, too. But do you remember he'd left me a note on the table?"

Leo paused, and then slowly nodded.

"It was one of his stupid riddles. He couldn't even tell me to my face that he was selling it. It took me an hour to decode when I dug it out of the trash, and the note said he had plans for the money. Probably some big expedition that would get him another *National Geographic* cover." She wiped her clammy palms on her thighs. "I was so pissed, I moved out that day."

Leo bent, putting his head in his hands. "Holy shit. He didn't mention any of this."

She was about to continue when his words crashed into her. "What do you mean? When did you talk to Duke?"

"When I called you back." Leo said this plainly, stating a fact. "The messages I left?"

Lily, mute with shocked confusion, shook her head.

"When you'd called me— I'm sorry," he said, neck flushing red. "I was arranging my mother's cremation. I— It wasn't a good day for me, and I know I was short with you, but—"

"What—your mother's—"

"—when I called back, I didn't even get a voicemail recording. I called the lodge, and Duke said you weren't at the ranch, and to leave a message with him."

The word *cremation* was looping over and over in her brain. His mother had *died*.

"You left a message with my father?"

He nodded. "Yeah, a few, actually."

Lily's jaw creaked open, words falling flatly out: "I never got a message. All I knew was what you told me the morning you had to leave: that your mother had been in an accident but was okay."

Leo frowned. "I told Duke that my mother had unexpectedly passed away from her injuries, and I wouldn't be able to leave Cora and return to Wyoming."

The words landed like a meteor falling from the sky; the impact shook her entire foundation. She'd been angry, acted impulsively. But that brief moment of fury meant that not only had she missed Leo's call, she'd also missed the messages from Duke that Leo's mother had died.

She'd been so stupid.

"I'm sorry," she said, voice muffled. "Oh my God. I had no idea, Leo." Slowly, she straightened and looked over at him. Guilt beat a heavy thunder in her chest as she got the next words out: "I didn't know you'd called. I didn't know your mom died."

"I—" Cutting himself off, he searched her eyes. "Yeah."

She felt displaced, disoriented as her memory of those bleak months after Leo left was suddenly like a window wiped clean. "I was angry at Duke for selling the ranch," she said, "but I wasn't surprised. He was never careful with my feelings. I wasn't answering his calls because I didn't want to hear whatever bullshit plan or excuse he'd concocted, and when days passed and I hadn't heard from you . . ." She shrugged. "I assumed you'd gone back to your city life and forgotten all about me. I, well, I threw my phone in the river."

Leo coughed out a horrified sound, running a shaking hand through his hair. The soft black strands immediately fell back over his forehead. "Then this whole time?" he croaked. "This whole time you thought—?"

"That you just never called me back."

His calm exterior broke, and he turned away from her, letting out a breath that seemed to have been trapped somewhere in his chest for the past ten years. She wanted to bury herself in the desert. She'd been so wounded, so young, so reactive, so alone.

"No wonder you were so mad in the boot shed." Leo bent, bracing his head in his hands and letting out a wry laugh. "Wow, okay, this explains a lot."

Feeling nauseated, she released a slow breath. "I wish I had known. I'm so sorry about your mom."

"No." He turned to look at her. "I can't imagine a worse combination of circumstances. I hate that you thought I just bailed."

She nodded, swallowing so she could speak. Her throat was suddenly so dry. "I know."

"Mom hung on for about an hour after I got there," he said, eyes on the fire. "I'll always be grateful that I got to say goodbye. She'd taken a turn for the worse when I was on the plane. After that I just—I don't know. I probably did forget about everything else for a few days—even you. I'm sorry, I see it in hindsight. I—I think something inside me broke, but I couldn't fall apart because—" He shook his head. "Cora'd been with Mom when she was hit by the car, and she was hysterical."

Silence blanketed the campfire; even the embers seemed to go still. The alternate versions of their past branched out into fresh paths in her mind, and for a beat Lily let herself flounder: *If I'd just kept my phone, or if Duke had driven into town to find me, or if the worst of it hadn't happened and Duke hadn't—*

No. Lily shut down those thoughts. If they *had* spoken? It wouldn't have mattered. Ten years older, Lily Wilder now understood that she and Leo never would have worked. It was a brutal truth, but it was what it was. They were from different realities.

She looked over at him. "I assume your dad never came back?" All she could remember him telling her was that his father left when Cora was little, that he hadn't been in the picture since.

Leo shook his head. "One of my mom's cousins in Japan tracked him down, and he basically said, 'Isn't Leo old enough to handle it?'"

"'It' meaning his *daughter*?" she asked, gaping. "What a piece of shit."

Leo nodded, shifting beside her. "You got that right."

Stillness—understanding—settled in the warm air. At only twenty-two, Leo had been tasked with raising his little sister on his own. "You stayed in New York?"

"Brooklyn. Our landlord was great. He didn't raise our rent—I think he actually lowered it and then kept it there for years. I'm sure it would have been cheaper to move, but Mom was gone. I couldn't leave the only place we'd lived with her. I couldn't do that to Cora. Mom had some savings, and the life insurance money helped. I finished school and got a job as soon as I could."

She blew out a slow breath. "And you raised her."

A proud smile broke through. "Yeah."

"That must have been so hard. On both of you."

"She's the best thing I've done with my life. She graduated from Columbia last week, did I tell you? She starts medical school in Boston in the fall."

Lily whistled, impressed. "Wow. Good for her." She looked over at him. "There's a lot in the middle that you left out about yourself, did you notice that?"

"Yeah." Leo glanced at her and shrugged, as if his own life were so inconsequential it was just an afterthought. "It feels a little like I'm only now coming out of a fog, to be honest."

"That's a long fog."

"No kidding." He laughed softly. "I had this realization the other night that for the past ten years I only had one goal—to take care of Cora—and I haven't done anything to plan for what comes next. I'm facing that now: What is my life going to be?"

She could be no help. Lily didn't even know what her own life was meant to be.

Leo bent, picking up a stick and tapping it against one of the rocks in a ring around the fire. She could feel him moving on, remembered the gesture, how he would change the subject with movement before words. His voice carried a new lightness when he spoke. "Can I ask you something?"

"Sure."

His unsure smile was a slow-growing assault on her libido. "What exactly are we going to find at the end of this trip?"

This was not at all what she expected him to say. "You're going to find *yourselves*," she said with exaggerated sincerity. "Your love for the outdoors and sense of adventure."

Leo's playfully skeptical face made her laugh.

"The treasure is mostly stuff that local companies donate," she relented. "But by the time the guests figure it out and crack the final codes, they're so proud of themselves it doesn't matter what's in the cave."

"So, you're saying it's in a *cave*," he detective-murmured, pretending to write this bit of information down on the palm of his hand.

Lily laughed harder. "That might not be the exclusive you think it is. There are a million tiny caves everywhere."

"Be honest," he said. "There will be Mardi Gras necklaces and fake jewels inside a plastic treasure chest, right?"

Their gazes danced together. "There might be yo-yos and branded stress balls."

Finally, she broke the eye contact, feeling too warm, and took her outer layer off, ignoring the way his eyes tracked her bare arms.

"Okay," he said, "well, I promise to be a good sport and to keep Terry in line as much as possible."

"What's his deal, anyway?"

"We went to school together, but he's more a friend of a friend, someone I see at weddings and stuff. He's never usually invited on these trips, for obvious reasons. If he gets to be a problem, I'll handle it."

She nodded, leaning back and settling her feet on a big rock bordering the fire.

"One last question," he said, "if we're still clearing the air."

Lily hummed. The fire was gently warm, and somehow it matched the energy between them. Calming. Thawing. Nothing was exploding and shooting heated sparks into the sky. "Go ahead."

"Whatever happened with Duke?" he asked. "Did you two ever work it out? Where is he?"

Laughing wryly, Lily pressed a palm to her forehead. How many cans of worms would they open tonight?

But the first words of her answer were drowned out by the abrupt sound of Nicole hollering, *"What the hell are you doing?"*

Before she even registered she'd moved, Lily was up, jogging toward the tents just as Terry yelled back, "Taking a fucking leak, princess!"

Lily paused, relaxing in relief before rounding a small grouping of rocks to reach the tent circle. In the shadows, Terry stood between his and Nic's tents, with his pants slung low on his hips and his—

"Oh *God!*" She quickly looked away.

"This fool was pissing on the side of my tent," Nic seethed, pointing to where Terry stood with his dick in his hand. "Are you out of your damn mind? Pull your pants up!"

"It's late," Terry reminded her snidely. "You told us not to wander away in the dark, didn't you?"

"Yeah, but you can take ten goddamn steps to pee!"

Deciding this wasn't a crisis that required both of them, Lily moved away, pulling in a deep breath. She felt whiplashed. On her left was Terry being Terry; on her right lingered the emotional contrails of her bombshell conversation with Leo.

Counting to three, she let the adrenaline clear from her blood. But it was slow to diffuse, and even after several deep breaths, her fingers shook; she still felt unsteady. The truth was all settling in now. She thought he'd left to help his mother recover from a broken leg, maybe a concussion. In Lily's world, people got injured all the time, but when she was young, no one she'd known had ever *died* from an accident. It'd never crossed her mind that when Leo had gone home, everything might have been so much more terrible than they'd understood. She'd seen herself as the wounded party for so long, but now had the nauseating realization that they were *all* simply the victims of shitty circumstances.

Leo stood nearby, an unspeaking and unmoving presence. She could turn around and go back to her spot next to the fire and answer the enormous question he'd just posed: *Whatever happened with Duke?* But an even larger part of her knew they could have the conversation and it wouldn't matter. The truth about tragedy was that once it struck, nothing on this wide green earth could make it any better. Leo had been her spark, had brought a glimpse of love and laughter and security into her life, but his departure had only proven what she'd already known: good things don't stick around.

The air away from the fire was cool and dry, and when Lily looked over her shoulder at him, she saw in his eyes that he knew it, too: their moment had passed.

He smiled, releasing her. "Sleep well, Lily."

Chapter Ten

NOT EVEN SEVEN days a week of the toughest Tabata class at the Upper East Side Equinox could have prepared Leo for the pain that greeted him every morning of this trip. By their fourth day, it was slightly easier, but that first step out of the tent remained excruciating. For the first twenty minutes every day, he could barely walk, and it wasn't just a sore ass and legs and back; even taking a deep breath was painful. Bending to spit out his toothpaste caused a frantic spasm in his side. He wasn't sure whether he should blame the cold, the dry air, the hours on a horse, or the nights spent sleeping on the ground, but he woke up feeling like he'd aged a decade.

Two full days had passed since he and Lily had talked at the campfire, and she was doing her best to avoid him. Sure, she'd asked him if he wanted more potato salad at lunch and told him to stop letting Ace graze along the trail as they rode, but they hadn't talked about anything meaningful since—had never returned to the subject of whether she and her dad ever reconciled. It felt like a code half-cracked.

From near a small cluster of rocks where Nicole had fashioned a makeshift hand-washing station—a jug of fresh water, soap, a couple of clean hand towels—Leo looked out at the slowly brightening morning, at the spires of rock crowded together in the distance. They'd passed a few signs of civilization over the last few days—the occasional piece of trash, a broken bike tire or marker along the trail—but it was easy to see how isolated they'd become, even a few miles out. This was desolate terrain, but breathtaking, alternating between flat sandy ground, steep drop-offs, and towers of carrot-colored rock faces. Wiry thickets of sage-green scrub grew thick and lush where the ground had been carved away and water collected. Spindly trees showed the persistence of life, finding purchase wherever they could. The sunrise hit the red rock from every angle, illuminating the landscape in startling shades of tangerine, rust, crimson, and wine. In a couple of hours, the sky would be almost startlingly blue. Already it was intensely bright, the air so parched his eyes itched.

With the soft nickering of horses and the smell of camp smoke filling the air, Leo could almost imagine cowboys thundering through this passage, the dust and cacophony of herds of cattle and horses.

Until a grunt rose from the ground, and Leo glanced down to see Walter half in and half out of his tent, shirt bunched up around his ribs, face pressed to the red dirt.

Leo dropped his toothbrush back into his toiletry bag. "Hey, Walt."

He looked up at Leo, eyes droopy and pitiful. "My ass is crying."

And Leo's spine felt welded in place. "It took me ten minutes to get my shirt on."

"Will I ever sit like a normal person again?" Walt asked, voice thin. "I don't even remember how it feels to approach a chair without dread."

Wincing, Leo slowly bent to help his friend up. "I'd like to take off my own back and beat Bradley with it." Together they hobbled their way toward the fire.

Nicole—already working on breakfast—watched with amusement as they attempted to sit gracefully down on a slab of sandstone. "It gets easier, I promise."

Walter looked betrayed. "You said that yesterday."

Leo glanced up in time to see Lily approaching with a pair of saddle blankets in her arms, and just like the past couple of days, she avoided his eyes. Her hair was braided under her Stetson, her jeans already dusty. She'd probably done more before six o'clock than most people did all day, and just seeing her in the muted morning light made his heart do an aching nosedive.

"You might also want to take some ibuprofen," Lily said. "We have a six-hour ride today."

Walter exhaled a terrified "*Six.*"

Nicole appeared, handing him a steaming mug of coffee, and he accepted it with a stiff bow. She gave the second mug to Leo before heading back to the table. It felt suddenly ridiculous that life could move on like this. A few days ago, he'd been in his safe but boring life, sitting in meetings or answering emails for nine hours a day; today he felt like he'd been yanked up and planted back on the earth upside down and inside out. In contrast, Lily moved around with more ease than before their talk, like they'd covered enough of their history to simply close the door and move on.

Leo wasn't sure if he wanted the door closed. He still had so many questions about the intervening years, and part of him—admittedly a new, unsteady part—thought he might want the door blown open instead.

He wanted to finish their conversation. He wasn't letting her evade him today.

His eyes lingered as she threw another piece of wood on the fire and carried a Dutch oven to where the flames had burned down to coals. When she straightened, she caught him staring, but he didn't look away.

"What the fuck is this?" Nicole was holding a burnt cigarette butt. "Idiot tourists smoking out here." She stomped over to the designated garbage bin. "Gonna set this whole goddamn canyon on fire."

"Did anyone hear rustling last night?" Walt asked. "It sounded like someone walking around outside."

"Probably just animals looking for supper," Lily told him. "We're the intruders here, camping on their dinner table."

Walter's cup wavered in his hand.

A tent flap opened, and Bradley emerged. He stretched in the rising sun, a little scruffier than when they'd arrived, but definitely more bright-eyed than any of the rest of them.

"God *damn*, I slept good." When he lifted his shirt to scratch his stomach, Leo noticed the way Nicole and Lily paused to watch and felt a hot swell of irritation in his gut. Bradley walked toward one of the larger sandstone ledges, propping a boot on the lip of a steep crevice, fists to hips as he surveyed the vista. "I feel alive out here. My heart is racing, my blood pumping."

Terry joined them a few minutes later, looking only marginally better than Leo felt. "I have a few suggestions for routes today," he said, picking up an apple.

"We've got it taken care of, Terry," Lily told him, ignoring his disappointment. "Get your tents packed and ready to go after breakfast. It's gonna be a long day."

———————

She hadn't been kidding. The heat of the day had sapped the riders of any remaining enthusiasm by the time they finally reached camp. Ace's shadow stretched long across the ground, distorted by piñon pine and scraggly patches of juniper that thrived there in the arid soil.

They secured the horses, then all gathered a safe distance from the edge of the mesa overlooking the vast canyon below.

"Jesus Christ, that's far down," Bradley said, attempting to see over the sheer drop-off. He lifted a hand to his forehead. "I'm dizzy just looking at it. Where are we again?"

"Maze Overlook. And careful," Lily warned with an outstretched arm. "If you fall, you die."

Obediently, Bradley stepped back.

Leo studied the section of canyon in the distance far below, with its intricate, serpentine formations. "It doesn't look real."

"It really doesn't," Lily agreed. "Can you believe that was all done by rainwater searching for the sea?"

"That makes me a little sad," Walter said.

Leo had never wished he could fly, but he did just then. There was something about the canyon that made him want to explore, to swoop from the top of one red rock pillar to another and down into the literal maze of intersecting slots. It was both exquisite and sinister.

"We're not going down there, are we?" Walt asked.

"No way," Terry said. "You pussies wouldn't last a day out there."

Walter stared at him. "Have *you* done it?"

Terry held out his arms as if this should be obvious. "Dude."

"Do you ever take people down there?" Leo asked Lily.

She reached into her pocket for her ever-present lip sunscreen, and it would take red-hot pokers to drag his eyes away while she applied it. "Sure, but only experienced hikers, and only certain areas. The backcountry is really remote. Some people go in by river or in high-clearance four-wheel drives, but roads only get you so far and you have to do the rest on foot." She pressed her lips together, spreading the balm. Leo swallowed heavily, ripping his gaze away.

Bradley let out a quiet laugh beside him, nudged him in the ribs. "You okay there?"

"You could do it one day, Walt," Nicole said. "You'd need a good guide, but it's not impossible. Look at you and Dynamite. Bet you never thought you'd be out here riding like a real cowboy, either."

Walter was still anxiously studying the Maze.

Lily turned back to a stretch of dirt behind them. "We're going to set up camp over there. But first." She turned to a supply crate that had been left ahead and dug inside, pulling out a small wooden box. "While Nic and I feed and water the horses, I want you to work on this together. You're gonna need what's inside here if you want to eat."

Walt stared at the tiny box in her hand. "Our dinner is in *there*?"

Terry rolled his eyes. "Yes, Walter, she's planning to feed us pellets that expand into real food in our stomachs."

"Cool," Walt murmured, excited.

Leo tipped Walt's hat over his eyes. "I think she means there's a key or something inside."

"That's exactly what I mean." Without looking at him, Lily handed Leo the box. "The key to tonight's dinner box is in here. But it's pretty tricky, so get to work."

Bradley already looked smug. "I don't want to disappoint you, Lily, but that slide puzzle the other day was just the tip of the iceberg. Our Leo here can figure out anything."

"I've locked myself out of my apartment four times, and Leo always got me in," Walter agreed.

Leo straightened, heating self-consciously under Lily's quiet focus. "You should see me play Tetris," he joked awkwardly.

Her brows rose in amusement. "I bet it's fascinating."

"Riveting." A tender green vine of infatuation wound its way through his ribs and squeezed. He swiped absently at his chest, as if he could bat it away. Lily was gorgeous and whip-smart and even more capable than she'd been all those years ago, but he knew better than anyone that their lives were puzzle pieces cut from two different pictures.

But as she let her gaze linger on him for a beat longer, the vine squeezed again, harder now.

She nodded to the box in his hands. "Well, good. Because I mean it when I say you won't eat tonight until you've got it out."

"I really hate you." Leo glared at Bradley across the wooden puzzle they'd been working on for nearly half an hour.

"Can we just agree ahead of time to do the dinner dishes to earn the key?" Walter called out to the guides. "My stomach is eating itself."

"Oh, sugar, you're doing the dishes, too," Nicole told him, smiling sweetly.

"If you would just focus," Bradley hissed. "We have to be getting close."

Close was meaningless. The puzzle box was only about six inches by six inches and made of wooden planks with a small maze inlaid into the surface of each one. Each maze contained a pin, and the object was to figure out how to slide each pin so its corresponding plank could be removed. The problem was that they had to work together to get every pin into its correct position, and even though Leo could see exactly how it had to be done, with three of their big hands stuffed into the tiny space it was challenging. After more than six hours in the saddle and with the proximity of dinner making their stomachs rumble, *challenging* became an understatement.

Which, he realized, was the point.

The upside, at least, was that with only the three of them, they were working relatively well together; Terry had gone off on his own, doing who knew what.

"What are you going to do about . . ." Bradley trailed off, tilting his chin to where Lily and Nicole were off checking on the horses. "I've known you for thirteen years and never once seen you look at a woman like that."

With a dry laugh, Leo told him, "I don't think that's going to be the vibe between us this week."

"What are you talking about? You two were up for a while the other night. Stars, campfire, tents. The scene writes it- self."

"We were just clearing the air." He shook his head. "She never got any of my messages. She didn't know about Mom. She thought I just left and forgot about her."

"Poor Lily," Walt said.

Bradley waved this off. "You can't talk about your mom dying if you're trying to score. You have no game, Leo."

Leo reached over to free one of Walt's fingers from where it'd gotten stuck. "She lives in Utah, I'm in New York. If you drew a Venn diagram of our lives, the circles wouldn't touch."

"I'm not talking about holding a commitment ceremony out here," Bradley said. "Just a little fun."

"It would be . . . complicated."

He looked around to make sure Lily and Nicole were truly out of earshot. "We could ask Nicole to take us on a walk to- morrow morning so you and Lily can play a little butter-the- biscuit."

"Bradley."

"Clean the carpet. Check the oil. Ride the flagpole."

"I understood the biscuit metaphor." Leo held a pin with his index finger and reached around the box to push another with his thumb. "I'm just ignoring you."

"Slime the banana," Bradley said, and Leo winced as Wal- ter gasped.

"That one is gross."

"I thought you were ignoring me."

"Shut up, I think I have it." Focusing, Leo used the side of his thumb to shift one of the pins into place with a click, and the wooden plank slid to the side to reveal a small opening.

"Oh my God!" Bradley said, jumping to his feet. "Leo, you fucking did it!"

Leo peered into the slot and could barely make out the glint of a small key attached to one of the sides. He tried to reach it but couldn't. The opening was too small.

"Can you get that?" he said, showing Walter.

Walt tried, but failed. "We need Terry's tiny hands."

"Where is Terry?" Lily said, approaching with perfect timing.

Walter shrugged. "Wandering."

"What?" Lily was immediately annoyed. "You guys are supposed to stay together."

Bradley was unconcerned. "He probably just walked a mile to pee this time to make a point."

"Relax," a voice called. Footsteps crunched through the dirt and everyone turned to see Terry emerging from behind a jagged rock. "Was out doing a little exploring."

"You're not supposed to leave camp alone," Nicole said. "If a cougar gets hold of you, I'm not hauling what's left of your body back to town."

"If a cougar gets me?" He laughed, sucking his teeth. "Come on, Nicky, you're not *that* old yet."

Nicole paused, then took a step forward. Lily blocked her with an outstretched arm. "Terry, do we need to review the rules?"

He laughed this off, too, taking a seat on a wide rock and nodding to Bradley. "Dude, did you buy the nagging-wife package of the expedition or what?"

Lily froze, letting out a quietly controlled "Pardon?"

But Nicole's attention had snagged on the bag at Terry's feet. "Terry," she said carefully, "what's that in your bag?"

Walt, happy to distract from the tension, clapped. "Yeah, Terry, what's in your—" When he registered that Nicole wasn't playing around, his expression straightened. "Wait. What *is* that in your bag? Isn't that Miss Lily's journal?"

All eyes swung to the backpack at Terry's feet. Tangled in the zipper was very clearly the yellow leather string that wrapped around the notebook Leo had seen Lily occasionally holding over the last few days.

Terry bent, trying to shove it out of view, but it was obvious to everyone what had happened: He'd taken Lily's journal.

"Are you crazy?" Walter asked, letting out a confused laugh.

Lily took a step forward, but Terry stood abruptly, grabbing the backpack and shuffling a few steps away. "Hold up."

The earth went completely silent as everyone grappled with what was going down. Dust kicked up around Terry's legs, and he slowly slid the backpack strap over his shoulder. He glanced away, like he might make a run for it.

"Uh," Bradley murmured, looking around at the rest of them, "what the fuck is going on?"

"Terry," Lily said, frowning, "that's my journal."

"It's your *dad's* journal," he corrected.

At the sinister timbre of Terry's voice, Leo put the puzzle down, ignoring the metallic click of the pins sliding back into place. Uneasiness spread in a queasy rush through him.

"Well, it's mine now," she said pointedly but calmly, "and I'd like you to give it back."

Terry's expression was an eerie paradox: eyes flat, jaw tense, wooden smile, nostrils flared. "I was just reading it."

"Right." She nodded slowly. "Without my permission."

"Still don't see what the big deal is." He shrugged. "I was just looking at some of Duke's maps. I don't think you even use them, do you?"

"Who's Duke?" Walt whispered.

"Her father," Bradley whispered back.

"Guys," Leo hissed.

Walt ignored this, asking Bradley, "How'd you know that?"

"Terry told me."

"Guys."

"When did—"

Halfway through Walt's question, Terry let out a scoffing "Idiots," and moved to brush past them.

Struggling to understand whether Terry was serious with this nonsense, Leo bolted forward, catching him with a hand around his shoulder. "Hey. We're not done here. Give Lily her journal back."

But instead of complying, Terry wheeled on Leo, hooking a fist into his jaw. Pain cracked across the side of Leo's face, and he stumbled back, weathering the shock and impact of the punch.

Surprised voices burst out from all sides, and Leo moved into action, stepping forward and shoving Terry's chest. "What the hell was that?"

"Jesus Christ," Terry said. "None of you have any idea how much money is out here, do you? Just keep going along with this fake—"

Walt shocked everyone by dashing in, swiping the bag off Terry's shoulder, and, like it was on fire, throwing it to Bradley, who threw it to Leo.

Terry charged forward, but Bradley and Nicole held him

back as Leo moved several steps away. He ripped open the zipper, and his stomach dissolved the second he saw what else was in there, just beneath the journal.

"Terry," Leo said flatly, passing the journal to Lily and looking up at Terry in stunned confusion. "Man, what do you need with a gun?"

"You brought a *gun*?" Walter shrieked. "I couldn't even bring my bidet!"

When Bradley leaned forward to look, Terry broke free of their hold, lunging for Leo. Ripping the bag from Leo's hands, Terry backed up, pulling out the gun. Looking around wildly, he reached for Nicole, and before Leo could process what was happening, Terry roughly grabbed her arm and jerked her back against his chest.

Lily let out a broken cry, and a spiraling shimmer of panic shot through Leo.

"Whoa, whoa, whoa," Bradley said, hands up and voice high with shock. "What's happening?"

"Terry," Lily said, her voice quaking violently. She immediately tossed the leather-bound notebook onto the dusty ground between them. "Terry. Hey. Take it. You can have the journal. It's fine. Just put the gun down."

Leo held his hands up. Fear scaled his chest like a jagged sheet of ice. "Let's calm down. We just wanted to know what's going on."

"What's going on is you're being a nosy little bitch." Spittle flew out with Terry's words, getting trapped in his mustache. "Go chase after the hot daughter some more, Leo, and just forget about this."

"Someone skin this man alive," Nicole seethed, gritting her teeth against the press of the gun.

"Nic," Lily whispered, "be quiet, honey."

"You're not going to shoot her, come on," Bradley said. "This is just a big misunderstanding. You'll put it down, and we'll keep the trip rolling along like before. We'll pretend this never happened. Right, Lily?"

Lily swallowed. "Of course."

"It's not that simple," Terry said. His eyes roved the scene: over their faces, across the landscape, behind him where the lip of the canyon loomed far too close. Scrambling forward, he bent awkwardly around Nicole's body and grabbed the journal before scooting away from the rest of them.

"Lily," Walt murmured, "what the hell is in that book?"

"It's just my father's notes," she said, and swallowed. "He can take it. It's fine."

"Okay," Leo said placatingly. "Terry, you have the journal. Let Nicole go."

"I'm taking her with me," he said, voice tight. "If you follow us, I'll shoot."

Anger and panic were a salty tide rising in Leo's chest. He couldn't let Terry leave with her.

He would worry later about what was in the journal, about the loose cannon Terry had morphed into, about what any of this was really about. Right now, he had to get the gun out of Nicole's face. His eyes shifted to where the barrel pressed into the soft skin of her cheek. Her eyes were squeezed closed, her pulse a riot in her neck. Without thinking, Leo exploded forward, grabbing her free of Terry's hold and tossing her behind him. Immediately, he wrapped a hand around Terry's fingers on the gun, wrestling it skyward.

A shot rang out, and everyone but Leo and Terry ducked for cover, screaming.

Terry wrenched the gun free, shuffling back a few more steps. If possible, his skin grew redder, face flushed with anger as he swung the shaking gun at Walt, then Leo, and finally to Lily crouched with Nicole in her arms, off to the side.

"*Just—chill the fuck out!*" he shouted.

"Terry," Bradley said, his voice shaking. "Man, put the gun down. I'm not fucking kidding here."

"I should have known it would be like this," Terry seethed. "Surrounded by a bunch of cowards. We shouldn't have come here as a group."

"Don't do this," Bradley said quietly. "Why are you doing this right now? Don't ruin the trip, man."

But Leo knew that ship had sailed long ago. Holding his shaking hands out where Terry could see them, Leo—with his heart in his windpipe—took a cautious step forward, and then another. "Terry. I'm going to reach for the gun, and we're going to put it down. You can take the book and go. Whatever you need. It isn't worth this."

Leo reached out, wrapping a hand around the barrel, but as soon as he tilted it to the side, Terry registered that he was fucked. Panicking, he reached with his other hand to try to claw at Leo's face, and before Leo knew exactly what was going on, the two were wrestling with a loaded gun between them. He heard Lily cry out his name. His heart was in his skull now, pounding, pounding; everything around them was dust and panic and noise.

Walt grabbed on to Terry's gun arm, trying to help Leo wedge the barrel from Terry's grip. The gun came free, falling to the ground in the melee. Bradley came for Terry's other arm, finally managing to drag Terry away. Furious, Bradley wrapped his fists in Terry's shirt, walking him backward.

"Are you out of your mind?" Bradley shouted into his face. His normally placid expression was tight with adrenaline and fury. "What the hell is wrong with you?"

Red dust had kicked up, leaving them all disoriented; Leo had no idea whether the rocky lip of the canyon was in front of him or behind him, so he carefully went down to his knees, feeling around to regain his bearings. Somewhere in the past thirty seconds, the shouting had stopped sounding like individual words and was now only a din. Squinting up into the gritty cloud, Leo reached forward to grab Bradley's calf, desperately yelling for him to let Terry go and get down.

So, Bradley did.

Terry's face went round with shock, eyes wide and arms flailing as the dust cleared and all six of them seemed to realize in unison that only the very tip of one of his shoes had any remaining contact with the fragile lip of the canyon. And even that slipped away as Terry's weight and momentum propelled him backward.

Over the edge, for just a heartbeat, Terry appeared to be running in place on top of nothing but air. Leo reached out, grappling into the emptiness—

But Terry was gone.

Leo was astounded at how fast a human body could fall. He had never—not once in his life—heard such silence. It was as if Terry had pulled all of the sound with him when he plummeted.

For two,

five,

ten heart-pounding seconds, they stared at the empty space that Terry's body had just occupied.

Delicate swirls of dust danced around them in the fading light. "No way that just happened," rasped Bradley.

"Maybe . . ." Walter wondered, "maybe he survived?"

Shuffling to the edge and staring down together, the group struggled to catch their breath. The fall was so far, it was impossible to see clearly from where they stood, but the five of them winced together when a tiny puff of dirt rose up from the distant ground.

Even if nobody said it aloud, they all knew he hadn't.

Chapter Eleven

NO ONE MOVED.

The numbness began in Lily's fingers, spreading up her arms with shocking velocity as she registered what had just happened.

"What did I just see?" Nic asked, voice high and thin. "What am I seeing *right now*?"

Bradley turned with wild, hysterical eyes and, as if his emergency glass case had been shattered, yelled, "*TERRY WENT OVER THE FUCKING CLIFF!*"

Butter in a frying pan, Lily's thoughts melted away. Nic's face, Leo's face, Bradley, Walter . . . they all told the same story. They'd really seen Terry fall over the edge into the canyon.

Her ass hit the dirt. Dread filled her like the cold, violent rush of ocean water into a cave, and something broke loose in the group. Chaos erupted: Bradley was still yelling. Leo yelled at Bradley to stop yelling. Walter yelled that his lower intestines were very sensitive to stress. Nic started yelling at all of them to shut the hell up and calm the hell down. Each one peered and gestured over the edge of the cliff.

But to Lily, all of it sounded like it was happening many, many miles away. White noise roared in her ears. This wasn't falling off a horse or breaking a leg. A person had died on one of her tours. A man was *dead*.

Get it together, Wilder. Fucking get up.

She scrambled to her feet, crossing the last few paces and jerking them all back from the ledge. When she hurled him away, Bradley rolled, coming to a stop on his side. He shoved a hand into his hair and groaned. "Holy shit, holy shit, I've never seen someone die before."

Lily's voice was white-knuckled calm. "Breathe."

"I can't believe this," Walter babbled. "Everything was so crazy and chaotic and . . . I can't believe—"

"Wait," she cut in, gut locking up. The last few moments before Terry's fall were a confusing snarl of dust and limbs and shouting. "Did someone *push* him?"

Walter pointed and stammered out, "Bradley did."

"*It was an accident!*" Bradley screamed. "Why would you say that?"

"She asked!" Walter screamed back. "I didn't want to be rude!"

"He had a gun!" Bradley cried. "What the fuck was he doing with a gun?"

"You're the only one who wanted him to come!"

"I didn't! But he—"

"*Everyone, shut up!*" Lily almost couldn't consider what had led up to this moment—Terry with Duke's journal, planning to take it *and* Nicole with him into the desert. The only thing she could think about was the way he'd been there one second, suspended in air, and gone the next. There was no way he'd survived. "I can't even hear myself think."

"Okay, okay. Okay," Bradley babbled. "We can handle this. Here's what's going to happen. We're all going to just turn around and go home, right? Terry took off. Terry left us. He's been saying this whole time that he doesn't need us to survive out here. What if he left? What if he left and we have no idea? It's possible, right?"

"Oh, that is not happening," Nicole warned him. "You want me to lie to the police and say Terry's still alive somewhere? Boy, I'd have to give myself back to God before I could do that."

"Bradley," Leo said soothingly, "it's going to be okay. Come on. We'll tell the cops exactly what happened. Terry had a gun. He held it to Nicole's head. We were all scrapping and it was confusing. You didn't do anything wrong."

"The hell he didn't!" Nicole shouted frantically. "If Walt says Bradley pushed him, then that's good enough for me. The rest of us are not taking the fall for him. Case closed!"

Lily bent at the waist, roughly pressing the heels of her hands to her eyes. This was bad. It was so bad. She was never getting out of this hole. A wrongful death suit was coming, maybe criminal negligence charges. Even if they all said Terry held them at gunpoint, she was supposed to ensure all the guests' safety. That meant no firearms, no illegal substances. It had never been an issue; she'd stopped searching bags ages ago. What the fuck was she going to do? Aside from dude ranching and bartending, this was all she knew. Lily had wanted to quit before, but that wouldn't even be an option now. How on earth would she survive?

But, she thought darkly, *making ends meet is a best-case scenario. Maybe I'll be in prison.*

The arguing around her seemed to grow in volume, but before she registered what was happening, a hand wrapped around her elbow and she was pulled to Leo's side.

"Bradley?" Leo's voice carried a rare waver beside her. "Bradley, what are you doing, man?"

The gun shook wildly in Bradley's trembling hand as he pointed it at Nicole, Lily, then back to Nic again. "That's *not* what happened, Nicole."

"Bradley." Now Leo's words were steely and low. "Think this through."

Awareness came at her like a train as the barrel swung her way again. "But I didn't push him!" Bradley yelled.

"Yeah, you're acting real innocent, aren't you," Nicole growled.

"Nic," Lily murmured, "you're not helping."

A handful of yards away, Walter bent, clutching his midsection and groaning. "Oh God, I'm gonna shit my pants."

Lily took a step closer, palms down. "Bradley. Put the gun down."

"It was an accident," he said, voice high and panicked.

"And we all know that!" Leo said. "Don't make this worse."

"Just let me think!" Bradley cried. "Holy shit, let me *think*."

"We start by calming down, man," Leo said slowly. "Calm down and put the gun on the ground. This isn't who you are."

"Do you even know how to use a gun?" Walter asked.

"Of course I know how to use a gun!"

Walter frowned. "The safety is on, though."

There was a tiny click followed by Walter's quiet "Oops," and Lily watched as Nic unsheathed her knife and, to Lily's horror, stepped up behind Leo to press it against his Adam's apple.

"Nicole Michelle!" Lily yelled. "What the hell?"

She ignored this. "Drop it, Brad."

"It's Bradley!" he barked.

"He's actually really weird about being called Brad," Walter offered. "If you want him to put the gun down, don't—"

"If y'all don't shut the fuck up and get that gun out of Brad's hands," Nic yelled, "I am going to open this man from his chin clean down to his testicles."

Lily's stomach withered as she met Leo's eyes. They were trained, unwavering, on her face. Now was not the time to tell him that Nicole was raised by parents who owned a butcher shop.

"You're liable here," Bradley told Lily.

"She's not the one who pushed a man off a cliff," Nicole volleyed back.

"You're our guides!"

"You signed a waiver!"

Bradley froze. "We didn't sign a *death waiver*!"

"That's literally what it is!" Nicole yelled. Lily flinched as a tiny line of blood ran down Leo's neck.

"Nic," Lily said as steadily as possible. "You're cutting him, honey."

"Who says you didn't push him off?" Bradley growled. "You hated Terry."

Nicole came unglued: "*Everyone hated Terry!*"

Undeterred, Bradley rolled on. "We have more witnesses than you do. We could say whatever we wanted."

"Bradley," Leo said, hands out, palms down, "get your shit together. Terry held us at gunpoint. We were defending ourselves. You're not going to shoot anybody, and you're not going to pin this on them, either. Don't make this worse. Come on, be reasonable. How would I explain this to Cora?"

Bradley took a gasping breath before dropping the handgun like it was on fire. He immediately burst into tears. "Shit. I'm so sorry." He collapsed to his knees. "I'm freaking out. Sorry, sorry. I wouldn't ever—"

Nicole immediately ran over, grabbing the gun and turning it around in shaking hands, trying to get the safety on.

Leo rubbed a hand over his neck. "Nicole—just—" He walked over, taking it from her, and calmly clicked the safety back on. "Is everyone okay?" There was a murmur of response and he turned to Lily. His eyes searched hers, and he lifted a hand to rest on her face. "Are you?"

It took everything in her to not throw herself into his body, to not wrap her arms around him and hold on until she'd convinced herself that he was safe. Nodding, Lily forced away the burning threatening the surface of her eyes. She never cried unless she was angry, and right now she was glowing with rage.

"*You're* okay?" she asked.

"Yeah."

"Good." She turned to Bradley. "*You.* Sit." Lily pointed to a rock about ten yards away, and he bowed his head, slinking away, wiping tears from his face.

Nicole glared over at him. "Tell me not to hog-tie him."

"Don't hog-tie him," Lily said flatly. "We need to pack up and turn around or call or . . . Shit. I can't think."

They were out in the middle of the desert, hours away from civilization, with a death to deal with. It was almost dark.

She watched Leo as he approached the ledge, bending and carefully retrieving the journal from a pile of dirt. Dusting it off, he brought it over to her. "I was worried this went over with him."

Grateful, she took it, remembering the way it felt like her heart had soundlessly evacuated her body when she watched Leo run toward Terry and the gun, hurling Nic to safety. Shaking off the memory, she gazed down at the worn, soft journal in her hands, feeling Leo step up close behind her.

In the aftermath of the chaos, adrenaline had left her weak and trembling. She couldn't help it. She leaned back against the solidity of his chest. Without hesitation, his hand came up, wrapping firmly around her hip, steadying her.

"It's okay," he said quietly. "I got you."

"Do we need to go down and get the body?" Bradley asked from the periphery. Four heads swung his way, four sets of angry eyes narrowed.

"I just mean," he said, hands up, "he's down there. I— I don't know what to do, okay? I'm sorry."

A chill washed Lily out for a beat, and Leo pressed more firmly against her.

"Can someone explain what the deal is with this note-book?" Walter asked, his voice rising. "And to bring a gun out here? Is that why? Was he *planning* to steal it this whole time? Why would he do that?"

"Duke was famous in treasure-hunting circles." Lily turned the journal over in her hands. "He kept everything he knew in here. He'd been adding to it for years. Maps, notes, riddles, codes."

"How on earth would Terry know about it?" Walter asked.

"I keep this with me all the time because I know people think it's valuable." She took a deep breath. "I didn't really know that until after Duke died. Apparently he had a big following online and his fanboys assumed he'd leave it to another treasure hunter. But he didn't."

Lily felt Leo go still behind her. Right, they hadn't finished that talk; he wouldn't have known that her father died. "People have contacted me over the years wanting to buy it or trying to convince me to give it to someone in that community," she said. "But no one has ever actually come for it before."

"So there's information about treasure in there?" Walt asked. "Do you think Terry was trying to find where Butch Cassidy hid his money or something?"

"Her father knew everything about the Wild Bunch," Bradley said from the side. "Every story, every trail."

Nicole shot him a ferocious look, and he shrank guiltily again but still added, "I'm just helping explain why I think Terry did what he did." He looked at Walt. "At one point, Duke Wilder was one of the most sought-after archaeological guides in the Southwest. He was on the cover of *National Geographic*."

"Did you know Lily was his daughter when you booked this trip?" Walter asked Bradley.

He nodded, staring at the dirt between his boots. "Terry told me, but just in passing. I didn't know about the journal." He looked up and met Leo's eyes over Lily's shoulder. "And I swear to God I didn't realize this was your Lily." The group fell dead-of-winter silent, and an awkward awareness heated the points of contact between Leo's body and hers. He made to move away before Lily stilled him with her hand over his. She heard his breath catch.

With the reassurance of Leo's body behind her, the chaos in her head slowly started to calm. She looked down at the journal in her hands, letting it fall loosely open. Two pages had been torn out from the very end, and then shoved back in, crumpled inside, as if he'd planned to take them but decided to keep the whole thing instead.

"What the hell?" she murmured, fingering them.

The first of the two was a map. It was one of Duke's aerial drawings of slot canyons; formed by water flowing through sandstone over millions of years, slot canyons were serpentine, intricate, sometimes as wide as a river, other times as narrow as a man's arm, and deadly. Without a map, it was easy to get lost and never make it out. But each major vein, every slot on this hand-drawn map was labeled with a tiny number or letter.

"Do you recognize where this is?" Leo asked, gently taking the page so he could get a better look.

Lily shook her head. "He had about twenty of these drawings in here, and each one covers too small an area for me to know exactly where it is," she admitted. "It's a section of the Maze, I'm sure about that."

"Maybe Terry thought it's where Duke hid something," Bradley offered, scooting a little closer to the group.

Nic glared at him. "Shut up, Brad."

The next torn page was a riddle in Duke's handwriting, and Lily's heart dunked down into her gut.

"What's that?" Leo said quietly near her ear.

She took a steadying breath. "A Duke Wilder riddle."

"Have you seen this one?" he asked her.

"I've seen it, but I didn't care," she said. "The journal is full of ramblings, and I've never had a reason to figure every one of them out. This and the map are the last pages."

Leo looked over her shoulder again as they read it together.

In the end, the answer is yes.

You have to go; I have.

You hate to go, but you will.

You'll need to go, but never there.

But whether you do or whether you don't,

I can assure you that suffer you won't.

If nothing else, you are free,

So, search the stump of Duke's tree at the belly of the three.

She read the words again and again, mumbling, "This is not the time for a fucking game, Duke."

"Half of it rhymes, half of it doesn't," Leo murmured.

"That's Duke for you." Finally, Lily exhaled a frustrated "What the *shit*."

Leo repeated the cryptic lines, puzzling this out. Lily could hear the hesitation in the way he seemed about to speak but then held his breath.

Turning, she looked at him. His face was so close, only an inch away. "What are you thinking?"

"That Terry was looking for these pages specifically," he said quietly enough so that only she could hear.

"Agree." Lily looked back at the page. "But why? Out of the hundreds of pages in here?"

"They were the ones at the very end, right?"

She nodded. "But they're no different from anything else. A map and a riddle—that's literally like every other page in here."

He stared at her, eyes unfocused as he thought this through. "I'm wondering what the odds are that Bradley is right," he whispered, "and Terry really believed Duke hid something out here—or knew something was out here and left it for someone else to discover. Maybe these pages were what Terry needed to find it."

"How do you take that from this riddle?"

Leo turned her to face him. "Read the first line again."

She scanned the words. *In the end, the answer is yes.*

"If the answer is yes," Lily said, understanding, "then what is the question?"

"Exactly."

Of course. This would be where he'd want her to start. Duke's approval echoed in her thoughts: *That's the first thing I'd ask, too, kid.* Lily closed her eyes, thinking. What was the one thing that people had asked Duke all the time?

The answer was as clear as day: whether he'd ever found Butch Cassidy's treasure.

When Lily looked up again, Leo was staring right at her. Understanding lit up his eyes the same way it ignited her. A sharp ringing began in her ears, clear as a bell. She'd never been a religious woman, but an eerie awareness spread like static along her skin.

"Are the pages so important right now, Dub?" Nicole

walked over and waved a hand in front of her face. "It's almost dark, and we have a dead man at the bottom of the canyon and another man who I still think we'd better hog-tie."

Lily hedged unsteadily, looking over at Nicole. "I think Bradley's right."

"See!" Bradley shouted from his rock but immediately shrank into himself when they all turned to glare at him.

"I think it's possible Duke found the treasure and hid it out in the desert again." Lily swallowed, looking back to Leo, who nodded. The torn pages shook in her trembling hand. "And if he did, I'm pretty sure this tells us where to find it."

Chapter Twelve

THERE WAS A long moment of quiet, and it stretched tighter and tighter like a rubber band as Lily's meaning sank in.

"Do you mean the *actual* treasure?" Walter finally said. "The—the Butch Cassidy money?"

Lily nodded, head spinning. "I think these pages have a hunt written for whoever Duke planned to give this book to. I didn't know any of his friends in that circle. So I have no idea who."

Bradley looked around the group, ran a hand through his hair, then fixed his gaze on her face, jaw working. "Finders keepers, right? Even if he didn't mean for you to get it, you have it now."

That one hit harder than she wanted to admit. It was the bullet she'd been avoiding, because if Duke had found the treasure, and hid it . . . then by definition he had hidden it from her. He hadn't specifically left *her* the journal; he hadn't left it to anyone else, either, but if he'd meant for Lily to have it, surely he would have told her that at some point.

"There's something about the phrasing here," Lily told them, pulling herself together. "He says, 'The answer is yes.' If I'm right, then the question is, 'Did you find the hidden money?'"

"What does the rest say?" Bradley asked, craning his neck.

She read it aloud, tucked the pages back inside, and passed the whole thing to Nicole with a shrug. "I have no idea what the other stuff means." Lily turned to Leo. "What else is in that bag?"

"Oh, um." He opened it again, looking inside. "Looks like a cell phone. No signal."

"Turn it off to save the battery," Lily suggested.

"Good idea." He did, and then handed it to Lily before returning to the bag. "Ammunition clip. A very big knife." He paused and turned wide eyes up to hers. "Zip ties."

Nicole walked over, took the strips of hard white plastic in her hand. "These aren't meant to keep the cords on your TV from getting tangled; they're zip cuffs."

"Jesus Christ," Lily mumbled, and a chill moved through them all.

"Whoa," Bradley said, and looked like he might be sick. "What did he need those for?"

"He was your friend," she said accusingly. "You tell me."

"That really wasn't like me back there," Bradley insisted, crawling a bit closer. "I panicked. I'm sorr—"

"Okay, okay. Let's calm down." Lily hoped she sounded more convincing than she felt. It was beginning to look like Terry hadn't just been an asshole, he'd been dangerous. She nodded for Leo to continue.

"GPS," he said, handing her the fancy Garmin she'd argued with Terry about at the start of the trip. "Some C-rations, water. Condoms—" He grimaced.

"I'm sorry?" Nicole barked. "*Who* on *earth* did that man think—"

Leo cut off this line of conversation, pulling more things out. "Satellite phone."

"At least that's helpful," Lily said. "Anything else?"

Leo dug around for a second before finally handing her the bag. "Nothing the rest of us don't have."

Bradley inched his way closer. "What the fuck was he thinking?"

"You know how Terry is," Leo said, and then awkwardly amended, "or . . . was. He was always down one rabbit hole or another on some bullshit conspiracy theory. I knew he was gross, but I never thought he was violent."

"The question is, what are we gonna do about it?" Nicole said. "The fire's out, and even if we use the sat phone to call for help, they won't be able to do anything till morning."

Lily shook her head, struggling with a vague sense that she was floating, imbalanced.

"Nic's right," she said finally. Lily hated it, but it was true. With the sun gone, the temperature had dropped. No fire meant it would only get colder *and* harder to see. The last thing she needed was everyone else stumbling around the edge of a cliff in the dark. They'd call first thing in the morning; she would keep everyone else safe tonight.

"Fire first," Lily told them. "We can figure the rest out after that."

———

Nicole dropped into the empty spot where everyone had gathered around the now blazing fire, wordlessly watching the smoke twist up into the star-sprinkled cobalt sky. A shooting star arced overhead, and not even Walter pointed it out. The mood was tense as they each marinated in their own panic. Even the crickets seemed to be holding their breath.

Finally, Leo took the first step into the conversation they all knew needed to happen. "Are we in agreement about what we'll say to the police?"

"Terry held Nic at gunpoint," Lily said robotically. "When you went in to help, he went over the cliff."

No one spoke. To Lily's surprise, the voice to rise out of the quiet was Walter's. "I wonder if we should just say he went over in the dark," he said, words trembling. "I'm worried the real story sounds made-up."

"Sweet Potato has a point," Nic said, and looked over at Lily. "Could say he wandered off against the rules, went missing."

Lily nodded, resigned. "Fine."

Across from Lily, Bradley began to fidget. "Should we talk about the possibility that there's a map to real treasure in your bag, Lily?" He looked around the fire, and slowly, Leo nodded in agreement.

"He knew who your dad was," Leo said. "He brought a gun and zip ties. Do we take this treasure thing seriously? Or is this a Terry-is-a-nutjob moment?"

"I'm not sure," Lily admitted, "but Terry was hardly the first person to come out here thinking he knew something big. People have been looking for this money for over a hundred years. My dad was local, which gave him an advantage, and he'd worked with various archaeologists and historians for decades, so he had about as much inside information as anyone did about this thing."

"What is *this thing*, exactly?" Bradley said. "Give us the whole story, not the brochure version."

Lily exhaled, unsure where to begin. "Duke started chasing treasure when he was a kid. He spent nearly every free moment learning about Butch Cassidy. He worked with some pretty famous archaeological teams, but his first love was always that particular story." Staring into the fire, she tried to put the words into some sort of order. "I told you a little about Butch Cassidy before, but that wasn't his real name. It was Robert LeRoy Parker. He was born here in Utah in 1866. When he was a teen, he took a job on a ranch where a cowboy named Mike Cassidy taught him how to ride a horse, how to shoot, and how to steal. Robert's parents were Mormon dirt farmers who worked their fingers to the bone and had nothing. Mike Cassidy knew how to get ahead, and that's what Robert wanted."

Lily glanced at each of them in turn and wondered if anyone was blinking. Even Nicole—who'd probably heard more of this stuff than she ever cared to—seemed to know something was different tonight.

"Fast-forward to 1889," Lily continued. "Gold fever hits, draws men from all over the country. Robert is in Telluride, Colorado—called 'To Hell You Ride' because of the saloons and brothels and gambling. He works loading gold ore onto mules to carry down the mountain. And just like his parents, he has nothing to show for it. But right there on the corner is the San Miguel Valley Bank, and because it's where they take the gold, Robert knows it's going to be loaded. He thinks about when the biggest amount will be kept there and who's working. But more important, he's thought of how to get away." Lily picked up a stick, dragging it in small spirals through the dirt at her feet. "Robert was a charismatic guy. He'd been getting to know the people outside of town, making friends, slipping them money, and stashing fresh horses at their places. So, the day of the robbery, he and his buddy Matt Warner wait till there's only one teller working. Matt holds a gun on the guy while Robert cleans out the safe. They get away, and news explodes about the robbery. Robert is hooked now but doesn't want to shame his sweet Mormon mama. He starts going by Butch Cassidy."

"So, wait," Walter said. "Was the Matt guy Sundance?"

"No. Sundance Kid was Harry Longabaugh. He was from Philadelphia. Like every other boy around that time, he dreamed about going west. He moved to Colorado, was a ranch hand until a freak storm killed off ninety percent of the cattle and the jobs, and got caught stealing a horse, a saddle, and a gun outside Sundance, Wyoming."

"So, when did he hook up with Cassidy?" Bradley asked.

"In 1896," Leo answered, and met Lily's eyes across the fire. She'd wondered how much of it all he remembered. How much he heard during his short time at Wilder Ranch or picked up from the books Duke kept around. She remembered lying on Leo's stomach, the two of them reading together in bed with a fire crackling nearby.

She also remembered setting her book down one night, coaxing Leo's out of his hand, and losing herself in him for hours.

As if he was remembering it, too, Leo blinked, shuttering his thoughts. "They met on the Outlaw Trail," he finished.

"Is it true they never shot anybody?" Walter asked.

Lily nodded. "Didn't need to. They slipped money to people who were in danger of losing their farms to the banks. So, instead of turning the gang in to the police, these people fed them, kept their horses, lied for them."

Bradley whistled, low and impressed, poking at the fire with a long stick.

"Yeah, and the banks and railroads were pissed," Leo added. "They got the Pinkertons involved, and they had a ton of agents and informants all over the country."

Walter looked genuinely worried. "Oh *no*."

"It all went sideways when Butch and his guys robbed a Union Pacific train in Wilcox, Wyoming," Lily said. "They blew up the car with dynamite and within twenty-four hours nearly every man on the Pinkerton payroll was on the hunt. But they weren't just scouting the trails. The Pinkertons tracked down every serial number on every note Butch's gang had stolen and passed the info to banks, railroads, hotels, and general stores. Reward for his capture was four thousand dollars. Then five thousand. Eight thousand. In 1899, Butch knew it was a matter of time before they'd be caught." She paused to glance around the campfire. Nobody moved.

"*And?*" Bradley said urgently.

"Story is that they hid their money somewhere along the Outlaw Trail," Lily said, "knowing that if they spent a single dollar it'd lead straight to them. Then they fled to Argentina."

"Wait a minute." Bradley threw a twig into the fire. "In the movie, they both died in a shootout there. Are you saying they hid that money, but never came back for it?"

"Some people think so."

Walter leaned forward to catch her eye. "And you think your dad found it, and instead of cashing in, he hid it all over again?"

"Either that," Lily said, shrugging, "or he's leading whoever he'd planned to give the journal to to the location of the original treasure." She bent her head, chewing her lip as she thought about how either of these possibilities made her feel sick to her stomach. "He sold our land in Wyoming and probably expected to live off that profit, so depending on when— and if—he found Butch Cassidy's cash, he might not have ever expected to need it. Duke used to say, 'Adventure over stuff, kid.' For my birthday he would make me solve a cipher in order to find a pack of gum he'd wrapped or take me on a hike and quiz me on landmarks and tell me knowledge was my gift."

Bradley looked around the campfire. "Someone Google how much the Wilcox robbery was."

"Google?" Nicole said. "With what? This rock and a fork?"

"They stole about sixty thousand dollars," Lily said, waving them off. "I'm sure they spent some of it somewhere, so let's say fifty thousand, give or take."

"That's it?" Walter said. "Terry was going to kill us all for *fifty thousand*?"

"But that was in 1899, right?" Bradley asked, looking around to each of them for confirmation. "It'd be worth way more now."

"Plus," Lily said quietly, "that was just one holdup."

Leo stared at her. "How much did Duke think they hid?"

"Altogether? About a hundred and fifty thousand dollars."

"A hundred and fifty thousand dollars in 1899," Bradley said, awed. "And I bet some of the gold coins are so rare it's almost unheard of. That'd be worth millions in today's money."

"At least ten million, Duke thought," Lily said, eyes on the fire.

Walter blinked. "It's funny because it sounded like you said ten *million*."

"She did," Leo replied, and everyone went very, very still.

"Holy shit." Bradley stood and began pacing the camp. "Holy shit."

Nicole stepped into his path. "Sit down. I still don't trust you."

He immediately complied.

"What's wild," Walter said slowly, "is that Terry knew to bring a gun and GPS and all that stuff with him. And how he was so into this treasure hunt." He looked over at Bradley, his expression perplexed. "But wasn't it *your* year to plan this trip?"

Everyone looked at Bradley now, too. His shoulders hunched. "So, okay, don't get mad." He smiled nervously. "But I told him he could come if he picked the spot and planned the whole thing."

"Jesus Christ, Bradley," Leo said. "You're the biggest flake I've ever met in my life."

"I was really busy!" he protested.

Leo glared at him. "Busy like when you were supposed to plan my thirtieth birthday, and we ended up at the Golden Krust? Or Walter's promotion?"

Loyally, Walter piped up to tell Bradley, "I actually think supermarket cupcakes are better anyway."

"Could we just throw them all over the edge?" Nicole asked Lily. "It'd be so much quieter."

"But if the treasure is real," Walter said, focusing everyone back on the subject at hand, "and Terry needed your journal to find it, doesn't that mean we have the map to the real treasure?"

"Hypothetically," Lily said.

Bradley looked around the fire at each of them. "We're

doing it, right? We're going to follow Duke's clues to Butch Cassidy's money."

"And what makes you think you'd get any of it?" Nicole said, glaring at him. "It's Lily's map."

"Because we had a code," Walter said. "Like the outlaws. Remember?"

Bradley grinned. "That's right, Walt."

"I think we're missing the point," Leo said. "Terry is *dead*. If we go back and tell the authorities that he fell, there's a good chance we won't be suspects in a murder case. Going off on a treasure hunt is a very bad look."

"But if our plan is to tell them that Terry wandered off anyway, why can't our story be that he wandered off and we went looking for him?" Bradley paused, seeming to wait for immediate dissent. At Lily's silence, Bradley continued, bolder now: "We were already planning on doing a fake treasure hunt over the next three days. Why not do a real one?"

"Dub," Nicole said quietly. "He's on my shit list, and Lord knows I hate to admit it, but—Brad makes a good point. Why not just go and see?"

Lily's eyes flew to hers. "I thought you said you couldn't lie to the cops."

"It's ten *million* dollars." She shrugged, like *Sorry, but you know I'm right*. And then she looked around at the rest of the group. "Whatever I say here stays here, okay? I'm just spitballing, but . . . We could go ahead as if we're going to look for him. How many times did he say he knew this place better than any of us? Maybe he took off and fell over. Maybe I can trick my brain into thinking that. Maybe," she said, her voice thick with emotion now, "we go looking for the money."

"How long would it be?" Walt asked. "Out and back?"

Lily studied the hand-drawn map, blood pounding in her ears as she nervously tapped a finger against her leg. "If we're riding to the Maze and then going by foot? Three days? Maybe four. But this is really treacherous country. It's not family fun or tourist friendly. You need a permit with your itinerary so they can find your body if you don't come back. We'd need to stop and get supplies."

"If you're leading us, we can do anything," Bradley crowed, confidence booming. "We'll just call the police on the other side. With the money. You're in, right, buddy?" He looked over at Walter.

After a beat of hesitation, Walter nodded. "This is my do-over, remember?" He looked at Leo meaningfully. "All of ours. When will we ever have a chance like this again?"

"It's not like taking an afternoon hike, Walter," Lily said. "It's dangerous. What we've done is the easy part."

"*That* was easy?" he said.

Lily met his eyes. "That was nothing."

The fire crackling was the only sound.

She expected someone to push again. She did not expect the words that rose out of the darkness to be Leo's: "But do you think we could do it?"

"Leo. Are you telling me you actually want to do this?"

"I don't know what I'm saying," he admitted. "But that riddle feels like something, Lil. I know you feel it, too." She blinked away, running a hand down over the goose bumps on her arm. *Lil.* No one had called her that in years.

And he was right; she did feel something deep in her gut that told her not to ignore this. Leo pushed on: "I know we all thought he was an asshole, but Terry believed it enough to bring a gun. To take Nicole hostage. Was he going to shoot us? Was he going to make Nicole take him down into the canyon?"

"Don't forget the zip ties," Bradley said. "You don't bring zip ties to fight bobcats and cougars."

Leo walked around the fire to kneel in front of her. He put his hand on the journal. "Terry needed what was in here. And you have it."

There was an ember of hope flickering faintly beneath her ribs; he stoked it with the unexpected hunger in his expression. What did he want her to say right now? It all felt like too much to process at once. Terry's death aside . . . she felt in her bones that the riddle was more than just a game.

And yet Duke hadn't given this diary to her. He hadn't told her he'd found the treasure, either. He was fine selling her favorite place in the world, leaving her poor and alone. She was tired of her life being decided by Duke Wilder.

Still. Was it worth just . . . looking?

"Walt and I are with Nicole," Bradley said. "We're in."

"I'm with *Dub*," Nicole clarified. "I'm with whatever she says. We're a team." After a beat, she added, "I mean, I do think there's a way to go ahead with the riddle and also not get into trouble about Terry."

Bradley turned to Leo. "What do you think, man?"

Leo was still crouched in front of her, but his gaze dropped to the dirt at their feet. The fire licked shadows across his face, setting the angles of his jaw and cheekbones aglow. After a moment he lifted his chin to meet her eyes again. "I'll do whatever Lily says."

Lily tried to kick down the tiny spark in her chest. She looked at the map again, and the words in Duke's handwriting.

The answer is yes.

"We'll sleep on it," she said. "We can't do anything until the morning anyway."

Chapter Thirteen

LEO WASN'T SURE how he managed to sleep as hard as he did, but he woke on their fifth morning in the desert with a shoulder so stiff it suggested he'd barely moved all night. He didn't remember dreaming, didn't remember a single second of consciousness between when he'd closed his dry, exhausted eyes and now. Grateful, given the alternative, he pushed up onto an elbow, clearing the sleep from his vision. With a spike through his gut, it all came tumbling back: the bewildering discovery of the gun, the view of Terry slipping over the lip of the canyon, the map suggesting there might be real treasure out here.

He wondered whether Lily'd gotten any sleep at all.

There'd been no animal sounds the night before, no creatures rustling around the camp. No birdsong greeted the day now. It was just after five thirty, and through the soft gray tent walls he could tell that the sky was the deep-sea blue of a morning still considering daylight.

And then, a sweet groan cut through the cool air—a sound he'd heard a hundred times in reality and a thousand times in his memory: Lily stretching as she got up for the day. Even separated from her by the fabric of his tent, he could picture it perfectly: her arms snaking above her head, the way her body twisted, catlike, from left to right. She would tilt her face to the sky, eyes closed, and let out that low, sexy sound that— more than once—had him reaching to pull her back into bed. Instinctively, his body tensed, responding with a rush of blood so intense it made him light-headed. Wild that, given the circumstances and the downright clusterfuck they found themselves in, his brain had no problem going directly to how good it would feel to have her warm body next to his.

Truthfully, he thought he could face anything with her at his side again.

She was awake, getting the day started, and he was about to do the same when he heard another voice only a few feet from his tent, closest to the campfire. "You get any sleep?" Nicole asked.

The glugging sound of water being poured into the kettle, the metallic scrape of the kettle set on the grate over the fire. "Not much. You?"

"A little."

They fell quiet, and he settled back down, propping his head on his hand, shamelessly eavesdropping. Blame it on the fog-like surreality lingering from yesterday or the way Lily seemed at once so familiar and so unexpected; he wanted to know how she was, and he didn't know if she'd be honest with him.

"Okay, Dub," Nicole said. "What're you thinking?"

Lily's answer was quiet, like she might be worried someone could overhear. "I went around and around all night."

"Same."

"We can't just ignore the situation." A quiet pause, and then, "Terry, I mean."

"Of course not. That's not what I'm suggesting."

"But you were right. Heading straight back won't make him any less dead."

"Sure won't." They were silent for a few seconds, and he wondered if they'd moved farther away, until Nicole spoke again: "Here's how I see it: You can have just shit, or you can have gold and shit."

"Nic, I'm not even sure Duke ever found anything, and if he *did* . . . I mean, that's just a lot to think about."

"I know."

"I thought I was done being disappointed by him." The way Lily's voice went thin, cracking at the very end, made Leo's chest ache.

"I know, honey, but here's a chance to maybe get something out of everything he did," Nicole said gently. "Say Duke didn't find anything. Say it's a game, or that we're wrong about the riddle. Then what? We're talking a couple days, tops. Down and back up. We don't find anything, we come back and tell the cops Terry took off and we went to look for him, thought we knew where he was headed but it was a bust."

"They'll eventually find his body at the bottom of the canyon below our campsite," Lily reminded her.

"Well, and what do we tell guests on day one? Not to wander off. We can all testify he did it before. Who's to say he didn't Peter Pan it in the dark? Not a soul would question that."

"I know."

"Worst-case scenario, we don't get the treasure, but we do

get a couple more days of hope and living a dream. And *you* get to stare at that hot nerd for a few more—"

"Nic. Shut up."

Wait. What?

Leo nearly had to smother himself with his pillow. If he could take out his eyeballs and roll them over to where the two women were sitting to watch Lily's expression while she said this . . . he would voluntarily be blind for the rest of eternity.

He barely made out her whispered "I'm *not* staring at him."

"Are you for real?" Nicole said, decidedly less quiet. "You're a worse liar than I am."

"I'm not!"

"Well, he sure is. That boy stares at you with the horniest eyes."

Heat crawled up his neck. He was positive Nicole was correct.

"Okay, now: Imagine if it's real," Nicole said, redirecting. "Imagine finding even a little bit of cash. Even if you think there's, like, a five percent chance that Duke found it, Dub, even a fraction of the Butch Cassidy money is enough to buy your land back. It could change our lives, girl. Isn't this fate? Right when your land goes up for sale, this chance lands in your lap?"

Leo stared at the tent ceiling, reeling. Wilder Ranch was for sale?

Several long seconds passed, and then: "I know."

"That's all you've ever wanted, hon."

This time, the "I know" was quieter.

Leo settled back onto his pillow. His heart twisted so painfully in his chest that he couldn't manage a deep breath.

That's all you've ever wanted, hon.

All he'd ever truly wanted was her.

He felt uncorked, like he'd been shoved into a tiny space and was bubbling over, too large for his old skin. He'd been ripped from his reality, torn from the monotony and routine and loneliness of his life in New York, and despite everything that had happened yesterday—despite the fact that he had no idea what the next few days would bring—there was no way in hell he was ready to go back.

He wasn't surprised to see he was the first guest up, but he also wouldn't be surprised to hear that everyone else was lying on their backs like he'd just been, staring at the roof of their tent, trying to figure out how to feel. His thoughts were a rubber-band-ball tangle, but he had to find Lily.

She was standing at the fateful spot at the edge of the canyon, staring out, holding a tin cup of coffee. Her dark hair wasn't braided; it hung soft and straight between her shoulder blades. Her frame was slight, wiry, and maybe it was the conversation he'd just overheard, but to Leo there was a vulnerable bend to her spine that made him ache to pull her into his arms. Afraid of startling her, he cleared his throat a few feet away and watched her jerk to awareness, the tiniest hitch of her shoulders.

"Hey." He came to stand beside her, fighting the urge to move even closer.

"Hey."

"At the risk of asking a stupid question," he said, "how are you?"

She let out a dry laugh, bringing her steaming mug to her lips. "Fucking dizzy, that's how."

"Yeah," he agreed, smiling warily out at the vista. "I'd say the same."

"This is not a situation I ever expected to have to face," she admitted.

"I'm sure."

"Not just the Terry part." She tilted her face to the sky. "Which is tragic, of course, but I meant what I said about people dying out here."

"What other part do you mean?" he joked.

She laughed, a surprised, sharp single syllable, but her smile quickly faded. "It's weird, you know? Because on the one hand, of course he found Cassidy's money. It makes sense. He was *the* Duke Wilder, after all. If anyone found it, he did. And on the other hand, to think he found it and didn't tell me is so terrible it's hard to comprehend."

"I absolutely get that." Leo squinted into his mug as he tried to put his next question into words. But in the end, it was pretty simple. "When did he pass?"

"About seven years ago."

He let out a low whistle. "Wow. It's been a while, then."

She took a sip, nodding. "He had a stroke." He felt her attention on the side of his face and turned to meet her steady gaze. "A few weeks after you left," she said. "A few weeks after the ranch sold."

Leo's heart landed in his stomach with a heavy thud. All of it at once, and she'd only been nineteen. It was too much.

"It took the hospital a while to get ahold of me," she said, "because I wasn't at the ranch and didn't have a phone." She laughed humorlessly, a sharp exhale. "He couldn't walk or talk. I brought him back to our cabin in town and the only thing he could say from that day on was 'Lily.' 'Lily' for water,

'Lily' to adjust his pillows. 'Lily' to change the channel. We'd have a nurse come in a few days a week to help so I could work; otherwise I probably would have killed him." She laughed so he'd know she was mostly kidding. "I guess a bright side to him selling the ranch when he did is that we had money for the medical bills. He lasted just under three years." Lily looked over at him and attempted a smile, almost like she heard in her own voice how flat and dissociated she sounded, like she was reciting back his diner order rather than opening up about the wasting away of her father.

"I'm not sure which is worse," he said sympathetically, "losing someone suddenly, or after a prolonged illness."

"Losing a parent you're close to," she replied immediately. "However it happens. I know how close you and your mother were. Taking care of him was hard, and I'm sure he and I both regretted a lot by the end, but Duke didn't even know me well enough to know how much you meant to me. I've been thinking: He could have gotten your message to me if he'd really tried. It may not have changed anything, but at least I would have known what happened to you."

He didn't know what to say, so he let out a muted sound of agreement, nodding. It would have meant something to him, too, to know she hadn't just forgotten him. "I guess I'm still trying to figure out how you ended up running treasure hunts and expeditions," Leo finally admitted.

"I was working at a bar in Hester," she said, "but I was so broke. The owner knew some people who needed a guide, and I knew the area. I did the trip as a favor, but they had a good time, I guess, and told their friends about it. Word of mouth and all that. It was about seven years ago now. It definitely wasn't my dream job, but it was a way to make money and get my horses back. I figured why not use Duke's crazy reputation for something?" She shifted on her feet. "Did you know I always imagined this?"

"Imagined what?" He looked over at her, holding his breath. Her tone had shifted into something lower, more secretive.

"Seeing you again."

Leo's heart punched his throat. "Same."

"Sometimes I imagined, like, going to New York with Nicole and bumping into you on the street or something."

"I thought if it happened, I'd be on a trip somewhere with the guys," he said, and it was so easy to recall this fantasy, the words just spilled right out of him, "and you'd show up with a husband and a few kids. I'd be dying to catch up with you but would have to escort drunk Bradley back to the hotel and I'd miss my chance. But then I always figured you were just living your best life on the ranch."

She shook her head, laughing at the ground. With the toe of her boot, she drew a circle in the red dirt in front of her. "I got a letter a day before y'all got here. From Jonathan Cross, the guy who bought the ranch. He's retiring and wanted to give me the first shot at buying it back."

"Are you going to?"

Lily let out a laugh through her nose. "With what money?"

He wanted to tell her, *I have some saved, it isn't enough—it isn't nearly enough—but it's a start,* and then realized that the idea was insane. It had been barely four days. He couldn't offer to buy her a ranch.

"Anyway," she said awkwardly, "I'm not saying everything is okay. It's a mess, frankly. But I'm glad you're here with me for all of this. I really missed you, Leo."

In the creaking silence that followed, Leo went still.

Lily stayed focused on the sky in front of them and he was glad for it. Direct eye contact right now would end him. After all, her steady, confident gaze was what had made him fall for her that very first day ten years ago. The heated weight of her attention had sent his hands closer, seeking bare skin more times than he could count. He knew he'd been the only person she'd ever trusted with her softest thoughts. So her admitting this feeling aloud made him jittery with adrenaline.

"I did everything I could to forget you," she continued, and when he glanced at her, he saw that her eyes were closed. "I made myself into a different person. I drank or slept around or worked endless hours. It didn't matter."

Leo had to count his breaths. He was all tightness and longing; there was no space for words. Finally, he was able to tell her: "Missing you was physically debilitating."

She turned, meeting his eyes.

Leo stared at her a beat longer and then looked down, studying his hands, rubbing a thumb over his knuckles. "I had to get to a place mentally where I didn't want anything. I had to sort of," he said, exhaling slowly, "turn everything off. But I'm here now. With you. I don't mean— I mean, you matter to me. Even if we don't know each other anymore. Whatever you need, I'm here for you."

She turned toward the ledge again. "My whole life I've assumed Duke was full of shit," she said. "And now, it feels like my only chance to get my ranch back relies on the assumption that he was *not*, in fact, full of shit."

"Is that what you want?" he asked her. "The ranch?"

She inhaled slowly, tapping an absent rhythm out on her

coffee cup. "I want that, yeah. I want my ranch, and a family, and to not worry that I might not have money to feed my horses and pay Nicole. I want what *I* want, for a change. What about you?" she asked him. "What do you want?"

When he smiled, he was sure she had no idea what was supposed to be funny—but his answer was almost the direct opposite of hers. "I want my life turned upside down."

She turned to look at him again. "What's that mean?"

"I'm in if you are."

Lily's hazel eyes took on a golden glimmer in the rising sun. "Yeah?"

"Yeah." *I might follow you anywhere*, he thought.

"I'd need to have complete control," she said, searching his eyes. "I'd carry the gun. I'd be the only one holding the maps. I don't trust anyone except Nicole." She paused. "And you." Another pause. "I think."

At this, his ribs formed a Faraday cage around a crackling electric heart.

She stared at him for several long seconds.

"Okay, then," she said quietly.

"Okay, then," he echoed. "Do we need to figure out the riddle?"

"We can think about it while we head toward the Maze," she said. "I'm not sure we have time to decipher it—sometimes his riddles took me weeks to untangle." Lily looked up at him. "But if there's a tree, I know it would be near the river, and I know some of his favorite spots down there. And we definitely know it's in the Maze. We'll need to drive there. I'm not willing to risk the horses, and we'd need to go by foot at some point anyway."

Goose bumps spread along his arms. "Okay."

"There's a guy I know who can help us, a little town not too far from here. But I meant what I said about the hike being dangerous," she warned him.

"We'll figure it out," he said, and she let out a long, slow breath.

"Fuck it," she whispered. "Let's do it."

An explosion detonated in his blood. His fingers itched to reach down and twist with hers. Leo wanted to punctuate this agreement with a shout aimed at the sky, his mouth on hers, his hands on her skin. It'd always been this way: his heart on his sleeve for anyone to see. He felt utterly lovesick again.

"This feels like a second chance." She tilted her coffee cup to her lips, draining it. "At the very least, failing to find anything here won't make my life any worse."

This had to be enough for now. Because bubbling in his veins was the realization that if this was real, she could have everything she ever wanted, and maybe he could, too.

Chapter Fourteen

"IS IT BAD that I don't really feel bad?" Bradley adjusted Bull-winkle's reins in his gloved hands, and Leo wondered how he'd react if he saw himself right now. His jaw was covered in whiskers, sunglasses smudged and a canteen at his hip. He looked, frankly, the worse for wear.

Leo certainly felt different. In some ways it seemed no time had passed between when he'd climbed off a horse for the last time in Laramie and when he'd mounted Ace at their first campsite here. In others, it felt like he had been asleep for the entire decade, not using any of his senses, any of these muscles.

"I feel bad." Walter straightened in his saddle. "I didn't like Terry, but I didn't want him to die."

Bradley took off his baseball cap and used it to scratch the back of his unruly hair. "I'm sorry he died, but I'm done feeling guilty."

Leo glanced at his friend, muting his surprise. Bradley

had apologized again, and everyone agreed that emotions were justifiably high, but Nicole'd told him she'd gut him if he tried anything like that again. She'd have to get in line behind Leo.

They rode in silence as the horses continued navigating the descent into the canyon. The six and a half miles of switchbacks were relatively wide, but the edge was still sharp enough that they stuck to the inside of the trail, acutely aware that only five of them rode this morning instead of six.

Lily assured them that the horses had done this before, and that to them it was sort of a game. She was right. They nickered and called to each other almost all the way down and around the mountain, ears forward, tails up. Calypso seemed to be the most enthusiastic. Leo wasn't sure whether it was because she didn't have the weight of a rider to carry or because she was specifically happy to be rid of Terry, but Lily and Nicole each yelled at her to take it down a notch at least twice before they'd reached the sandy washout below.

The trip had obviously gone off script, so after a break where the guys handled lunch and Lily and Nicole took care of the horses, it was another three hours at least before they stopped just at the edge of the town where they would meet Lily's friend Lucky.

She'd used the word *town* generously.

"This is it?" Leo asked when they finally came to a stop at the vague beginnings of a dirt road. It was nothing more than two dusty walkways set parallel to each other and a few small, rickety buildings.

"Looks like Redneck Radiator Springs," Bradley mumbled.

Leo glanced around. "That's an insult to rednecks."

Deflating, Walter admitted, "When you said 'town,' I was hoping we could get massages."

"You could get off your horse," Nicole said, "and I'll step on your neck for free."

Walter blushed hotly and Bradley stared blankly at them. "This is the most bizarre flirting I've ever witnessed."

"Welcome to Ely. Population . . . I don't know. Two?" Lily ignored the commotion behind her and pointed to a tan double-wide with a tin awning on the front. "That's the ranger station. If we're going through with this, then we'll want to steer clear." At Leo's continued wide-eyed appraisal of the town, she added, "Reset your expectations, city boy."

"As with the 'bus depot,'" Bradley recollected. "Or what you're calling 'toilet paper' out here."

Lily leaned forward, urging Bonnie into a walk, and Leo sat up in the saddle, signaling to Ace to follow. "Who's Lucky?"

They passed another old, crooked building with the word EAT painted onto a wood board outside. A pair of ATVs were parked haphazardly—he doubted there were any actual parking spots anywhere—and a couple of mountain bikes leaned against an empty flagpole. "He was a good friend of Duke's."

The horses' hooves clip-clopped along the dusty ground.

"And he'll be okay with you just stopping by?"

"I hope so, because there was no way to make an appointment." She looked over at him, grinning, and it sent a thrill down his back to see the old fire come to life inside her. "He's mostly around for the idiots who bring their giant trucks out here and end up high-centered on a trail or in a ditch."

Sure enough, at the end of the "road" was another double-wide. The land around it looked like a 4x4 graveyard. There was also a small barn that was a lot nicer than the trailer, and a paddock with a handful of horses inside. Bonnie immediately whinnied to them, which set the others off as well.

"Guess she's been here before," he said, nodding to Bonnie.

"This mare loves it here," Lily drawled in a voice that implied she did not share the sentiment.

"Not your favorite place?"

"Nope." Lily looked over at him and let out a scoffing laugh. "This tiny town represents what I fear my entire future will be: dry, dusty, and decrepit."

———

An hour later, they crowded around a table in the ramshackle building with the EAT sign out front. It was more bar than café, but it had beer, a jukebox, a couple of cramped but real restrooms in the back, and many, *many* photos of Duke Wilder on the walls: the framed *National Geographic* cover of Duke; him with a team from Princeton, huddled around a large tarp weighed down by a collection of dusty artifacts; photographs of him on horses, on a motorcycle, hiking in Moab, sitting at a campfire under the stars. There was even one with a front-tooth-less five-year-old Lily at his side holding a huge set of deer antlers.

"Wow, Lily," Walt said with breathless admiration, "your dad really was famous."

They took it all in for a long, silent minute. The magnitude of Duke's history seemed to fill the room as they sat in the first actual chairs their asses had seen in days and sipped ice-cold beers out of mismatched glasses. Thanks to the quintessential aging cowboy Lucky—wiry, mustached, and skeptical of the men—the horses were now happily munching hay in his stables, and the treasure seekers had a borrowed Jeep parked out front. They also had fresh water and supplies in their packs, a few pairs of boots better suited for rocky terrain, and a handful of paper maps spread out between them.

Lily stared down at a topographical drawing of Canyonlands. More specifically, she studied the Maze, a trailless sandstone puzzle of interwoven canyons with dead ends and the threat of death by drowning and/or dismemberment at every turn. It was the most remote part of any of the Canyonlands National Park districts, and because it could take rescuers days to reach someone if there was trouble, every party heading down was required to have their itinerary approved with a permit. Obviously, they wanted as few people to know what they were up to as possible, so they'd risk descending into the canyons without one.

Leo watched as Lily and Nicole went over the map. Lily jotted down notes and sketched routes, referencing something in Duke's journal or recalling some random fact she pulled out of thin air. Lily, he knew, could handle just about anything, whether it was the horses or managing an entire ranch alone or knowing every plant or rock or animal out there. Even a decade ago, she'd never needed Leo for a thing, but he wanted her to want him anyway.

They all leaned over the table, tracking Lily's finger as it moved along the wavy line of the Green River. "The map has to be of a section somewhere along here. Unfortunately, this is miles and miles of undeveloped land." She growled in frustration.

"I feel like I'm looking at one of those Magic Eye things

they used to have at the mall," Walter said, unblinking. "You know, where you stare at a bunch of lines and suddenly it's a picture of a cat?"

"An autostereogram," Leo told him. "A picture within a picture."

"How do you even know that?" Lily said, catching his eye.

Bradley snorted. "Because he's a fucking nerd."

Leo nodded to the papers spread out in front of her. "How do you know any of *that*?"

She leaned back in her chair and rubbed her temples. "I feel like I don't know anything right now."

"You don't recognize anything here?" Walter asked. "A spot that might have been important to Duke?"

Nicole drew an imaginary circle over the map with her fingertip. "If we were flying overhead, we'd say the location in Duke's map is probably around here. It looks small on his drawing, but that's a big area."

Leo pulled the sheet with the riddle across the table. "Let's see if anything here jogs your memory."

"'*In the end, the answer is yes,*'" Lily read, and glanced up to catch his eye. "So, we're assuming that means yes, Duke found the treasure. Next, '*You have to go; I have.*' Again," she said, "I think that means he's already gone on a hunt, and now it's the reader's turn."

"Right," he agreed. "But then, '*You hate to go, but you will.*' What could that one be?"

Lily shook her head in confusion. "If he wrote this for one of his friends, it might be an inside joke, and we'd have no way of knowing."

"Unless it's to lead anyone who finds this to Butch's hiding spot. It could be universal."

She nodded slowly. "Okay, so then what is a place we all hate to go, but we will go?" After a beat, Lily shook her head again. "And then, '*You'll need to go, but never there.*' Those two lines . . . I'm not sure." She tapped the bottom of the page. "I feel like we should be able to figure out where this is. It says 'Duke's tree.'"

They all grew aware in unison and looked up, searching the photos on the walls. After a few moments, they turned their attention back to the riddle. None of the photos showed a tree.

"What does 'belly of the three' mean?" Bradley asked, leaning in.

"Duke used to call the bends in the rivers 'bellies,'" Lily said slowly, "and this part here"—she pointed back to the full map of Canyonlands—"definitely looks like a three." She drew her finger along a series of curves in the Green River. "But even if this is the right location, getting to it won't be like walking up to a safety-deposit box. It's a literal maze down there. I feel like I'm missing something." Discouraged, she stood and made her way to the jukebox.

Leo watched her go and considered following. Sometimes Lily wanted company when she was working things out, but more often she didn't. He resisted the ache in his chest and the urge to stand and move to her. Lifting his beer to his lips instead, he looked around the space, wondering how many beers Duke had had in this very spot. The old man must have loved seeing photos of himself everywhere.

His eyes snagged on the bartender, a good-looking guy in his thirties, and then followed the path of his heated focus . . . straight to Lily. He was definitely not looking at her like a man who was wondering whether a customer needed a refill. Tossing a rag down, he began to make his way around the bar toward her. Before he'd even registered his own decision, Leo shoved back from the table, jealousy and possessiveness streaking a hot path through him. The chair scraped against the battered wood floor and in three steps he was standing behind her.

Close behind her.

Leo wasn't sure which of them was more surprised by his sudden appearance, but Lily let out a soft "Oh, hi" and now he was stuck there in his self-inflicted moment of machismo. But the heat of her, the awareness of her body so close to his, made it impossible to move away. He rested one hand on the yellowed glass of the machine and ran a finger down the list of songs.

"This one," he said, tapping the plexiglass over "Rock You Like a Hurricane." "All the boomers say it's a banger."

With a mischievous laugh, Lily clicked *F* and then *4*, and the opening notes of Fleetwood Mac's "Go Your Own Way" warbled out of the tinny speakers instead.

"Ouch," he said, mock-wounded. "Burn."

"It seemed more fitting." Her little smile down at the jukebox told him she meant this with more of a wink than a slap, and he found himself staring at the tiny freckle on the back of her neck. She had two freckles: one there, another just above her left hip bone.

A memory speared him, of a sun-soaked afternoon off, with Lily splayed naked across his bed. As if it had happened only hours before, Leo recalled the sunbeam through the window, warm along the backs of his bare thighs, the feel of Lily's hip bone under his lips as he kissed that tiny mark.

His heartbeat was suddenly too heavy for his body.

Leo didn't think she realized how close they were when

she bent forward, pressing her ass to his crotch, but on instinct he reached for her hips, gripping her with a quiet "Lily."

She straightened, startled, turning to face him and leaning back against the jukebox. Her eyes narrowed in suspicion. "What are you doing, Leo?"

He glanced back over his shoulder. The bartender was behind the bar and watching them with a dickish smirk on his face.

"Came over to see if you were okay. You seemed frustrated with the map and riddle."

"Because you remember how much I love it when someone asks me if I'm okay?" she asked, staring straight at him.

No.

"Or," she said quietly, "is it that you didn't want me standing alone at the jukebox?"

She could see it all over his face, and there was nothing Leo could do to reel it in; the memories were flowing now in a rush through his mind: the nights he'd spent lying in bed at the ranch—before she'd given him the time of day—wondering what she would feel like against him. He'd close his eyes and imagine kissing her, touching her skin, tasting the water that ran down her neck when she emerged from the bank of outdoor showers. And, just as sharply, he remembered the dizzying relief of that very first touch: her palm sliding under his T-shirt, pressing like a branding iron to his stomach.

They were all covered in dust, they had a dead man in their wake and were about to descend into one of the most dangerous places in the United States in search of a treasure that might or might not be out there, but Leo hadn't felt this alive since Lily'd slipped that hand under his shirt and pulled him into the shadows with her. With a startling slap of clarity, he decided right in the middle of a nothing bar in a nowhere town that he would not let go of her so easily this time. If there was a one percent chance that she would take him back, he would try.

"Yeah, you're reading that right," he said, meeting her eyes squarely. "I didn't want you alone at the jukebox."

She put a hand flat on his chest and hesitated for a conflicted handful of seconds before forcing him back a step. "Well, knock it the fuck off."

Lily stepped around him, but to his relief she didn't walk to the bar; she went to her backpack, digging for more quarters. Slowly, he exhaled. That could have gone much worse. He knew better than to follow her again, though, and figured it couldn't hurt to cool down. With Bradley's knowing smirk trailing after him, he moved past the table and toward the men's restroom.

It was dark inside the cramped room, from the heavy grained wood to the dim bulb that glowed overhead, and it took his eyes a few seconds to adjust. An exposed pipe sagged from the buckling ceiling. The sink leaked and stood crookedly in the melancholy half-moon of a rust-colored stain on the floor. The urinal was in a disconcertingly damp corner, looking like it could be dislodged from the wall with only the vibration of a heavy truck rumbling past, with a lone framed photo above it. He'd take a moment to appreciate the luxury of indoor plumbing, but he wasn't all that confident it actually worked. With his tangled thoughts full of Lily and the renewed, familiar fire burning in his blood, he stared, dazed, at the wall in front of him.

Slowly, the photo came into focus. It was old and yellowed at the edges, with scribbled handwriting in the corner.

A structure . . . scraggly trees . . . a man. Leo arched a brow, amused—Duke must have made quite an impression on the bar owner if even the john was a shrine to him. In this photo, he was far younger than when Leo had known him, but the mustache, dark hair flattened by the trademark Stetson, the cocky lean: it was definitely Duke, clear as day.

Realization felt like a shot of adrenaline as the words from the riddle crashed into Leo's thoughts: *So, search the stump of Duke's tree at the belly of the three.*

He leaned closer still. Down in the corner, almost too faint to make out, were two words scribbled in pencil. *Duke's Tree.*

Holy shit.

Chapter Fifteen

LILY LOOKED UP from the jukebox to find Leo Grady, whose weirdly possessive self had left her only minutes ago looking chiseled and gorgeous in soft worn jeans and a white T-shirt, emerging from the men's room looking like a . . . a goddamn sandwich board. And wet.

"What on earth?" she mumbled, trying to decipher the object shoved beneath his damp shirt.

Hair dripping, Leo hurried toward her, grinning as he opened his wallet and threw down more than enough money to cover a handful of beers.

"What did you—?" she began.

"Lads, Nicole," he called to the group, walking briskly. "We're leaving. Quickly."

Smoothly, he dug his hand into the front pocket of her jeans and tugged the car keys free, spinning them on his finger and winking as if he knew exactly how the brief intrusion into her pants sent an electric thrill sparking between her legs. Tossing the keys to Bradley's waiting palm, Leo grabbed her wrist and pulled her behind him toward the exit.

As he dragged her out the door, Lily looked back over her shoulder in time to catch a thin trail of water silently seeping beneath the men's room door.

"Leo, what's under your sh—?"

"Get in the car," he said, cutting her off again. "All of you. *Now*."

Scrambling, they shoved a bewildered Walt into the rear cargo area and tumbled into the back seat while Nicole and Bradley jumped into the front.

"What happ—?" Bradley began as the bartender ran outside, shouting.

"Just go," Leo urged, slapping the back of the driver's seat headrest. "Go, go, go."

Without needing further instruction, Bradley turned the engine over and peeled away with a roar. "This is it!" he yelled, rolling down the window. "This is the shit we came for!"

Specks of dirt swirled into the Jeep, orbiting like stardust, and a wild energy took over. Nicole reached to crank the radio playing crackly honky-tonk. "I don't know what that was about," she said, "but goddamn if I don't feel like an outlaw."

Lily turned in her seat to face Leo, ready to demand he explain precisely what the fuck that was all about, but he beat her to it, already pulling the item from his sodden shirt. For a handful of seconds, words fell away, and she held her wind-whipping hair from her face as she stared down at the framed photo in his hand. The glass of the frame was streaked with water, but the image inside was protected. It was a photograph of her father, standing outside a tiny one-room cabin. The tilting wooden structure itself was flanked by two trees, and a brown-haired, bushy-mustached Duke leaned against the tree on the left, holding a beer and smiling easily at the camera.

"Duke's tree," Leo said proudly, tapping the words scrawled beneath the glass with an index finger. "'So, search the stump of Duke's tree at the belly of the three.' If we can figure out where this photo was taken, we won't even have to bother with the riddle. This is it!"

Lily would have sworn the breath was being slowly pulled from her lungs. "I know where this is."

Leo stared at her. "Wait—seriously?"

"I think so," she said, nodding. "The few times Duke took me with him on cartography outings, we'd stop at this little cabin down in the canyons. Well, more shack than cabin and I haven't been there since I was little, but . . ." She chewed her lip, mind spinning. "I think I know generally where it is."

Bradley shouted, slapping the steering wheel. "Yes!"

Shaking her head, Lily said, "I've never seen this picture."

"To be fair," Leo answered, "it was hanging in the men's room."

She looked over at him, blinking into awareness. "So you decided to *steal* it?"

"At the time it seemed easier than asking your buddy at the bar if he was willing to part with his urinal art." He paused. "There was, however, a slight plumbing mishap when I took it down."

"'A slight plumbing mishap'?" she repeated, stomach sinking.

"The less you know, the better," he told her. "I think this frame was nailed into an actual pipe. That restroom was definitely not up to code." Lifting the bottom of his shirt, Leo used it to wipe his face. Lily's eyes dropped to the hard planes of his flat stomach, the line of soft, dark hair just above the waistband of his jeans. "You might not want to go back there for a while."

"You could have just taken the photo out!"

"I got excited." Leo looked at her and let loose that reckless grin again. "Besides, I overpaid for his shitty watered-down beer. If you think about it, I paid for this, too, just indirectly." At her look, he relented. "I'll send him a check, okay?"

"Why not just," she said, flabbergasted and enunciating every next word for the apparent man-child in front of her, "*take a picture of it?*"

He barked out a laugh. "With what? A pint glass? You took our phones."

"This is so awesome," Walter said from behind them, his knees tucked to his chin. "I feel like we're in *The Goonies*."

Lily leaned her head back to collect her thoughts. If she was right, and the photo was taken in front of the little cabin, they might have the biggest clue yet about where they needed to go. Once her temper cooled, maybe she'd be able to thank Leo for simply grabbing it and bolting. After all, why waste time?

Nicole rolled down her window, and the hot air thrashed deliciously through the Jeep. Lily glanced down at the picture again, trying to build a plan in her mind. The entry points into the Maze tangled into a blur. She was too amped up by photo-stealing, key-grabbing, jukebox-possessive, bathroom-destroying Leo—the quiet man unraveling right in front of her eyes. He'd barely said ten words that first morning, but now he seemed *alive*—and the sight of him bursting out of his shell was bliss. Like time melting away.

Her blood streaked white with adrenaline as she remembered the way his hands had curled around her hips and pulled her against him. *I didn't want you alone at the jukebox.*

She threw him a dirty look. Yes, they needed this clue, but there had been so many other ways to handle it—other than simply ripping the frame from the wall. If Leo couldn't keep a level head, what hope was there for the rest of them?

"I didn't want to leave it to chance!" Leo yelled over the wind, correctly reading Lily's expression.

"But Axl is a nutjob!" she yelled back. "Maybe you noticed the pair of shotguns over the bar?"

Bradley smacked the steering wheel again. "Why does everyone have a gun?"

"His name is Axl?" Leo's expression cleared. "*That* guy? The bartender?"

Lily paused, searching his eyes to understand. "Yeah, why?"

"I am just . . ." His face tightened again with an odd mix of amusement and violence. "I'm trying to wrap my head around the idea that you hooked up with a guy named *Axl*."

Her mouth closed, eyes widening as shock rippled through her. "What did you just say?"

He passed a hand down his face. "Forget it."

"How did you—?"

"What do you mean 'how'?" he cut in, coughing out a laugh. "He looked at you like he had the *right* to."

"That was—" she began, irate, before starting again. "It was nothing. It was forever ago—and forgettable."

"Uh, guys," Walter murmured from the back. "Not to interrupt, but—I think we're about to die."

In unison, every head in the Jeep except Bradley's swiveled just in time to see a giant black truck barreling down the road behind them. It slowed, weaving and hovering, barely six inches off their back bumper, while the driver leaned heavily on the horn. Bradley let out a war cry, raising a fist to pound it on the tinny ceiling of the Jeep.

"I was born for this moment!" he shouted to the sky.

Raised on tires the size of a house, the truck had floodlights on the roof and a custom hood emblazoned with a hand-painted bald eagle, wings spread, talons carrying an American flag. Behind the wheel, to Lily's complete lack of surprise, was Axl. One of his idiot friends leaned out the passenger-side window, shouting something.

Leo let out a delighted laugh. "You've got to be kidding me! Look at that truck!"

"We are absolutely going to die," Walter groaned.

"You can't make this shit up!" Leo crowed. "That is the exact truck I would have chosen for him!"

But Bradley wasn't having it. He floored the Jeep, which responded with a chugging hiccup before hopping ahead, causing Axl to hit his own gas pedal with a vengeance. Both cars barreled down the bumpy, broken road; one wrong move, and the Jeep would be flattened by Axl's vehicular tribute to small penises everywhere.

"He's so mad!" Bradley yelled, delighted. "Jesus Christ, Lily, what did you do to him? Doesn't he know you're his hero's kid?"

"Yeah, but they knew I never gave a shit about the treasure!" she shouted over the roaring wind.

Bradley extended an arm out of the driver's-side window and raised his middle finger, yelling, "Want your picture back? How about you suck my dick?"

Axl and Idiot Friend's faces went red and they screeched ahead, cutting in front of Bradley and slamming on their brakes. The Jeep skipped across the road, stuttering as Bradley reacted, veering to the left to avoid hitting the truck's rear bumper. A horn blared and Bradley screamed, steering harder to the left to avoid an oncoming car and swerving down a side road that was even more riddled with potholes than the one they'd been on.

Axl spun out in a tornado of dust before righting his truck again and barreling after them. A gunshot sounded, and another, and dirt ahead of the Jeep exploded with the pellets.

"They're shooting at us!" Nicole screeched.

Leo reached for Lily, protectively cupping her head with his arms and pulling her into his chest. "They actually brought a *gun*?"

"I've got Terry's bag!" Walter yelled above the chaos. He pulled the handgun out, waving it. "Guys! Want me to shoot back?"

"*NO!*" everyone shouted in unison, and Leo reached over the back seat, carefully easing the gun away from Walter. Lily pressed her hands to her face, struggling to not throw up.

Leo's cool hand came around her neck, and she put aside the way she wanted to punch him in the stomach and let herself be coaxed down. Resting her forehead on his thigh, she focused on breathing, on ignoring the violent jostling of the Jeep and the horn behind them and the reality that this road probably ended in half a mile and they'd be staring down the barrel of a shotgun all because of a photo Leo stole from a bar.

He gently smoothed hair from her face before reaching to the back of her neck, massaging. She wanted to scream with how good it felt.

Leo's voice came from beside her ear. "It's going to be okay."

"I'm so mad at you."

"Breathe now. Be mad later."

"I will."

She felt pressure on the top of her head and realized he'd placed a kiss there. Lily instinctively clutched at his thigh as another gunshot whipped past.

"These idiots are terrible shots," Nicole said. "How hard is it to hit a car?"

Bradley yelled for everyone to hold on, and Nicole whooped loudly just as the Jeep took a sharp right turn, bouncing across a field, jostling them around for what felt like an eternity until the wheels jerked over a bump and finally hit smooth asphalt again. "We're losing them!" he yelled over his shoulder.

There was the screaming of metal and road, and Lily bolted up as everyone cheered, looking back to where Axl's truck had landed in a ditch and rolled limply to the side. Bradley slowed the Jeep to a reasonable speed as Axl and his friend jumped out, half-heartedly chasing them for several paces before stopping in the middle of the road to shout.

Walter stretched forward to lean his head out of Lily's

passenger-side window. "He'll send you a check for the picture frame!" he yelled back to them.

Axl and his friend got smaller and smaller in the distance, and Bradley eased up on the Jeep's accelerator.

"Holy shit, that was insane," Leo said, running his hands through his hair. "Wouldn't it have been better for him to—I don't know—*stay and turn off the water*?"

"I've seen those restrooms," Nic said. "You probably did him a favor."

"I can't believe you dated him," Leo murmured, dark eyes cutting to Lily with a heated depth.

"I never said I *dated* him."

He smirked and she smacked his shoulder, but the eye contact lingered. He was so jealous.

Jesus, why did she like it so much?

Walter continued to look out the back window. "Do you think we should go check on them?"

"They were literally shooting at us thirty seconds ago," Nicole reminded him incredulously.

"Cell service works out here," Lily assured Walter. "They'll be able to call for help." She watched as the truck got smaller and smaller behind them, finally disappearing from sight. Lily leaned between the front seats, pointing ahead for Bradley. "Keep on this road," she told him. "Another ten miles or so, and you'll take a left turn just after we pass a canyon on the right."

He sent her a salute, meeting her eyes in the mirror before blinking forward. He was glowing, and Lily would wager he'd never been this happy. When she looked over to Leo, his head was tilted back, eyes closed as the wind passed in warm bursts over his face.

Breathe now. Be mad later, he'd said.

It was what she promised herself she would do even as he reached out and soothingly covered her anxiously tapping fingers, pulling her hand onto his thigh.

"Goddamn, I'm so glad I'm here," he said.

Chapter Sixteen

BY THE TIME they arrived at their campsite for the night, the air was electric. They had a map, they had Duke's clue for the next step, and Lily knew where they needed to go. Leo's chest and limbs were buoyant, and everyone tumbled from the Jeep, energized.

Leo and Bradley unloaded the packs and tents. Nicole and Lily worked to dig out a safe campfire spot while Walter went off in search of anything resembling firewood. When the fire finally crackled in the fading sun, they gathered around a flat rock nearby and laid out all of the materials, planning their route deeper into the Maze the next morning. Lily traced their path with the tip of a pen, indicating how long each section should take, where they'd stop to rest, and where they'd camp before making the final push into the more treacherous caverns. With luck they'd find what they all desperately hoped was still hidden there.

"I need you all to promise you'll do exactly what I say," Lily told them.

"We will," Leo assured her.

She scowled and he could only guess she had taken the *be mad later* part of his advice to heart. He'd feel bad about stealing the photo if . . . well, he wasn't sure what would make him feel bad after a dude she'd hooked up with chased them out of town with a loaded shotgun. Frankly, Leo wished he'd taken a few bottles of booze, too.

"We'll go down here," she said, indicating a spot on the map that looked a lifetime away from where they were currently camped. "If I'm right, the cabin should only be about two miles upriver once we're in."

Holy crap. Suddenly, his life in Manhattan felt remote to the point of fiction. His days spent at a desk, sitting down every morning to create a new unhackable algorithm, home every evening to his little apartment, the constant rumble and hum of a city beneath his feet—all of it could not feel more foreign. He looked over at Lily's profile, and a cord pulled tight from his throat to his gut. He hadn't felt this *present* in so long. Air hit his skin differently, landed in his lungs with more of a punch. He was aware of his pulse pounding and the handfuls of times he'd laughed out loud in the past few days. Here was color, and sound, and heat. *She* was here. He wasn't sure how he would manage to leave her at the end of the trip.

But when he took a breath to calm his vibrating nerves, he realized the air was *actually* electric now: lightning flashed on a vista in the distance, and the heavy gloom of a storm loomed, unsettlingly low, hovering like a swollen, alien spacecraft. It was wild to see the actual momentum of a cloud: the gray mass blotting out the sun as it charged closer, dropping rain like a curtain of silver from sky to earth.

Lily had noticed, too. "Shit. That one is going to hammer us." She looked to Nicole, and then around the group. "Okay. Get your stuff set up and get in your tents. We're not going to be able to cook tonight, so grab a few energy bars from the Jeep—but don't go crazy. Whatever we have has to last us two more days."

They scrambled to stand and dispersed to find their packs, pull their tents open, and start erecting them. Lily helped Walter, and by the time Leo's was up, she was just reaching her own pack. He jogged over to her, helping her tug it from its storage bag.

"I got it," she said, jerking it out of his grip. She flattened the tent on the ground, dumping out the narrow sack of metal stakes. Picking up her small mallet, she began anchoring the corners of her tent into the dry earth.

Crouching beside her, he pulled one corner tight and used his own mallet to pound in a second stake, quickly reaching for another.

Beside him, he sensed that Lily had gone still, and did a double take when he glanced over to find her glaring.

"What?" he asked.

"What are you doing?"

"I'm helping," he said, confused.

She reached forward, yanking the stake from his hand. "Do I look like someone who needs help putting up a tent?"

"Of course not." Carefully, he reached for the last stake. When he paused, their eyes met, and he had to tamp down the longing in his voice. "I'm just helping you get it done faster."

Slowly she stood and stared down at him. There was an

oddly charged scent to the sky; it felt like the sizzling humidity of the thunderstorm was settling directly on top of them.

"Can I have a word with you in private?"

He looked down at her tent—still just a pile of fabric and poles on the ground—and then at the gray clouds barreling in on them. "Now?"

"Now."

Without waiting, Lily turned and stalked away, disappearing into the dusk behind a large rock formation.

He jogged after her, rounding the corner to find her farther away than he'd expected, pacing in the space between two hulking red boulders. She stopped when he approached, wheeling on him. "What do you think you're doing?"

He paused. Somehow, he suspected they weren't talking about the tent anymore. "What do you mean?"

"The stunt at the jukebox?" she said. "Rubbing my neck in the car? Coming over to help me with my tent?"

"Is it that unheard of for someone to help you?"

"You know that isn't what I'm saying. It's the *way* you're helping. What are you doing, Leo?"

The tight set of her jaw and angry vulnerability in her eyes told him she knew exactly what he was doing. He might as well admit it. "I want to be near you." She gaped at him, and he added, "I still have feelings for you."

She shook her head. "No."

"No?"

"No," she said again. "Stop it."

His heart sank. "Lily—"

"Do you know how hard it was to move on?" Her nostrils flared, and he caught a tiny glimpse of her chin quaking before she got it under control.

Nodding, he assured her, "Of course, I kn—"

"I realize you called—I get that now—but I didn't know that then. The hope I had that you might come back didn't just go away one day, Leo. It was a constant ache." She pressed a white-knuckled fist to her chest. "For *years*." She clamped her jaw shut, staring at him with unmasked pain, immediately mirrored in his own chest. "Those promises we made meant something to me. I get that what happened was just as heartbreaking for you. I *get* that. But when you do this kind of thing—talk about feelings, touch me? For you, maybe it's just a vacation romance, but it takes me right back to the hardest time of my life. If you'd been there for me—even from New York—I could have weathered anything. But you weren't. And I can't go through that again."

Leo took a step toward her but recoiled when a fat raindrop hit him on the forehead. "I want to have this conversation," he said gently. "But—can we talk in my tent? It's about to start pouring."

"And I get that your life went to shit for a while, too," she continued, ignoring this. "But mine has been terrible ever since you left." Her eyes grew red-rimmed and watery when she said the next painful truth out loud: "I hate my life. I fucking *hate* it. With the exception of my horses and Nic, I've got nothing." She took a few deep breaths through her nose and shook her head. "And so, what gives you *the right* to come back into my life and touch me, and look at me like that—like it isn't completely presumptuous—"

The sky opened up with a deafening crack, swallowing the rest of her sentence.

"Lily," he yelled above the cacophony of the rainstorm on rock. "Let's go back!" Big cold sheets of rain fell in their narrow crevasse, and he stepped forward, lifting the sides of his windbreaker to cover her, but she shoved him away.

"I don't need you to protect me from the rain, Leo." Water streaked down her face and soaked her blue-checked shirt, leaving her bra visible, every curve defined. He dragged his eyes back up to hers. His head was a blur, emotions rolling around in him like boulders.

"I don't need you," she insisted again, but this time with less heat.

"Okay," he said gently. "I'm not doing any of this because I think you need me. I'm doing it because I want to." He looked around, searching for the right words and finding only the simplest ones. "I want *you*."

"I don't want you to want me."

He closed his eyes, reaching up to wipe the rain off his face. When he opened them again, rain thoroughly drenched her, from the soaked ends of her hair to her lashes, her cheeks, her lips.

Under the pressure of his attention, she licked away the water, but the movement and the way she looked at him only made his longing worse. Unbidden, he remembered the first time he ever made her come. Long after her cries dissolved, Lily had looked down where he'd been lying between her legs, breathless. Her eyes were hazel, with a darker coffee-brown ring around the irises, but right then, her pupils swallowed them up, made them black with lust. Her dark hair had been a chaotic halo around her head. Shirt and bra pushed up over her chest, shorts hanging loose around one ankle. She'd looked like a star that crashed through the ceiling: blown open and depleted but still illuminated from the inside.

"*Stop it*," she said now, reading the hunger in his expression.

"Sorry." He squeezed his eyes closed, tilting his chin toward camp. "Let's—let's head back."

But she didn't move. "Why do you always look at me like that?"

Leo didn't know what to say. He didn't know how he was looking at her, but obviously he couldn't keep the infatuation from his eyes. He was falling in love again. Had never fallen out of it. Leo broke his gaze from hers. "I'm sorry."

He froze when she reached up and dragged the pad of her thumb across his lower lip, staring at his mouth like she wanted to eat it. Longing corkscrewed through him, but then she blinked, clearing the heat from her gaze.

"No," she said quietly, and then, with more force: "I am not doing this."

He was frozen, his heart scaling the length of his windpipe. "*Lil*," he said. "What am I supposed to do right now?"

She tilted her face to the sky, exhaling a devastatingly broken "*Fuck*. I don't know."

He reached forward, pulling a strand of hair away from her lip. "It's okay."

"It's not."

If she wouldn't lead them to camp, he would. But as soon as he turned, she caught him around the wrist, pulling him back, and in a blaze of movement, captured his face in her hands and took his mouth with hers.

An explosion detonated in his blood, propelling him forward, forcing a gust of air to escape her throat when her back collided with the rock face. Her kiss was hot and angry, but when she sucked in a breath, it pulled cool air across his lips and tongue, and the sensation was like a whip cracking, tripling his desire. He couldn't get enough. Her softness, the sound she made at the back of her throat, her taste. His entire life he'd wanted nothing the way he wanted her, and the feel of her wild kiss dissolved any restraint he had. They were drinking rainwater from skin, kissing so deeply he could feel her moan vibrate through him.

Her hands formed fists in his shirt, holding him captive for the savage scrape of her teeth across his bottom lip, the hungry stroke of her tongue. He groaned, giving her all of him, his lips and chin and neck, to bite and suck; her hands slid down his front, digging up inside his shirt. He must have felt like a fever come to life against her cold palms. She gasped, nails dragging down his chest, over his nipples; the sensation like becoming a tuning fork, struck. His frantic hands moved over her cheeks, neck, and down, cupping the gentle curves of her breasts. He licked the water that fell from her skin, sucked her jaw and throat, releasing fragments of his hectic thoughts about wanting her, missing her, losing himself in the way she gripped his collar like she'd punish him if he stopped.

Leo worked free the buttons on her shirt, spreading the cotton open and kissing the soft skin he exposed inch by wet inch, neck and collarbone and sternum and down, curling a finger around the strap of her bra and easing it off her shoulder to bare her breast to him. With his sanity pooling in the water at their feet, his palm came over her, feeling, remembering; his fingers closed around the peak in a teasing pinch.

Lily's sounds cut through the storm, her body responding helplessly, nails digging into his shoulders, urging his mouth to where she wanted his kiss and jerking in pleasure as the heat of it closed around her nipple. He switched to the other side, frantic, lost in the taste of her, thinking he'd drown in this rain before he'd move his lips away from her skin. With a cry, Lily pulled him up, fists in his hair, claiming him again with a fevered, gasping mouth, her lips and tongue cooled from the rain.

The kisses slowed, languid and deep, and he cupped her face in his hands, nipping gently at her lower lip before coming back for—

Lily jerked her head abruptly to the side.

"Shit." She squeezed her eyes closed in a hard wince and pressed her palms to his chest, shoving him away. "*Shit.*"

The air cooled, and his stomach sank. She reached for her shirt, closing it in a shaking fist.

"Lily—"

Without another word, she turned, jogging past him and back to camp.

Chapter Seventeen

THE RAIN WAS there and gone again just as quickly, but when Lily climbed out of her tent the next morning, everything was a mess—herself included. The fire was out, her boots were wet, and she'd kissed Leo. Hungrily. Aggressively. Unabashedly.

And she was dreading seeing him today.

Slipping into a pair of dry boots, she surveyed the damage around camp. The dirt was baked hard by the sun and unable to readily absorb much rain. They'd pitched the tents on high enough ground that the bulk of the water had run off and collected in slippery depressions or rushed to lower elevations, but their gear was wet, and nearly everything was slick with red mud. A morning that was supposed to be quick and orderly would be twice as much work.

The sky brightened behind the giant hoodoos, the gentle pinks and golds a bashful apology for last night's unexpected downpour. Lily got the fire going again and set her boots as close to the flames as she dared, draping her clothes over the branches of a gnarly juniper to dry. She was starting the coffee when she heard the muted footsteps of someone walking through mud.

Lily assumed she'd see Leo first that morning. Hell, she wouldn't have been surprised to find him waiting outside her tent for an explanation. God knew he deserved one. Thankfully, it was only Nicole.

"Well, well," Nic said, running a hand through her wild blond curls. "Half expected to hear Leo's tent collapsing last night."

The image sent a jolt of awareness straight through her, pinging parts of her body that ached to be touched. She could have gone to Leo's tent. She'd definitely wanted to. He would have let her in, too. Lily knew he would have said or done whatever she asked. He always had.

"Thanks for pitching mine," she told her. "I don't know what I was thinking."

"Oh, I know what you were thinking." Nicole swung a leg over a wide rock and sat facing her. "And normally I'd tell you to get yours and ride that boy like a bronco, but I thought we were focusing on this." She pointed out to the canyons and the wild, coiling landscape that would undoubtedly need all their attention over the next two days.

Lily carefully measured coffee grounds, avoiding Nic's eyes. Nicole was risking just as much as Lily was. They would both be liable if something went wrong. Leo was a distraction they didn't need. "We're doing this," Lily assured her. "I didn't have my head on straight last night, that's all. It would never work between us anyway."

"I don't know about that." Nicole tilted her head. "Anyone who says money can't solve problems has always had money." She lifted the pot of boiling water and poured it slowly over the grounds. "We find this treasure, and your whole outlook'll change. Hell, maybe I'll buy out the property next to the ranch. Imagine the spread!"

Lily liked this plan, a lot. Too much to look at it directly. "What if it's not for sale?"

Nic winked. "When you got money, everything's for sale."

A throat cleared behind them, and they turned to see Leo clutching an armful of wet clothes. All three of them knew exactly why those clothes were wet, and Lily's cheeks burned.

"Okay if I put these out here?" He nodded to the small tree where Lily'd hung her own sodden pile.

Nicole stood, her lips stretched in a smug smile. "I'm gonna pack up my tent and wake the others."

Leo took care of the clothes, and Lily handed him a mug of strong coffee.

"Can we talk about yesterday?" he asked.

"I'd rather not."

He took a sip and stared down into the dark liquid. "Okay. Sure."

But she knew it wasn't okay. *She'd* pulled him back. *She'd* kissed him.

"I need you to not . . ." She trailed off. *Look at me like that.* She blinked over to the fire, searching for the words there. "I shouldn't have kissed you. I'm sorry."

"I don't think you're sorry you did it." She looked up at him, surprised. "And *I'm* not sorry you did it. If you did it again, I wouldn't stop you."

"I won't," she told him firmly. "We're not teenagers anymore, Leo."

"I wasn't a teenager when I worked at the ranch." He

smiled but held up his hands when she set her jaw and glared at him. "Okay. I'm done."

With a wild flame of golden waves atop his head, Bradley walked over, still yawning. "Jesus. That was some storm last night." He poured himself a mug of coffee, oblivious to the tension hovering over the small campfire. "Thought we'd get washed right out of here."

"Nah." She waved this off. "That was nothing."

Walter joined them, too, scruffy and shuffling sleepily over. He looked like he belonged out here. The rugged look worked. Lily poured him a coffee while he found a place to sit.

"What about when we go down today?" Bradley asked. "Can we expect more rain?"

"I didn't even know it rained in the desert," Walter said.

"We get about ten inches a year," Lily told them. "Mostly in the spring." She looked up to where the sky had gone from sherbet-hued to bright blue. The air felt calm. There wasn't a cloud in sight. "The ten-day forecast had about a thirty percent chance for showers yesterday, but normally we'd be pretty high up, so I wasn't worried. Should be clear the rest of the way, though."

"Just slick as shit, so be careful," Nicole added.

"Can I ask what might be a dumb question?" Leo asked, staring down as he flipped a short stick along the backs of his fingers.

"Shoot," Nicole answered.

"Now that we have this photograph and we have an idea of where we're headed, what exactly are we expecting?" He looked up, squinting at Nic and then at Lily in the weak morning sun. "Once we get down there, let's say we find the cabin.

Hopefully we find the stump. Do we think that's where Duke hid everything?"

"It's possible, but I'm guessing not." Lily winced. "You remember how my dad lived for puzzles and games? Well, if a code or riddle near the stump doesn't tell us where to go to find the money, hopefully it will at least tell us our next step. I bet you my left arm that if this treasure hunt is real, he left ciphers all over the place."

If it's easy, Duke whispered in her memory, *then it isn't worth it.*

Bradley leaned in. "But where are we now relative to where we're going today?"

She pulled out her big map and pointed to where she'd marked a giant square. "This is where we are now." She dragged a finger several inches over. "And this is Jasper Canyon. We're headed there."

"It all looks very . . . wavy," Walter said through a grimace.

"Yeah. Those are elevation lines. We're going down to river level." They'd all seen the river in the distance; they knew how far they still had to go. "We'll have to leave the Jeep soon and go on foot. It's not going to be easy."

The guys looked at each other, and Lily looked at Nicole. It was going to be a rough couple of days.

Bradley was the first to break the silence. "Then we'd better get started," he said. "Let's eat and get out of here."

There wasn't much variety—instant oatmeal, nuts, and berries—but they savored the last of their fresh food, knowing their next meals would have to be light, nonperishable, and heavy on the protein. Nobody mentioned Lily's and Leo's clothes—mostly dry now in the heat of the fire—but they hung there like guilty shadows.

They took down the tents and loaded everything into the Jeep, driving a few slow hours on the increasingly bumpy and treacherous road before deciding that it was time to take the rest on foot.

They checked their packs and determined what they absolutely needed to have. No way was Lily leaving the gun in the Jeep, so along with Duke's notebook, she zipped it, her satellite phone, and Terry's phones into a gallon-size plastic bag.

Leo put his hand on Terry's phone in the bag. "Should we take those? Will it look bad?"

"Nah. I grew up with every ranger in the county. They're good guys but it's not FBI headquarters down here."

Those who needed to switched out their shoes, and they each packed a change of clothes, and enough energy bars, beef jerky, water, and C rations to last a couple of days. Nic took the first aid kit and everyone had their sleeping bag and tent strapped into their hiking pack, but—

"Keep it as light as possible," she reminded them. "I know you want to take everything, Bradley, but I promise you won't need cashmere down in the Maze."

He looked quietly insulted, but then removed a bundle from his pack and put it back in the Jeep.

And then, they set off in relative silence. The mood was thick with hope and apprehension . . . but maybe the quiet energy Lily sensed in the group was also focus. They'd never done anything like this in their lives, and here there was an intermittent cairn to guide the way, but no obvious path.

"Do you remember how bad cell service was at the ranch?" Leo said, surprising her with how close he was.

She looked over her shoulder at him, confused. "What brought that up?"

"I don't know. I was just thinking about how pissed the guests would get when they realized there was basically a square foot of space on the entire property where we could *occasionally* get a signal. It reminded me that I haven't checked my phone or email or anything for days. I think that summer was the last time I was this unplugged."

"What do you think's happening online?" Walter said, frowning down at his feet.

"Same thing as every day," Leo said. "Somebody's mad. Somebody's lecturing. Cat memes."

"Someone's posting a shirtless bathroom selfie on Instagram," Bradley said.

Leo barked out a laugh. "Half your feed is shirtless bathroom selfies."

Bradley glared at him. "Not *half*."

"Those hell rectangles have turned you guys into zombies," Nicole said. "Instagram? Twitter? If you hate 'em so much, delete them."

"Of course we hate them." Bradley laughed. "That's the point. We go there to feel superior and angry."

"Not Walt," Leo said. "He's got almost a million followers on TikTok; they can't get enough of his pure animal content." He looked over at Walter as they navigated a relatively flat section. "What was the one that went viral first?"

"The one about responsible ferret ownership," Bradley said, laughing.

Walter shook his head. "No, it was about the mating habits of the common fro—" His words were cut off with a sharp cry as he lost his footing, crumpling to the ground and sliding a few feet down a rock face.

"Shit!" Nicole scrambled over, falling to her knees to check where he was clutching his ankle, rolling in pain. "What happened? Are you okay?"

He grimaced, pointing at a pile of loose stones hidden behind the tangled limbs of a fallen juniper. "I slipped on those rocks," he said, voice tight through clenched teeth.

They moved him to flatter ground, and Leo kneeled at his side, gingerly working his boot and sock off.

"Oh shit," Bradley whispered as they all stared at his quickly swelling ankle. A purple bruise was already blooming beneath Walter's pale skin.

"How bad is it?" Lily asked.

Leo felt along the bottom of Walter's foot. He sucked in a pained breath and swore when Leo pressed near the top of his ankle.

He pressed again and pain seemed to wash Walter out, making him look sweaty and pale. "Don't push there again, please," he said weakly.

Leo looked up at Lily, expression crashing. "I think it's broken."

"Can you move it?" Lily asked Walter.

He tried to turn his foot and immediately gasped sharply. "No."

Lily sat back on her heels, dread creeping like fingers along her skin. "Well, that's it, then."

"What? What's it?" Bradley asked.

"Walter's hurt," she said. "We'll need to turn back."

Bradley took his hat off and tossed it into the dirt. "God-dammit."

"*Brad*," Nicole barked. "Don't be a dick."

"You guys, I'm really sorry," Walter said. "Maybe we can wrap it and see how it is in the morning? Help me up."

They helped him stand, checking to see if he could put any weight on it. He cried out almost immediately. Lily met Nicole's eyes. They both knew what it meant: No expedition. No money.

No ranch.

And a dead body in the canyon.

Disappointment felt like a punch to Lily's gut, and she dug into Nic's pack for the first aid kit as Leo and Nic got Walt seated again.

"We have to go back," Lily said, squeezing the cold pack until it popped and the contents grew cool. She carefully placed it against his ankle. "I was already worried about getting everyone down there. It's questionable whether you could make it on both feet, never mind one." Lily gave him a sad smile, knowing how guilty he must feel. "Better safe than sorry."

Leo and Bradley stared down at Walter while Nicole handed Lily the elastic bandage, and they worked to get his foot stabilized and wrapped.

Bradley cleared his throat. "Leo and I will go ahead on Duke's hunt."

"We will?" Leo said with an incredulous laugh, and Nicole snorted.

"Are you fucking crazy?" she asked Bradley. "You could barely find an outhouse."

"Okay," he said, considering. "If you're worried about

how it would work, how's this: Leo and Nicole will take Walter back. They'll let the police know Terry disappeared, but that Lily and I went looking for him. Meanwhile, we'll keep searching for the money."

"No," Lily said. "We're not splitting up."

"After all of this we're just gonna quit?" he asked, voice rising.

"Brad," Nicole warned.

"Bradley," Walter corrected under his breath.

"No way, man." Bradley started to pace. "Something's out there." He pointed to the Maze, looking at each of them. "How many times in our lives will we be able to say we did something like this? Something daring and risky with a mega potential payoff?" He turned to Lily. "You're just going to live out your life not knowing whether your old man ever found the most famous treasure in American history? This is it, you guys, our big adventure. We can't turn back now."

"You could do this, Dub," Nicole said to Lily, quietly.

Lily turned her face up. "*What?*"

"You've been there. You know the journal, you know the games—you know Duke. It *has* to be you."

"Right," Bradley said. "Like I said. Nicole and Leo, take Walter back, and Lily and I can keep going."

Lily stared down at the wrap on Walter's foot, thinking. No matter how much she wanted this—the money, her ranch, and a definitive answer about whether her father kept the biggest win of his life from her—could she do that? Just . . . send Walter to a hospital and keep going? Wasn't it already terrible enough that they'd left Terry at the bottom of the canyon?

But . . . having them go back and contact the authorities

would at least show they'd tried to do the right thing. It wasn't a terrible idea . . .

"Leo," she said abruptly.

Bradley blinked, confused. "Leo?"

"I'll go with Leo." She straightened, jaw tight in false confidence with this decision.

Bradley balked at this. "Why not both of us?"

"Fewer inexperienced hikers mean fewer risks. Leo was an Eagle Scout and has more outdoor experience than any of you." She paused. "And frankly, I don't think I can do it without him. Duke wouldn't have made this easy, and I'll need Leo to figure out whatever codes he's left for us."

Leo met her eyes and she blinked away. She'd asked him once how he figured things out so quickly. He'd explained that he saw codes and puzzles as pictures in his head. He would shift things around, mentally sliding pieces or numbers together and apart until he had a solid visual of the solution. Then, he said, he would poke at it, check and recheck his conclusion. If it was a code, he'd confirm the translation of every number, letter, or symbol. If it was a puzzle, it was easier: he'd figure out where to move each piece, and he'd know he was right when he did it manually.

To Lily, it seemed like magic. She didn't understand how his brain worked without the help of his hands, but she didn't need to understand. She'd seen it, and right now she needed that brain.

"You can't leave me behind," Bradley said.

"You don't make the decisions here. And to be honest, I don't trust you under pressure. You've already pointed a gun at our heads and gotten us into a high-speed car chase."

"Technically, Leo got us into the high-speed car chase," Bradley grumbled.

Leo watched her, his hands gripping the straps of his backpack. Lily knew it was the only way forward, but her heart stuttered with adrenaline at the thought of being alone with him and trying to keep her head on straight. "You guys take Walter back. Leo and I need two days," she told Nicole meaningfully. "Tell the rangers that Terry wanted to try different routes and wandered off on his own, and Leo and I went to look for him."

Nic nodded, eyes intense.

"Wait for our call," Lily said. "Let us worry about getting within service range."

"What if you don't call?" Walter asked.

"We will." None of them voiced it, but they were all thinking the same thing: they'd call . . . unless they ended up like Terry.

Chapter Eighteen

BY THE TIME they got Walter back to the Jeep, his ankle was about twice its normal size and turning a sickly blue. Bradley was definitely not happy about the change in plans, but despite his guilt and need for adventure, Walter seemed somewhat relieved to be heading back.

Honestly, Leo wasn't sure how he felt. The distance between the safety of his cubicle and the spot where he stood could be measured in galaxies, not miles. The danger they faced was real. Terry was dead. Walter more than likely had a broken foot. Leo and Lily could easily drown or be crushed to death out there and never be heard from again. His mind drifted briefly to Cora, wondering what she was doing, how she'd handle it if anything happened to him.

And yet, the hum in his blood was anticipation, not fear. The adrenaline of adventure and the prospect of being with Lily again coursed through him. He could sense the war inside her—the attraction, the fear—and knew that this had to be her choice. Nearly everything in her life had been forced on her. He wanted her to choose him.

They unpacked the bags, reevaluating what they truly needed in order to consolidate supplies down into two packs. Terry's pack was some kind of high-tech, expensive mountain-man thing, so Lily took it from Bradley, loading it up. Leo saw her hesitate when she pulled out the Ziploc bag with the journal, phones, and gun.

"I'd still take it," he said. "They won't need it."

With a resigned sigh, she shoved it all in the center of her change of clothes.

When everything was ready, Leo helped get Walter settled in the back seat.

"You sure you know what you're doing?" Bradley asked him with a mixture of concern and envy.

"I think I know what I'm doing," Leo said warily. "But even if I don't, Lily does." He glanced back to where she and Nicole were talking quietly a few feet away. "Let's just be glad she's willing to keep going."

"You are in so deep," Walter said with a pained laugh.

"Yeah, yeah, it's adorable, but come on," Bradley said. "If I have to go back with Mom and you get to keep playing, you'd better keep your head in the game." He motioned between the three of them. "We're splitting this, right? So don't get distracted because you're busy getting your dick wet."

Leo pulled back, feeling his temper slam down, a heavy pulse right in his temples. "Bradley, what the fuck?"

"I'm sorry to be crass, but this is serious!" Bradley stepped away from the Jeep, shoving a frustrated hand through his hair. "Walt and I need to know that you've got this."

"I know what I've got to do," Leo said. "Do you?" He

ticked the instructions off on his fingers. "Get Walt to the hospital. Go to the police and tell them that Terry took off and we're looking for him. If we find the money, we'll get whatever we can carry, and call you the second we have a signal." Leo held his gaze and then braced his hands on Bradley's shoulders. "You've got to trust me. Okay?"

Reluctantly, Bradley nodded.

They all straightened when Lily and Nicole joined them again.

Nicole adjusted the ice pack around Walter's ankle. "How're you doing?"

"Okay," he said. "Sorry again for messing everything up."

"No need to be sorry," Lily said. "It could have been worse." Her words echoed for a beat. "Obviously." She squeezed her eyes closed and took a deep, steadying breath. "Y'all were real cowboys this week," she said, looking carefully at each of them, and a tender filament in Leo's chest burned at how good she was at being a host, even now. "You aced your do-over. You should be proud."

Lily and Nicole shared a glance, and then Nicole moved in to hug her. "You stay safe." Nicole turned to Leo. "And *you*. Bring her back in one piece or I'll cut off all your protruding parts."

"Noted," he said, and turned to Lily. "Do we have everything?"

Lily checked her pack one more time. "I think so."

"Wait!" Walter called. With a dust-caked hand, he reached up, shoving his dark curls off his forehead. "I just wanted to say to Miss Nicole and Lily, this has been one of the best trips we've ever, ever done." He looked at Bradley and Leo. "Right, guys?"

"Except for the death," Leo agreed, "it's been great."

"Right," Walter said, laughing nervously, "obviously except for that. So, I just wanted to say thank you. I won't ever forget this experience."

With a reluctant smile, Lily leaned over and hugged him. "You're a sweetheart, Walt. Don't let Nicole into your pants."

"*Hey.*" With a scowl, Nicole climbed into the driver's seat, and Leo watched Bradley get in the passenger side. The engine roared to life, and Nicole looked out the window at them. "See you in a few days, Dub."

Beside him, Lily nodded, expression intense. The guys waved, and they watched as Nicole tried to gently navigate them over the bumpy road.

Finally, the Jeep disappeared from view. "Think they'll be okay?"

"They'll be fine." She hitched Terry's pack up on her shoulders. "It's us I'm worried about."

They headed back out, retracing their steps, more conscious of the path and the pitfalls this time. They hadn't *talked*, but there seemed to be an unspoken truce between them, an acknowledgment of what had happened last night and an understanding that it wouldn't happen again. They just focused on the journey in front of them.

After about half an hour, though, the reality that they were truly alone seemed to loosen something. They dusted off conversation, warning each other of things to avoid or pointing out sights on the trail. Leo asked her about a flowering plant (creosote bush), and the clucking of a small bird with a gray

cap (chukar), and she asked him a little more about Cora:
What was she like, did she have a significant other, what kind
of medicine did he think she'd go into? The going was faster
with just the two of them, and they talked as they hiked over
loose red dirt softened by bulges of grass and shrubby plants.
When Lily veered right, the makeshift trail became more rock
than soil and began to slope sharply down, requiring most of
their concentration. They walked for miles, his thighs burning
in the steep downhill grade.

"Step directly on my footprints here," she tossed over her
shoulder.

He did as she said, changing his stride so his steps mirrored hers.

She pointed. "See where the dirt is darker over there?"

He nodded. Just off their path, the dirt was bumpy, covered in some kind of organic matter. "What is that?"

"Cryptobiotic soil. It holds moisture when it rains and
helps with erosion, but it can take hundreds of years to grow,
and it's super fragile. You never want to walk on that."

He was careful to follow her steps as they navigated
ground that became more gravel than dirt, then more solid
rock than gravel. Gradually, the terrain narrowed into a slot
canyon. Sheer faces of rock rose above them, tunneling them
in, blocking out the sun. He was reminded of being in the city
and stepping into a narrow gap between buildings.

He reached out, letting his fingers trail along the rock wall.
Some parts were flat, some curved like waves. The surface was
almost striped, with layer after layer of sedimentary rock
carved by floodwater over millions of years. It didn't feel like it
should be real.

"Have you ever heard of Manhattanhenge?" he asked her, turning sideways to fit through a particularly narrow section.

"Manhattanhenge?" She laughed. "Sounds made-up."

"In the city you don't really see the sun rise or set because the buildings block the horizon. But twice a year the sunset aligns with the east-west streets, and if you stand in just the right spot—I like East Forty-Second and Third—you can see it."

She stopped and turned with a faraway look in her eye, like she was trying to imagine a day without a sunset. Lily shook her head, clearing it. "I can't decide if that sounds awful or weirdly magical."

He looked up at the thin strip of sky overhead, a highway of blue stretched between red rock rooftops. "Probably both. I went to a party with Bradley one night, and just as I was ready to lie about why I needed to head home, he pulled me outside. There was a huge crowd, and it was like the whole city got quiet for a second while we watched the sunset together."

"Do you miss it?" she asked. "The city?"

Leo hummed, thinking. "Don't get me wrong, I do love New York. It's where I grew up, where my mom was, and where Cora is. At least for another month or two. But I am so restless there. I'm up for a big promotion at work, and honestly, if I don't get it, I don't know what I'll do. Maybe switch firms."

Leo thought of the last Manhattanhenge he'd witnessed. He'd been on a date—he couldn't even remember her name now. Maggie? Margie? It had been clear from the very first moment that there was no chemistry. And even though the sunset that night had been beautiful, it was nothing like the sunsets here: the sky spilling fire onto the crooked rim, all with space to breathe. It made sense why Lily would never want to leave.

"Do you think you'll get it?" she asked.

"The promotion? Probably."

This made her laugh. "You don't sound particularly excited. Isn't it a good thing?"

He shrugged, smiling at her. "More money, less fun."

"Money's good," she reasoned.

"I guess."

He felt Lily watching him and knew how it sounded. But to admit to her that a promotion suddenly felt like a trap, that since he'd come on this trip he almost couldn't imagine working inside ever again, and that being out here made him see how rote and sterile his life in New York really was, would also be admitting her role in this epiphany. So much of it was about being near her again, and she'd explicitly asked him to keep those things to himself. So he did.

They spent the next hour scrambling over and under chockstones wedged between the vertical walls. He wasn't claustrophobic, but it was disorienting to not be able to get his bearings with the help of the sun, sky, or mountains. The sharp severity of the rock terrain here made for slow going. Not panic-inducing, exactly, but the unease of having only one way out combined with the physical exertion had started to wear on him by the time the slot opened up again. How did Lily make this look so easy? They were both breathing hard when she stopped to check the map, but she seemed completely calm otherwise. He hadn't noticed how cool it was in the shade until they were back in the sun, and he reached for his canteen. The air was dry and filled with dust.

She reached up to wipe the back of her hand across her

forehead. She was awash in color and light, her skin reflecting the golden cast of the rocks all around her. She was so beautiful, it nearly took his breath away. "Ready?"

Leo nodded, jerking his gaze back before taking a long drink and tucking his canteen into his pack. "Yeah."

"We're still going down, but we'll take the easier way. I think you're a little too tired to rappel." She folded up the map.

"I'm not tired," he lied.

She ignored this. "Step in my steps," she reminded him. "And don't stand on the edge of the rocks."

Unfortunately, Leo didn't have Lily's balance, and it took his hands and his feet to navigate part of the descent.

"This is the easy way?" he asked.

"Not if you're gonna bitch about it the whole way down."

He opened his mouth to say something sarcastic, but when a lizard darted out across his hand, he jerked back in surprise, his foot slipping. One second he was there, and then he was gone, free-falling, and wondering if this was what Terry felt.

The ground disappeared, gravity sending him down a speckled slide of shale and gravel in under a second, Lily's scream already seeming impossibly far away. He reached for whatever he could find—plants, branches, rocks—his fingers clawing at the dirt as the world flipped upside down and then right again over and over. His stomach rolled around inside him; his legs felt disconnected from his body. Something cut into his palm, scraped against his face. The wind was knocked from his lungs when he finally landed on his pack at the bottom of . . . somewhere.

His ears rang; dirt and grit burned his eyes and clouded his vision. He wasn't sure where he was until Lily was there, out of breath and passing frantic hands over his chest, his legs, his face.

"Leo—" Her voice cut off abruptly as she pushed his pack off his shoulders, feeling down his arms, squeezing, pressing her fingers to his neck to feel his pulse. "I thought you died."

He tried to sit up, but everything hurt. Especially his ass. "I might wish I had," he said, groaning.

"Does anything feel broken?"

He looked at his hand; he'd cut it on something but not too bad. She traced what he imagined was a scrape on his cheekbone and frowned. He tested everything else: elbows, wrists, knees, feet. It all seemed to move. "I don't think so."

She sank to the ground, pulling him to her. "I really thought you died," she said again, voice suspiciously thick. Lily held his head to her shoulder, pressing his face to her neck, and the sweaty heat of her skin made him dizzy all over again.

"Lil, I'm okay." He tried to pull back, but she tightened her hold on him, and his suspicions deepened. "Hey," he murmured, wrapping his arms around her, slowly rubbing her back. "Look at me. I'm okay."

Finally, she allowed him to tip her chin back and look at her face. His heart took a sharp, delicious nose dive in his chest. This steely, wary woman was crying. Over him.

He reached up, running his thumb over her wet cheek, and she reluctantly turned her watery eyes up to his. Leo would voluntarily fall down that hill a dozen more times if it meant she'd look at him like that every time. "See? Not dead. Not missing any teeth, am I?" He smiled.

She scowled at this, not ready to joke yet. "You're really okay?"

His smile widened into a grin despite the pain. "I'm really okay."

"Okay." She took a shuddering breath and nodded, eyes searching his features to reassure herself. "Leo?" she said softly.

He gazed up at her lips, leaning forward. "Yeah?"

She lightly cuffed the top of his head. "I told you to watch your step."

Chapter Nineteen

IT TOOK A good twenty minutes for Lily's adrenaline to sort itself out, and when it did, the powerful roar of the river reminded her that the hike down into the Maze was supposed to be the easy part. She could hear Duke's gravelly voice: *This is Canyoneering 101, pal. Don't tell me you're not prepared for this.*

Leo came to a limping stop behind her, voicing her thoughts: "Whoa. That's more water than I expected."

Looking out at the river, Lily felt her stomach sink. Whitecaps jutted up, crashing down on each other, tangling. Small eddies whirled in graceful spirals; fat, glossy pillows of water pushed up against unknown obstacles. And from the way the water ran flat right in the middle, Lily knew it was deep.

No, Duke, I am absolutely not prepared for this.

No river crossing is worth your life, her father drawled in response. *Did you pack your stuff watertight?*

She took a deep breath to steady her nerves. Their packs

were water-*resistant*, at best, but she'd expected calm water to her shins. It was part of the reason she'd planned the descent where she did, to cross here. Putting aside the possibility of ruined maps and waterlogged sat phones, if their things got wet and they were unable to start a fire, unable to change into dry clothes . . .

Lily didn't finish the thought. Never in all her life had she imagined her own death, but if pressed, she'd say what anyone who was at least part optimist probably said: she expected to die when she was old, after a long, happy life. She absolutely did not expect to die in the Green River, chasing her father's lunatic dream.

Leo shrugged off his pack, checking the zippers and ties, making sure his tent and sleeping bag were secured in their straps. Lily dropped hers to do the same.

He looked around. "It's greener than I expected, too."

Most of the vegetation here would never survive the dry conditions in the surrounding desert. The river created its own riparian zone, one where Fremont cottonwoods and Russian olives offered dappled shade, where dense clusters of shrubby plants and spring grasses grew with their feet in the rushing water.

"It's been a wet year. Might not look like this next spring."

"Let's hope we're still around to see it." He nodded and blew out a steadying breath. "Okay. We can do this," he said, squinting as he looked upriver. She could see him come to the same conclusion she had—it would be worse the closer they got to the confluence. "We just need to go slow."

She picked up a branch and threw it in, gauging the current's speed. Immediately, it submerged, bobbing a few feet downriver before spinning quickly in a tiny, hungry whirlpool. Lily groaned.

"Still, we should cross here," he said, "and then set up camp nearby to dry our shoes." He quickly looked over at her, anticipating her argument. "We can spare a few hours, Lil. We can't hike in wet boots, and we can't cross a river like this barefoot."

He was right, but she hated it. Hated how complicated this was becoming, hated how she'd failed to plan for everything, and hated even more that her desire to push forward outweighed her desire to call it quits. "It makes tomorrow's hike longer, but I'm not sure what we can do about that." She gave him a once-over. He looked solid and was barely limping, but still: "You sure you're up for it? You took a pretty big fall."

"I'm good." Leo bent and began rolling up his pants. They were expensive—lightweight nylon-spandex—and she was slapping herself for not bringing something like that along. Then again, when would she ever have imagined a detour like this?

Deftly, he managed to get them to midthigh, and Lily felt her thoughts come to a dusty, coughing stop.

She'd forgotten his legs. Or, more likely, she'd forced herself to not remember them quite so vividly. His thighs were unreal: defined and thick; the most surprising part of a body that was otherwise so lean. Broad shoulders, narrow waist, then thighs that could crush her like a walnut. Jesus, Lily had loved those thighs.

Pulling her brain up from the free fall, she looked down at her jeans. She wouldn't be able to roll them high enough to stay dry, but crossing this river in only her underwear, with

Leo beside her, sounded like number ninety-nine on her list of one hundred things she did not want to do, just above stabbing a fork in her leg.

Still, fuck it.

Without looking at him, she kicked off her shoes, unbuckled her belt, unzipped her jeans, and shoved them down her legs. She tried not to think of her own thighs, and the way they'd looked the last time Leo had seen them. She wasn't nineteen years old anymore. She worked hard and ate heartily when she could, but unlike Leo, she had never set foot inside a gym. Rolling her jeans into a ball, Lily pushed them deep into her pack along with the wasted energy of worrying about her body. Looking great in her underwear wouldn't get her across the river any faster. She put her hiking boots back on and then straightened, setting her backpack on her shoulders and buckling in as if she did this every day.

Lily registered that he'd gone suspiciously quiet. "What?" she said sharply.

Leo cleared his throat. "Smart." He paused again, and when she glanced over at him, he quickly tore his eyes away. "Would it make you feel better if I took mine off, too?"

Her "*NO*" rocketed out of her, too fast.

Way too fast.

Leo smirked. "Then let's go."

Together, they approached the edge and stared down at their entry point. The water was unsettlingly murky and dark.

"Unbuckle your waist and sternum straps," she reminded him.

If either of them stumbled, the weight of their giant packs could flip them over, pull them under. The bags could snag on an obstacle and trap them. Yes, with it unbuckled, Lily could easily lose everything in there—including her pants—but considering the alternative, she'd take it.

She'd crossed this river before, many times, but never when it was this full or this swift. It was the danger of being deep in a low canyon—rainfall could quickly flood them out. Last night's storm had been short, but it was a rager. When Lily looked up, she could see a few tiny waterfalls pouring over the edge of the red rock just from where she was standing. It wasn't going to get easier if they just stood there and watched.

Lily put one foot in, facing the oncoming current, sidestepping into the water. And then, once she'd found her footing, she kept her eyes on the opposite shore, careful not to get dizzy looking down at the river swirling around her legs.

"Try to stay on the sandbar," she said.

To her right, Leo stepped in slightly upstream, and her heart tugged insistently at the realization that he was protecting her by breaking the current. He reached out, grappling for her hand, and together they moved in tiny shuffle steps through the knee-deep water.

And then, only about five feet in, they abruptly dropped to their waists. Leo sucked in a sharp breath at the frigid temperature, and she looked over at him, stomach sinking. They weren't even to the middle yet.

"We're going to have to hold our packs up," she told him. "We'll just have to hope that it doesn't drop much deeper in the middle."

It would throw them off balance, but if they moved slowly, they should be okay. Shrugging out of their packs, they carefully raised them above their heads.

"Just one step at a time," he said, meeting her eyes steadily. "Are you okay?"

Lily nodded, her focus on the opposite shore, allowing herself only tiny peeks down at the river even though she could no longer see the bottom. The water was icy rushing over her waist, her ribs. Her feet slipped around rock, around small branches and reedy detritus. Every step was a slow process of extending a leg out only a few inches, feeling around, finding solid footing, carefully shifting her weight forward. She sensed the same careful focus in Leo.

Everything was okay so far. But still . . . Lily felt uneasy. There was an instinctive, dark hum in her blood.

"This feels like a bad idea," she said.

"We can do it," he murmured, eyes on the other side. "One step at a time. We're almost halfway."

They hit the deep, quiet middle and, to their surprise, the water rose only a few inches up their torsos. Leo looked over at her in triumph. "See?" he said. "Almost there."

She smiled, but a sharp sound ripped from her throat as her next step landed wrong, her foot sliding off the slippery edge of a jagged rock. Lily cried out, arms struggling to hold her bag overhead under the increasingly taxing weight. Leo looked over, eyes wide. "You good?"

A *yes* was on her lips, but then, suddenly, she wasn't good. Her balance veered sidewise, and to compensate Lily did a quick sidestep, but all that did was bring her into a small eddy; she leaned to steady herself, tripping over an invisible obstacle. Her foot was swept out from under her, and she fell backward, submerging entirely for a shocking, gasping second.

The current twisted her torso, flipping her legs over and pulling her downriver, leaving her panicking, kicking for footing.

Lily came back up, coughing, blinking into the bright sun, desperate to get her bearings. The water was punishing and unsympathetic, rushing past her in a gleeful torrent. Suddenly her soaked pack was the least of her worries. When she'd lost her balance and slid downstream, her foot had slipped into a tangle of branches and rock . . . it was trapped. She had nothing to hold on to, nothing to reach for, stretch for, to pull her up. Leo took a few precarious steps toward her, reaching one arm out, but he couldn't hold his pack steadily one-handed. Nearly dropping it, he immediately pulled his arm back, struggling to maintain his own balance. Both of them dropping their packs into the water would be catastrophic.

"Lily," he said, voice steady. "Tell me what's happening."

"My foot is stuck." She tried to keep the panic from her voice, but she felt it rising anyway, hot and bloating, pushing aside reason. When she jerked her leg back, attempting to pull free by sheer force, she discovered that it wasn't only that she'd stepped into a tangle of branches. Something was hooked around her ankle, and she couldn't twist her way out of it without losing her balance again. Lily could reach down and work it free, but she'd have to sacrifice her bag, and she wasn't ready to do that yet. "I can't get free without dropping my pack into the water."

He looked at her, and then over to the other bank, only about fifteen feet away. His dark eyes returned to her face, searching. The chaos of the morning had already delayed their start, and now the sun hung low, a lazy globe in the cloudy sky. Even if they sacrificed both bags and swam for the shore—even if by some miracle they made it out of the canyon before sunset—they would still have miles to walk in the dark, soaking wet, before they'd reach a phone.

"Are you stable there?" he asked.

"If I just stand still," she said, teeth chattering, "I think so."

"I'm going to get close enough to throw my pack on the shore, and then I'm coming back for you, okay?"

Lily nodded, holding on to his gaze like a tether. The water was pushing at her hips; fighting it with her body weight left her with the sensation that it was accelerating, that the river was trying to battle her. The outside of her bag was already drenched, but the possibility that something inside there could still be dry—the sat phone, the gun, *my God, the journal*—made her determined to hold it up, hands shaking as water dripped down her tired arms.

She needed him to hurry, but her heart twisted around itself at the idea of him rushing to get there and back, of him getting stuck, of both of them trapped and unable to even reach for each other. She was slapped with the frantic reminder she'd felt earlier: that if anything happened to him, she didn't know what she would do. Lifting her chin, ignoring her thundering pulse, Lily urged him to get moving. "Be careful."

"I will." With one final glance over at her, he turned forward, one foot out, then another, faster now, taking risks he hadn't before. A few times, his foot slipped, but he managed to catch his balance. Lily watched the tense muscles of his arms using the pack to balance his weight. She had a ball of lead in her throat. Leo stumbled, nearly pitching forward, and she cried out his name; panic felt like it was filling her, cold and terrified as her arms gave out and she had to rest the pack on top of her head so she wouldn't drop it entirely.

Breathe in, breathe out.

Watching him wasn't helping; it was making her more terrified. *All I can control is myself,* she thought. *Leo is capable, he is calm under pressure. Just stay still, and he'll come for you.* Lily tried to relax into it, pushing against the way her thoughts recoiled at dependency. She opened her eyes as she heard his pack land safely in a tangle of sagebrush, and he immediately turned, using his arms to propel his momentum quickly over the uneven riverbed.

Beneath her, something shifted, and in an instant her foot was free, but she had no solid stance; the river victoriously tugged her forward, pulling her legs out from under her again, dragging her away from Leo. The last glimpse she got was of his eyes going round in shock, the shape of her name on his lips. Icy water filled her mouth, her eyes, and she was fighting to remain at the surface, spluttering and coughing before slamming roughly against a rock. With a burst of light, the impact knocked the wind out of her. Water rose in a pummeling force, reaching her neck, pinning her to the stone.

Lily couldn't see anything, couldn't *think* of anything except maybe this was how she died. *I hope Leo finds the money,* she thought. *I hope he finds it and buys the ranch in my honor and lives there alone with the horses and Nicole. I hope he never fucking gets over me.* A laugh bubbled up and out of her throat, but it turned into a sob when Leo surged from the water in front of her, hair plastered half in his eyes, tiny stars of sunlight gleaming off the spiky tips of his lashes. He reached forward, dragging her away from the rock and hoisting her and her sodden pack onto his back as he trudged forward, one step at a time against the forceful current, determined.

They reached the shore in a tumble, and Leo rolled Lily over onto the grass, crawling after her and cupping her face as she coughed out water.

She felt hysterical now that they were on land, hiccupping and gasping for breath as the shock wore off and understanding hit her: if Leo hadn't gotten to her when he did, she would have drowned.

He reached back, pulling his soaked shirt off and using it to carefully clean her up. "Lily," he said gently. "Breathe, honey. It's okay. You're safe."

Giving in to the crash of emotions, she reached for him, pulling him down and over her. His torso landed on hers, solid and warm through her wet clothes, and she spread her hands across his bare back, stretching her fingers wide to cover as much of the broad expanse as she could. The strong *bum-bum-bum* of his heart pounded with reassuring vitality against her sternum. Lily wondered whether he could feel her heart, too. She wondered if he was remembering the first time they'd made love—Lily's first time ever—and the way he'd collapsed on her afterward, just like this. That night his heart seemed like it was trying to drum its way out of his body and into hers.

It all could have ended back there in the river, and for what? Some money?

"What are we thinking?" she managed. "This is so *dumb*."

Leo pulled back, passing his hand over her cheek, over her hair. "We're thinking a shot at getting you your ranch back is worth a little wrestling with a river."

In spite of herself, she coughed out a wry laugh. "For a second there, I really thought I was going to die."

From the way he looked down at her, gaze moving over every one of her features, Lily could tell he'd thought the same thing. "I had to let you go once," he told her. "You think I'm letting that happen again?"

Chapter Twenty

A LONG BEAT passed, Leo's words echoing between them before he grimaced, pulling away.

"We should get you dry," he murmured.

They climbed up onto the bank, and Leo immediately began to pull together sticks and twigs to build a fire. Lily wanted to help, but it felt like she'd been paralyzed. By his confession, by the near-death experience in the river, by the reality of their present circumstances. For a second time that day, adrenaline dumped a relieved deluge into her bloodstream, and she was suddenly shaking so hard she could barely take another step forward. She closed her eyes, clenching her jaw, trying to get her shit together when she felt Leo's body move closer.

He held the sleeping bag from his bedroll between them, shielding her.

"Take off the rest of your clothes. They'll need to dry overnight. You can wear my dry clothes."

Lily stared at him over the top of the bag. "Leo, you don't—"

"You're shaking so hard you're going to fall over. You know it's going to get cold as soon as the sun drops." He turned away, jaw tight. "I promise I won't look."

"I don't care if you look." Lily tugged her sopping shirt up and over her head, feeling weak and unsteady. Socks were peeled away to expose pale, waterlogged feet. After a brief hesitation and a glance up at him—he was still looking studiously away—she unlatched her bra and stepped out of her underwear.

"Okay," she said quietly.

"Here." With his eyes closed and face turned away, he moved to hand her the rolled-up bundle of his spare clothes. "Put those on."

His neck was red, cheeks splotchy with heat. A vein in his neck pulsed.

"Okay," she said again once she was dressed. "I'm decent."

Leo stepped forward, draping the sleeping bag around her shoulders. And then he bent, picking up the pile of her wet clothing and his T-shirt, and moved several yards away to spread them across a flat stone still warm from the quickly setting sun. He pulled her tent and sleeping bag out of their straps, laying each out on warm rock surfaces. He lined up their hiking boots, dug into her bag, and showed her that although the beef jerky was wet, the phones, gun, and notebook—packed wisely in the middle of everything—were still safely dry inside the Ziploc bag.

"Thank God," she said quietly.

"Yeah."

Lily watched as he unselfconsciously stripped his pants and socks off and placed them beside everything else. She should have been more surprised by the sight of his skin, or by the fact that she was suddenly looking at so much of it. His broad shoulders, tapered waist, thick thighs were all bared to her; smooth and defined. Leo was more muscular in this grown-up body. But his body was still *his*, and looking at him now— especially with the panic wearing off—made a yawning ache grow inside her.

He left his boxers on as he gingerly stepped barefoot around their makeshift camp, going back to collecting branches, twigs, dried grass.

Once her legs were working again, she moved to his pack—the dry one—and pulled his tent free.

"We'll have to share this, I guess," she said.

"I'll set it up." Leo grinned at her from where he was crouching over the kindling, holding the flint. "Your job is to sit there and watch me."

Heat flooded her cheeks and she tried to figure out if he was teasing her for getting mad at him last night or implying that it was a hardship somehow to have him doing a rugged mountain-man routine in nothing but a pair of wet black boxer briefs.

And then she decided she didn't care. Lily settled down on a rock, allowing herself this tiny window to enjoy watching him. Carefully, he started a fire, surrounding it with a small ring of stones. Once it was going and he was satisfied it wouldn't fizzle out, he sat across from her, holding his hands out to warm them.

"Want this?" she asked, meaning the sleeping bag.

"No, I'm good." He met her eyes, adding, "Really."

It was still probably in the high sixties, and without a breeze the air wasn't bad at all. But although her body had stopped the violent shivering, she still felt mildly feverish. Lily pulled the sleeping bag tighter around her shoulders.

"Would you like a protein bar or a protein bar for dinner?" he asked, laughing.

She bent down to dig into his bag. "Luckily we have seven hundred of these." She pulled out a couple of bars for each of them, tossing his one at a time over the top of the quickly growing fire.

He caught them and gave her a playful wide-eyed look of disbelief. "Living on the edge."

"You know me. Almost died, nothing can shake me now. What about you? You got pretty banged up yourself today."

Leo ripped open a wrapper and took half of a bar down with a single bite. He looked at the cuts and scrapes. "I'll heal."

"I'm sorry I dropped my pack in the river."

He shook his head, finishing the protein bar. "You're alive. That's just stuff, and it'll dry."

"Not by bedtime."

Leo leaned forward, poking at the little fire. "We can share my sleeping bag."

As he stared at the flames, Lily stared at him. *Can we?* she wondered. He was always so calm, always adaptable. She realized, watching him, that he met challenges as if they were an expected part of his path. By contrast, she resented every tiny roadblock.

Maybe it wouldn't hurt her to try to enjoy the adventure rather than quietly burning up over the possibility that her father hid treasure from her. She couldn't change the past, after all.

"Are you really okay?" she asked. "Not too sore?"

Now that he was practically naked, Lily could see some scrapes on his left arm and a bruise blooming on his ribs.

He nodded, smiling at the fire. "That was one crazy fucking day."

This made her laugh, and he looked up at her, pleased at the sound. Her heart tugged. Lily could simply look at him and know how he felt. How wild that, in this way at least, they hadn't changed at all.

Don't fall in love with him again, she thought.

"I'm really trying to imagine how we're both going to fit in the bag, though," he said, lifting his chin. "You'll have to keep your hands to yourself."

Tearing off a piece of her protein bar, she lobbed it at him.

But instead of it hitting him in the forehead like she'd planned, Leo ducked, catching it in his mouth.

Lily screamed, pointing. "Shut up!"

He was so proud, it was hilarious. "Did you see that!"

"Okay," she said, "but can you do it twice?" She lobbed another piece, but the arc was flat. That one hit him in the chin.

He shook his head, slapping his hands on his thighs. "That was a bad throw. Doesn't count."

"Okay, okay."

She tried again. It was high, and he had to lean to the right, but he caught it, chomping proudly.

"Who knew you were gifted in the art of catching flying food?" she asked, bending to take a bite for herself. "This must be a new skill."

He nodded, opening his second bar. "I am full of surprises."

Isn't that the truth. Lily stared at him, long and lean. Her nerves hummed. She wondered how good it would feel to have that smooth honeyed skin pressed all along her front. She wanted him for a blanket.

Lily had to be careful, though: keep her focus, not make this about being alone with Leo in the middle of the wilderness. They weren't just there for themselves, after all. Their friends were relying on them. Her future was riding on this.

But when he looked up at her, smiling shyly, every coherent thought flew out of her head and she found herself blurting, "I like how you're just sitting over there mostly naked like it's totally normal."

He smirked at her, completely at ease in his body. "Well, someone is wearing my clothes and my sleeping bag."

"Are you cold yet?"

He shook his head. "I'm good."

Honestly. Lily stared at him, wondering if he was really so dumb as to pass up that opening.

He did a double take when he caught her expression. "What?"

She shook her head, smiling. "Nothing. Good." Turning her attention back down to her food, she said, "I'm glad you're not cold."

"Wait." He paused. "Were you inviting me into that bag with you?"

"Too late."

He laughed incredulously. "Just last night you kissed me

like I was returning from war and you haven't acknowledged it once."

"I know," she said quickly. "You're right. Ignore me. I just got wrapped up in the moment."

She looked down, picking at her bar, but could feel the press of his focus on her. Finally, he said her name: "Lily."

"Hmm?"

"Ask me again."

She laughed. "No."

"Yes."

"No."

He stood and walked over, bending to get her attention. "Lily, I'm *freezing*." His eyes were dancing, sparkling playfully in the sunset. "I'm so *cold*. Please help me."

"You liar." She couldn't resist him, though, and opened the sleeping bag, holding her breath as he settled beside her. Warm like the sun, smooth and solid. Lily couldn't help it— she leaned into him, and he wrapped his arm around her shoulders.

Leo's voice was a soft hum. "Mmm. This is better." He rested his chin on the top of her head. "You feeling okay?"

She nodded, pinning her lips together with her teeth. She hadn't felt this kind of sweet, physical ache in forever. Deflecting, she said, "These boxers you gave me have little pizza slices all over them. Are you twelve?"

"Oh, I'm sorry, would you prefer to wear my other pair?" he asked. "The invisible ones?"

Lily laughed, looking up at him, and the instinct to prolong the joke disappeared as a bulb burst somewhere and their smiles straightened. Oh no, they were thinking the same thing. Specifically: how weird it was that they were here, huddled together under a sleeping bag, on this insane adventure, all alone.

She reached out, brushing his hair off his forehead. "Thanks for saving my ass in the river."

"Thanks for kicking my ass earlier when I fell," he said, and then smiled down at her, eyes on her mouth.

Grinning, Lily asked him, "Are you perhaps suggesting I was too hard on you?"

He nodded, leaning forward, and she met him halfway, pressing their foreheads together. Lily lifted her hand to the side of his face; his stubble was soft, and she loved the gentle scratch of it. He reached up, cupping her jaw and sending his fingers into her hair. The simple touch on the nape of her neck sent a drugged, ravenous sensation across the surface of her skin. Her lips hovered barely an inch away from his.

"Don't do this if you'll feel shitty tomorrow," he said.

The request sent a cooling realization through her. Tonight-Lily wanted those full lips on hers. But Tomorrow-Lily might wake up feeling unsteady and unsettled all over again. In her experience, nighttime hunger had never been a good mix with daylight rational thinking.

She turned away. "Okay. Sorry."

Beside her, his disappointment manifested in a quiet stillness, a held breath, and then Leo shrugged out of the sleeping bag. "I should get camp ready."

She knew she should help, but the sunset was a streak of pastel orange and purple, the fire was crackling away peacefully, and Leo was practically in the buff—the view was now firmly planted in Fantasies She Never Knew She Had.

As soon as Leo had the tent set up and his bedroll and sleeping bag laid out inside, Lily's body sagged. Her bones felt like they were softening inside her; all she wanted was to crawl into an actual bed and lose herself to oblivion. They went about the quiet normalcy of preparing for sleep: brushing teeth, refilling canteens with water and treating it with tablets. He checked their clothes and assured her everything would be dry in the morning. And as the sun gave its final wink over the rim of the canyon, the temperature seemed to drop immediately. Leo opened the flap to the small tent and gestured for her to lead the way.

She climbed in and pulled up short when faced with the reality of the sleeping bag situation. It was a one-person bag, in every dimension. They'd both fit, but barely.

"Could we unzip it and use it like a blanket?" she asked.

He reached up, scratching the back of his neck. "We could try. I just worry that it won't keep us warm. Especially if it drops into the forties again." Leo paused, attempting to read her silence. "I won't try anything."

A weight rolling over inside left her mute for a second. She *wanted* him to try something. If she was being honest, she wanted every moment of downtime they had to be spent touching. But that was the infatuation talking, and Leo was right—she shouldn't do anything if she didn't know what it meant. Because what *could* it mean? What was he going to do? Turn down a promotion, leave New York, and move here? How would she even adapt to that? The idea of having him in her life every day, of growing dependent on that connection, made her pulse rocket, her body instinctively rebelling.

"I'm not worried about that," she said. "I'll, um . . ." She gestured to her body, in his clothes. The jeans were baggy, and she was sure with both of them in there, it would be too warm in them anyway.

She slipped them off and he busied himself with climbing into the bag first, shoving his body as far to the side as he could and holding it open for her.

Was there a word that meant both *perfect* and *terrible*? It was this moment. Leo in nothing but black boxers. Lily in a T-shirt and his boxers with little slices of pizza all over them. She wiggled down into the bag beside him and the reality of just how close they'd be all night hit them both, as it essentially meant she was sliding across his naked torso. She couldn't help the laugh that tore from her, and Leo's eyes were squeezed shut, his lips trapped between his teeth. "Great," he said, and laughed. "This is fine."

She tried to work out which would be worse: facing him, or pressing her ass up against him? They both seemed to agree without discussion that facing each other was better; that way, at least they could keep a few inches of space between their hips. While she tucked her arms between them, Leo worked to maneuver his around her. His left arm became her pillow, the other looped around her torso, and then the terrible dissolved and it was . . . only perfect.

She wondered if he was remembering, too, how this was the way they used to sleep—by choice. How his tendency to roll away to the cool section of sheets was slowly eroded by her sleep-clinging tendencies and he eventually relented and held her in the tight cage of his arms.

Lily let out a jagged breath against his neck. "This is cozy."

His throat was so close to her lips that she felt the vibration of his voice. "It sure is."

"Are you okay?"

He nodded, tucking his chin over the top of her head. "I'm good."

They fell quiet, and in one ear she had the crash and flow of the river, and the other the steady drum of his pulse. Lily expected sleep to take forever, but some bone-deep instinct was tripped, and she felt drugged by his warmth and proximity and safety. She was asleep almost immediately, falling sweetly into blackness, and the tendrils of a dream stroked the edge of her thoughts just as she felt Leo's lips move against her scalp.

"I love you," he said in her dream. "I don't think I ever stopped."

Chapter Twenty-One

LILY WOKE UP with her face pressed to Leo's neck. His arms were banded around her, his breath slow and even. Everything inside her felt tense and hungry. His chest was broad and hot, skin so close to her lips it made her mouth water. The smell of him hit her like a lusty hammer, and she pulled her head back slightly, needing air, dizzy with the sudden wave of desire.

But she could pull back only so far; the sleeping bag was tight, and it meant that she could really only move her head. The second she did, she sensed that he wasn't asleep, either. His chin tilted down, reacting to her movement, his breath warm across her lips. Even in the pitch black, she knew that their mouths were barely an inch apart.

"Are you awake?" she whispered.

His voice, when it rose out of the darkness, was deep and gravelly. "Yeah."

"What time is it?"

"I'm guessing around midnight."

"Have you slept at all?"

Lily heard him swallow. "I'm having a hard time."

"Because of me?" she asked quietly, but he didn't say anything. "Leo? Because of this?"

"Yeah," he admitted.

She lifted her head. "Is your arm okay?"

"It's fine." He swallowed and attempted a laugh. "The arm isn't the problem."

Right. There was no way to miss the way he'd gone hard the second she woke up, so fast, almost like he'd been focusing solely on not doing so. "I'm sorry," he added.

Was he kidding?

"Don't be sorry," she said. "It's hard to ignore that we're, like"—she laughed out a breath—"*pressed together*." She swallowed back a quiet moan when his hand spread over her lower back.

The way his thumb moved in a steady, sensual circle felt practiced, *experienced*. It set a jealous warning light glowing in her thoughts.

Darkness gave her bravery. "Do you have a girlfriend?" The thought blackened. "Or wife?"

He went still. "Seriously? Lily. No."

Instantly, she felt like a jerk. She knew he wasn't the kind of guy to cheat. "Sorry. That was a stupid question."

He laughed. "It was." But then he let out a tiny creaking noise in his throat, a realization dropping: "Do *you* have someone?"

"No." She turned one hand over, resting her palm on his chest. "It's hard to date in this line of work. Most of my . . . whatevers have been guests."

"'Whatevers'?"

"Hookups," she said. Blood rushed to her face. God, it sounded so sleazy. She didn't want to have to admit how pathetic her love life had been.

But Leo had gone stony and silent.

"What about you?" she asked. "Do you date a lot?"

"Are you really asking me this right now?"

"Yes?"

He exhaled a slow breath through his nose. "I've dated a little."

"Oh. Cool."

"Bradley will be more than happy to tell you that I'm a commitment-phobe, but it isn't that." He went quiet, and with nothing else to notice, it was impossible to miss how his pulse had ratcheted higher. "I think the problem is that I'm not the kind of person to fall in and out of love."

And now *her* pulse was pounding. The implication landed heavily.

But she asked anyway: "What do you mean?"

"I mean, I fell in love once and stayed there."

"Leo . . ."

"You don't have to feel the same. I'm just explaining where I am. It seems important to not leave anything unsaid." Pausing, he added, "Though I admit maybe when you're trapped with me in a sleeping bag . . . after we've both almost died, might not be the best time. Shit, I'm sorry."

Her body took over, responding to the idea of him lying here, wanting her, holding her while she slept, doing everything she'd asked him to do when the truth was that she wanted this just as much as he did.

She slid her palms up his bare chest, setting off an explosion of need in her blood, and Leo sucked in a sharp breath, going very, very still. Beneath her hands, his pulse hit so hard she felt it reverberating along his skin. Her fingers rose over the curve of his chest, dipped into the hollows of his collarbones. She gave thanks to the darkness, because feeling him without being able to see him heightened every other sensation. Lily noticed the definition of every cord in his neck, how the length of his throat stretched unbelievably long under her touch. His jaw was a sharp edge against her fingertips, his lips full and softly parted, panting when she ran her index finger over them.

She whispered, "Come here."

He paused, but she felt the fight in him fall away. Digging her fingers into his hair, she leaned in, opening her mouth over his neck, sucking. A groan escaped her throat; he tasted so good, it made her feel feral, made her body press into his, hungry and sleepy and hot.

"Don't play with me," he said, and his voice vibrated against her lips. "Lily? I don't have it in me to say no, but don't do this out of pity or obligation."

"I think you know me better than that."

"You know what I mean."

Her head was foggy, her body so wound up it was hard to pull coherent thought forward. But even if she'd been fresh at sunrise with a cup of coffee in her hand, she wasn't sure she'd know the right words to say. What did he think was possible between them? He was in New York. Lily was here. Living in wide-open land was as natural as existing inside her own skin, and she was never going to carve the shape of her life around a man again.

But being this close to Leo felt just as natural. It felt right to share her body with him. And even more than that . . . it

felt right to let him into her world. She hadn't wanted to figure out how to build something lasting with a lover in years,
but the thought that she could try with Leo flickered like a
firefly around the edges of her thoughts, teasing.

"I'm just lying here in the darkness," he said, "trying to
imagine going back to my life the way it was last week, and I
can't. I can't even imagine what that would look like."

"What does that mean?"

"I don't know what it means, exactly. I guess it depends on
what you want."

"I don't know." She drew absent circles on the side of his
neck. "Right now? I want you. Right this second, I want to
feel you. But I guess if you need something more permanent
than that, then . . . don't kiss me."

Please kiss me, she thought. Her pulse was rioting. His
breath was warm and still sweet with the mint of his toothpaste and mouthwash. The kiss in the rain, against the rock,
had been bruising and angry, but right now she remembered
every other kind of kiss Leo could give and she wanted them
all. Sweet, deep, searching, frantic. Her breath seemed to
hover in her throat as he thought it over.

And then, just when Lily thought she might cry out in
needy frustration, his full mouth slowly came over hers. Like a
match had been dragged down the walls of her veins, a fire exploded in her blood, and she didn't let him pull away, chasing
his lips, opening to him, soft and pliant. The kiss felt nothing
like last time; none of the anger and hurt, only pleasure that
promised to stretch her to the breaking point. God, she'd forgotten the undiluted bliss of kissing Leo, of focusing every
drop of energy on the way his lips felt, the wet slide and drag of
them, the teasing licks and deep, sweet invasion of his tongue.

She couldn't keep her hands still; there was too much to touch and feel. Everything from the shape of his mouth to the heat of his skin to his perfect, quiet sounds felt tailor-made for her. Outside there was the rush of the river, the swirl of wind through sagebrush, the insistent clicks and chirps of insects. But in here there was only breath, the sound and feel of kissing, the soft noises they couldn't hold inside.

Maybe they would just kiss like this until morning. Maybe the sun would rise, and they'd still be here, unable to get enough of how it felt to lick and taste and suck. Lily suspected that kissing Leo could satisfy her forever, but then he made a fist in her hair, licking a hot path up her neck, and something turned over in her. Her body cautioned that without deeper relief, she might crack open and spill fire everywhere.

A warning bell rang, quaking in her arteries, pounding down every limb. Lily wanted him with a broken-glass intensity. Her hands were greedy, gliding everywhere she could reach, palms flat, fingertips a blaze of sensation. Leo's arms tightened, pressing her flush against him, and he read her posture, rolling forward when she rolled back, and inside of the tight sleeping bag he came over her, hips shifting between her legs, arching forward when she rose, and the relief of him there, the compound bliss of his weight and the pressure of him—desperately hard, just where she needed it—made her cry out. She was nothing but hollow ache. If he reached between them and touched her, he'd know without words that there'd never been anyone that turned her on the way he did. Leo dug down, but not for that. He bunched his shirt up her body and over her head, tossing it somewhere to the side. She wanted to cry at how good he felt when he came back against her, the slide and heat and solidity of his bare chest on hers.

He pressed forward, rocking into her, and his mouth rested on hers, open and overcome, and when he quietly asked her, "Does that feel good?" she wanted to bow down in gratitude to the universe that, no matter what else happened to him when they'd been apart, these essential elements of Leo—sweet and attentive and inquisitive—hadn't vanished.

Her brain flashed, *How did we ever end? How did I not get on the first plane to New York, or demand he get on the first plane back to me?* What she'd felt for Leo—what she felt for him still—was too big to name or tame, too big to shove back in a box when he went home. And if he stayed, she couldn't even promise not to fuck it up, but it wouldn't be because she didn't want him.

His mouth sucked her neck, his hips shifted forward and away, grinding so good, and even through the boxers—the pair he wore, the pair of his she wore—it was enough. No, not just enough. It was perfect, he was exactly what she remembered, exactly what she'd needed. Moving together like this, Lily felt the pleasure stretching, and shoved her hands beneath the fabric of his boxers, cupping his backside, pulling and urging him harder, faster, and his mouth came to hers, open and soft and distracted. Could anything but love tear her into pieces so quickly? With a flush across her skin, pleasure seared through her, warm and metallic, flooding her vision with spots of light until she slowed to a breathless stop beneath him.

Leo stilled. "Did you?"

Nodding, she pulled him forward, urging, and Leo's breath was hot on her chin, his sounds turned broken and tight. Lily reached up, digging her hands into his hair, dragging her teeth along his jaw, and his deep groan cut through the tent, vibrating in her bones. He jerked away, reaching between them, coming with a shaking moan.

In the deep silence that followed, her head was full of laughing gas; her heart felt like a wild creature had spawned in her chest cavity. Leo braced above her, breathless, and she ran lazy hands up his sides, counting ribs with her fingertips.

He let out a raspy laugh, lowering himself to rest on his elbows, half of his body out of the sleeping bag. "Holy shit." He reached for his pack, digging in. Lily cleaned up with the disposable wipe he handed her while he unzipped the sleeping bag a bit, letting some cool air wash over their heated skin.

"That was some quick thinking," she said, tossing the wipe somewhere in the tent.

"I have two pairs of boxers, and you're wearing one of them," he reminded her, catching his breath. "Somehow that realization penetrated at the critical moment."

With the sleeping bag unzipped, he had room to collapse onto his back, and ran a hand down his chest, groaning.

"You okay?" she asked.

Eyes closed, he mumbled a quiet, happy sound, rolling back into her and throwing a heavy arm around her waist, pulling her flush against him. "Come here."

But Lily was suddenly wide awake. How was she supposed to manage this feeling growing like a vine inside? She was elated and scared and anxious and relieved and still deeply, *deeply* turned on. The shape of him moving against her felt like a physical echo. She was suddenly insatiable, pressing her face to his neck, feeling the throb of his pulse, wanting *inside* him somehow. Wanting him inside her.

Leo.

Lovesick City Boy.

All over again, she couldn't believe he was really here. He smelled like sweat and soap, like the sagebrush-filled air of the canyons. She wanted his hands on her skin, his mouth moving frantically everywhere. She was aware of every point of contact between their bodies: her face to his neck, their naked chests pressed together, their hips, her leg wound around his muscular thigh. The memory of the sound he made when he came echoed in her cranium. And had anything ever been sexier than the way his labored breaths expanded and contracted the wide expanse of his rib cage?

God, she was a mess.

Lily pulled back, running a hand up his chest. He'd always been game for round two.

"Hey," she whispered, waiting. And then: "Leo?"

His lips parted and she felt her desire rise, anticipating the sound of his voice.

But instead, a quiet snore rumbled from his throat.

Chapter Twenty-Two

LEO AWOKE TO the sensation of Lily wiggling her way out of the sleeping bag and frantically whispering, "Shit, shit, shit."

He rolled to his stomach, eyes blurry but not so blurry that he missed the view of her scrambling to find the shirt he'd pulled off her and thrown aside.

"Hey," he croaked.

Startled, she wrapped a forearm across her chest, wrestling her way into the T-shirt. Her hair was insane, like she'd just wrapped a palm around a plasma globe. Her right cheek was bright pink from where it had been pressed to him, and her answering "Hey" was abrupt and stressed out.

"What's wrong?" he asked.

Lily lifted her chin. "Look at your watch."

He dragged a heavy arm out of the sleeping bag and blinked down. "Shit."

"Yeah."

Somehow the morning had blown right past them. It was after nine thirty.

"I have no idea how we slept so long," she said.

"Warm and comfy."

"You were *out*." She shoved her hair behind her ears. "Such a dude." And then she ducked out of the tent.

He followed her and stretched in the morning sun. Wearing nothing but boxers, soaking in the desert air on his bare skin felt fucking amazing.

His balled-up pants hit him directly in the face, and Leo caught them before they fell to the ground. "It appears you'd like me to put these on," he said dryly.

"We have to get rolling." She tugged on her stiff jeans before pulling her shirt off and tossing that to him as well. He stared at her breasts just . . . right there, in front of him, like it hadn't been a decade since he saw them last.

She reached for her bra, now dry on the rock. "Put your eyes back in your head," she said, laughing. "It's supposed to hit eighty-five today, and we have nearly four miles to hike."

"Four miles is an hour, maybe two if we stop for water," he told her.

"Not down here it isn't."

He pulled his shirt on and was immediately hit with a desire so heady it made his eyes roll closed. The shirt smelled like Lily. It was still warm from her body. Pulling it down over his torso, Leo looked to where she sat on the rocks, tugging her socks and shoes on.

But I guess if you need something more permanent than that, then . . . don't kiss me. What a joke. Like he would have been able to stop himself.

There was so much he hadn't said, and in the light of day he was glad. Things like how he was considering giving up his life as he knew it to be near her. Besides, his life was different now; he wasn't tethered to New York in the way he'd been since his mother died. He was still figuring out how it would look, what he could even do for a living if he moved to be near her. He was organized and worked hard; in truth, if he wanted a job and not a *career*, Leo could probably find something relatively easily. He wouldn't mourn leaving the office life behind; continually trying to outsmart some of the best hackers in the world had been a fun challenge at first—but in the last few years, the reality that even if he created the perfect code he would have to write a new one the very next week meant the job had lost some of the early glow. Still, even that had allowed him some creativity; if he got the promotion, he would be in meetings ten hours a day. And the point of moving would be to be near Lily, he reminded himself. A job was a means to an end, a means to make ends meet. A life was what he could have with her.

He shook some dirt off a sock, and then paused. *Slow down, Leo.* Even Walter would probably tell him to cool it. Lily was quickly and methodically packing up everything while Leo stood there slowly pulling his clothes on and thinking soft-focus thoughts about what their forever could look like. He didn't even know if she'd want that.

As if on cue, she asked, "Can you pack up the tent?" with only a thin layer of exasperation.

In minutes, he had it disassembled and stored. Lily spread the map out on a rock. "There'll be some pretty tricky bouldering here," she said, pointing to a section about a mile away, "but that's not what I'm worried about."

He waited, but she didn't elaborate. Finally: "What *are* you worried about?"

Lily took a deep breath through her nose, staring at the map. "I'm worried the cabin isn't there anymore. It was ancient then, and that was twenty years ago. The photo is from even before that."

"Even if the cabin has fallen down," he said, "the stump will still be there. At least presumably, right?"

"Right, but a stump is a lot harder to find from memory than a cabin is."

"Good point."

They shoveled a few protein bars into their mouths, chugged down lukewarm instant coffee, and set out. Immediately, Leo understood why Lily had been in such a hurry. By 10:15, it was hot as literal hell. Dry, too, in a way that made his skin feel too tight. Upside: whenever they found a patch of shade, they could stand in it and feel like the temperature dropped at least a full ten degrees. Downside: there just wasn't that much shade in this part of the Maze, and when they got to the part where there was, the sun would be the least of their worries. Some sections were so intricate and narrow, they could go in and die of thirst or heat stroke before they found their way back out again.

About a full hour into the slow hike—over boulders, finding narrow paths through scratchy blackbrush—Lily turned to speak over her shoulder. "Should we talk about it?"

Leo grinned at her back. She knew he wouldn't bring it up again. Now he had to wonder if it'd taken her the entire hour to get that simple question out. "We can, sure."

"I don't want to hurt you," she said outright, and his stomach rolled. Great start. "And so if what happened last night upset you at all, I want to say I'm sorry."

Her shoulders dipped and flexed as she scrabbled up and over a boulder and then reached back to help him. But Leo was tall enough to reach the top and pull himself up. "I'm good," he told her. "Thanks."

She stopped to catch her breath at the top, squinting at him with the sun at his back. "Were you responding to what I said or was that about the rock?"

"The rock," he said. "I'm thinking about the other part." Digging the water out of his pack, Leo took a long drink and then admitted, "I'm not sure where you're going with this, so maybe just get it all out. I already told you where I stood."

"So that's true, then?" she asked. "What you said last night?"

"Which part?"

Even flushed from the heat, her cheeks went pink. She had to turn and keep hiking before she could answer. "That thing you said about how you fell in love ten years ago and never moved on," she called back.

"Yeah." He leapfrogged across a few rocks to catch up. "Can we stop, please?"

She relented, ducking into the shade between two large red sandstone pillars.

"I want us to be able to look at each other when we have this conversation," Leo said, following her into the dark, cool space. Lily leaned back against one side and he leaned against the other, facing her. "I want to be very clear that it's okay if you don't feel the same."

She gnawed her lip, and for a brief second, her eyes teared up. She blinked the moisture away. "I think I might."

His chest took on a euphoric, caving-in feeling. Leo fought the urge to raise his fists in victory. "Okay."

"But it's not as simple as it was then."

"Probably not," he agreed. "But I lived my life in the most

responsible, boring way imaginable for the past decade." Leo looked to his left, out of their little crack in the rock and to one of the most beautiful views he'd ever seen, red stone and tanzanite-blue sky. "I think I'm done with that. Things are easier now that Cora is grown, and I'm not afraid of making a huge leap. When I was twenty-two, with every bone in my body, I wanted to stay in Laramie with you. But I couldn't." He paused, studying her, hoping she understood the sincerity of his words. "I can now."

She winced, searching back and forth between his eyes.

"I still love you," he told her. "In hindsight, if I'd never come out here, if I hadn't seen you again, I would have just kept moving forward with a life half-lived." Leo took a step closer, gently crowding her space. "I see you doing the same thing, Lil. You're just trying to get through every day."

"Leo—"

"There's probably not a life for me in Hester, but there's a life for us somewhere else if you want to try to find it."

She stared at him for several silent heartbeats. "This is *crazy*. You've known me for a week."

"Five months plus a week, with a little gap in between."

She closed her eyes, tilting her face up. "I need you to understand that I can't shape my life around someone else ever again. Every day has been dictated by another person's shitty choices, or my own circumstances resulting from another person's shitty choices. I realize I'm being rigid here, but I have to be. I can't bend to suit what works for you."

"Then let me bend," he told her.

Lily stared at him. "What does that even mean?"

"It means you figure out exactly what you want your life to look like, and I find a way to fit into it." He reached forward, drawing a strand of hair from where it was stuck to her lip. "Maybe you get a job on a bigger ranch, and I—"

"I can't work for someone else's operation like that." She seemed to hear the stubborn edge to her voice and softened. "I know myself, Leo. I'd be frustrated all the time."

"Then we set a goal and work toward getting our own ranch."

"Leo, you're on the verge of getting a promotion."

"Exactly. We'll save up faster."

She set her jaw, shaking her head. "We have to find this money."

"Why is that the only way?"

"Never mind the whole dead-body situation," she said pointedly. "It's the only way I can imagine right now. If we don't find this money, whether you're here or not, I'll have to keep doing some version of this. And this isn't the life of someone in a relationship."

Leo nodded, thinking this through. If she was even able to keep leading her tours, she'd be gone most of the time. He'd be alone in Hester, or some nearby town, working an hourly job just to have the privilege of seeing her a couple of days a week. He wasn't saying he wouldn't do it, but he did see her point.

He cupped her face and rested his lips on hers. "I guess we'd better find that treasure, then."

————

They set back out, talking every now and then and pointing to things occasionally, but for the most part their focus was entirely on not breaking an ankle on the increasingly treacherous landscape and looking up every so often in search of this tiny cabin in the middle of the most remote part of Utah. Leo sensed Lily's anxiety begin to bloom the closer they got to where she expected it to be, the longer there was literally no sign of other humans ever having stepped foot this far out.

The trip to the cabin should have been the easy part, but now it was sinking in that this adventure could really be over fast. One night down and then back out of this canyon, calling the whole thing off, left with the fallout of Walter in a cast and Terry dead.

Suddenly the sky went dark and the temperature dropped perceptibly.

Lily picked up her pace when they hit a flat stretch, just before a bend in the river, and Leo heard her sharp "Oh my God!" just before the first ball of hail hammered him on the back of the neck.

The first few pieces to land were small, maybe the size of a pea, but then a hailstone the size of an ice cube landed near his foot, and Lily took a golf-ball-size one to the shoulder. But it didn't matter, because her exclamation wasn't about hail anyway.

It was about a cabin only a hundred feet away.

Chapter Twenty-Three

ALL THEY COULD do was cover their heads and force their way in through the rusty, crumbling door. They burst inside, laughing and breathless.

"Oh my God with this weather!" Lily wiped her face. "I give up. Clear forecast, my ass."

Leo laughed. The tin roof of the tiny cabin was intact—mostly—the walls warped and crooked but with no major gaps. Hail flew in sideways through a blown-out window, clattering with eerie menace on the floor until they managed to pull one of the tents out and hang it around the jagged frame. It turned the light inside a strange, soft blue. Lily spun in a slow circle, taking it all in.

"Holy shit, it looks exactly like I remember," she yelled above the hailstorm.

It really was more shack than cabin, with only one room, maybe ten feet by ten feet, with an old, rusted-out woodstove in one corner, a dusty trunk in another, and . . . that was it.

There was no table, no chair, let alone anything to sleep on. It was, in design and location, only a place to provide shelter, not comfort. In the corner directly across from the door, the wood floor had rotted away, leaving a hole with dirt and rock visible beneath.

There was nothing even for them to explore, and so they turned and stared at each other, their smiles jubilant and wild. They'd found the cabin. Somehow they were one step closer, and with each step, this stupid, crazy, amazing, far-fetched plan seemed more and more possible.

Lily looked past him and her expression cleared, then she stepped to the wall, running her hand down the dates etched there. There were at least thirty of them scraped into the wood, ranging from dates too old to make out, to about ten years ago, and next to each were initials.

Most of them were *WRW*.

"William Robert Wilder," she said, tracing with a finger. The hail had stopped, and now rain pattered gently down on the tin roof. "That's Duke."

He touched a crooked *LFW*. "Is that you?" Leo asked, remembering. "Liliana Faith?"

She nodded. "He started exploring when he was around eleven, I think." She dropped her hand. "Closer to where he grew up, though. Near Laramie. His parents would tell him to get out at sunrise and be back for dinner." She laughed. "He went on a backpacking trip in Moab when he was about four-teen, met up with a group of researchers from Princeton, and just started hanging around all summer until finally they let him help with their digs. He lost a finger when he was fifteen, and didn't even call his parents. Just quietly left the dig and took himself to the ER."

Leo let out a low whistle. "He told me he lost it chopping carrots at the ranch."

"He was absolutely fucking with you." She grinned. "Anyway, he and Mom met in school in Salt Lake. He was studying history and archaeology, and she was studying marine sciences. Marine sciences!" Lily exhaled a dry laugh. "Then he brought her to the *desert*."

"Yikes."

"Right?" she agreed. "They moved to Hester after they got married and helped my uncle work the ranch in Laramie half the year. What was she supposed to do in either of those places? Duke got to join all sorts of teams going out on expeditions. His life stayed interesting and full; hers just got tiny, and he was gone all the time. Not to mention they were broke." She touched one of the dates—1987—carved there. "Sometimes I can't really blame her for leaving."

Lily's mother: the one subject she'd never really opened up about. He wanted to tread carefully. "I think you can blame her for leaving *you*."

Lily shrugged, dragging her fingers down the wall. "Yeah."

"How old was Duke when he died?"

She thought for a beat. "Well, it was seven years ago, so . . . fifty-three."

"So young."

She looked at these carvings for a few seconds longer. "Yeah. Hard living."

"Do you have any contact with your mom?"

Lily shook her head. "She visited a few times. But she never asked me to come with her. I think she just needed to start over."

This last sentence felt like an old, dusty echo, and ignited a spark of anger in Leo's chest. "That was my dad's line, too," he told her. "It's bullshit. Once you have a kid, you don't get a do-over."

"Honestly," she admitted, "I was closest to my uncle Dan. He loved horses the way I do. I lived for summers at the ranch with him. It was hardest when he died, but by then I was seventeen, and I could see the future where the ranch was mine and I could do what I wanted for the rest of my life."

They fell quiet, staring at the carvings in the wood, until a tiny hitch in her breath made him look more closely, leaning forward to be able to catch a view of her face. Quickly, she wiped a tear away.

"Hey, hey," Leo said, trying to turn her to him. "Talk to me."

Her face was red and angry, and she stepped into his arms. "Do we really think Duke found the treasure?" she mumbled into his chest. "What kind of a monster does that? Do you know how that money could have changed our lives? To think that he managed to find it and turn it into some kind of game? It makes me feel crazy."

He tightened his arms around her. "I know."

"I'm serious." She looked up into his face. "We're doing this, we're moving forward and chasing this thing, but in here"—she tapped her temple—"I'm constantly flip-flopping between 'This is exactly something my dad would have done' and 'There is no way he found the money and hid it again; not even Duke was that big an asshole.'"

Lily shook her head. "I thought all of his trips and treasure hunts and stupid riddles were a waste of time, and I resented him for it. But look at me now: I'm in a cabin at the bottom of a canyon, looking for his clues on a tree stump. How fucked up is that?"

"Lil," Leo said quietly, "it's okay to want this, and go after this, and still be mad, too." Reaching up, he cupped her jaw. "You don't have to pick one or the other."

"Am I crazy?" she asked.

"If you are, then I am, too."

She nodded, and her eyes dropped to his mouth, expression softening. Abruptly, she tore her gaze away, looking past him and toward the tent-covered window. "I wonder if we should keep going."

Leo touched her jaw, turning her face back. "I seem to remember someone saying the rain could be dangerous."

It seemed like she unconsciously pressed closer to him even as she said, "But Nic and the boys are expecting to meet us tomorrow."

"Nicole will check the weather," Leo told her, heating under her wavering resolve. "She'll yell about it but know we were delayed by the storm."

He bent to kiss her just as she stretched on her toes, meeting his mouth with soft, eager lips. The rain outside felt like it was sitting on this little section of canyon, stuck between peaks, and they both knew further exploration was futile until it let up.

Or maybe they were both happy to have an excuse.

"I guess you're right," she said between kisses. "And look how dark those clouds are."

He hummed against her.

"Sun will set soon . . ." she said.

It wouldn't, but he wasn't about to correct her.

So Leo nodded, sucking on her bottom lip, her jaw, running his hands up underneath her shirt to cup her breasts. "Might as well find another way to kill the time."

He hurriedly spread out the sleeping bag, and Lily stepped back, undressing while he watched. It was only late afternoon, but the canyon walls cast the inside of the cabin into shadow. Lily stared at his face and he followed the path of her hands as she dragged every piece of her clothing off with deliberate slowness. He could barely suck in a full breath, watching her.

The sight of her teasing him this way meant his undressing was far less seductive—a shirt discarded as quickly as possible so he didn't lose sight of her fingers flirting with the strap of her simple cotton bra; jeans kicked off in an effort to not trip when she hooked her thumb into the waistband of her underwear and slid them down her legs.

He hadn't seen her naked in so long, and for a while, looking and touching and tasting was all he could do. But when he drew his tongue over her and her back arched from the sleeping bag and her hands dug into his hair, Leo felt like he was waking up, as if the intervening ten years had been a nightmare, as if he'd just closed his eyes at the ranch and a lifetime of anguish passed behind his lids, and then he opened them again and found Lily exactly the same: skin flushed, soft thighs open, heels digging into the bed, wanting him.

Inside their tiny cabin, he loved her with his mouth and his fingers until she cried out, pulling him up and over her. He'd forgotten the width of her smile and the mischief in her hazel eyes, the way her kiss could turn from sated and soft into searching and *biting*, the way she rolled over onto him, pinning his hands over his head, scraping her way down his body to taste and lick, to make him crazy.

His hands dug into her soft tangle of hair, touching and tugging and begging with his fingertips, and she scaled back up his body again, rolling him over her. Wrapping her arms and legs around him in a wild coil of clasping limbs and arching hips, asking him with words and gestures to touch her and tell her what he felt.

She asked him if he wanted to—of course he wanted to—and they dug around, finding the condoms in the bag.

"There's a joke here about a dead man's condoms," Leo told her, pulling out the box Terry had packed.

Lily pressed two fingers to his lips. "Let's make it later."

He couldn't believe that his hands were shaking as he tore open the packet and rolled on the condom, but they were. Sex was sex, but love was a different language, and Leo hadn't spoken it in ten years. He felt rusty. Whispering as he focused on the task at hand, he said, "I do want to point out that they're ribbed for her pleasure."

"Literally no woman cares about this."

"Well, don't tell Terry. It was the one thoughtful thing he ever tried to do."

"Leo, I swear to God."

He sat back on his heels looking at her, running his hands up her shins and over her knees.

"I want you on me," she said, so simple. Leo threaded his fingers with hers and lifted them over her head. She slid her legs around his thighs, pulling him close, and then, with a mind-bendingly perfect shift forward, he was there.

I want you on me, she'd said, like he could ever forget what worked so well for her. All he wanted to do was watch her come undone from above. He wondered if, looking down, the stars ever felt like falling, lovesick, onto the planets. The instinct was in him when he was over her, moving, unable to believe that she was real and her quiet sounds were real and the way she looked up at him was real. *Just fall. It's okay.* She had to see this truth tattooed in his eyes and scrawled across every feature: that he had always loved her, was loving her still. Leo would love Lily Wilder forever.

He'd realized—after he'd left her, after he'd managed to pick his head up and return to class and go through the motions of finishing his education—that when he learned a new action, his brain would use spatial cues: turn left here, take these stairs, touch this, go deeper. And then a different part of the brain would take over; the movements wouldn't be guided by the environment anymore but by the innate sense of space, of where to turn because it *felt* correct; left versus right was habit, directions were instinct, and muscles reacted.

I guess we never forget those, Leo thought, watching her neck flush and lips part. He slowed, pulling her leg higher, tilting. Her eyes were greedy, tracking over his face, his shoulders, between them, back to his mouth. He could notice all this because making love to Lily was hardwired.

Her neck arched, nails dug in. Leo recognized that tightness in her expression, the hope that the moment was imminent and fear that it wasn't. He reached down, remembering, stroking her with the pad of his thumb, and witnessed the clearing of tension when pleasure hit her like a flood. The telling sound tore from her, thankful and overcome and amazed; her body beneath him was a fevered riot of shaking, clutching relief. It could have ended there, he truly meant it, with her collapsing limp and sated, but it didn't. She wouldn't. Lily wanted what he'd just had—the same view, but from beneath: planets staring up at the stars.

What a relief to find she was hardwired just the same, there was no left or right for her, either, just hips and rhythm and the unreal heat of her hands. Just heat and the delirious wet of her kiss until Leo was grasping at the sleeping bag under her head, clawing the ground, pushing them with desperation across the makeshift bed until they were a wrestling madness. Strong legs squeezed and she was over him, pinning him, finishing him, staring down with victory at the mess she'd made of him.

Chapter Twenty-Four

AS THEIR BREATHING calmed and their bodies cooled, they talked about everything. About Archie's Bar and the handful of people in her life who mattered a little, and about Nicole, who mattered the most; about the little restaurant near Leo's apartment where he and Cora would have okonomiyaki on Thursday nights because it tasted just like their mom's. He talked about how much he loved his sister and how disorienting it was to be facing a future where she didn't have to come first in his every waking thought.

He talked about how Cora was silly in a way he never had been, how no one made him laugh as easily or as hard, how she was wonderful with friends but terrible with money, which was entirely his fault. He described her: long black hair, a dancer's posture, a long neck, and a surprisingly loud laugh. They talked so much that by the time they'd finally drifted to sleep Lily felt like she knew Cora, could hear her bursting giggles, could imagine Leo watching her with adoration. Lily could imagine this little sister she would take on a ride into the sagebrush-covered hills of Wyoming; she wanted to make the city girl fall in love with nature.

In reality, Lily and Cora would probably have nothing in common except for Leo, and yet somehow, she imagined that would be enough.

Consciousness came thickly, dim light hovering outside the cabin. Staring at his sleepy face, part of her knew she should be more careful. Lily's first instinct was always to draw away and leap to the worst-case scenario, which, being honest, was usually her life. But she was tired. Couldn't she have this? Even if only for a few more days?

Rolling over in Leo's arms, Lily kissed the center of his chest, his cheeks, his lips. He startled a little, his smile taking shape against hers.

His eyes drew open. "Hi."

"Good morning."

He kissed her again, before glancing at his watch.

"Let me guess," she said, and then tilted her face up, pretending to smell the air. "It's seven."

He laughed. "Six forty-three. Not bad."

Leo's hands slid down her ribs and along her waist, coming to a gentle rest on her hips. He hummed in appreciation, kissing his way to her neck, pausing to gently nibble on the skin there. Her mind became fuzzy along the edges as she imagined how easy it would be to spend the rest of the day like this.

Unfortunately, her bladder had other ideas, and nothing on the trail was ever as simple as running down the hall to the bathroom. Lily groaned, letting her head fall to his chest.

"Later," he said, palm flat and warm on her breastbone.

She felt Leo's eyes follow as she dragged herself from the warmth of the sleeping bag and out to where her clothes were scattered across the buckled wood floor. She heard shuffling and looked to see him propped on his elbow, watching her without an ounce of shame.

"You going to treasure hunt like that?" She stepped into her underwear, slipped the straps of her bra over her shoulders, no longer self-conscious.

"Maybe." He lifted his chin, motioning for her to continue.

She pulled her jeans up over her hips and his hand slipped so casually below the fabric of the sleeping bag that she wondered if he even realized he was doing it. She wanted to catalog the way he looked at her, the heat of his gaze, the way she felt almost drunk with the weight of his attention.

And as much as she'd like for it to continue, she reminded him why they were there: "That stump isn't going to find itself."

With a groan, he climbed from the sleeping bag. They split up and hurried through their morning routines. Thankfully Lily had perfected the art of peeing outside and washing with nothing more than a little biodegradable soap and water.

Clean and packed again, they met out front, where disappointment immediately descended. Grass and weeds and clumps of sagebrush crowded the small building, but it was clear there weren't any stumps.

"This can't be right." Lily pushed aside the limbs of a leggy creosote bush to get at the ground below. Straightening, she turned in a circle, tapping a finger against her thigh.

"We know it's the right place," he said. "Your dad's

initials are in there. This cabin is right at a bend in the river, too. Isn't that what you said he means by 'the belly of the three'?"

"We could be at the wrong belly, but why would 'Duke's tree' be somewhere else?" she asked herself. "He was here all the time, and it's not like there are a bunch of cabins everywhere. What am I missing?"

She walked farther into the clearing, her footsteps startling a canyon wren picking through the brush. She reached for her backpack. "Come on."

Leo didn't hesitate before swinging his own pack on and falling into step beside her. "Where are we going?"

She pointed to the canyons ahead. "Up."

He followed her gaze. "Oh."

"Just so you know," she said, visually scanning the landscape for the easiest path forward, "I'd never let a group of tourists do any of this, but I need a better vantage point."

"I'll be sure not to mention it in my Yelp review."

Fortunately, the washout curved upward with plenty of hand- and footholds, and enough ledges that they managed to get to the top without too much trouble. They were only about fifty feet in the air, but they could make out some of the river and the snakelike canyons that surrounded it.

"Would you get service up here?" Leo asked.

"Sometimes," she hedged.

"I'm wondering if we can get a satellite map to load."

She pulled the Ziploc bag free, tucking the gun into her waistband for the moment, and dug her own satellite phone out. After a few attempts to power it up, she realized the battery was dead. She must have forgotten to turn it off in her haste to move everything over to a new bag. "*Shit.*"

His brows came together in a frown and then, "Would Terry's still have power?"

"Oh my God." Lily found it and pressed the power button. Neither of them breathed until the tiny satellite image loaded on the screen. They both whispered celebratory curses, and quickly high-fived.

"I think I understand Bradley's love for gambling now," he said, laughing. "Every tiny bit of encouraging news is like a shot of dopamine straight to my brain."

"There's not much battery left," she told him, cupping a hand over the screen to block the sun. "The maps'll take a second to load." She pointed out toward the river. "Do you see those two really sharp switchbacks? At the confluence and then there, just above it?"

He followed her attention and nodded immediately. "They really do look like threes. But which bend is the 'belly'?"

"We're at the outside of the bottom of the three. I'm wondering if we need to be up there, at that sharp bend."

He laughed. "You're telling me we have to cross back over?"

Lily groaned. "I know. But it doesn't look too bad." She chewed her lip, thinking. "I don't remember ever seeing anything there, but what else can we do?"

"We check it out," he said. "Should we call Nicole and have her get on Google Earth? I know we don't have much power left, but—"

Terry's sat phone came to life in her hand, vibrating as a blur of notifications loaded, all for texts in a group thread called the Lost Boys.

They stared down at the screen. "Who are the Lost Boys?" Lily asked.

Leo shook his head. "No idea."

"Some of these delivered *today*," she said, uneasy.

Who was frantically trying to contact Terry in the middle of his supposed vacation?

She clicked to open the thread. There were four people in the group: Terry, who it became clear was using the handle *Rufio*, along with a *Pockets*, *No Nap*, and *Latchboy*.

"Peter Pan," she said. But the conversation that loaded wasn't messages full of concern. There were *Game of Thrones* gifs and dirty jokes, a few texts where Terry talked about the trail, and then some back-and-forth about Nicole and Lily . . .

"Oh," she mumbled, grossed out, and scrolled past those quickly before Leo could see them.

Too late.

Leo jerked the phone from her hand. "What the—"

"It's fine. He was a pig. This isn't a revelation."

She leaned her chin on Leo's shoulder, reading.

"They're talking about the trip," he said, scrolling. "He was keeping someone up to date on where we were. Man, this is so weird." He shook his head.

Three days ago—when the group's plan changed—the texts turned more frantic.

No Nap: Rufio.

Pockets: Rufio, dude.

Latchboy: Terry where r u

No Nap: We lost your trail man, check in.

"Lost his trail?" Leo said. "What the fuck does that mean?"

She pointed to the date. "It's from the day after he fell. His friends obviously don't know he's dead."

Leo continued scrolling.

Pockets: Dude I thought we were busted that night at the roost. Where'd you go?
No Nap: TERRY, dude answer your phone.
Latchboy: He's just gone, wtf
Pockets: Did you get the book?

Leo lingered on that text, his thumb hovering. "Are they talking about Duke's journal?"

Anxiety climbed Lily's spine and she reached around him, pushing the thread up, scrolling to read through the rest to see where it ended.

No Nap: Terry, let us know what we need to do
Latchboy: He's not answering. Go with Plan B.
No Nap: Let's meet where we planned. Roger on Plan B.
Pockets: Terry, I swear you'd better not be double-crossing us or you're as dead as they are.
No Nap: Let's move to a different thread. Fuck this dude.

Awareness landed like an explosion. They looked at each other, realizing they'd been taking their time the last two days, completely unaware that someone had been working with Terry, and been following them.

"I don't understand." But Lily was worried that she did, in fact, understand. They'd already known that Terry came to get Duke's journal. But to think Terry had accomplices? That their group was being followed? A shiver ran through her when she remembered the cigarette butt, the rustling at night. She'd been so distracted by Leo and the possibility of what Duke had done that she'd let down her guard. "Son of a bitch."

Leo shook his head, stunned as he read through the texts again. "They think Terry has double-crossed them," he said. He looked up, and then scanned the vast canyon below. "Whatever plan B is, they could be anywhere."

"If they were following us . . ." she said. "If there's any way they know where we were headed . . ."

"Then they might have beaten us there," he finished, turning to face her.

His eyes pulled to hers. The race was on.

Chapter Twenty-Five

IF THEY HAD been in a hurry before, it was nothing like this. The competitive fever that blew through them was palpable, turned Leo's vision wavy as they scrabbled down the cliff. Ankles, knees, and elbows collided with rock and thorny brush—skin and joints be damned. They'd been through too much to lose, and knowing someone was on their tail—knowing someone else believed just as fervently that there was treasure to be found—lit a white-hot fire under their asses.

They didn't talk much. Leo worked on committing the photo to memory and Lily looked around and behind them a lot. She seemed to have a solid map of the river in mind now that she'd seen it from above. They tried to stay on as much of the flat rock terrain as they could, but eventually had to go farther down, into the more varied and green landscape near the water. They got to the river's edge and hiked over small boulders, through marshy patches—leaving as few tracks as possible—and once Lily started searching for a good place to cross, he knew they must be close. Ahead of them was a wide bend, curving sharply enough to the left that it hid the river upstream from view.

Lily stopped just before it, at a section with fast-moving—but relatively shallow—water.

"This is probably our best bet," she said. "Belly of the three." She squinted out at the water. "I can't believe I didn't think of this sooner. I've been down here a hundred times and don't remember seeing a cabin. But there must be one at that bend."

He remembered the section she meant, remembered looking at it on a map and wondering how some of the land in between hadn't been completely washed out in high-water years. The turns of the river at that point were a white-water rafter's dream, and the slot canyons hugging the river there had been carved and recarved over centuries into intricate, lacelike mazes. It was the perfect place to hide something: without detailed, specific directions, it would be next to impossible to find their way in, and even harder in the near darkness to find their way back out again. Urgency and excitement were twin mallets: *Go. Faster. Go faster.*

Lily gazed down at the water with a wariness Leo could see her trying to fight.

"Take your time," he reminded her.

"We don't have time."

"We absolutely have time to cross carefully."

With their first step, ice-cold water rushed over their ankles, submerging their boots.

"I guess dry feet are out," Leo said.

At its highest point, the water reached his knees, but even so the current was fast and strong. He held on to Lily's hand

and, with their eyes on the opposite riverbank, they made it across without incident.

She didn't bother to consult a map again, just charged up-river, ducking into a tangle of cottonwoods, hugging the line of the red rock to her right. After another half a mile or so, worry grew in Leo's chest. Without the distraction of conversation or kissing, the reality of what they were doing seemed to press down on his brain, pins into a pincushion. Really, what were the odds anything remained out there? Who was Terry working with, and how many of them were there? Why had Terry brought Bradley, Leo, and Walter along when he could have set up a trip with Wilder Adventures on his own? Even if Leo and Lily were a half day ahead, how long would it take them to crack the code? How long until they could—

"You're too quiet," Lily said, holding a cluster of thorny branches back so they didn't whip into his leg when she passed through. "Are you freaking out?"

"Yes."

She laughed, peeking at him over her shoulder. "Me too. But we're in too deep."

"Way too deep," he agreed.

Still . . . he couldn't imagine where a structure would even be. Where the landscape was open, it was wide open: rocks, low sagebrush. And where it was narrow, it was tight: high-walled canyons and claustrophobic shadows. So he nearly ran into her back when Lily stopped abruptly.

"There."

He caught his balance by holding on to her shoulders and trying to see what had pulled her up short. He saw the same thing he'd been seeing: the river, cottonwoods, dirt, rocks, rocks, and more rocks. But then the shapes came into focus.

He wasn't staring at a disorganized tumble of broken boulders. He was looking at a collapsed stone chimney covered in layer upon layer of red rock dust. He was looking at crumbled and rotting planks of wood buried beneath wild sagebrush tangles and thorny bushes. He was looking, very clearly, at a dust-covered and brush-obscured tree stump.

"Holy crap," he said. "Duke's tree."

In hyperaware unison, they whipped their attention behind them and all around: no one. He listened for the sounds of people: nothing. Only the river roared nearby, cascading over a small pointy cluster of rocks and crashing onto a shallow stretch of pebbled riverbed.

Lily ran to the stump, falling to her knees and dusting it off. "Hurry, Leo."

He joined her, setting his pack on the ground and helping her wipe the bumpy surface clean. The dirt had been there too long undisturbed, ground into the rings and crevices. Cursing, he scratched at it with a blunt fingernail.

Clearly the thinker of the two, Lily poured water over the top, washing away the last few layers of dirt. At first, the pattern looked like nothing more than holes burned into the wood, but something tripped in his brain.

He bent at the waist, examining it closely. There was a series of perfectly round charred marks, each only a bit smaller than the diameter of a pencil eraser.

"Is it one you recognize?" he asked.

She shook her head. "Not really. He used mostly letter codes with me. Caesar. ROT cipher. Atbash."

He turned his attention to the task at hand. There were seven distinct groupings, spaced a couple of inches apart. The first was a series of three dots, stacked vertically, with a single dot to the left at the bottom—like a backward L. Beside that were two dots, side by side, horizontal. Next, there was a single dot, low on the line of the pattern. The next was two dots stacked on top of each other vertically again. The fifth were two again but positioned diagonally. The sixth were two dots stacked vertically, and then a third positioned diagonal from the top left dot. The seventh cluster was the same as the fifth.

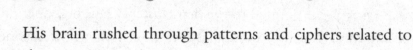

His brain rushed through patterns and ciphers related to numbers, positions, shapes.

Four, two, one, two, two, three, two.

Is it a dice cipher? Rosicrucian?

No. Position is clearly important.

The longer he stared, the more his ability to think was thwarted by the heavy, thrumming sense of a ticking clock. He felt understanding just out of grasp; maddening. They might have only a matter of minutes to figure it out, cover the stump, and head out in search of whatever was encoded there.

Leo rubbed his eyes. "*Fuck.*"

Beside him, Lily let out a little growl. "What if there's more to it?" she asked. "Are we missing something, or is this it?"

"Burning it in was smart." Reaching forward, he traced the seven distinct groups with a fingertip. "I think it's spelling something. We just have to figure out if it's a numeric code or something else."

She shuffled to the other side of the stump to see it from a different angle. "Maybe we're looking at it wrong."

"The more I stare," he told her, "the more I feel like I can't see anything."

Her breath escaped in an audible gust. "Oh my God. Leo. You're a genius."

"What'd I say?"

"You said you can't see it." She grinned. "It's flat, but it's written as *braille*. Duke didn't use it often, but he knew it. He taught me forever ago."

She let out a little squeal and he peered down, realizing she was right. He scraped through his brain, trying to remember the braille he'd learned for an Eagle Scout badge.

"Okay." She pointed to the first cluster. "This first one, the backward L? Means a number is next. So, I think the second pattern is a three."

He stared at the others. "Right, and doesn't this dot mean a capital letter?"

"Yeah," Lily said, nodding excitedly.

"I'm almost positive this is *B*," he told her. "This one is *e*. And I'm pretty sure this one is *s*."

"I think you're right, but . . ." She pointed to the last one. "That means this is *e* again."

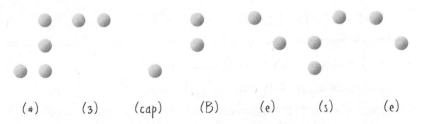

(#)   (3)   (cap)   (B)   (e)   (s)   (e)

Frowning, Lily sounded it out. "Three-*Bese*? 'Bese' is not a place. It's not even a word." She looked up at him dubiously.

He scrubbed a hand over his face. "I know."

"*Wait.*" Lily's voice was so loud and forceful that he startled. She dug for the notebook in her bag and pulled it out, extracting the other loose page that Terry had torn free—the intricately drawn and labeled map of a section of the slot canyons. It looked like a dense network of capillaries. "There." She set it down on the stump, smacking it with a hand. "Look."

They leaned in and studied it carefully. The start of the map was a single entry point—a wide-open crack in a boulder. From this first opening sprouted about ten smaller arteries, and each of those secondary branches had numerous tertiary and quaternary paths that got smaller and smaller as they branched away. The first series of branches were labeled with numbers, and the paths that broke off from branch one were labeled *A*, *B*, and *C*. The second had six narrow branches labeled *A* to *F*. And the third, labeled with Duke's careful *3*, was deeper and had branches labeled up to *J*.

"Three *B*," he said. "Right here."

"What's *e*, *s*, *e*, then?" Almost as soon as the words were out, she slapped a hand down on the stump again. "East, south, east! Leo, these are the turns inside the Three-B slot canyon." She reached out, gripped his arm. "These are the actual directions."

He leaned across the stump, fitting his lips to hers, feeling her smile curve against his. Adrenaline dumped into his veins. They were really going to find it.

"Are you ready?" he whispered, leaning his forehead into hers.

She nodded, kissing him again, teasing. His blood became helium, stars popping behind his closed lids. The words *I love you* hovered on the tip of his tongue.

But some sounds were so distinct Leo would know them

anywhere. The sound of his mother's voice, for example. A police siren. An egg cracking. Before his brain cataloged the sound, his body tensed.

Feet crunching through dry branches.

A gun cocking.

Chapter Twenty-Six

"HELLO, LOVEBIRDS," A voice drawled from behind Leo. "Hands where I can see them."

Lily peered around him, eyes wide, to find two men standing in the shadows.

The one holding the gun was taller, big, and filthy, with a blood-soaked rip in his pants and cuts and scrapes down each of his meaty biceps. The other one wasn't faring much better. He was wiry and short, his blond hair matted with dried blood near his temple. A dirty bandage clung to the back of his hand. Both were wearing the same camo-chic style Terry favored.

The Lost Boys, she assumed.

Blinking across the stump at Leo, she took in his blank shock. Still facing her, he slowly raised his hands, mirroring her own movements. It was crazy, but her first thought was to wonder whether, before this trip, he'd ever had a gun pointed at him. Leo's life was normal. He worked in a cubicle and went on wine-tasting tours. He made cheese in France, for crying out loud.

A week with her, and he had a dead friend, another with a broken foot. He had a deep gash on his cheek, and a pistol aimed at his skull.

Biceps used his gun to gesture to his friend. "Jay," he said. "Get their bags."

"Looks like you're bleeding, Jay," she said, taking no small amount of pride that at least she and Leo hadn't made it easy for them to follow. "Take a little spill?"

He glared and yanked her pack off her back so hard she stumbled forward, catching herself right before she hit the ground. Leo angrily charged, shoving Jay back, and in the commotion, she reached around for—

Cool metal pressed to her forehead.

"I wouldn't do that," Biceps said.

Jay jerked her back to her feet while Biceps pulled Terry's gun from her waistband. Fuck.

Leo's eyes went wide. "You had that in your pants this whole time?"

"Not the *whole time*," she said.

Jay made quick work of searching her pockets while Biceps went through their bags, carelessly tossing whatever didn't interest him to the ground.

"Let me guess," Lily said through gritted teeth as Jay took a liberal handful of her ass while digging into her back pockets. "Friends of Terry's? He left us days ago, you know."

"Yeah." Jay moved on to Leo, patting him down.

"Do you know where he went?" she asked, playing dumb. "We woke up, and he was gone."

Ignoring this, Jay lifted his chin to his friend. "Kevin. Find it yet?"

Biceps—Kevin—pulled Duke's journal from her bag and held it up victoriously. "Yup." He flipped through the pages before tucking it into his back pocket and nodding to the stump. "Three B-e-s-e, so helpful. Thank you."

"You're welcome." Leo cleared his throat. "But I hate to break it to you: the code is a red herring."

Lily tried to keep her expression neutral.

Jay frowned, stepping closer. "Excuse me?"

"The code on this stump," Leo said. "You think it corresponds to a map in there, revealing the treasure's location, but I'm betting it won't. Terry—" He cut off abruptly, wincing a little. "Terry is really smart, and he had plenty of chances to take the journal. He probably studied the whole thing and realized Duke didn't really leave anything important."

"Didn't leave anything important?" Jay repeated, swiping at a trail of bloodstained sweat that ran from his temple down into his eye. "How do you figure?"

"Why else would Terry leave it with us?" Leo asked, and Lily finally caught on. If these assholes took the journal, she and Leo would be completely screwed. "Seeing as you guys are here without him . . . he must know something we don't."

"Like what?" Kevin asked, frowning. "What would Terry know?"

Lily shrugged, joining in. "If I knew that, I wouldn't be standing here."

Kevin blinked for several silent seconds. "Huh." And then his expression cleared. "Why *are* you here, then? If you're so sure it's useless?"

"Why . . . are we here?" She floundered. "Well. We're—we're here—"

"We're working our way through Duke's clues for closure," Leo cut in. "This is Lily Wilder, you know. *The* Lily Wilder? We're finding a way for her to finally be able to say goodbye to her beloved father."

"That's right. Closure. It's hard for me to talk about."

Jay's eyes narrowed as he studied her. "Closure. I'm not buying it." He sucked his teeth and shook his head. "You're just trying to get us to leave the book. Fuck you."

Inwardly, she growled in frustration.

The two men leaned their heads together, discussing, but the attempt at secrecy was completely undone when Jay quietly said, "Either Terry's in there already, or we beat him here," and tilted his chin toward the slots, as in, *Let's go.*

Kevin looked over his shoulder and nodded at Leo and Lily. "What about them?"

"You could take us with you," Leo offered quickly. "Lily is better at cracking Duke's codes than anyone."

"Like you wouldn't try to knock us on our asses the first chance you get."

Leo gave a tilt of his head that said, *That's fair.*

"Besides," Kevin said, waving the journal, "we already have the directions. We don't need you anymore. So I guess this is where we say goodbye." He reached into his pack and pulled out a set of zip cuffs exactly like the ones Terry had.

With Jay pointing the gun at Lily, Kevin crossed to Leo, pulling his hands behind his back and securing them together with an unnerving series of clicks. Next, he instructed him to sit, and bound Leo's feet at the ankles. When it was Lily's turn, he did the same and put them back-to-back in the grassy clearing.

For a brief moment, Lily wondered if the two men planned to shoot them anyway, but Jay reached into her bag, took a protein bar, and tossed their packs out of reach. Biting into the bar, he threw the wrapper on the ground at her feet. "Hope you don't get hungry."

Kevin snorted. "You're a dick, you know that?"

"But I'm not a killer." Jay shrugged. "Whatever happens now is between them and nature."

Kevin pulled Duke's journal from his pocket and waved it at her. "Thanks again. If you see Terry, tell him to choke on it." Sparing a last glance at their belongings strewn over the ground, he gave the packs another kick. With a little smirk, Kevin added, "Good luck, *Lily Wilder*."

The sun was high overhead. They hadn't even attempted to figure out their bullshit situation yet, and Lily was already sweating.

"I can't believe that just happened," Leo said. "I think we just got robbed and zip-tied by the two dumbest humans alive."

"Can you still see them?" He faced the direction those two idiots had taken off in.

"Yeah." Leo leaned to the side. "But just barely. They're still walking along the rock wall."

"Tell me when you can't see them anymore." Her mind raced, sorting through every possible escape route. She hated Terry for bringing those guys along with him. If he hadn't already been dead, she'd have pushed him off that cliff herself.

"Okay." Leo was quiet for a moment before he spoke again. "Lily?"

"Yeah?"

"I want you to know that last night was the best night of my life."

She paused, frowning. "You know we're not going to die out here, Lovesick City Boy."

A laugh. "I know. But I could hear you doing that heavy rage-breathing thing and I wanted to distract you."

"I'm seeing red," she admitted, her heartbeat so strong it seemed to quake her skeleton. "I can't believe they got the journal. I can't believe we're tied up here while they—"

"Lily."

"—waltz in there and use everything my dad dedicated his life to—"

"The first time I had sex with someone after you," he said breezily, interrupting her, "I asked her to call me 'cowboy.'"

In spite of the situation, she burst out laughing. "I'm sorry, what?"

Behind her, he nodded. "We were . . . you know, and it wasn't working for me for obvious reasons."

"Which were?" A cord of jealousy threaded through her rib cage.

"She wasn't you?" he said, a grin in his voice. "I felt guilty and awful and sad, and I just blurted it out. 'Call me cowboy!'"

Lily bent forward, cackling, surprising herself. "I never even called you cowboy."

"I know!" He leaned back against her. "It had been so long since I left, and I was desperate to prove to myself that I

could still—but God—I mean—that poor woman. She probably told that story to her friends hundreds of times."

"If it makes you feel any better," she said, "I barfed on the
first guy I was with after you."

"You were so sad you actually *vomited*?"

"I was so sad I got hammered, and *then* vomited." She
paused, realizing what he'd just done. "You distracted me.
Cowboy."

"Gave you a second to calm down." She felt him lean to
the side again. "The meatheads are gone. And we have to figure a way out of these before they come back." He tugged on
his restraints.

It was her turn at serious. "No one knows me the way
you do."

He grew quiet, the air warm and heavy all around them.
"Remember that later when you're trying to tell me why we
won't work out. But first . . ."

A swarm of anxieties flapped wildly in her chest. She
tamped them down to focus. "Right. I have a couple ideas."

"Such as?"

"If we can push on each other to stand, you can try to
break them."

"Break them? With the strength of my love for freedom?"

She laughed. "Have you never been arrested before?"

"Is that a serious question? I create investment algorithms.
I'm usually in bed by nine. In what situation would I have
been arrested and restrained with *zip ties*?"

"Okay, so that's a no I'm hearing."

"Have *you*?" he asked incredulously.

Lily ignored that can of worms and returned to the problem at hand. "It's easier with your hands in front but still pos-

sible from the back. I'm not sure I'm strong enough to break this kind, but you probably are. You bring your arms down with enough force that you snap the restraint near the weakest point."

There was a long pause with no response. "And the next option?"

"Those two numbnuts didn't check for the knife in my boot."

"You have a knife?"

"I forgot about it when I was pissed off and plotting Terry's redeath," she told him. "See? It's good you calmed me down."

It took more than a few minutes of work, but eventually Leo managed to get on his side facing the right direction and maneuvered his way down so that his hands were near her boots.

"Can you unlace them?" she asked.

"I think so? It feels like I have ten thumbs." With his hands trapped behind him, he fumbled a lot before he managed to get one boot untied and loosened.

"Okay, I'm going to try and push it off," she said. "But if you can help?"

"Yeah . . . okay . . ."

"But push on that—"

"Can you squish your foot in a little?"

"How the hell do I *squish my foot*?"

"I don't know, just—like, try to *feel* small in your boot."

"What the fuck does that mean?"

With the sun passing its highest point in the sky, they were a sweaty mess by the time they managed to extract her foot enough that the knife fell to the ground. Leo worked to pick it up with his mouth and then grasp it with his hands, and maneuvered his way back up against her.

"Okay," Lily said, blowing the hair from her damp forehead. She'd barely moved from her spot, but she was exhausted. "Take it out of the sheath, and carefully try to cut my tie."

Shaking his head, he passed the knife to her. "You do it. Something tells me you're way more proficient with a knife than I am."

She took a deep breath before gingerly feeling along the restraints, deciding where to cut, and carefully working her fingers down to the spine of the blade.

"Hold still," she told him.

He laughed nervously. "Trust me, I'm not going anywhere."

A few minutes passed of her sawing lightly, checking the progress, trying not to cut him too badly while also trying to keep her fingers from going numb and dropping the knife.

"Lily, in case we don't actually get out of here—"

"We will."

"In case we *don't*," he repeated, "I really do love you."

She bit back a smile but stayed focused. "You're pretty great yourself."

"Wow. Be still my heart."

"Just be still." He hissed in pain, and she froze. "Shit, sorry."

"Keep going. It's only a flesh wound."

She drew in a breath and continued. "I think I'm . . . almost . . . there . . ." And with a small snap, the tension in Leo's shoulders disappeared, his arms going limp.

"Oh my God!" He scooted himself around, shaking his

hands out before grabbing her face, pulling her in for a kiss. "You did it!"

Adrenaline and elation flooded her bloodstream. "Quick, quick."

With shaking hands, Leo cut the ties on his ankles and then hers. Blood rushed to her fingers like pins and needles. Her muscles ached as she pushed herself to stand, legs tingling, feet almost numb. Both of their hands were streaked with blood, but nothing looked serious. With a final burst of energy, they limped to where their bags lay, shoved everything inside, and jogged as fast as they could back the way they'd come, escaping into the shadow of the canyon.

Chapter Twenty-Seven

THEY SCRAMBLED THROUGH dry brush and jagged boulders, jogged along the riverbank, and—checking frequently over their shoulders—ducked into the cooler shadows, where Leo hoped they would be hidden away, out of danger, while they figured out what the hell to do next.

After several beats where they stood, bent at the waist and catching their breath, Lily straightened and collapsed back against a rock wall. Elation had clearly worn off, and what remained in her posture was only the heavy weight of defeat. "This sucks."

If there ever was treasure, someone else had just taken all of Duke's clues and their hard work and snatched it from right under their noses. For as much as his brain took the testosterone-fueled story line and ran with it—*go after them, take back what's rightfully ours!*—Leo knew that was unrealistic. For one, there were two men back there, armed and clearly emanating that unhinged Terry vibe. But more important, Lily was on the verge of completely losing her shit, too, and at least one of them had to keep their head on straight.

Frankly, he only sort of cared about the money. Well, obviously he did—he wasn't an idiot—but mostly he was fighting for *them* right when Lily looked like she had no fight left in her. Would a windfall of cash make everything easier? God, yes. But more than anything he was desperate to help Lily have a life that brought her actual joy. Few feelings were worse than hopelessness. He would know.

There was a wilting lean to Lily's posture as she sat on the ground, half-heartedly eating a protein bar and staring blankly at the rock ahead of her. Leo didn't need to be a mind reader to see that she was in the midst of a doom spiral. Not ten days ago, he'd been sitting at Cora's graduation dinner, having his own spiraling realization that she didn't need him anymore and he had absolutely no idea what it would even look like to live his life for *himself*.

"If twenty years pass before I see another protein bar," Lily said, chewing and swallowing with effort, "it will be too soon."

"Fair."

Seemingly unconcerned with the dirty earth beneath her, Lily lay back and stared up at the crystalline sky, caged in by looming rocks overhead. "So, to recap, not only do I *not* have any money, not only did we just get robbed at gunpoint, but tomorrow I'll have to call the police and deal with a dead body and I don't even know where to start."

"I really think it'll be okay," he said. "And at least we can just get it over with and move on with our lives."

She closed her eyes, exhaling slowly.

"Is now a good time to remind you that I know you better than anyone?"

"Leo, I don't—"

"Just hear me out," he said. "I have a small but nice apartment in New York. I know it isn't ideal, but this time, you could come back with me. Just for a little bit, until we can figure out what's next for us. I've been good about saving money. It's not enough to buy your land back, but I'm likely to get that promotion, and maybe if I work for another year and we save every penny, we can move upstate where we can get horses."

"What would I even do in New York until we can move?"

"You'd pretend you're on vacation."

"What about Bonnie?"

"Nicole could take care of her and the others until we're able to bring them out to wherever we end up. I'd take care of you."

Lily's face said: *What about me makes you think that I want to be taken care of?*

"I'm just trying to find a way we can be together," he said, succumbing to frustration. "If you don't want that, then it's a nonstarter."

"I do." She closed her eyes again, reaching for his hand and setting it over her heart, covering it with her own. "I'm sorry. But you're right. I'm sitting here trying to imagine moving somewhere. I can't. I can't leave Nicole. And Leo, I have *maybe* three hundred dollars to my name. I would be entirely dependent on you and—I can't," she repeated quietly.

"Now that Cora's tuition is paid off, I make enough to support us. I don't care about the money."

"But I do." She rubbed her thumb over the back of his hand. "You'd go from supporting one woman in your life to supporting another. I don't want us to have that kind of relationship."

"I don't see it that way at all."

She barreled on, ignoring this. "I could sell Duke's cabin, but who the hell is buying land in Hester?" She looked at him. "I can only do this by my own bootstraps. You can't fix this for me."

Leaning over her, he tipped her hat back and bent to kiss her, just once. "Okay. I won't push."

"Trust me, I like that you're pushing," she said quietly. "There's just no easy answer."

"We'll figure it out," he told her. "But probably not today. Let's go for a walk."

They stood, sore and bruised and filthy but still there. And, at least for now, still together.

Tomorrow, he thought bleakly, *I might have to say goodbye*.

———

Up on top of a small ledge overhang, they sat with their legs dangling, fingers entwined. It was afternoon—just after three—but it felt like they'd been awake for a year. In front of them, the sky was a flawless jewel. Lily's backpack was open beside her, and even with her clothes inside, it seemed empty without the journal.

She pulled Terry's satellite phone out and turned it on. Leo supposed he should be grateful that Jay and Kevin hadn't taken it during their backpack raid. "I'm gonna let Nic know to pick us up tomorrow."

He nodded, watching her dial the number from memory. Tinnily, the sound of the phone ringing reached him.

"Hello?"

"Hey, it's me." He didn't hear more than the loud, amorphous sound of Nicole's voice. Lily shook her head. "It's a bust." Another pause. "I'll explain it all later, but Terry was working with some guys. They followed us down here and took my gun, tied us up." She paused, and Leo could hear the disembodied sound of Nicole yelling. "Yeah, I'm serious. Nic—Nic—just listen. If you could pick me and Leo up where we went down, we'll try to get there by around two tomorrow afternoon." She paused again and looked over at him, saying, "Nicole says Bradley had to fly home, and Walt is recovering at a hotel in Moab." She turned her attention back to Nicole. "I guess it'll just be you picking us up, then. Prepare for a big night at Archie's before we send Leo back to New York."

Ouch.

Lily said goodbye and pulled the phone away from her ear, hitting End Call before dropping it in her backpack. She stared down for a few seconds and then let out an angry growl.

"I hated that journal," she said, "but it's worse that Terry's asshole friends have it now. It was all I had of Duke's."

He didn't know what to say. Her relationship with the journal was complicated as hell, and Leo couldn't pretend to understand the extent of it. Instead, he squeezed her hand.

She pulled out the photo of Duke leaning against the

tree, releasing Leo's hand to hold the photograph in both of hers. Someday, when the disappointment wasn't so fresh, maybe they'd be able to talk about her dad, and how this trip changed her feelings about their history. But today was not that day.

"I'm so mad," she said quietly. "And I am *desperate* to know whether those assholes found anything."

The words exploded from him. "God, me too. It's killing me."

She laughed. "On the one hand, I think, 'Fuck those guys. I hope there's nothing.' But also: I want to think we were close."

"I agree."

Tapping her fingers on her thigh, Lily leaned closer to the photo, narrowing her eyes. She looked up, frowning, and then stared down, more intense now. "Wait."

There was something in her voice that caught his heart in a hook, sent it casting out into a pool of adrenaline.

"Wait, what?" he asked.

She pointed to it. "Am I seeing what I think I'm seeing?" Lily handed him the photo and squeezed her eyes closed. "Describe this. Tell me everything you see. Every detail."

"Why?"

She shook her head. "Just humor me." He stared blankly at her for a few beats, uncomprehending, unwilling to latch on to the weird twinge of hope in his pulse until she reached out blindly and tapped the picture again. "Do it, Leo."

"Well, okay. It's, um, a black-and-white photo," he said. "It's a picture of a cabin in the canyon. It's tiny, made of wood, looks to be about ten feet across the front at most. There are two windows, small, identical. And between them is a chimney. And Duke is leaning against the tree on the left, holding a beer, smiling." He exhaled slowly. "Duke's tree, the stump we found."

"Our left or his?"

Leo blinked over to her, confused. "The left side of the photo. He's leaning against the tree with his right arm."

"What hand holds the beer bottle?"

He looked down again. "His left."

"Exactly. How many fingers do you see?"

His stomach seemed to drop straight out of his body and over the cliff. "Oh, shit."

He looked up at her to see she was already shaking her head, eyes open now and smiling. "It's impossible, right? He only has four fingers on his left hand."

"Then how—?"

She took it back. "It's a red herring. It's intentional. Only someone who knew Duke could figure it out. Leo: this photo is a mirror image."

A mirror image.

Duke wasn't leaning against the tree on the left. He was leaning against the one on the right, and they hadn't even looked for that one.

"But did you see another stump?" Leo hadn't seen anything other than rotting wood and crumbled stone.

"No." Lily grinned over at him. "But we wouldn't have if it was buried under the collapsed fireplace."

Leo let out a breathless "Oh my God. We have to go back."

Lily turned, frantically digging into the bag. "Give me Bradley's and Walter's numbers." He rattled them off, and watched over her shoulder as she texted the group: Photo was a mirror image. Don't come for us yet. We'll call when we know more.

Lily hit Send before shoving the phone back into her bag.

"Take two?" she said, grinning so wide he could count her teeth.

"Take two."

Chapter Twenty-Eight

THE CLEARING OPENED up in front of them and, once they were positive no one else lingered nearby, Lily and Leo raced toward the crumbled chimney—right back to where they'd been barely two hours ago. Though both their hands were covered in cuts and scrapes, they hardly noticed as they dug through the pile to unearth a stump that was in considerably worse shape than the one on the other side.

Years of being covered by rock and other debris meant it hadn't dried out and aged in the same way. Some of the grain was swollen; sections of bark had rotted and sloughed away. Hopefully whatever remained would still be legible.

Leo leaned in to study it while Lily hovered behind him, her heart in her windpipe. "Do you see anything?" she asked. "Is it braille again?"

"There's definitely something here." Reaching into his bag, he pulled out his canteen and poured water across the surface, just like she had last time. "Right? Do you see those dots?"

She crouched next to him, and though the markings weren't as pronounced, she agreed they were similar to what they'd seen earlier.

But she was tired, and the longer she stared, the more they seemed to swim in front of her, turning into nondescript, blobby masses. "Looking at this makes my brain malfunction."

Leo picked up a stick, swiped an area of the earth flat and clear of leaves, and began drawing the patterns in the dirt. After a few minutes, he pulled back. "Does that look right?"

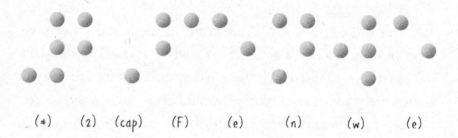

(*)   (2)   (cap)   (F)   (e)   (n)   (w)   (e)

She compared the drawings to what had been burned onto the wood. "I think so?"

Below the drawings, he slowly wrote *2, F, e, n, w, e.* "I'm less confident this time around," he murmured.

She pointed to the final series of dots. "But if this is an intentional dot and not a spot of decay on the wood, that would turn this final *e* into an *o*."

"Right," he agreed. "But if the *two* is the slot canyon, and the *F* is which crevasse we turn into, then the next four letters are directional turns deeper into the Maze, an *o* wouldn't make sense."

"The way you've drawn it looks right to me." She looked up, hyperaware of every sound.

"Do we really think the first code was a decoy? Is that something Duke would do?"

"It is absolutely something he would do. I almost feel stupid for not anticipating it."

He gazed down at the dirt and up at the log, back and forth, confirming. "If the photo of Duke is a mirror image, then this is definitely the right tree stump."

"Let's roll with it," Lily said, tugging on his sleeve. She looked back up the path toward the slot canyons, paranoid and unable to shake the feeling that they weren't alone. "Those two idiots might not be the brightest stars in the sky, but assuming we're right about the tree, it's only a matter of time before they realize that the earlier directions were wrong. And if they find us, I don't think they'll just zip-tie us again."

Feet crunched through leaves behind them and this time Lily knew she hadn't imagined it. She whipped around, knife in hand, and saw a man backlit in the low-hanging sun, standing about ten yards away. They both pushed to their feet, Leo shoving her behind him, shielding her.

Lily moved to shove *him* behind *her* when she heard Leo's relieved voice: "Dude."

"Bradley?"

"Goddamn, there you are." Laughing as he took in their expressions, Bradley shook his head. "You both look so panicked. It's just me."

Leo and Lily exchanged a brief, confused look.

"How—what are you doing here?" Leo asked. "Nicole said you'd gone back to New York."

Bradley looked momentarily surprised. "You spoke to— Oh, right. I told her I was flying home, but really I just couldn't handle knowing you two were going on without me." He winced self-deprecatingly. "This was the most fun I've had in my life, and I couldn't miss it. So tell me what's happened! I bet it's been insane." He gave a wild Bradley-mountain-man shout and grinned at them.

Lily imagined that in any other circumstance Leo would walk over and embrace his friend. But he didn't move from her side—and she didn't lower her knife. She also couldn't shake the weird feeling that coiled in her gut like a rattlesnake. Why would Bradley risk coming into the canyon alone? Why, if he trusted Leo, wouldn't he meet them back in Hester, as planned?

Oblivious to the vibe, Bradley approached and gestured down to the stump. "Is it the same tree as in the photo? Holy shit, you guys. You found it!"

Lily noticed Leo use his foot to subtly wipe the code clear in the dirt, and her stomach dropped. Something was definitely off. When did Bradley leave Nicole, and how did he find them so fast?

Unfortunately, Bradley noticed, too, and a shadow moved over his features. "What? Don't be like that, man."

"It's weird," Leo said quietly. "You showing up here? I'm just thinking it through."

Bradley's laugh was forced. "Come on. What's weird? It's me. Here to help. Teamwork, right? Isn't that what Lily told us this is all about? What's the code?"

Leo scratched his jaw and looked away, wincing.

"Seriously?" Bradley said, wounded. "It's *me*. What's there to think about?" He reached out to jovially smack Leo's arm. "Already this treasure has messed with your head."

"It isn't that." Leo looked back over his shoulder, toward the direction the other men had disappeared earlier. "The guys who held us at gunpoint today weren't surprised that there were only two of us down here. I'm trying to figure that out."

"What guys?" Bradley asked, shaking his head.

Leo ignored this. "We knew they wouldn't be surprised to hear that Terry bailed, because we read his text messages. But how did they know we split up if Terry hadn't answered them since? Who told them we split up?"

"Sorry, what are you talking about?" Bradley leaned down to catch Leo's eyes. "Someone held you at gunpoint? Was it the guys from town?" He wrinkled his brow. "Lily's bartender boyfriend?"

Unease bled further into Lily's mood, sending her pulse racing. "You're working with them," she said quietly.

Bradley blanched. "*What?* With who?"

"There were four people in that text thread." Leo tilted his head. His expression cleared. "How would Jay and Kevin have known to come here if they hadn't been told about the photo of Duke? The texts said they lost track of us after we left the overlook."

"Bradley must've called them," Lily said. "Maybe when you took Walt to the hospital. Unless . . . No one ever bothered to look in your backpack. You could have called them the night of the storm."

Bradley looked genuinely shocked for a beat.

And then his expression broke, and he burst out laughing, bending at the waist. "Shit, I couldn't hold it." He straightened, wiping a hand down his face. "This isn't how I wanted this to go down. I don't know why I'm laughing, dudes."

Unsettled, Lily threaded her fingers through Leo's, taking a step backward. "Leo. Let's go."

But Leo stood firm, staring at Bradley. "We texted you." He swallowed, pained. A glance at him told her his expression was washed out, sick with shock. "We texted the group and said the photo was a mirror image." Leo looked around them, and Lily realized that the sounds earlier weren't her imagination. Jay and Kevin were nearby, hidden in the shade, had been standing there the entire time, waiting to see how this would unfold. "What I don't understand is how you got the message if you were already here. There's no signal."

"There is if he's forwarding everything to a sat phone," Lily said.

Bradley reached into his pocket with a heavy sigh and pulled out the small device. "Damn. Didn't think you'd catch that." He grinned. "It's easy to hide shit in a bag if no one actually checks. Jesus, Lily, what's the point of having rules if you don't enforce them?"

Lily stepped forward in anger, but Leo stopped her with his arm across her chest. "You've been here the whole time," he said. "You started down the night you left Nicole, didn't you?"

Pocketing the phone again, Bradley held up his hands. "Guys, seriously—this doesn't have to be so tragic. Just put down the knife and head home. Let us go in there and get the money. We'll laugh our asses off about this whole thing later."

Red flooded her vision, blanketing everything around her in a fiery glow. "'Just . . . head home'?" she repeated. "'Laugh our asses off'? Are you kidding me right now?"

She glanced to Leo, who couldn't seem to pull his attention from Bradley's face. "You pushed Terry," he said tonelessly.

Jay and Kevin stepped out into the dappled late-afternoon sun. "What'd he say?"

Bradley waved them off. "Don't worry about it."

Jay pulled his gun out, resting it meaningfully against his leg. "What's that mean, Brad? 'You pushed Terry'?"

Goose bumps moved like icy fingers along her skin.

"Bradley. And I didn't *push* him," Bradley said irritably. "He let the situation get out of control when he pulled a gun in broad daylight. It was his own fault he went over the cliff."

"But Terry's *dead*, man?" Kevin, to his credit, seemed genuinely upset by this.

"He is," Bradley said. "And like I said, it was his own fault."

Kevin had barely moved, clearly unable to process this. Finally, he looked over at Leo and Lily. "Terry died, and you lied to us?"

"'*Lied*—'?" Leo cut off, coughing out an incredulous laugh. "You held us at gunpoint and tied us up with zip cuffs. I didn't exactly feel like we were betraying your trust."

Bradley's patience snapped. "This is a stupid fixation! Get over the Terry of it all. You weren't even there to see what a disaster he was. I was trying to pull him away from the edge and he was freaking the hell out. Did I push him? Maybe! It's all a blur! I did you a *favor*. Now there's one less person to split the money with."

"We wouldn't even be here if it wasn't for him," Jay seethed.

"You guys know him from Reddit, for fuck's sake!" Bradley shouted. "I've known him for years. Terry wasn't the super-rugged outdoorsy dude you think he is. Wearing a vest with seventy pockets doesn't make him capable, it just makes him overdressed. Yes, he knew more about Duke Wilder than any of us, but only on paper. He couldn't even keep his mouth shut and be likable for four days! And there were so many chances to take the journal, but he was as stealthy as a grizzly bear in a wind chime factory. He couldn't even zip up his fucking backpack properly."

Lily was so mad she was practically levitating off the ground. She nodded to Jay's gun. "His aim better be good because if I get to you first, I'm gonna reach down your throat, grab your balls, and show 'em to you."

"Lily," Leo whispered in warning.

Bradley grinned at her in genuine delight, showing a row of pearly teeth. He pushed his golden hair off his forehead. "You are so different than any woman I've ever seen Leo with." He stepped forward. "I know you won't believe me, but I'm genuinely bummed about how this is going down. It didn't have to go this way, you know?" He gestured behind him, as if the decision that led to all of this was just past where they could see. "The original plan was to take the journal and pass it off to these guys. But Terry left it sticking out of the bag, and Nicole noticed, and it all went to hell. I'm just here for the cash. I'm not here for all this drama."

"The cash?" Leo said. "You don't need this. You have—"

"An associate professor's salary and a fuckton of debt. It's impossible to get out from under it," Bradley admitted, looking vulnerable for just a moment.

"Dude. How much—"

"Enough," Bradley cut Leo off. "We've been planning this for so long, it just really pisses me off that it got this complicated."

Heat rose to the surface of Lily's skin. "Are you implying that you have some claim to this money because you've spent so much time planning to steal my father's journal? Are you really saying that right now?"

"Like I said, it's a finders keepers situation, darling," he told her. "Those were clearly Duke's rules, too. You can't even tell me you're sure he wanted *you* to have it." Lily made to bolt forward again, but Leo held her back. Bradley laughed. "You're so fiery. I like you, Lily Wilder. I think you liked me, too."

Then he winked at her.

She lifted her chin to meet his gaze. "Eat shit, Brad."

This only delighted him more. "I get it, Leo. I get why you were so hung up on her for so long."

Beside her, Leo was not amused. "Why did you even bring me and Walter here?" Leo asked. "You could have come with Terry and done this on your own. You didn't have to drag us into it."

"Do you really think Lily wouldn't notice if her journal went missing?" He grinned proudly at Leo. "Terry was the one who'd done all the digging into Duke Wilder's past. He was the one who convinced me the money is still out here. But I was the one who thought to distract her with her ex-boyfriend."

Leo, finally, looked genuinely wounded rather than angry. "You said you didn't know Lily was the girl from the ranch."

Bradley shrugged. "It wasn't that hard to piece together, dude."

"This is boring as hell." Jay pointed his gun at Lily, and Leo tensed at her side. "Can we get back to the point here?

The first directions were wrong. Drop the knife and take us to the right place."

When she didn't move, he swung the gun at Leo. "Think real hard, Lily Wilder."

Lily calculated how long it would take to reach Bradley and knew it was no use. Opening her fist, she let the knife fall to the ground.

"Good," Bradley said, and bent to pick it up. "Now tell me the correct directions."

"Yeah, I don't think so," Leo said.

Bradley smiled, walking closer and lifting his hand to move a strand of hair off Lily's face. Leo reached out, grabbing Bradley's wrist, as a gun cocked off to the side.

"Leo," Bradley said quietly. "Brother. Take us there, or leave us with all the information, but don't make this worse than it has to be."

"Why are you risking your job, our friendship—everything for this?" Leo asked. "Why didn't you just talk to me? I don't get it."

"You *wouldn't* get it," Bradley said simply. "Mr. Responsible would never get himself into this situation, and I admire that, but I got mixed up in some stuff you wouldn't understand and am in so deep these guys are going to straight-up kill me if I don't get my hands on a lot of cash. Want to save my life? Help your best friend out."

Leo shook his head, looking away. Bradley waved Kevin forward. "He needs encouragement, I guess."

"It's getting dark," Lily said, and Kevin stopped. The sun had begun its steep descent; shadows were growing longer by the second, and in the canyon, the sky went from dim to dark in a snap. Within an hour, they could easily step off a cliff or

walk right into a clump of prickly pear. There was a good reason why you didn't wander around at night in the desert. "We
won't be able to see a fucking thing."

"Good thing we're prepared," Bradley said.

Kevin opened his bag and pulled out three heavy-duty
Maglites. "What?" he said in reaction to Lily's expression.
"You think we're going to have a fucking sleepover and start
fresh in the morning? We go now."

Jay waved his gun at Leo. "Lead the way, my man."

Chapter Twenty-Nine

BY THE TIME they followed the curve of the rock cliff from the stump to the entrance of the slot canyons, the last of the light had been snuffed from the sky. Lily couldn't even appreciate how it seemed like the stars spilled in a blanket of glitter overhead. The moon was muted behind a froth of clouds, but the beams of three flashlights swung back and forth across the trail, Bradley and his two assholes hovering right behind them.

Louder than the shuffle of their footsteps through the brush were her own racing thoughts. Lily cycled through one possible escape after another. Maybe they could run? Maybe they could duck behind one of the canyon walls and lose them in the dark. But could they lose all three of them, and for how long? She had neither a light nor a gun. What if they cooperated and Bradley didn't find what he was looking for in the end? Finding the right entrance was one thing; they'd still have to navigate the correct turns through narrow passages full of chockstones and puddles and God knew what else—in the pitch-black darkness. They could easily come up empty-handed. Then what?

She was no closer to an answer when Leo stopped in front of what looked like a narrow hallway carved into the sandstone wall.

"Can I just reiterate how insanely stupid this is?" he said. "Every one of us could die in there."

Bradley leaned in, peering past him into the darkness. "You're not wrong, but wasn't it just the other day when Lily reminded us you were an Eagle Scout and have more outdoor experience than any of us? That she needed you to solve the puzzles? Really helpful intel." He poked Leo in the shoulder. "You go first."

Leo's jaw clenched as he stared forward into the slot. "I'll need more light." He glanced back. "And the map."

After a moment of consideration, Bradley opened one of the packs and handed him the torn-out map and a small head-lamp. Bradley was smarter than he looked; given the chance, Lily definitely would have cracked him over the head with one of the Maglites.

"Don't be a hero, man," Bradley warned quietly.

"Yeah" was all Leo said before slipping the lamp on.

The beam of light sliced through the dark, and when he reached back to squeeze her hand, she squeezed back, tighter. With a deep breath, he took his first step inside.

2 . . . F . . . e . . . n . . . w . . . e.

They walked about two hundred feet—sidestepping, single file in the claustrophobic darkness—before the narrow path opened up and, just like Duke's map predicted, split into at least ten directions. It was like a circular atrium with hallways branching off. Leo led them to the second one from the left. "Two," he said. They slid down into the narrow crevasse, which thankfully broadened after the first couple fissures, each of which Leo marked aloud. "A . . . B . . ."

And so it went. They climbed over boulders and squeezed down impossibly narrow slots, keeping track of each opening until they reached the sixth, F. Leo looked down at the compass on his watch, locating the direction of the first turn: east. They tripped and stumbled their way east, and then north, and then west, deeper into the disorienting maze with only darkness and possible death in front of them.

Despite the chill, Lily was sweating when Leo stopped, facing a narrow hole in the rock. He angled his light inside.

"Is this it?" Bradley said, and it was impossible to miss the edge of exhilaration in his exhausted voice.

Leo looked down at the page again. "Should be."

Kevin's voice carried from behind. "It better be."

Bradley moved to the front to stand next to Leo. "It's mad narrow," he murmured. "We have to crawl in."

To Lily's surprise, he didn't send Leo in first. Instead, Bradley went, disappearing into the darkness. His echoing voice reached them. "Holy shit."

Leo followed, then Kevin, and then Jay pointed the gun at Lily's head, forcing her to crawl through before him.

The tunnel was narrow enough that Lily had to army-crawl for about five feet, her heart in her throat, choking on panic. And then cold air hit her face and she fell onto soft ground. Leo rushed over, helping her up as she looked around a space that was about twenty feet in diameter.

A secret room, worn away by the elements over hundreds of years, in the middle of solid rock. The ground at their feet was sandy washout; a thin strip of stars was visible overhead.

The walls were smooth and dry, with a narrow shelf carved into the wall of stone opposite the entry tunnel.

"Code boy," Jay said to Leo. "Go check that out."

Haltingly, Leo approached. His headlamp swept across the front of the rock shelf, most of which was hidden in darkness. Lily was afraid to breathe as her brain unhelpfully supplied every booby trap scene in every movie she'd ever watched. Leo reluctantly reached forward to feel around.

"Oh my God."

Everyone crowded closer. "What is it?" Bradley asked.

Jay stepped up right against Leo's back, hovering. "Dude, is it big?"

"Give me some space." Whatever Leo found seemed wedged in there, and it took a few tugs before he pulled a wooden box free.

Lily coughed from the dust. It was about the size of a shoebox, plain and framed in metal with a flimsy padlock holding it closed.

Bradley tilted his head back, yelling a triumphant "Fuck yes!" His voice was almost deafening as it echoed around them, tiny pebbles falling from the vibration. "Duke, you never let us down!"

Leo set it on the ground and backed away. Lily rushed to him.

Jay stepped forward and nudged it with the tip of his boot. "It's not very big."

"Might have a key inside," Bradley mused, crouching in front of it.

Jay looked up, squinting into the beam of Kevin's flashlight. "Open it, Brad."

Bradley was trembling with excitement as his palms smoothed over the wood, but he paused in his exploration to speak through clenched teeth. "It's Bradley."

Just beyond the beam of the flashlight, Leo's hand found her own, and they stepped backward into the shadows. Bradley used his Maglite to easily break the padlock and flipped the top open, staring down.

"What?" Kevin said, approaching. "Is it—?"

They fell silent, and Bradley slowly bent to pick up a thin scrap of paper. "What the fuck is this?"

Jay snatched it from him and growled. "It's just a bunch of *numbers?* Is this a code?" He walked it over to Lily, shoving it in her face. "What is this?"

She stared at the long string of numbers, uninterrupted by spaces. Shaking her head, she admitted, "Duke never did codes like this with me. I don't—I don't know it."

Kevin swiped the paper from Jay's grip, marched over, and grabbed Leo by the shirt collar. He dragged him backward, slamming him against the rock wall. At the sound of Leo's pained grunt, Lily started toward him, but Bradley clamped a strong hand around her arm, holding her back.

"You think this is a joke?" Kevin said, in Leo's face now. He thrust the paper at his chest. "What the fuck does this mean?"

Leo glared at him. "I did what you asked. I got you here." He nodded to Bradley. "He's the archaeologist. You guys fucking figure it out."

Jay smirked and ran a hand through his hair. "Kevin, do your thing."

Bradley banded Lily's arms behind her back as Kevin—

twice Leo's size—hurled his giant fist into Leo's stomach. When Leo bent to protect himself, Kevin went for his face, the blow hard enough to knock him to his knees. Leo tried to fight back, but his punches barely seemed to land, and Lily screamed, her voice reverberating but not loud enough to block out the sound of Kevin's fists landing on Leo's face, his stomach; of his boot landing kicks to Leo's ribs over and over.

Finally, Bradley shouted, "Enough!"

Lily tried to bolt forward again, but this time Bradley grabbed a fistful of her hair, violently forcing her head back. She could see Leo crumpled on the ground, hear every one of his pained breaths.

"Leo, say something," she begged.

He spit a bloody mouthful and looked up at her through one swollen eye, trying to grin. "You'd probably choose a protein bar for every meal over this, right?"

"This isn't going to work," Bradley said. "He just needs the right motivation, that's all." He dragged her forward to where Leo could see and spoke to Leo as if to a small child. "Leo, they're numbers. Numbers are your jam. You just have to figure out what they mean. Okay?"

Leo stared up at him, face bloody, smile gone and eyes full of rage.

Bradley tugged on her hair again, forcing her to her knees and brandishing a gun. Leaning in, he loudly whispered, "Gee, Lily, sorry for the déjà vu." He turned to Kevin. "Get him up."

Kevin dragged Leo to his feet and tossed the paper at him. Leo lifted his shirt, wiped at his eyes, at his forehead; the shirt came away stained red. His hands trembled as he peered down at the writing with an intensity Lily had never seen before.

"What does it say?" Bradley asked in a quiet growl.

"It's twenty-five numbers with no spaces," Leo said. "This could take weeks to decipher."

"Bummer that we don't have weeks, then." Bradley lifted his chin. "Feel free to have a seat and use the journal to work it out. We're not leaving until you're done."

All Lily could do now was wait.

———

A person could think a lot in a few hours.

Bradley sat beside Lily with their backs against the wall, gun resting idly against his thigh while they watched Leo work. For minutes, and then hours, Leo didn't write anything down, didn't use the journal. He just stared, mumbling to himself, working out sequences and codes before seeming to disregard them almost as quickly.

Kevin and Jay paced and talked in low voices, and eventually slumped to sleep on the ground. Bradley sat silently, watching Leo, then watching Lily watching Leo, lost in his own thoughts.

Lily had never been a trusting person. In fact, except for Nicole, there wasn't a single human she'd trust with her horses, never mind her life. But it occurred to her that when they'd heard Bradley's voice at that stump, she'd never considered that he and Leo might be in this together. Instead, she was scared for Leo, and beyond the obvious danger, she was scared for his heart and what it would mean that the man he considered family betrayed him so deeply.

So far, he was doing exactly what she'd expected him to—

remaining calm and stoic in the face of danger—but after this, and God she hoped there'd be an *after this*, she knew the pain of this betrayal would land, and hard. She hated it even more than the burn of her father's journal being taken from her and the two of them forced to help someone else find this treasure. In that moment, it felt like it was her and Leo against the world. Lily would have done anything to keep her man safe, but right then she could only sit back and trust him. Her competence couldn't save them right now.

"Stop that tapping," Bradley said, surprising her by stilling her hand on her thigh. "God, it's like a hammer in my skull at this point."

She hadn't realized she'd been doing it. "Sorry. It's just a habit."

"Well, it's fucking annoying."

She glared at him, wanting to claw his face off. "You ruined a decade-long friendship with the best man you know," she whispered to him. "For *money*."

"He and I are damaged but not broken," Bradley assured her. "Every relationship has a low moment."

She laughed sadly. "A low moment. You're delusional."

"Look at you two," he said, smug. "You're trying to tell me nothing happened out here with you? If it wasn't for me, you and Leo would have never reconnected, so he should actually be grateful."

"Fuck off."

Bradley turned his head to watch Leo bent over, staring at the code. "When we get out of here, he and I will talk it out."

She wanted to punch him. She wanted to swipe the gun and pistol-whip each of them before blocking them in there with their stupid box and this stupid—

"Breathe, Lil," Leo murmured, glancing over at her. "Don't let him get you riled up."

A rush of emotion pushed up from her chest and into her throat, salty and hot, at the awareness that even when injured and intensely concentrating on an urgent task, Leo was still keeping an eye on her.

She nodded, replying quietly to him, "I won't. I'm okay."

Bradley laughed softly. "You are so whipped, Leo."

"You don't know the half of it." Leo pushed his hair off his head and leaned closer to the paper again.

Lily didn't know how many hours had passed, but her throat was dry and she was exhausted. It was freezing, and even the slow appearance of dawn through the gap in the cave's ceiling didn't promise much warmth. She really had to pee. She looked up just as Leo's eyes went wide. His brows lifted—hope soared in her chest—before slowly straightening again. He'd found something.

About fifteen minutes later, he said simply, "I think I've got it."

Jay and Kevin bolted awake. Leo managed to stand, and Lily pushed to her feet. Bradley pulled her back when she made to move toward Leo.

"Well?" Bradley asked. "What does it say?"

Leo held Lily's gaze before blinking over to Bradley. "You're not going to like it."

Bradley stared at him for a long moment. "Read it anyway."

"It says 'Beat ya here.'"

Bradley rushed to the code, and Leo rushed to her, crushing her to him, breathing in.

"What do you mean?" Bradley said, picking up the scrap of

paper Leo had set on top of the box. "The note just says 'Beat ya here'? Are you kidding me?"

Ignoring him, Leo put his hands on the sides of Lily's face and bent to look at her. "You okay?"

"Yeah." She gripped his wrists, needing to feel his pulse under her fingertips. Strong and alive. "You?"

"I'm fine." He was lying. She'd seen the way he'd absently cupped a hand over the ribs on his right side all night long. Even now, he worked one of his wrists free of her grip, lowering a hand to support his side. There were scrapes everywhere on his face, a nasty cut over his brow, and even in the lingering darkness, she could see bruises blooming under his eyes.

Leo was jerked away, and Bradley shoved the paper in his face. "Explain how you got that."

Slowly, Leo explained the code, that it was called Fougère, named for the French spy who invented it, that it was a way to group numbers to form letters. He wrote out the code and explained how he got the answer, even though Lily was pretty sure Bradley didn't understand any of it. Leo said he went through every alphanumeric code he could think of, and none of them spelled anything but nonsense. This code, though, spelled a specific phrase. And Fougère was definitely code that Duke Wilder would have known.

Leo's exhausted words were cut off by the sound of someone throwing a flashlight against the stone wall.

"What the fuck do we do now?" Kevin said.

Bradley paced the length of the room. "Duke's taunting us. It's all a game to him." He stopped pacing to narrow his eyes at Lily. "'Adventure over stuff,' isn't that what you said his motto was? Sanctimonious son of a bitch really thought people would be satisfied with the thrill of the chase and he could keep the money himself." He ran a hand through his hair and looked at Jay and Kevin. "He got the money. We take them with us. We go back to Duke's place and tear it apart if we have to."

Chapter Thirty

SHUFFLING OUT OF the narrow confines of the slot canyons meant it took them all a few seconds to adjust to the brilliant morning light. The sun was fresh, the sky cloudless and almost blindingly blue. But even bloody and half-blind, Leo could still make out the blobby shapes of five people standing not ten yards away.

One of the figures burst forward. Leo startled, protectively shoving Lily behind him before realizing the body sprinting toward them was Nicole. She wasn't headed for Lily, though. Instead, she stormed straight past them, barreling into Bradley and sending a brutal fist into his stomach. The hit sounded like she'd swung a baseball bat into a bag of flour. Literally blindsided, Bradley let out a sharp groan, doubling over.

Jay and Kevin went for their guns, but four other guns cocked in warning before they could reach them.

"Rangers?" Lily said, just as the uniforms registered in Leo's brain.

"You fucker," Nic seethed, grabbing Bradley's hair and cracking her knee into his face. Blood gushed from his nose, and Leo's old instinct remained—to move toward his friend, to protect one of his own—before he remembered. Bradley wasn't included in that circle anymore. Finally, another figure jogged forward, dragging Nicole away swearing and kicking at the air.

Leo watched as a female ranger aimed her pistol and moved with purpose toward the man Leo thought had been one of his best friends.

"Let's see those hands on your head, sport."

Bradley did as she instructed but backed up a couple of steps. "Hey, whoa. I'm just here with these two"—he motioned to Leo and Lily—"following the same information everyone—"

"Hands on your head," the ranger repeated calmly, "and get down on your knees. You can tell me all your stories back at the station." With her free hand, she tugged a pair of handcuffs from her belt, flicking them open.

"What?" Bradley cried, teeth gory with his own blood. "Wait. Hold up. Leo. Tell them. I'm with—"

Leo's voice was quiet but steady: "He's not with us."

Saying it felt like a knife to his stomach.

"You have the right to remain silent," she told Bradley, extracting the gun from his waistband and handing it to the fourth ranger. "Anything you say can and will be used against you in a court of law. You have the right to speak to an attorney . . ."

Leo turned from the sight of his oldest friend being arrested, and watched as Lily ran to Nicole. The two women embraced, and at Lily's relieved sob, all of the tension diffused out of the moment. Suddenly Leo felt like he could breathe again, no longer holding it in, struggling to keep himself together long enough to get Lily to safety.

With the reprieve, however, came torment, and he now felt every punch, every brutal kick, every ounce of betrayal and disappointment. Beneath him, his legs seemed to morph into a different substance, no longer flesh and bone but shoddily built and rubbery. He fell gracelessly as the cops marched Bradley, Jay, and Kevin out toward the river, where, in the distance, a helicopter whirred to life, misting water everywhere.

"Leo," Bradley called. "Dude, tell them we're cool!"

Leo ignored him, pulling his knees to his chest, pressing the heels of his hands to his eyes. "Holy shit," he mumbled over and over, trying to breathe more deeply. His head throbbed, his mind grappling with this new reality.

Voices rose around him—Lily telling the rangers what had happened, Nicole explaining how it hadn't sat right with her that Bradley left, that the one person who was most enthusiastic about every part of this trip would just disappear right at the end.

"I was sitting at Archie's," she said, her voice muffled by the constant low ringing in his ears, "and I thought, 'Why did he keep asking me how much money I thought there would be and how we'd split it up?' He'd been all about the adventure, but then suddenly it was, 'How are we gonna split it up?' and 'Are we gonna have to give some of it to the government?' Why was he so obsessed with it one minute, but flying to New York the very next? It didn't add up."

When Bradley had left, she thought maybe he just wanted to weasel out of questions about what happened to Terry, but then Lily called and told her the Lost Boys had held them at gunpoint. That's when Nicole had put it all together.

"But how did you find us *here?*"

"They traced your call from the satellite phone," Nicole said. "But honestly, we knew to look for a trail, and these assholes are just really fucking sloppy."

The rangers' voices faded, footsteps approached, and he felt two arms come around him.

"Hey, you." Lily coaxed him to lean against her. "Come here."

Her lips pressed to his neck, his cheek. She ran a careful hand over his hair. "You're a mess, honey, look at you."

"I still can't believe it," he told her. "Bradley."

"I know." She set her mouth against his temple. "I hate him for this. God, I hope someone beats his ass in county." Scooting around so she was kneeling in front of him, Lily caught his eye. "You okay?"

He nodded, but the motion made him wince.

"I'm worried he has a concussion," she said to someone over the top of his head. "Leo?" She kissed his cheek. "Honey, do you think you can walk?"

"Yeah." But when he tried, his legs didn't want to cooperate. Nothing felt solid. Everything hurt.

Nicole came to his other side, and the two helped him stand. A head rush hit him like a hurricane, and he weaved in place, so queasy that his vision dotted black.

"Easy," Lily murmured. "Take your time. They're just getting the shitheads situated in there. They'll wait for us."

He closed his eyes, bending to rest his forehead on Lily's shoulder while he got his bearings. Leo felt like he was falling forward into her, but she was steady and strong against him.

"How did you manage to get a helicopter?" Lily's voice was a gentle vibration against his skull. He didn't know how she was so calm right then. Maybe because it was her turn to be steady, and Leo's turn to be lost.

"I slept with that guy Joe, remember?" Nicole said. "He flies that thing."

"Oh my God, *that* Joe?" Lily laughed. "Why did you kick that hot man out of bed? I thought—"

"Hey," Leo growled. "I'm standing right here."

"You're making jokes!" Lily sang. "That has to be a good sign. Let's try to walk, okay?"

She put her arm around his waist. He took one step, then one more, and slowly, supported by two women who were stronger than any man he knew, he hiked the distance to the chopper. He was glad Lily was okay. He was glad Nicole had slept with a helicopter pilot, that she got the rangers there in time. He was glad he'd grabbed the one important thing from the cave. He was glad they were alive, but it was hard to celebrate: his temples throbbed, his ribs were screaming. But just thinking about what happened . . . it felt like his heart had cracked in half.

He made it inside the chopper and was situated in a seat near a window. The last thing he remembered before passing out was asking Lily whether he had anything in his pocket.

Chapter Thirty-One

LEO MISSED EVERYTHING that followed because he was essentially comatose for six hours.

Well, not really comatose; the doctors said he didn't have a concussion but was in shock. Lily was glad he got to miss the odd bedfellows of tedium and stress over this reentry into society. While he was taken to the county hospital about thirty miles west of Hester, Nicole, Lily, and a subdued Walter gave their statements at the police station. Given that they'd already told the police they were out looking for Terry, they stuck to that story. Luckily, Bradley wanted to avoid outright murder charges and gave the same version of events.

It turned out to be a good thing Terry had signed the liability waivers for everyone. Less lucky for Bradley, though, was that he couldn't avoid criminal charges altogether.

Walter, emerging from his final conversation with his handcuffed former friend, used his crutches for balance as he sat down heavily in one of the plastic chairs beside Lily and

Nicole. He told them what Bradley was up against: two charges of kidnapping, two charges of conspiracy to commit aggravated assault, two charges of threat of violence, and one charge of aggravated robbery. "He's looking at, at minimum, three to five years."

With a quiet "Thanks," Walter took his backpack from Nicole. "I declined to cover his bail but told him he was allowed to write us letters of apology from jail." He cleared his throat. "I also told him he looks terrible in orange."

Nic barked out a shocked laugh, gazing at him with fondness. "That's right, sugar. Let him rot."

"I don't want him to rot," Walter corrected, "but I wouldn't mind knowing he has time to really think about what he did to Leo. I'm not sure I can ever forgive him. He didn't uphold the Outlaw Code."

Lily stepped forward then, wrapping her arms around his shoulders, mindful of his casted foot. "But you did."

When Joe and the female ranger—Officer Pochuswa— came back several hours later to tell them they'd retrieved Terry's body, Lily didn't know why she started to cry. The finality of it all hit her hard. The relief, too, maybe. But also the realization that, even after everything that happened, nothing would really change. Even after Terry's death, their failed attempt to find the treasure, the wild way that she and Leo crashed together, and the fact that she'd been held at gunpoint three times in a matter of days, she'd have to keep bringing people out to the trail to put food on her table and take care of her horses.

Nothing they'd done in the past week had made any difference. In fact, it had only made things worse. Because from that day forward—whether it was next week or ten years into the future—she'd always imagine Leo out there: his big hands loosely holding the reins while he coaxed Ace into a smooth lope; eyeing Lily knowingly over his tin coffee mug, flirting even in the cold shock of the morning; climbing over her in the sweet confines of a cabin, kissing his way down her body.

Lily assumed her meltdown helped convince the police that she was blindsided by the news, because Officer Pochuswa put Lily in her truck and personally drove her to the hospital to be with Leo.

She was directed to a sleepy ER bay with five beds, the other four of them empty. Bright light streamed through tall windows, and the entire space had the feel of a hospital from the past, plunked down in the middle of some quiet countryside. Leo was still asleep when she got there. It meant that Lily could take his hand and just . . . look at him.

As expected, he had stitches in his temple, some more in his cheek. He would have an impressive shiner under his right eye, and his bottom lip was cut and swollen. They'd taken his shirt off and his ribs were bruised but not wrapped; thankfully nothing seemed to be broken. There were wires taped to his chest and attached to monitors. She had to assume it was out of an abundance of caution, because his heart rate beeped steadily, his blood pressure an even 110/70. Despite the beating he'd taken, he looked healthy and sun-kissed. She loved this face. She loved him. She couldn't imagine finding another face anywhere that she would love this much.

She looked at his hands instead. They were strong: long fingers, muscular, with prominent tendons that made her want to bend down and bite. Turning his hand palm up, she ran her fingertips over the paths of lines there. Except for random cuts and scrapes, his skin was mostly unmarred and smooth. His hands were only mildly calloused, nails meticulous. There was no sun damage, no scars. They were city hands. These hands belonged to a man who lived in a high-rise and jogged in an urban park and would get a promotion when he returned home.

She and Leo were from two different worlds.

She bent, resting her lips on his knuckles, and began the mental process of saying goodbye. Her stubbornness had served her well, even if it was a double-edged sword. It meant she was unbending, but it also meant she was a survivor.

So she told him, while he was sleeping, that she was sorry. She knew she was uncompromising, but she couldn't move to New York. And she didn't want him to move to Hester, either, didn't want him to pretend he could be happy in a town that had one general store–café and one bar. He might think he remembered what it was like to be in the middle of nowhere, but the only time in his life he'd come close, he was falling in love on a beautiful ranch with a well-stocked kitchen and the luxurious semblance of "rustic." Leo Grady didn't have any idea what it would feel like to have to drive one hundred miles to a Target.

But even when she laid out the justification for pulling away, she realized—objectively—it wasn't healthy to be so unwilling to try. She heard Leo's arguments in her head, saying they could figure it out, that there was a way forward. She knew Nicole would yell at her that if she was so miserable without him, why not come up with a solution. But Lily wouldn't, and when Leo opened his eyes and sleepily blinked at her, and then smiled in relief, she knew exactly why: because when he'd left her before, what was hardest was the way it let a tiny voice take up permanent residence in her mind, telling her she wasn't worth it. She hadn't been enough for her mom to stay, wasn't enough for her dad to stick around for long. And Leo had never come back for her. Lily had survived all of that, but she didn't think she could survive trying to make it work with Leo again only for him to realize she wasn't worth living in the middle of nowhere.

"Uh-oh," Leo said, drowsily reaching out to tuck a strand of hair behind her ear. "She looks serious."

She tried to laugh, but it came out thick like a sob. She hadn't realized her eyes had filled until the wet heat of tears streaked down her face. What was it with her and crying lately? She was not a fan.

Leo frowned and reached forward to swipe at her cheek with a thumb. "Lily, there's . . . a watery substance coming from your eyeballs."

She smacked his hands away, laughing through tears. "Shut up."

He gazed at her. His eyes were so soft and adoring, they pulled a sharply defensive "*What?*" out of her.

But Leo laughed. "Not yet, sweetheart."

"Not yet what?"

"You can't break up with me yet."

Pulling back, she reminded him, "We aren't even together."

He grinned at this, eyes sparkling. "Wow, you are delusional. Two people who 'aren't even together' don't make love the way we did."

"Leo, we already talk—"

"I know what we talked about." He reached out, sweetly capturing her chin between his thumb and forefinger. "I'm not giving up."

Heat filled her chest, and she knocked his hand away again. "You don't get to decide for me."

"But you can decide for me?" he asked, but gently.

So gently, in fact, that she was left staring at him in mute shock.

"Anyway," he said, rolling onward, "I'm not deciding for you. I've just decided—for me—to not give up on us." Unruffled, he tucked his hand back beneath his cheek. "For me, unless you tell me to get out of your life and never contact you again, I'll be here." He gazed at her steadily. "Do you want me to get out of your life and never contact you again?"

When she couldn't pull an answer from the foggy cloud in her mind, he nodded. "Good, because all of those voices in your head telling you that I wouldn't be happy with you long-term or you're not worth giving up my life for are just thoughts, Lil. Just because thoughts are loud or constant doesn't mean they're right."

"You left me," she said starkly. "I know why, but still. You promised before that we would be together forever, and I can't hurt like that again."

"Neither of us knew what we were promising. We were kids." He reached forward, brushing away another tear. "You knew me when I was at my happiest. My mother was alive. I had everything I needed. I'd never known sadness." His dark gaze held hers. "I have, now. I'm an adult who has lost his mother, lost his twenties, lost the love of his life. My life in New York is soulless. You don't know what it's like being with you again." He stroked her jaw. "You have no idea how alive I feel just looking at you from a hospital bed while I've got stitches in my face and a monster headache."

Lily swallowed, unable to turn away, drowning in watery, sloshing feelings she couldn't repress. She *did* know how alive he felt.

"So, are you willing to let me figure out a scenario that works for us, to try?"

"To try," she repeated slowly. "You mean, to try being together?"

He nodded, humming. "I'm just asking for permission to come up with some ideas to run past you." He winked playfully. "You can opt out at any time."

This made her smile. "Well, those terms are pretty hard to refuse."

"Good." Leo leaned forward, carefully pressing his bruised mouth to her cheek. "I have faith that we can do this. I love you. You don't have to say it back. But I do. I love you."

She stared at his perfect hands and his battered face and his eyes that seemed to see straight through her. It would be a lie to hold it in: "I love you, too."

His eyes softened and he spoke quietly. "That is great news."

Finally, she looked down, not sure how to tell him this next part. "They found Terry's body."

Leo went still. "I'm glad."

"I don't think there's a problem there. For us, I mean." She shifted in her chair, reaching forward to fidget with the corner of his hospital sheet. "But Bradley . . ." She met his eyes again, and her heart twisted at the pain there. "He's in a lot of trouble."

Blinking away, Leo fixed his gaze on the beeping monitor. "I'd imagine."

She bent down, resting her lips on his uninjured temple. "It'll take some time to get over that one," she said quietly. "The treasure hunt was a bust, but maybe we get out of town for a little while. Just the two of us."

At this, he seemed to remember something. "Can you hand me my jacket?"

She looked on the table beside his bed, where his jacket and shirt were neatly folded. Extracting the coat from the pile, she handed it to him and watched as he casually peeled the monitors from his skin. She'd been around his body for over a week; she didn't know why the view of his torso in a hospital bed was suddenly sending her into wavy, heated territory.

Leo dug into one pocket, frowning when his hand came out empty, then dug into the other. He released a little "Ah," and handed her a familiar scrap of sepia paper. "Read this."

She took it, already knowing what it was. "Why are we doing this again?" she asked, worried his head wound was worse than she thought.

"Tell me what you see," he said, recalling her words from yesterday on the ledge, dissecting the photo of her father. She looked down.

7611179107651167211110969

"Numbers," she told him blankly.

"Read them." She glanced at him incredulously, but he only nodded to the paper in her hand. "Humor me. Please."

So, she recited the numbers: "Seven, six, one, one, one, seven, nine, one, zero, seven, six, five, one, one— Jesus, Leo, how did you get anything out of this?"

"Just finish," he said quietly.

She looked back down. "Six, seven, two, one, one, one, one, zero, nine, six, nine." She counted them. "Twenty-five numbers. No spaces."

"Duke had no way of knowing I'd find this, but you're lucky I did."

She hesitated. "Why?"

"Because it's a computer code."

"Wait. Duke used a computer code?"

"It appears he did. At least a little. It's old. We use Unicode now, mostly, but ASCII was used for order-entry computer systems for years. Your dad might have been an old, traditional dog, but he was crafty enough to use every kind of code he could find. He might have even anticipated that ASCII would be obsolete one day, if it wasn't already—making it even harder to solve." He frowned. "I don't actually know when he would have hidden this in the cave."

"So," she said, trying to follow, "it's an old computer code that translates to 'Beat ya here'? Because that is absolutely something my dad would have said."

Leo nodded. "In ASCII, there are numbers corresponding to capital letters, lowercase letters, numbers, symbols. The fact that there weren't spaces between the string of numbers made it hard at first to know what I was looking at," he explained. "I mean, it could have been anything—even a code he made up himself. But because I'm used to seeing numbers grouped for code, I first looked at them in doublets." He pointed to the paper. "The fact that there was an odd number told me that maybe he mixed capital letters with lowercase to make it more complex—capital letters are two digits; lowercase are mostly three."

She was lost. "I don't understand."

"It's okay. The only thing you need to understand is that most people also probably don't read ASCII, so in many ways it was perfect. Bradley didn't know, and his friends definitely didn't know."

She smiled blandly. "Well, good job to you for figuring it out, I guess."

He laughed. "You really don't see what this means?"

"No."

Leo rested his cheek sweetly on his folded hands and smiled at her. "It means I could tell them anything I wanted."

Chapter Thirty-Two

LILY SNIFFED, SWIPING a hand over her face before scooting her chair closer to the bed.

"Leo," she said with forced calm.

"Yes."

"Are you telling me you lied to them back there?"

He nodded, ignoring the way his cheek throbbed in pain. "Yup."

Her expression flattened in disbelief. "The note doesn't say 'Beat ya here'?"

"It does not."

"It's not the . . ."

"Fougère?" he supplied, and shook his head. "That's not a real thing."

"You made up a code to *trick them*?" she asked.

"Sort of? Not really. I faked it."

"What would you have done if Nicole hadn't been there with the cops?"

He shrugged. "That was a problem for Later Leo."

"Then do you even know what it says?" Lily's jaw had gone rigid, the tendons above her collarbones tightening. "Leo, stop fucking around."

"I'm tempted to give you the satisfaction of solving it yourself."

She scoffed. "I promise I never needed that satisfaction."

Relenting with a smile, he said, "The real trick was trying to remember ASCII without writing it down. Once I realized what it was, I didn't want them to see me work it out. I had to do every letter in my head."

"Impressive."

"I thought so, too. So, while I was pretending to solve it and write down wrong letters, I was mentally high-fiving your dad for using a mix of capital and lowercase."

"Why?"

"Because if by chance they put together that my fake Fougère code was a doublet or triplet code, then the three *E*'s in *Beat ya here* should have been the same number. But—"

"Leo," she said with strained patience, "I swear to God if you don't tell—"

"Look at home," he said quietly.

She wrinkled her nose. "What?"

"That's what it says." He watched her reaction, how her expression crashed in disbelief. "It says 'Look at home.'"

"At whose home?"

He gazed steadily at her.

"At—at *my* home?"

"Who knows," he said. "But if your dad really was the one writing this, and hiding it, wouldn't it make sense that it would mean his home?"

"Which is also my home," she said on an exhale.

"Exactly."

She bent, cupping her head. "If you're telling me Bradley was right this morning . . . that this money has been right under my nose this entire time . . ."

"Worth looking, isn't it?"

Leo could sense Lily's apprehension as they approached her place. Her old truck barreled down the road, and she attempted to manage expectations. She reminded him that the cabin wasn't that impressive, that she was never there, and that when she was there, she never had time or money to fix it up. After everything they'd been through, her mood was understandably all over the place. She was hopeful and pessimistic, giddily disbelieving and anxious.

Inside, Leo was a mess, too, but he had decades of experience keeping his emotions hidden from the surface. Each of them had a mountain of therapy in their future, but right then, this tendency was serving him well. Did he want to climb out of his own skin? Of course. Was he losing it at the possibility that the treasure was still there? Absolutely. Was he worried about facing another devastating letdown? Hell yes. So he focused on Lily instead—on reassuring her that he didn't care what her house looked like, reassuring her that even if the money wasn't there, he was still all in on *her*.

But when they pulled up, they stared out the windshield, wordless, for several quiet ticks of her engine.

"See?" She studied his reaction so closely he had to carefully school his expression.

Because, in fact, the cabin was as bad as she had described.

From a distance, it had looked like a sweet log cabin nestled in a cluster of cottonwoods. Knee-high desert grass rolled up all the way to the foundation. A little creek babbled nearby. The fencing and small stable were old but lovingly maintained.

The house, however . . . well, it leaned—a lot—settling unevenly into the earth. The roof needed to be patched at least, probably replaced entirely. One of her porch steps had caved in, rotten and crumbling. Screens were missing from windows. The front door was water damaged and had to be hit with a determined shoulder in order to open.

But inside, it was clean, tiny, and surprisingly sweet. Her furniture was a simple navy blue sofa, two chairs, a battered but carefully polished coffee table. What looked like a hand-crocheted rug made out of strips of fabric decorated the scratched hardwood floor in front of the fireplace, giving the room a homey feeling. The dining room was small; the four-seater pine table looked handmade. Her kitchen was tidy and bright, appliances old but clean, fridge whirring loudly.

"It's nice, Lil."

She huffed out a quiet laugh. "I'm sure it's nothing compared to your Manhattan bachelor pad."

"This is at least twice as big."

"It's seven hundred square feet," she replied flatly.

"Two and a half times as big, then," he joked.

She rolled her eyes, but a smile pulled at the corners of her mouth.

"What's with the walls?" he asked, hoping the question wasn't rude.

That the house had been built by someone who was not employed in construction seemed almost comically apparent.

The walls were dotted with round, flat nail heads, haphazardly hammered at random intervals as if they alone were holding the entire structure together.

"Hell if I know," she said with a tiny edge in her voice. "I stopped trying to understand him a long time ago. He built this place for my mom, who didn't want to stay in an old trailer during the winter months. It ended up being a waste of time, since in the end, she left anyway."

"And you took care of him here, too? After the stroke?"

"Yeah. It's not a lot of space, but it was just the two of us, and a nurse when I had to work. He spent a lot of time in his chair by the window, looking out at the mountains."

As much as he hated to imagine Lily left to care for Duke by herself, he hated the idea of her living in this crumbling cabin alone even more.

Lily left him to look around, but she immediately got to work. And in what he assumed was one of the two tiny bedrooms, he heard Lily pulling things out of her closet, opening and closing drawers, banging on the walls to feel where something might be hollow or full of something other than wood. She stomped along the floors, checking every surface, every wall, every floorboard to see if it wiggled. He joined in, peeling back rugs, looking for false backs in her kitchen cabinets.

"Where do you think he would hide something?" he asked.

She paused her work tapping every brick in the fireplace to give him a dramatically excited expression. "Oh shit, do you think I should be considering that?"

He ignored her tone. This was Lily on defense; she was trying not to hope.

"I *mean*," Leo said patiently, "let's brainstorm what he might have thought would be a location nobody would ever think to look in. He was actually brilliant, Lily. He'd have known that anybody who suspected he kept the money here would have looked in the closet. They would think he hid it in the floor somewhere. They would look in the cabinets. So, if Duke thought there was a chance *you* would be the one to make it to the cave and left *you* that note, and he sent *you* right back here to your own house, what is the place where he would think you had never looked before and only you would look?"

She sat down on the couch, pinning her hands between her knees. "I don't know."

"Let's just let it sit," he said. "Look around. Think about the space, if there were any meaningful places in here."

"Leo, there's only so much space to consider."

"Exactly," he said. "That makes it easier and harder. Duke would have to be really creative to hide something here."

She sat back, looking around as if with new eyes. As usual, her fingers tapped against her thighs, and by now, he'd heard the rhythm so many times he found himself tapping along with her. They sat together—*quick tap, slow tap, quick, quick, quick, quick. Quick tap, slow tap, quick, quick, quick, quick . . .* and then everything seemed to come to a stop inside him.

"Lily."

She paused. "What?"

"What is that?" he asked, pointing to her hand. "What is that rhythm you always do? Is it a song?"

She looked down, almost like she didn't realize she was doing it.

"No. It's just my dad's knock," she said. "It was our secret knock. From when I was younger. He would be gone a lot, and I was alone here. It's how I knew it was Duke at the door. Of course, he could have just used his key like a normal person, but he always did like to make an entrance."

Leo stared at her, heart thundering in protective anger . . . and understanding. "Do it again."

They did it together once, and then again, and he jogged to the desk, finding a piece of paper and a pen to write it down as she repeated it: *short, long, short, short, short, short.*

On a hunch, he opened his phone browser, typing in a search.

"It's Morse code," he said.

"What does it spell?" She came up beside him, staring down at the piece of paper.

L I L I L I L I . . . Lili.

"Lily," he said. "But with an *I*, not a *Y*. Just a repeat of Lili over and over."

"Do you think it's important?"

"Maybe? It's how Liliana is spelled . . . But maybe not. It's not a location," he said. "Not a spatial cue or direction."

He looked over at her, but her attention had been snagged by something. She was staring up at the wall.

The wall—the *walls*—covered in nails.

He saw it now. The nails weren't haphazard; they were in patterns, patterns *everywhere*. Single nails, or careful lines of three of them in a row. Dots and dashes everywhere.

Words literally hammered into every inch of the cabin.

"Have these always been here?"

She shook her head. "He did it the year after my mom left. I figured he'd finally lost it or was just working through something." Lily let out a quiet cry, cupping her hand over her mouth and then speaking behind it. "My name. After his stroke, it was all he could say. Do you think he was—"

"Trying to tell you something?" Leo asked, voice tight with excitement. "Saying Lily over and over?" He gaped at her. "Given that his secret knock was your name, and he couldn't speak after his stroke except to say your name? Yeah. I think he was."

She pressed a hand to her forehead. "Oh my God. The riddle."

"What?"

She recited the section from memory: "*You hate to go, but you will.* Leo, Duke knew I hated going into Ely. When I was a kid, there was never anyone there to hang out with; Duke would take me with him and spend hours at the bar, talking with the locals who all worshipped him, and I would be at the jukebox dropping quarters in, picking from the same selection of songs over and over." She lifted a hand, fingers shaking against her temple. "And *You'll need to go, but never there*. The photograph was in the men's room—I'd use the ladies' room." Her expression froze in shock as she stared at Leo. "That riddle was only for me to solve. Duke left this for *me*. This all ends with my name."

They stood in stunned silence for two beats before exploding apart and rushing to opposite walls, scanning wildly for *Lili* in the nails, feeling along logs, calling out patterns.

They didn't need to have Morse code memorized, just needed to find it in the patterns of nail heads—two rounds of a dot, a dash, and four more dots. She pulled a dining chair to the wall in the living room, standing on it so she could see near the ceiling, meticulously scanning. Leo did the same at the front of the house, from ceiling to floorboard, working his way from the fireplace to the front door to the shorter logs under the window where Duke liked to look out at the mountains, and

there

beneath a coat hook, under her winter coat and scarf, about halfway down at waist height, was a log that was just a tiny bit crooked, sticking out a bit more than the others, and on it, the telltale pattern hammered in.

Dot, dash, dot, dot, dot, dot. Dot, dash, dot, dot, dot, dot.

"Lily!"

She ran over, tracing her fingers along the string of small iron nail heads. "That's it," she whispered.

He stepped forward and felt along the entire length. This log was at the juncture between the front door and the wall, and only about three feet long. "It's been cut," she said, looking at him, awestruck. "The face was carefully cut away. See the seam?" Lily bent, looking closer. "I never knew this was here."

"Nobody would."

His heart had turned into a wild animal, throwing itself against the confinement of his breastbone. The hammering pulse echoed the code of her name all the way down his arms. He ran his hand up her back, needing grounding. "Does the log come out?"

She curved her fingertips around it, looking for a good place to grip. When she rocked her hand forward and back, the front gave a little. Lily pried it harder, pulling down on the very upper lip where the curve met the seam just above, and with a quiet pop, the front came off, revealing a hollowed-out space inside.

Lily gasped, looking into the darkness before reaching in.

"I don't see any—oh." She pulled her arm back, fingers clutching an old, wrinkled envelope. On the front, written in handwriting Leo recognized as her father's, were the words:

> For Lily,
> To hell you ride.

And inside were a key and a single gold coin.

Chapter Thirty-Three

AT 8:43 THE next morning, Lily stood in front of Elk Ridge Bank—the current site of what was once the San Miguel Valley Bank—sucking in short, shallow breaths.

There was a plaque:

MAHR BUILDING
1892
SITE OF THE SAN MIGUEL VALLEY BANK
BUTCH CASSIDY'S FIRST BANK ROBBERY
JUNE 24, 1889

"It's okay if it's nothing," she said robotically. "We don't know whether he even found it."

She'd said this before, about fifteen times on the drive from Hester, Utah, to Telluride, Colorado. She could say it a hundred times more, and Leo wouldn't begrudge her for a second. Neither of them had slept a wink the night before; the anticipation and looping *what-ifs* were a grenade to both concentration and rest.

Hope was a dangerous drug, and Lily was standing at the precipice between two worlds: one that promised everything she ever wanted in life, and another where she'd have to figure out how to make the life she had into the life she wanted.

She squinted into the tinted glass. "What if they're not open yet?"

"They opened at eight thirty," he said.

He took a step closer behind her, wrapping his arms around her middle. He could feel the way her body fought every breath, forcing the air back out as soon as she inhaled. There was no room inside her for anything except this tension.

"Even if there's nothing in there for you," he said, lips pressed to the soft skin below her ear, "you don't have to ever go back to the way it was before."

She nodded, quickly, absently.

"I'm here now. You aren't alone."

She exhaled a little more and was finally able to pull in a deeper breath. "I know."

"I love you. I'm not ever going to leave you."

Lily leaned back into him. "Say it again."

"I'm not leaving." He kissed her neck again. "And I'll stand here with you for a week if that's what you need, but if you're ready, all you have to do is open the door and walk inside."

She reached forward, wrapping her hand around the brass bar and swinging the heavy glass door open. Refrigerated air hit them in a blast, a refreshing wall of cold. They both needed a bath and a square meal; Leo hadn't realized the true depth of his dishevelment until he stood in the gleaming lobby in the same torn clothes he'd worn out of the hospital only nineteen hours ago.

And there was no covert entrance to be made: a Monday, and with the internet in everyone's palm, the bank was quiet inside. It made it easy to spot the moment a man stood from a desk just beyond the bay of tellers, staring directly at them as he smoothed his tie down the front of his shirt.

He walked over leisurely, wearing a mysterious smile; the heel-toe click-clack of his dress shoes seemed to echo from all sides of the wide lobby.

In Leo's grip, Lily's hand grew sweaty, her fingers tightening around his, and he squeezed back reassuringly. "It's okay," he said under his breath.

"Well, all right." The man—tall, narrow, with a receding hairline and a forehead that shone like the marble tile he'd just crossed to reach them—smiled wider, revealing a set of oversize teeth. With his gaze fixed only on Lily, he said, "I could hazard a guess, but just to be sure, I think you'd better tell me your name."

Leo turned to take in her reaction, wondering whether she could see the answer to all of her worries unfolding right this second. With her brows cinched close in mistrustful surprise, her chin set defensively tight, Leo saw the way she strangled that hope down with a tight fist.

"Lily Wilder," she said. "And you are?"

"Ed Tottenham." He reached out a hand for Lily to shake. "Christ on a cracker, Lily Wilder, I was beginning to think you might never show up."

Chapter Thirty-Four

Laramie, Wyoming
Two months later

THE FOUR FLUTES pressed together in a celebratory clink, but Nicole's glass came in hot, sloshing and spilling champagne down her hand.

"Fuck." Unfazed, she bent, licking a long streak from her wrist and up along the back of her thumb.

Walter tracked this with his eyes before meeting Lily's gaze, had a brief but visible internal meltdown, and then tossed back his full glass.

Lily brought her own flute to her lips, closing her eyes as the fizzy drink tickled her nose and popped tart and bright across her tongue. She'd never liked champagne—to be fair, she'd rarely had an opportunity to try it—but Leo had driven into town to shop specifically for that night's dinner and brought home a case of what he promised to be good bubbles. She was determined to understand what everyone else tasted.

As usual, Nic voiced what Lily was already thinking:

"Tastes like carbonated cough syrup." Nic smacked her tongue to the roof of her mouth, frowning. "*Blech.*"

Leo grinned at them, charmed and uncomplaining. "I'll have yours," he said, starting to reach for it.

Nic ducked away, tilting her glass back and draining it. "I never said I had a problem with cough syrup."

Laughing, Leo stood and moved to the kitchen to grab a fresh bottle. He had happily spent five hundred dollars on a case of champagne that his girlfriend and her best friend wouldn't appreciate. Most nights it was just the two of them. Leo cooked while Lily wrapped up the evening chores in the stables, and they clinked the necks of their beer bottles together over the long knobby table in the expansive dining room, curling up with books or a movie after all the work was done. No matter what their bank statements now said, Leo had fully— and blissfully—embraced the simple life.

Tonight was special, though. They would transition to beer at some point—all signs pointed to debauchery ahead— but for a reunion like this, bubbles were called for. Walter had flown in from New York that morning; Nic had driven over from . . . well, next door. Last week she'd closed the deal on the fifty acres of sagebrush and riverbank adjoining Wilder Ranch.

"To Nicole being a landowner," Lily said, refilling their glasses for a proper toast.

Clink.

"To Leo and Lily reopening Wilder Ranch," Walt added.

"Next summer," Leo quickly clarified, his voice a little tight under the awareness of everything that still had to be done. Buy horses, train them, outfit the lodge and cabins for guests, hire staff. And, of course, take a couple of trips overseas.

It was the compromise they'd made with her dead father: at least two months every year spent making her world bigger.

Clink.

Leo's smile softened, and that thing that had been knotted inside Lily as long as her earliest memory seemed to loosen a tiny bit more. *I love you*, his expression said. *I'm not ever going to leave you.* Maybe by the time next summer rolled around, it would sink in that this was real and that anxious knot inside her would be a loose rope, or even better still, a skein of cashmere, a soft strand of silk.

"Are you going to let us see that letter?" Walt asked, and at her nod, Leo stood, disappearing into the office and returning with the folded yellowed sheet.

Walter took the paper from him. "How many times have you read it?"

"Probably a thousand." Lily chewed her lip for a beat before adding, "It's going to take some time for it all to feel real."

"I bet." She watched Walter read, feeling like she knew the contents well enough to track the words as his eyes moved across the page.

Dear Lily,

If you're reading this, it means we've finished the trip and you're about to open a box with your future inside. I hope you enjoyed this adventure. It's taken me a few years to get this right, and now that you're reading it, I hope we can say that we had the time of our lives.

But knowing how much you grew to hate my riddles and seeing as how I'm probably standing right behind you as you read this, I also hope you don't turn around and wallop me for making you do it. This old dog loves his familiar tricks, and I can't tell you how proud I am that we did this together.

I think this is the first time I've left you a note you didn't have to decode. Ha! Even I don't want to spend that much time translating something. Besides, if you've found this, you've earned the right to an easy read. (And even if I could say all this in person, you know I'm not very good at it.)

Do you remember when you were little, I used to call you Grasshopper? You would hop from spot to spot in the front yard, swearing that you had to land on a stick or you'd melt into the lava. Back then you liked the treasure hunting, too. You were my little sidekick.

I think you stopped liking all that stuff when your mom left. I get it. Maybe it would have happened anyway as you got older, but I imagine her leaving had a lot to do with why you started hating what I love. You always loved horses, but once upon a time you loved hiking and treasure hunting, too. I wanted you to get back into it, but I get why you didn't. It took your mom away from us, and it took me away from you, too. I couldn't ever resist it, though, and I know you have something you love just as much, so I hope someday you'll understand.

I found most of this money about a month after your mom left. You were at the ranch with your uncle Dan. I didn't have a plan. I wandered in places I'd never been before. I even got lost once or twice. I made my way into that final cave, and there it was, all this cash, all these old coins, packed up in about fifteen dusty wooden crates. Honest to God. The first time in my life I went out into the desert without a thirst for treasure was when I found the one thing I'd been searching for my whole life.

It took me a few weeks to get it all out of there, and then I didn't know what to do with it. Part of me thought, "This is when Lily and I start a new life of our own choosing," but even by then, I think we would have chosen different things. I would have wanted to keep searching the land for something to surprise me. You would have wanted to stay put with your horses.

But then that got me thinking, too, "Has she ever had a choice? Is this what she would choose if she'd seen the world beyond this border?"

I hope all of this makes you understand why I sold the ranch. That place never made me feel anything but trapped. I know you love it there, but I don't want to feel tied to that land anymore, and I don't want you to simply fall into your fate. That's my decision and I stand by it. I want to tell you something important, and maybe if we've made it through this crazy hunt together and you're still reading, there's a chance you'll hear it.

You're barely an adult. Don't tie yourself down to a place or a person yet. Don't let your world be small until you've seen more of it.

I know you love that ranch. But it will mean something different when you get out in the real world and choose it. That's what I'm giving you. With this money, I want you to travel. There are horses all over the world, Lil. Go ride 'em. I want you to explore, and branch out, and be brave. If, at the end of a year, you still want the ranch, then buy your own land and make a name for yourself that way.

I see how you might just return to Laramie and be

there forever, and never understand why I couldn't
do it, why I couldn't stick it out in one place. Maybe
after you travel, you'll get the travel bug, too, and
you'll want to make that part of your life the way I
have. Or, maybe you'll hate it, but then at least you'll
know how your heart is built and you can tell me to
shove it with real wisdom. At least you'll have choices
in front of you, which is the only thing I want for you.

Most of all, I just don't want you to end up with a
life half-lived.

So. Open this safety-deposit box.

And live.

—Duke

"I tell you what." Walt covertly wiped his eyes before passing the paper back to Leo. "That hunt would have been a lot
easier if Duke had been there."

"He wouldn't have helped, are you kidding?" Lily reached
for her champagne, washing her laugh down with a sip of bubbles. "And I can't even imagine how homicidal the ASCII
code would have made me at the end. It would have taken me
weeks, and then to decode a note telling me to look at home?
Homicidal. Thank God for Leo."

"But only you would have figured out where the key is,"
Leo reminded her. "Only you had the right pattern—*LILI*."

Nicole reached for the bottle, leaning across Walter and

momentarily distracting him with a boob pressed to his fore-arm. Pretending to be oblivious to the way his eyes followed her when she straightened, she filled her glass to the brim, bending to suck when the champagne flowed over the lip of the flute. "I can't get over that he wanted to do this with you." She wiped a hand across her foamy upper lip. "I think it's sweet."

"Of course you do," Lily said, "because everything turned out okay."

Beside her, Leo leaned back in his chair, sliding his hand across her shoulder, fingers digging with unconscious familiarity into the hair at the nape of her neck. "Feels weird to be even a little grateful to Bradley and Terry, though. If they hadn't dragged us there, we never would have known."

Murmurs of agreement rippled around the table.

More than anything—more than the crime, the sheer magnitude of the treasure, or the unlikely band of misfits who managed to pull it all off—the media loved discussing how her dad hid everything he unearthed back in Telluride, the city where Butch Cassidy robbed his very first bank. Bills, coins, jewelry, documents. *What a rascal,* she'd thought with a sharp laugh, and then it had broken into a terrible sound. She'd crumpled down right in the middle of the bank after that nice man took her hand, realizing that Duke really had found the money years ago, years before his stroke, certainly before he sold the ranch. And then the safety-deposit box had swung open and the letter fluttered onto the marble floor at her feet.

Fifteen million dollars in today's currency. The number still didn't feel entirely real. After negotiations with the authorities, a chunk of it went to the national parks, historical societies, and Southwestern tribal lands. The rest of it was divided between them. Walter was looking at places but still weighing his options, noting there were 1,500 Petco locations across the continental US, Mexico, and Puerto Rico. Lily was hoping he'd been waiting to see where Nicole ended up, and she, of course, used her money to buy the ranch next door.

The rest of the money allowed Leo and Lily to buy Wilder Ranch back from Jonathan Cross, but it was the media attention that already had it booked solid for the next three years. And just because she was wise enough now to know what she wanted didn't mean she wouldn't still honor her dad's wishes— however misguided. The interest was what they would use to travel. First up: a trip with Cora to Japan to meet relatives she and Leo had never known.

"What a crazy story," Walt said.

He could be talking about Butch, or Duke, or what they'd all gone through in May. But when Lily looked at Leo, she thought the craziest story might be this one—that she fell in love when she was nineteen and lived through a decade of loneliness and scrabbling only to wind up right back here, saved by the history she'd figured was her curse, living blissfully with the man she'd convinced herself was lost forever.

They finished the bottle, and another, and then the beer came out—along with the playing cards. There was shouting (Nicole) and wrestling (again, instigated by Nicole), and it all devolved into laughter and chaos and drunken pledges of lifelong friendship. They planned their first new-group trip, and Nicole teased Walter for claiming to be wearing his "dressy" T-shirt. They harassed Nic and Walter to just kiss already—and they did, Walter's cheeks turning the color of a sunrise over red rock as their lips met under the celebration of their friends' obnoxious cheering.

But when the small hand on the clock hovered around the two, Leo gave Lily that look, the one that told her he was done sharing for the night. He stood and pulled her up off the floor, guided her to their bedroom.

Back down the hallway there were hoots and hollers—which weren't wrong. Lily would tell them to shut the hell up, but secretly she liked showing it off: this ranch and this man and this bright, insatiable love she'd once thought was only for other people. Leo told her happiness was her best accessory. Security didn't come easily—she was a work in progress, and that meant she spent just as many days wondering when it would all fall apart as she did realizing the dream was real—but tonight, she wanted to skywrite this feeling, wanted to shout her euphoria into the serpentine echo of the Maze.

Leo peeled away her clothes in the pitch black of their middle of nowhere paradise and kissed his way up her body, from knees to mouth, arriving over her with a smile he fit against hers.

"Did you give Bonnie the grain?" he asked. "I left the bag on the barrel in the tack room."

She nodded. "As if she'd let me forget. Did you put away the leftovers?"

He laughed. "What leftovers? Nic ate everything."

Leo asked if she'd closed the side gate—she had. Lily asked if he'd called his sister back—he had; she was coming for a visit before her first term started. Did he set the coffee maker to brew at five in the morning? *Yes, Lil.*

The horses wouldn't care how hungover they were tomorrow.

And then he came back to her, focused, hands hungry and roaming, body moving over her, then into her in the darkness.

And on that night in mid-July, with their best friends down the hall and their horses fed and sleepy out in the pasture, there was nothing else they needed to do. All there was to think about was this version of their forever. Leo paused at the quiet sound of happiness that escaped her. He pulled the blankets over their heads, and they made love right there, right back where they started.

Acknowledgments

WHEN WE FINISHED *The Soulmate Equation* in 2020 and started to think about what we'd like to do next, we knew one thing: we wanted FUN. In a year that kept us home and away from family, friends, readers, and each other, we were ready to get out into the world—even if only through our characters—and have an adventure. We were nervous at first. The seeds for *Something Wilder* had been quietly taking up space in the backs of our brains for years, but it was part of a conversation with one of our heroes, Sarah MacLean, that became our mantra: be fearless and take big swings. Movies like *Romancing the Stone* had adrenaline, and adventure, and deep, heart-clenching swoons. We felt post-pandemic romance needed more of *that*.

This book was the most fun thing we've ever written, but as usual, it takes a lot of people to turn it into what you're holding today.

Holly Root is our dream agent; even ten years in, we're just as smitten. Our wish would be for every writer to have someone this brilliant, badass, loving, hilarious, and gently terrifying on their side. Kristin Dwyer is our PR rep and our Precious and we would be absolutely lost without her. Both these women started their own companies, and seeing them conquering the world makes us Mama Bear proud. Hell yes, Team Root Literary and Leo PR!

Listen, we know our acknowledgments run long, but what can we say, our love is loud: Simon & Schuster has been our publishing home since day one and we adore everyone there like family. Jen Bergstrom, not many authors have a publisher who would probably get in an actual fistfight for them, but we do! (Can we say that in acknowledgments? We want the public to know this fistfight is entirely hypothetical, but even so, Jen would win.) Enormous thanks to our fabulous editor Hannah Braaten, Rachel Brenner, Mackenzie Hickey, Lauren Carr, Eliza Hanson, Abby Zidle, Aimée Bell, Jen Long, John of the Mustache Vairo, Lisa Litwack, Andrew Nguyễn, Anabel Jimenez, Sally Marvin, Jonathan Karp, and the entire Gallery sales team. You are all stupendous humans.

To badly quote *Tommy Boy*, Kate Dresser could sell a ketchup popsicle to a woman in white gloves. Thank you for having a vision for us and our books and pushing us to take big swings. You are the epitome of competence porn (and we're dying imagining your face while you read that). We are better writers because of you. We love and miss you endlessly.

Thank you, Margo Lipschultz, for diving in, for doggedly helping us find those saggy sections, and for helping make this book what it is. We're sending Walter to you—with doughnuts in hand. Jen Prokop, you are The Closer, you are brilliantly surgical, you are a *star*. We are so thrilled to see your editorial brain at work. We are indebted to Philip Atkins for the canyoneering, Canyonlands, trail safety, and map guidance.

Our families have had us home for almost two years now and they are ready to push us out of the nest. (But—ha!—we pushed them out first.) Thank you to K, O, V, R, and C for being the absolute loves of our lives. By this point our two families have pretty much become one, and nothing makes our hearts happier.

To the bookish friends we look up to, we love you: Kate Clayborn, Kresley Cole, Jen Frederick, Sarah MacLean, Jen Prokop, Erin McCarthy, Sally Thorne, Sarah J. Maas, Sarah Wendell, Susan Lee, Helen Hoang, Erin Service, Katie Lee, Christopher Rice, Cassie Sanders, Tessa Bailey, Rosie Danan, Rachel Lynn Solomon, Rebekah Weatherspoon, Leslie Philips, Alexa Martin, Sonali Dev, Gretchen Schreiber, Alisha Rai, Jillian Stein, Liz Berry, Candice Montgomery, and Catherine Lu.

We've thanked BTS in three of our books so far, and our gratitude seems to grow daily. If you've never been part of a fandom—and especially if you've never been ARMY—it might seem impossible that people you've never met can mean so much. But they can be the difference between a bad day and a good one, a hard year and one full of connection and hope. Thank you Kim Namjoon, Kim Seokjin, Min Yoongi, Jung Hoseok, Park Jimin, Kim Taehyung, and Jeon Jungkook for being joy personified. ARMY will always wait for you.

To every librarian, bookseller, blogger, BookTokker, and reader out there, we hope this year is full of love, health, happiness, and most of all: adventure. We all deserve it. Thank you for reading our books and shouting your love. Thank you for your gorgeous pics and hilarious and/or heartbreaking videos. None of this happens without you, and we are endlessly thankful.

Our favorite things to do together: write, ride Tower of Terror, and scream-sing our faces off at concerts. The last two years have meant we've only been able to do one of those. We have a lot of catching up to do, and so many adventures ahead.

About the Author

CHRISTINA LAUREN is the pen name of writing partners/best friends Christina Hobbs and Lauren Billings, the *New York Times*, *USA Today*, and #1 internationally bestselling authors of twenty-eight books, including the Beautiful and Wild Seasons series, *The Unhoneymooners*, *Twice in a Blue Moon*, *The Honey-Don't List*, *In a Holidaze*, and *The Soulmate Equation*. Find them at ChristinaLaurenBooks.com or @ChristinaLauren on Instagram and Twitter.

/